A FILTHY BUSINESS

BUSINESS

A THRILLER

Other Titles
by William Lashner

The Victor Carl Novels

Writing as Tyler Knox

WILLIAM LASHNER

A FILTHY BUSINESS

A THRILLER

Text copyright © 2017 by William Lashner
All rights reserved.

Published by Thomas & Mercer, Seattle

www.apub.com

Amazon, the Amazon logo, and Thomas & Mercer are trademarks of Amazon.com, Inc., or its affiliates.

ISBN-13: 9781477817858
ISBN-10: 1477817859

Cover design by Faceout Studio

Printed in the United States of America

For Chase, who is everything that Phil is not.

Let not our babbling dreams affright our souls.
Conscience is but a word that cowards use,
Devis'd at first to keep the strong in awe.

—Shakespeare, Richard III

I. Salesman

1

THE MAGAZINE WRITER

The magazine writer drove her rented car past sagebrush and cactus, heading ever deeper into the bowels of the desert and toward her interview with the outlaw.

She wouldn't even have known this rutted stretch of dirt was navigable if the outlaw's lawyer hadn't told her exactly how far to go past the Sinclair station before turning. She had reset the trip odometer on her rental car to zero as soon as she saw the dinosaur. At the 23.4-mile mark, she spotted a line of overhead electrical wires snaking to the right. Beneath the wires appeared something that might once have been a road. She reset the trip odometer as she steered off the asphalt.

The instructions from the lawyer had been explicit: she was to tell no one of her plans; she was to come alone; she was to bring neither cell phone nor any kind of tracking device. When she noted that the instructions were a perfect recipe for disappearing without a trace, the lawyer said she could bring a gun for protection if she chose.

"Cell phones terrify him," said the lawyer, "but he's not worried about you with a gun."

She didn't doubt that last part for a minute. The outlaw was being hunted by both the FBI and a horde of criminal assassins out for a posted bounty, and he had successfully stayed one step ahead of his pursuers. He was handsome, she knew from the photographs all over the web, well built and cocky; he'd look smashing on the cover of one of the magazines she wrote for. This interview would be the greatest get of her journalistic career, but it wasn't just a story she was after, and it was this other thing, this bitter and more pressing thing, that caused her to clench her jaw in determination as she drove through her fears along that ragged road.

The shack first appeared well in the distance, a listing structure marooned by time. It was a mere ghost of what it once had been, and what it once had been was nothing much. She stopped the car, checked her odometer, looked at the building. A single black line ran from the electric wires to the shack, the splice very much jerry-rigged. Slowly she turned on to the merest indication of a drive wending between the cacti.

After slamming the car door shut, the magazine writer clutched her bag and examined the barren landscape: not a truck, not a car, no signs of humanity but the shack and the thick black wire that connected it to the grid. The windows were caked with dust. The midday heat was ferocious. A hot wind swirled the dirt around her shoes. This couldn't be the place; this was an abandoned piece of nothing in the land of nowhere.

She had driven into the desert not just to find the outlaw, but to find a piece of herself hard enough to do what needed to be done. She worried that it didn't exist, this hard place within her, and in this arid wasteland her worry was solidifying into certainty. She thought of leaving, going back to the comforts of her life, but the thing that needed doing compelled her to grip the hot iron handle of the door and give it a yank.

The door pulled open with a squeal of its hinges. She peered into the gloom. An intermittent crackle and hiss came from somewhere inside. She stepped hesitantly forward. The door banged shut behind her.

It took her eyes a moment to adjust. The shack was lit by a yellow bulb hanging from the ceiling and the thin light that made its way through the dusted windows. Neon beer signs affixed to the walls flittered noisily on and off, on and off. Behind a makeshift bar, a man, morose and gray, sat motionless on a stool. Behind him, on a hutch, stood a strange stuffed animal the size of a tall squirrel, flanked by two large jars filled with some foul purple liquid. In one of the jars an eyeball pressed against the glass, peering out. The bar top was dusty, the bottles on the shelves behind the barkeep were dusty, graffiti was spattered on the timbered walls. A pair of ceiling fans stirred the air but still the room was stifling, and it smelled like an armadillo had recently crawled beneath the floorboards to die.

The barkeep stood, nodded at her like she was expected, and pointed at her bag. She handed it over and he gave it a cursory search, raising his eyebrow only as he lifted the camera—as if the gun he'd undoubtedly found was only to be expected—before handing back the bag, gun and camera included, all without saying a word. Then he tilted his head toward one of the tables scattered across the sandy floor, along with half a score of chairs.

She sat facing the door, laid her notepad and pen on the splintery tabletop, placed the bag on the floor. The neon hissed, the stink wafted, the fans whirred. As she looked about she noted something in a darkened corner, something small, curled, and covered with sand. She was still trying to make it out when the door squawked open and the fierce light of day smashed into the shack's interior. The magazine writer raised a hand to shield her eyes even as she reached for her handbag.

When the door slammed shut and the glare died, it took her a long moment to link the man standing before her with the handsome outlaw she had been expecting. This man dragged his left leg behind him like it was a piece of meat, this man's face was scarred and his hair was greasy, this man wore a black patch over his right eye. Yet as he shambled over to the bar to say a few words to the barkeep before making his way to her table, she could perceive, inside the wreckage, the man he once had been. To see the outlaw in this condition was to see her hope wither like a newborn abandoned in the desert.

"Thank you for agreeing to meet me so far off the beaten road," said the outlaw, now sitting across the table from her. His voice was raw and hushed, a thing scarred. "Ginsberg's bar is only one step up from an outhouse, and a short step at that, but it's about the only place I can safely show my face anymore without getting it shot off. I find it has other advantages, too. I might not be much to look at anymore, but compared with the rest of the mutants that patronize this joint, I'm a veritable matinee idol. In the land of the blind . . . well, you know. And here I can sit and drink alone for hours without being disturbed by the bonhomie and laughter at the other tables because at Ginsberg's place there is no bonhomie or laughter, only the strangled gurgle of despair. Ah, but at least we have his home-brewed beer to cut the edge."

The magazine writer looked up from her notepad to see the barkeep carrying two beers in heavy glass mugs. He slammed the steins down so that waves of beer sloshed onto the table. Without a word he turned and trudged back to the bar. The outlaw hoisted his mug.

"Cheers," he said, before pouring a good portion of his mugful down his throat. He let out a loud sigh, wiped his mouth with the back of his hand, and looked at her expectantly.

The magazine writer took a sip from her mug and reflexively spat out the mouthful. The outlaw didn't flinch, not even from the splatters that landed on his chest and arms.

"I should have warned you," he said. "Even skunks won't drink this piss. But at least it's warm."

The outlaw took another long swallow as he squinted at her. His one-eyed stare was disconcerting. She tried asking something but he waved it off, as if he had no interest in her well-prepared interview questions.

4

"I could read the disappointment on your face when you saw me scuffle through the door. I'm not what you expected. So let me guess your lede coming in. You were going to call me a crusader for justice ghosting across the land. You had heard about that gang of motorcycle marauders in New Mexico that ended up in a bound heap by the side of the road. You had heard about that tech millionaire who's now in a Mexican jail on charges of sex slavery. You had heard about the so-called Salt Lake Killer who mysteriously stopped killing. You had heard all this and for some reason you were going to attribute it all to me.

"Oh, I've seen the sites about me on the dark web, I know what they say. Defend one girl from a band of thugs, fight it out on the grounds of some crappy tourist camp in West Virginia, and suddenly any mysterious piece of justice gets pinned to your ass. But you see me now and you are having doubts. We all want our champions to be strong-legged and two-eyed and as good-looking as underwear models. I used to be just that, but I am not that anymore, and you are wondering now what is true and what is myth.

"Let me assure you of one thing before we continue. Whatever I tell you of my story from here on in is going to be raw truth. I'm through lying. Every lie I ever told was designed to hide the biggest of my secrets, but I'm beyond secrets now. Anyway, you didn't come for the truth—reporters never do—you came for the legend. So I figure we'll start at that tourist camp and then loop back for the dirty truth of how it all began."

The magazine writer reached into her bag, pushed aside the gun and the camera, and pulled out a silver digital recorder with a small LCD screen. She asked if it was okay if she recorded the interview.

"Okay?" he said. "I'd be disappointed if you didn't."

The magazine writer had hoped the physical presence of the outlaw would grant her the strength to do the thing she needed to do, but this wreck of a man was not at all what she expected or required. If she would find her strength, it would come through his words. His story would determine her future course of action, and in a very real way her future itself. She pressed a button and a tiny red spot on the screen began to glow.

"They were coming for her, all right," said the outlaw, leaning forward as he spoke into the recorder, his scarred voice taking on a newsreader's self-serious timbre. "What had been done to her was utterly unconscionable, and now they were coming to finish the job. Only I was in their way. We had been trying to run, the girl and I, but after a Pontiac nearly slammed us off the road, I realized running wasn't going to work. We had been betrayed. They were trailing our every mile. The only choice was to make a stand. I turned into the mountains and found a tourist camp on a patch of gravelly dirt. I left the car in the open like a neon sign blinking on and off. Vacancy, No Vacancy. If we were going to have it out, I figured sooner was better than later. The girl was most likely going to die at that tourist camp, and so was I, but a choice had been made, and so there I was, steely eyed and rock jawed, putting my life between them and her. I knew the names of those that were coming, I knew their skills, their utter savagery. And I knew they would be led by a pure piece of killer.

"But I was a pure piece of something, too."

He looked up. "Too much? I noired it up for you, gave it the staccato rhythm of gunshots so your copy would sing, but maybe I overdid it. Now it sounds so damn heroic it makes me want to vomit. Or is that the beer? But wasn't that the angle you were looking for? I was going to be the righteous warrior, the noble protector of the innocent. And don't doubt that the girl I was protecting, a young woman, actually, was an innocent. She was all rainbows and unicorns and stuffed bears. So the protectee you got right, it's just the righteous warrior part that needs work.

"Okay, so here, now, in the interest of truth, I need to make the first of my confessions. The role I was playing at that tourist camp—defender of the innocent, the hero's role—was not my usual part. Through most of my life I had cast myself onto the other side of the equation. In fact, those henchmen coming for me with teeth bared and guns drawn, they had once been colleagues. I had been a henchman, too. We had all been part of a syndicate dubbed the Hyena Squad. And here's the kicker: the utterly unconscionable thing that had been done to that girl had been done by me.

"Can people change? Did I change? That's for you to determine. How I went from one side to the other is the beating heart of this story. And don't think you can figure out the why of it on your own. Don't think one look into my eye will give you the answer. You'll be looking for a spark of conscience, some glimmer of humanity, and you'll find it because you'll mistake reflection for fact. But all you'll have seen is a shard of yourself staring back from the vile sack of jelly still in my skull.

"My eyes have always been dead as pennies. It just took the right person to recognize that fact and make it worth something. Someone to see the value in the darkness, to refine it as one purifies a discarded mass of slag until what remains shines with the brightness of gold before sending it out into the world to do its damage.

"Someone like Mr. Maambong."

2

Gold Dog

I was recruited by Mr. Maambong as a henchman for the Hyena Squad out of a multitude of deserts, the most literal of which was the scorched and arid landscape of Nevada. This was the before, when I was still full of piss, good-looking as hell, and undamaged enough to be optimistic about my life and prospects.

"Good morning, Mr. Cannizare. This is Dick Triplett, senior account executive with Gold Dog International in beautiful Carson City, Nevada, the gold capital of the world. The reason for the call is sometime back you requested information about the precious metals market. I wanted to personally introduce myself and get some fresh, free information out to you in this morning's mail. Now, Mr. Cannizare, have you ever invested in the precious metals market before?"

You already know that my real name is not Dick Triplett. In accord with my promise to tell you only the raw truth, I must also confess that Mr. Cannizare never requested information about the precious metals market, our boiler room was in a strip mall outside the Carson City city limits, and to be a senior account executive with Gold Dog International was an achievement on par with putting your pants on with the zipper in front. Even the old alcoholic who swept the office once a week was a senior account executive if ever forced to answer the phone. Our receptionist, Shelly Levalle, a fifty-year-old bottle blonde with hair higher than Lincoln's hat, was the vice president of communications, meaning we senior account executives were subordinate to her, which you would understand if you ever saw her breasts.

We were all working for Joey Mitts, an ancient, chain-smoking blob of con with yellow teeth and a nose like a tennis ball. Joey was a legend in certain desert circles; he was a former brothel proprietor, a former member of the state assembly, a former Carson City casino operator. Each of these positions had ended with an indictment, but Joey had a connected Vegas lawyer on speed dial and he had beaten each and every rap. "They can't do nothing to an honest man," would say Joey Mitts, "which is why I'm always in the shithouse."

Outside Joey's private office were nine desks with phones in a room that smelled of coffee and flatulence, and from those desks we cheerfully sold promises to deliver gold to doomsday preppers from sea to shining sea. As Joey told us incessantly, "Selling gold is selling money, and if you can't sell money, then you're in the wrong business, chum." "Chum" was one of the words Joey threw at us instead of our names, which he never seemed to remember. We were pally, buddy, amigo, brother, captain, cousin, Tom, Harry, and Dick, from which I took my nom de plume of gold dust.

"I'm sure, Mr. Cannizare, that you know the secret to making money on any investment is proper timing. That's especially true in the metals market and I am happy to say that your timing has never been better. Now, Mr. Cannizare—can I call you Luigi? Great! Now, Luigi, if I could show you an opportunity in the gold market, an opportunity that you just could not say no to, are you in a financial position to take advantage of my firm's initial recommendation of ten thousand dollars?"

Gold Dog International consisted of Joey, Shelly, a guy in India working the website, and a rotating roster of salespeople hammering the phones. We were mostly young, mostly male, mostly wearing shorts and T-shirts and flip-flops because the air conditioner was crap, all of us recruited by Joey himself. On the sound system we ran a continuous loop of the last five minutes of a frenzied day on the New York Stock Exchange, with desperate traders calling out prices and the crowd noise rising to the famous triple chime of the bell. And we worked the phones all hours of the day, 8:00 a.m. on the East Coast to 8:00 p.m. on the West Coast, weekends included; it didn't matter much when we called, our customers were always home and delighted to talk because they were generally alone and lonely and so old they barely remembered their names.

Nothing sells gold more effectively than a sense that the nation is going straight to hell, and so Joey bought his leads from a wild roster of religious and political organizations that predicted the coming apocalypse, or the coming rapture, or the coming economic collapse of America, or the coming election of another stinking Democrat president. And if you were stocking up on freeze-dried MREs or water storage kits or yellow pandemic suits, you could be assured Joey already owned your name and number. In support of these leads, Joey himself wrote the script. "Just read what I wrote, cousin, and don't do no freestyling. This ain't surf school. We're selling gold and this is the way we do it."

"Luigi, I understand that's a big chunk of cash, but it does take money to make money, am I right? Let me tell you something you already know: this whole damn country is going down the tubes. Our man in the White House is being thwarted every which way by the socialist rabble-rousers looking for their own box of chocolates. And if the mullahs in Iran drop the big one on Toledo, you're going to want more than a few dollar bills in your wallet, am I right? That's where our opportunity comes into play. History proves that when the US dollar dives, gold does what? Absolutely! We're on the same page, Luigi."

The job was to be on the phone. We weren't paid to sit around and gossip about Joey's past, or Shelly's breasts, or the latest bit of action we picked up at the Carson City casinos, although we did, incessantly. We weren't paid at all, unless we closed. Joey's shop was pure commission, and that's the way we liked it. You didn't work for Joey Mitts to hedge the upside.

On my desk, beside my laptop on which I typed up the official paperwork, was a sheet of leads, a calendar where I jotted numbers for callbacks, and an egg timer. The egg timer was the second most crucial piece of equipment next to the phone, far more valuable than the laptop or the calendar. As soon as I had a lead on the line I flipped the timer and started in on the script. If I couldn't make the pitch, get a series of responses, and be on the edge of closing in three minutes, then I was off to the next number on the lead sheet. Some of these old-timers would take half a day with you just for entertainment purposes and then tell you to call back next week after they talked it over with their wives. Are you kidding me?

"Luigi, one of the great advantages of trading with our gold program is the ability to utilize leverage. Now follow me closely on this. Gold's trading at about twelve hundred dollars an ounce, right? Let's say you put in fifty thousand dollars, that's right, let's not be pikers. If the price goes up to fifteen hundred dollars, which it will in a few months' time, trust me on that, you'll have made thirteen thousand dollars. Not bad. But we make our money not just on what we own, but on what we control, and if you use leverage to control three times as much, suddenly you're making something like forty thousand dollars. That's a boatload, Luigi. Better yet, that's a boat. Do you see how I got that number? Isn't that the type of security you're seeking for yourself and your family?"

On breaks I would pass by Joey's office and head out the back door to stare at the terrain and smoke a cigarette. In the distance was nothing but the wind moaning its disappointment over a barren tract of wasteland. I was the highest-grossing senior account executive at Gold Dog International and the pay was pretty damn sweet, but still I was stuck in the wilderness. Like everyone else I had dreamed my future, and being just another drifting piece of desert trash wasn't it.

Don't get me wrong, I was grateful for the job. It was tough out there for my generation. We were scrambling for the scraps left by the generations before us, and they hadn't left much. The selfish bastards had outsourced the jobs that had kept them fat and happy for decades, had buried us in debt when we tried to get the education they said we needed to make a go of it, and had left us to fend for ourselves without health care or pensions in a freelance economy that was really as free as a set of shackles. Our generation did what we had to do to get by, showing off our tits on YouTube, or interning for peanuts with billion-dollar corporations, or selling gold certificates out of a boiler room on US Route 50. I once had a job in a law firm in Sacramento—that's right, I'm a lawyer, put that in your little notebook—but when the boomers crashed the economy, that job went to hell and no one else would touch me. I was in scramble mode, and I ended up scrambling to Joey Mitts.

And I'll tell you something you might understand. I didn't feel even a twinge of guilt at milking the geezers out of their end-of-the-world stash. It was their generation that had raised the generation that left us nothing but crumbs. If I was pulling out a piece of someone else's inheritance, I figured I was just getting my share. And it was almost too easy. These old-timers had been primed by their favorite newscasters and political hucksters before I ever dialed their numbers. The world was going to hell, only gold would keep them afloat, and I was offering them a seat on the boat.

"Now Luigi, our commission is only three percent. Based on the lever-age, we can overcome that with a fractional move in the market. But I need to know now, am I wasting my time here, Luigi? Are we talking the smaller investment or the big move at fifty thousand dollars? Color me impressed. And what about your wife, is she going to step in and tell you to stick your

money in a mattress? Why, I'm so sorry to hear that, Luigi, but I'm sure she'd want you to grab hold of the security you deserve in these difficult times."

I got the usual cheer from the other senior account executives when the printer started churning out the completed investment documents that would be overnighted to Luigi Cannizare. I'd call again in a few days and make sure the papers were signed and the check sent. Once the check cleared, my wallet would thicken with cash. Now I just had to get Joey's approval. I slapped a few high fives, pulled the paperwork from the printer, gave Shelly a wink, and headed back to the big man.

"Luigi Cannizare, fifty thou," I said as I tossed the documents onto his desk, tipping his ashtray. "Boom."

The office was small, thick with smoke, sprinkled with bottles emptied, ashtrays filled, subpoenas ignored. Joey, his elbows on the desktop, took a long drag from his cigarette and let the smoke slide out his toadstool nose.

"Tell me, captain," said Joey. "You read him the script?"

"Yes, sir."

"Every bit of it?"

"Every bit that counts," I said. "Every bit that got him to yes. What about a smile, Joey? I'm killing your leads. Don't I get a smile?"

Joey glanced down at the mess of ash and butts now spread across the wood in front of him, and swiped at it with the back of his hand.

"Are you banging Shelly?"

"What? Joey? No. No way. Give me some credit, she's freaking fifty. And that was one of the things you told me at the start."

"Yes it was," said Joey Mitts.

"I wouldn't do that to you, Joey. Not on my worst day. You're like a father to me."

Joey stared at me a bit and then stabbed his butt into the ashtray. "I got a call from the attorney general's office about a Roger Ludkins. Do you remember Roger Ludkins?"

"Ludkins?"

"His daughter says he was never informed that there was interest charged on the margin loan, or that the loan would be called if the price of gold slipped."

"Everything was spelled out in the documents he had to sign."

"The attorney general says that's not enough. It needs to be explained in the sales pitch. Something about a contract of adhesives or whatnot."

"Adhesion."

"That's it, yeah. Adhesion. He wants to interview the senior account executive on the case." Joey lit another cigarette, inhaled deeply. "Dick Triplett."

"Good luck finding him," I said, smiling broadly.

"Who did you use for . . ." He shuffled quickly through the document pack I had just brought in. "For Mr. Cannizare?"

"Look, I doubt this Ludkins can remember the size of his shoe, the way he was drifting in and out during our talk. He asked me if I was his son."

"What did you say?"

"I said, 'I miss you, Daddy.'"

"I'm gonna have to let you go, pally."

"What are you talking about? I'm making you money, here, Joey, real money. So Dick Triplett disappears. Who cares? I'll be Tim Johnson, I'll be Buddy Bernstein, I'll be Dudley Downright Upright—it doesn't matter as long as I'm selling, right?"

"How many times did I make it clear you got to read the script? I had a lawyer go over it, it's clean. That's the point."

"Joey," I said, putting a line of pleading into my voice, "from now on it's word by word, I swear."

Joey just stared at me through the smoke, like he was staring into a mirror and not liking the view.

"This isn't right," I said.

"Since when does that matter? Don't worry about it, pal, you'll land on your feet, your type always does. There's a guy. His name is Maambong. I met him when I was still in politics. A serious guy, if you know what I'm talking about. He's looking for someone. He's got other candidates, but it's something you might should look into."

"What is he, Nigerian?"

"No."

"What's his racket?"

"Whatever it is, you won't play your bullshit with him if you know what's good for you." He handed me a slip of paper. "Give him a call. And try telling the truth for once, sport, it might pay."

"I doubt it," I said. I rubbed my fillings with my tongue, tasting a copper that wasn't there, and looked around at the dim, filthy office, the sun-bleached desert outside the window, the old mass of gristle that had been chewed and spat out onto the seat behind the desk. I always seemed to get cast out of whatever Eden I found myself in, even Edens as crappy as this. "Believe it or not, Joey, I'm going to miss this place."

"Then you shouldn't have banged Shelly."

"What was I going to do? Have you seen the tits on her?"

"Seen them?" said Joey Mitts, a sad resignation in his croak of a voice. "I paid for them."

3

Viva Las Vegas

There was a time while I was living in California that I tried my hand at surfing, and in that period I learned a lesson. When an ocean wave is slamming you face-first into a rock, it's difficult to appreciate the pattern of dips and swells flowing like a mathematical equation across the surface of the sea.

I didn't waste any time in packing my belongings after Joey Mitts gave me the sack. One thing I had practiced over the years when things inevitably turned to crap in my life was stuffing my belongings into whatever bags I could find and burning rubber out of Dodge. Into the narrow backseat of my gray 911 Turbo, bought used when I was still flush with lawyering cash, I threw a couple suitcases of clothes. Into the front trunk I jammed a box of personal items, which, if you know anything about Porsches, meant there wasn't much in this world I considered personal.

I gave a celebratory whoop as I motored south out of Carson City. Time to move on, and good goddamn riddance. But I had given a whoop when I left the call center after Joey had gotten his mitts on me, and a whoop when I left the law firm after that dustup with Boggs, and a whoop when I left law school for the firm, and a whoop when I quit the Walmart for law school, and a whoop when I graduated from college, and a whoop when I left my father's house in New Jersey at last and for good. I had to admit, each successive whoop was starting to seem less celebratory and more forced. This whoop was the yelp of a beaten dog.

I had no job, no income, no lover, no friends, no family I could rely on, and not even an addiction to keep me entrenched in the present tense. I was as rootless and free as you could be in America, nothing to lose, which sounded a lot better when Dylan was singing it. Let's just say that when the landscape becomes a metaphor for your life, it's better not to be driving through Nevada. And I was headed where every loose tumbling weed of humanity heads when things go wrong: Las Vegas. But in Vegas, at least, I had a dice-thrower's chance of getting back on track.

"Mr. Maambong. This is Phillip Kubiak. Joey Mitts suggested I give you a call."

"Ah, yes, Mr. Kubiak," said Mr. Maambong in a precise voice, with an accent I couldn't quite place beyond being west of California and east of Kazakhstan. "We've been expecting your call. And how is our dear friend Mr. Mitts?"

"Prickly as ever. He mentioned you might have an opportunity for me."

"We have an opportunity, yes, for the right person. The question is whether that person is you."

"What exactly is the job, Mr. Maambong?"

"Does it matter, Mr. Kubiak?"

"Shouldn't it?"

"The opportunity pays extremely well."

"Then maybe it doesn't."

"All you need to know is that we service a specific type of clientele, and to that end we require a specific type of employee. Whether or not you are of the satisfactory type will require a face-to-face meeting. Are you still in servitude to our friend?"

"Not since twenty minutes ago."

"Excellent news," said Mr. Maambong. "We are not above poaching, but it can be an unpleasant business. We will be in Las Vegas next Wednesday, perhaps we could meet then. The suite elevators at the Aria, let's say at two in the afternoon."

"I'll be there, Mr. Maambong."

"Splendid," he said. "Come ready to travel."

Approaching Las Vegas in the dead of night, I came out of the mountains to see the lights of the strip beckon like a vision of promise in the distance. Even at that late hour the spotlights were blazing, the video billboards were whirling, the crowds were thick. I drove past the Wynn, the Venetian, the Bellagio, Paris, New York–New York, and every possibility under the moon floated in the air like motes of gold. Vegas is a city of maids and moguls, of fish and whales, of sweaty mobs and tanned, perfect bodies in air-conditioned cabanas. Wherever the line between the sides was drawn, I was in town to get on the right side of it. But as I pulled into the cement self-park behind the Excalibur, all to take advantage of the thirty-nine-dollar room rate, I knew just where I stood.

There is nothing longer than a Vegas week spent alone. I drank desultorily and whored perfunctorily and watched porn halfheartedly on the in-room television. I ran the loop at Red Rock Canyon in the early-morning hours, just as the sun kissed the flanks of the rugged rocks. I tried to discover what I could about this strange Mr. Maambong on the net and came up empty. I dropped a blue suit at a dry cleaners and fiddled with my résumé. I took a day to drive out to the Grand Canyon and had an ice-cream cone on the South Rim and then drove back. I swam in the piss-warm Excalibur pool.

The day before my interview I checked out of the Excalibur and into the classier and more expensive Hard Rock, in case Mr. Maambong happened to ask where I was staying. Wednesday morning I breakfasted early, took a quick swim, picked up my suit at the cleaners, printed my résumé on bond paper in the hotel's business center. I shaved my jaw and my ears, plucked the hairs from my nose. I was brushed and bright and spiffy when I pulled into the front of the Aria and casually handed off my Porsche to the valet as if nothing could be more natural.

I was sitting on a green couch in the Aria Sky Suite lounge, beside a square vase of white orchids, when she came for me. "Mr. Kubiak, my name is Cassandra. I'll take you to Mr. Maambong now. Follow me, please."

In the ride to the high floor I tried not to give this Cassandra the up-down and failed, but she wasn't paying me the least bit of attention. Red hair, green eyes, pale skin, loose white blouse, tight black skirt, green high heels. Her head was bowed, her neck was long, the toe of one shoe pointed to the elevator floor. She was a perfect piece of porcelain, and in the presence of her flawlessness I was as inconsequential as the elevator carpet. If I had a hammer I would have tapped her into smithereens. Mr. Maambong, Mr. Maambong.

"Cassandra," I said, "could I ask a question?"

"Of course."

"What exactly does Mr. Maambong do?"

"This and that," she said, no smile cracking her faultless face. "And sometimes the other thing." The elevator doors hissed open. "This way, please."

Cassandra led me through the wood-paneled entrance to the suite and then parked me in the parlor. I watched the twitch of her tight black skirt as she left the room. With its plush couch, its tasteful gray walls, the swirl of colors in its painting, it was like sitting in the waiting room of a topflight plastic surgeon. I opened my briefcase and pulled out my spiffed-up résumé. My leg bounced as I wiped my hand on my pants.

"Ah, Mr. Kubiak, you have come." The accent was familiar, the tone as formal as the phone call. The man who stood before me was tall, stick thin, bald as a coffee bean, cinnamon roast. His suit was white, his shirt red, his tie thin and black. He leaned heavily on a cane and wore dark round sunglasses.

I leaped to my feet with embarrassing alacrity. "Mr. Maambong," I said, reaching out a hand to shake. "Phillip Kubiak."

"Yes you are," he said, lifting the cane in his right hand as an apology for not taking hold of my clammy palm. "You had an easy trip, we hope. And we assume you are keeping yourself busy."

"Well, you know Vegas."

"Indeed we do, Mr. Kubiak."

"Call me Phillip."

"No thank you. Where are you staying?"

"The Hard Rock."

"Ah, youth. Good. The pool, we are told, is a scene. What have you there?"

"My résumé."

"A résumé, how charming." He took my proffer, glanced at it for a moment, and then with his oversize hand crumpled it into a ball and tossed it onto the floor like a sneeze.

"Maybe I should have put Harvard on it," I said.

"It would not have mattered. This is not the kind of employment you get with a résumé. A résumé only tells us what you think we are looking for, but we can assure you, Mr. Kubiak, you have no idea. We knew most everything on that piece of paper before we accepted your call, and we have learned more in the time since. Now let us find out the rest, shall we?"

4

THE TEST

Mr. Maambong sat across from me, his hands braced on his cane, the too-bright Vegas light reflecting in horizontal slashes off his dark round glasses. "You are lost in a desert," said Mr. Maambong. "It is broiling hot, you are weak with thirst."

"Where's the desert?" I said.

"It does not matter. It is just a question. You are weak with thirst and you see a tortoise on its back, its little green legs waving helplessly in the air. On the tortoise's belly is a jug of water with a red cap on top. Drawn on the red cap is a black *X*. What do you do?"

"Am I a cyborg?"

"You are you."

"Am I dying of thirst?"

"You are weak with thirst."

"What's the difference?"

"That's for you to decide."

"Then I drink the water," I said. "If I don't drink, I'll be too weak to get out of there. I gamble that the black *X* doesn't mean poison. If it does, either way I die, so I do what I have to do and take the chance."

"No need to explain, Mr. Kubiak," said Mr. Maambong, with a smile that showed off a set of canine teeth longer than his incisors. "This isn't a math test where you get credit for showing your work. How did you lose your position at Gold Dog International?"

"Joey Mitts fired me."

"Why?"

"For going off script."

"Why did you go off script?"

"There were so many cautions and caveats in Joey's script I couldn't keep the customers on the line long enough to close, so I made modifications. The job was to close."

"Was your deviation from Joey's script the only reason?"

Ahh, the rub. I had learned over the years to tell people what truths they wanted to hear, which usually meant lying through my pearly teeth. It was a surprisingly effective strategy for dealing with clients and adversaries both, and I was damn good at it. You could say I was a natural born liar. But Mr. Maambong was neither a client nor an adversary, he was something other, and it was tricky determining what lies he wanted to hear. Adding to the difficulty, a man named Bert was sitting behind me, tracking my pulse rate, my heart rate, my perspiration rate, my blood pressure. With straps across my chest, a cuff on my arm, wires taped to my fingers, and a band tight around my skull, I felt like I was in some apocalyptic form of Japanese Jeopardy!

"I also slept with the receptionist," I said.

"Shelly Levalle?"

"You know her?"

"Indeed we do, Mr. Kubiak. She has been with Mr. Mitts for decades. Her breasts were legendary in the halls of the Nevada Legislative Building. Well done."

"When I was hired, Joey told me she was off-limits."

"And yet you had relations with her anyway."

"If that's what you would call it."

"What would you call it?"

"Sunday afternoons?"

"So tell us, Mr. Kubiak. These Sundays you had with Shelly Levalle that cost you your job. Were they worth it?"

"Truth?"

"That is all we are asking for."

"Well, you've seen her breasts."

We were in the dining room of the suite. There was a kitchen counter with a coffeemaker, there was a potted tree, there was one wide window, its slatted blinds partially open. Mr. Maambong had watched impassively as I was trussed like a turkey by Bert, a plump, sweaty man in white shirt and black tie. The straps and wires were linked to a box that was plugged into Bert's laptop, the screen of which was tilted out of my vision.

"Is all this necessary?" I had said as Bert placed his straps.

"Oh yes indeed," said Mr. Maambong. "It is crucial that we get truthful answers to our queries. We wouldn't want you trying to bluff your way into our employ."

"I wouldn't think of doing such a thing."

"Ah, Mr. Kubiak, if we didn't already know you were lying just then, we'd be disappointed. Are we ready, Bert? Excellent. Now in these kinds of proceedings, it helps to get a baseline. Tell us something false."

"My name is Dick Triplett," I said.

"Now tell us something true."

"I'll be the best employee you ever had."

Mr. Maambong turned his head toward Bert to get a sign. "Let us try this once more, and this time with feeling," he said calmly. "Tell us a lie."

"I enjoy watching hockey on television."

"Good. Now where are you staying in Las Vegas?"

"I'm at the Hard Rock."

"And before that, Mr. Kubiak, where were you staying?"

I was about to blurt out some face-saving untruth, but I stopped and looked at those dark round glasses, so much like the eyes of a beetle and just as inscrutable. "I was at the Excalibur."

"You sound embarrassed."

"Wouldn't you be?"

"Indeed." Mr. Maambong glanced at Bert and a smile broke out on his face. "Finally we are getting somewhere."

After that the questions came fast as tennis balls from a machine, bizarre hypotheticals mixed with queries about my actual past, all while Bert validated the truth of my answers.

"You are in a dark wood," said Mr. Maambong. "It is a cold day. You have a handgun but no hunting license. You see a buck lying on the snow, alive but with a bullet hole in its belly and blood all around. Do you shoot it to put it out of its misery, shoot it for its antlers and meat, shoot it because you can, or walk on because you don't have a hunting license and there are rangers in the woods?"

"Am I weak with hunger?"

"That's not part of the question."

"But I admit to being a bit peckish so I don't shoot it at all, instead I start carving it up for the meat. I don't want the antlers. What would I do with a set of antlers? But I can eat the meat if I'm hungry. Maybe I'll eat it raw, because I won't want to set a fire with the rangers prowling around."

"What do you want, Mr. Kubiak, from this job?"

"Money."

"Anything else?"

"Sex. Maybe with that Cassandra."

"Mr. Kubiak, listen now. If you, by chance, get this position, you are not to have sex with Cassandra. Ever. She is off-limits to you. Is that understood?"

"Yes, sir."

He tilted his chin toward Bert. "Good. That is one thing about which we need to be clear."

"It's clear enough."

"Now we all want money and sex, to want such things is to be a breathing human being. Tell us what else you want."

I paused a moment to figure out the truth for myself. "I suppose I want to be somebody."

"What does that mean?"

"It means when I walk through a crowd in the street I want them all to know exactly what I am."

"And what is that, Mr. Kubiak?"

"Better than they are."

"You are on the beach in Maine. A lobsterman has pulled his traps from his boat and one of the creatures has escaped. It is scuttling toward the water, scuttling toward its freedom. The lobsterman doesn't see. What do you do?"

"I pick it up for dinner."

"It snaps at your finger with a claw. You can feel the bite in the bone. You drop the creature and howl as it continues toward the sea. What do you do then?"

"I step on its head and then boil it red."

"Are you a good lawyer, Mr. Kubiak?"

"I'm crackerjack," I said.

"Then how did you lose your position at the firm of Peel & Boggs in Sacramento?"

"The economy tanked," I said. "The firm contracted. I was let go in the contraction."

"Bert says you are telling the truth," said Mr. Maambong, "which means you believe what you are telling us, but we all know that is not the whole truth."

"I'd go with Bert."

"What would Mr. Boggs tell us if we called him right now? Would he say it was the economy?"

"Did you talk to Boggs?"

"Do you think you walked in here by happenstance, Mr. Kubiak? Do you think we are concerned about your GPA in college as listed on your résumé? Do you have any idea what we do?"

"No, I don't."

"Exactly. Why were you let go by the firm of Peele & Boggs?"

"Boggs and I had a falling-out," I said.

"Over what?"

"Ask me about a frog on the highway or something. Would I swerve or run it over. I'd swerve to run it over."

"You had sex with Mr. Boggs's wife," said Mr. Maambong. "What is he, in his sixties?"

"She was a trophy wife."

"And how did Mr. Boggs end up in the hospital with a broken jaw?"

"He didn't appreciate my brand of polish," I said.

Mr. Maambong smiled his canine smile and leaned forward. It was as if the beetle eyes of his sunglasses were peering deep inside me, beyond all the shields I had built around my darkest truths. And he was pleased with what he saw.

"When did you first realize you were different from everyone else?" he said.

"I'm not so different."

"What would Joey Mitts say? Or your Mr. Boggs? Should we get the numbers from Bert for that answer or are we going to stop kidding ourselves?"

"What do you want from me?"

"How old were you?"

"I was seven," I said. "It happened when my grandfather died. I wasn't sad. I was supposed to be sad, and I pretended to cry. I rubbed my eyes, but it was an act. What I really wanted to do was watch TV."

"He was a nasty man, we suppose, not worth the tears."

"Not at all," I said. "He was the sweetest. But I just wanted to watch cartoons. And I knew that was wrong. So I rubbed my eyes to fool my mother. I don't know if it worked, but she gave me ice cream and put me in front of the TV because I was so sad. But I wasn't sad. I had ice cream and cartoons. Why would I be sad?"

"When was your first fistfight?" said Mr. Maambong.

"The very next day. Barry Sonenfeld. He said something about my shoes."

"Something nasty?"

"It didn't matter."

"I think we have enough," said Mr. Maambong. "Thank you, Bert. You can free Mr. Kubiak from your chains of truth. We are done here."

"If you knew all this about me from the first, why did you drag me down to Vegas? What the hell was the point?"

5

Copper

I won't deny he got to me, Mr. Maambong, with those ridiculous animal questions and the beetle gaze of his dark glasses. I won't deny that his test touched some nerve deep inside that jangled everything and sent me spinning. I won't deny that when I left that suite the taste of copper was so strong in my mouth I couldn't stop myself from spitting right onto the carpet of the corridor.

I could still taste the copper as I sped out of Las Vegas on the same route I had taken just a few days before on my Grand Canyon jaunt, past Henderson and Boulder City, flying over the Colorado on the Hoover Dam bypass on the way to Kingman. I was still then blind to the root pattern of my life, but the flavor of a sucked-upon penny was as familiar to me as cheap rye had been to my father. My teeth tingled of copper when I was fired by Joey Mitts, when I decked Old Man Boggs, when I found myself cheating on my wife with some scag I found in a bar with soft hands and a preference for the rough. Copper was the taste of my condition, and somehow Mr. Maambong had tapped into the mother lode.

But then he'd surprised me. "The point of the test, Mr. Kubiak, was to see if you measure up."

"You knew the answer before you started."

"Actually, no, we did not. But we've found that you measure up better than you might imagine." He laughed at my expression, his laughter loud, dark. "Don't look so surprised, Mr. Kubiak. You passed with flying colors. Have you ever been to Miami?"

"No, actually."

"Then it will be a pleasant excursion. We are having a get-together at our house in Miami in a few days. It is by the sea, it is quite lovely."

"Does that mean I have the job?"

"Not yet."

"So this is another interview?"

"A competition, let's say. There will be other candidates."

"How many?"

"More than a few."

"It must be a hell of a job."

"It is that indeed, Mr. Kubiak. With quite the upside. We'll have a hotel room waiting. Don't be late."

As I headed south to Kingman, as I ripped east across the massive wastelands of Arizona and New Mexico, and then farther east into Texas, the desert landscape seemed less a metaphor for my life than something to be passed through with all possible speed. I had hopes that this long ride, this furious run toward my future, would strip the taste of copper from my mouth once and for all. Copper was the flavor of my failure; I was driving now toward success. This time I wasn't going to allow anything, or anyone, to get in my way, which was why east of Amarillo I ditched Route 40 and headed southeast, through the center of Fort Worth and into the guts of Louisiana.

I had one loose end to bind before Mr. Maambong got hold of it and started unraveling the dark truths of my past.

***

Saint Gabriel is a bleak little oil town on the east bank of the Mississippi. I had been there twice before, so I had a sense of the ways and means of the place. Out of Baton Rouge I headed straight south and then took a left onto the small road that ran right through the belly of the town, such as it was, keeping my windows up to avoid that slicked oil smell from the refineries. I passed the bright-red shack of Big Jake's Bar-B-Q without stopping. I'd pull in on my way out of the city for some of Big Jake's famous pulled pork, but I knew enough not to fill my gut with dead pig before my appointment at the Louisiana Correctional Institute for Women. Something about the stink of the place could cause even the dead to rise.

"Give me a kiss. That's right. And another. Oh, you look so good, Phil, I could take you out back and eat you like fried chicken."

"It's good to see you, too."

"I'm glad you came. Sit down, I need you to do some things for me."

"I'm just passing through."

"You're working with them lawyers in California, right?"

"Not anymore."

"What happened?"

"The economy."

"Damn thing's no good for no one no more. The whole country's cracking up with poor. So what then are you doing with yourself?"

"I'm between things."

"I know what that means. Nothing is what that means. But you're still a lawyer, right? Because I need you to talk to Silverman for me and I think he'll listen better to another lawyer. He's not doing any damn thing. Tell him to start doing something."

"There's not much he can do. You lost at trial, you lost your appeal, you were denied federal habeas corpus."

"I hear the ladies in here talk. Every one of them but me is getting a new hearing. There's always something to be done. You tell that Silverman to get the hell off his ass. I'm getting old and ugly in here."

"Not ugly," I said, meaning it.

"Oh, you," said my mother. "Give your moms another kiss."

My mother had been the low-rent belle of Belleville, New Jersey, when she birthed me. Those eyes so blue, those lips so red, the way she shook her thin hips in those short shorts. I didn't realize how lucky I was to suckle at her breasts before she grew bored with the whole breast-feeding thing at three weeks and put me on the bottle. My strongest childhood memory of my mother is her squinting at me as she smoked a cigarette, as if I were as indecipherable as a Frenchman. I never knew what she was thinking and she felt the same about me. Whether I was crying because I had crapped my diaper, or crying because I was hungry, or reaching out my arms for a hug, it didn't much matter; she couldn't read me for the life of her.

"For God sakes, Helen, his diaper is full of crap," my father would say, coming home from his job with the Belleville Public Works Department to find me in a state.

"I didn't realize," she'd say, sitting on the couch with a cigarette and a magazine.

"Why the hell do you think he was crying?"

"How should I know?" She'd flip the pages with the fingers holding her cigarette. "He's a baby. That's what they do."

This regular give-and-take was relayed to me by my father long after my mother had left, in the nights when he was waxing nostalgic over his bottle of Old Overholt, shedding the occasional unapologetic tear. He would tell me he loved my mother with all his soul despite her failings, that she continued to be the love of his life even after she deserted him and her child and ran away with Jesse Duchamp, that he'd take her back in a heartbeat. She couldn't help herself when it came to men like Jesse Duchamp, he told me, she was just built that way. And I suppose she was.

"What's with your eye?" I said.

31

She reached up and pressed the bruise above her right cheek. "That reminds me. I also need you to get two thousand dollars to a man named Louis Boudin in Winn Parish. Can you do that for me, Phil?"

"Two thousand dollars?"

"That's right."

"Jesus, Mom."

"To Louis Boudin. Write it down. Boudin, like the sausage."

"What sausage?"

"He's somewhere up there in Winn Parish, just ask around. His daughter's in here with me and she's country crazy. She pounded my face and told me if I don't get her daddy the money, she's going to slice my throat like a pig hanging from his hindquarters."

"Just out of the blue she hit you in the face?"

"That girl's got a knife hidden in the leg of her bed. She'll slice me just like she said."

"Tell the guards."

"That's not how it works in here."

"Have you been borrowing money again?"

"How else you expect me to get my cigarettes and sodas? It's not like you're sending any hard currency. Your dad was good at posting money to my account but then he got the liver cancer and that was that, just when I needed him most. God, I loved that man."

"No you didn't."

"Think what you want to think. We had something beautiful."

"You left him first chance you had," I said.

"Not the first chance," she said. "Just the wrong chance."

My father plucked my mother right out of high school. He was in his early thirties, large and handsome; he had stepped into the prize ring a few times—without winning any prizes I might add—and played first base on the municipal softball team. She was stunning in that willowy and naughty high school way, too damn good for the pimpled schoolboys swarming around her. My father caught her eye flashing around some of that sanitation money and my mother was naive enough to snap at the lure. I was the product of their torrid fling, and the precipitating cause of the disaster that was their marriage.

"I miss your father, Phil. I do."

"Okay."

"Do you believe me?"

"Does it matter?"

"To me it does. But with him now gone, what was I going to do about money other than borrow it? You sure don't send any. And Jesse would have been stocking my account if he didn't up and die on me, too."

"Jesse Duchamp didn't just happen to die, Mom."

"He's not here to help, is he?"

"Because you shot him in the head."

"There's a story behind that, though. Just ask Silverman when you're talking to him about my case. He'll tell you the truth. My lord, Phil, you do look tasty. You got a girl?"

"No."

"Why not? A face like yours, they must be lining up. Don't be so picky. I got a right to some grandchildren, don't I? You never should have let that wife of yours go. She had the hips for bearing children."

"Has a man named Maambong been in touch with you?"

"What kind of name is Maambong?"

"Not Nigerian."

"Who is he, another lawyer?"

"He's just a guy. I'm sort of up for a job and he might end up giving you a call. Can you do me a favor and just tell him I was a sweet little kid if he calls."

"You want me to lie?"

"Stop laughing. I need this job."

"B-O-U-D-I-N."

"Like the sausage."

"You were a monster, Phil, but you were my monster."

"If this Maambong calls, he doesn't need to know all the details about the hamsters and stuff. Or the shoplifting. Or that time I stole your drugs."

"I'm still mad about that, young man."

"That was then and it's all different now and I need the job. But you can tell him I didn't cry when Grandpop died if you want. He already knows."

"You didn't cry?"

"But nothing else, all right?"

"Why didn't you cry?"

"I don't know. I didn't feel like it."

"I didn't cry, either, you want to know the truth. He wasn't as nice to me as he was to you. Did you cry when your father died?"

"No."

"Well then, we are different. I cried for him, I did. I mean, who was going to take care of me in here with him gone? Is it a good job, Phil?"

"Good enough that if I get it I could start sending in money for your account."

"Okay, then. But you'll talk to Silverman."

"I'll talk to Silverman."

"I got to get out of here. These women are all criminals. And you won't forget about Louis Boudin in Winn Parish."

"Hey Mom, let me ask you. When you shot Jesse Duchamp in the head in that motel room in New Orleans, was there any kind of weird taste in your mouth?"

"What kind of taste?"

"Like you were sucking pennies or something?"

"No, of course not. That's like crazy."

"Good."

"Who sucks pennies? All I could taste, Phil, was love. I never loved him more than when I blew his brains across the room. Funny how

that is. I have something else to tell you. I thought you should know.
I have a girlfriend."

"That's nice."

"Her name's Lana. She's a blonde. Not a real blonde, but still."

"I'm happy for you, Mom. Let's try not shooting her, too."

I wasn't thinking of the dead Jesse Duchamp as I skittered through
New Orleans on the way east, past the cheap southern beach towns
of Mississippi and Georgia, but his ghost haunted every mile. He had
destroyed my family, crippled my father with a sorrow that all the rye
in Jersey couldn't drown, driven my mother to murder and a life of
imprisonment. He was a killer himself, let's not forget that, with a string
of homicides in botched convenience-store robberies across Ohio and
northern Pennsylvania committed on his way to his ill-fated meeting
with my mother at the Stone Horse bar in Belleville. Yet the only thing
more frightening than running into a Jesse Duchamp was being a Jesse
Duchamp. He had become for me the exemplar of where my natural
inclinations, if unchecked, might lead: to a cheap New Orleans motel
room with someone else's wife holding the gun that was about to blow
apart my skull.

Along the panhandle, dropping into the dangle of Florida, past
the retirement havens of The Villages, skirting past the fantasy lands
of Orlando, down the same interstate that up north cut less than five
miles east of my hometown, I made my way with determined speed to
a brighter fate. The address Mr. Maambong had given led me across
Biscayne Bay, past an immense medical center, and then up and around
an island of extravagant homes that surrounded some exclusive country
club.

A closed gate fronted a modernist expanse of white concrete and
glass, with soaring curved lines and its name in steel letters above the
ivy-covered wall: Fisi.

"I'm looking for Mr. Maambong," I said into the speaker box at the gate. "My name is Phillip Kubiak."

The response over the intercom was mere static, and for a moment nothing happened. Then the motor started churning and the gate slowly slid open. I drove my Porsche across the tiled cement of the drive toward the front door. When I climbed out of the car, the house's front door was open and Cassandra was waiting for me. Her copper hair waved gently in the wind, her bright-red lips twitched.

"We expected you much sooner, Mr. Kubiak. You must have driven east with extraordinary care. In the right lane maybe, with your blinkers on? Well, hurry in, we're just about to begin the festivities."

6

Chess

"You've barely touched your beer," said the outlaw to the magazine writer in that foul-smelling shack. "Give it another chance. They say it gets better with a little airing."

The magazine writer lifted her mug and with eyes closed tried again. This time she expected the vinegary rankness beneath the stench and was not disappointed. The sip stayed in her mouth, a small victory.

"See, every terrible thing is better in its second helping," said the outlaw. "The beer is just one of the ways Ginsberg keeps the crowds out of his bar. A single glance at the decor is enough to know that he likes his alone time. And let's not forget the dead animals. Look at the deceased kangaroo rat curled in the corner, speckled with sand that has blown in through the wallboards. Look at the mounted head of the big horn over the door, mangy and marble-eyed, much like Ginsberg himself. And then there's the ugly little stuffed thing behind the bar. It's a meerkat, a kind of mongoose from the Kalahari. Ginsberg bought it to scare off the scorpions, but the taxidermy was done in some cheap Chinese sweatshop and now it smells vaguely of rotting horse. Yet Ginsberg has grown attached. Think on that a moment. His one true friend in this world is a stuffed meerkat. I would consider it pathetic, except it is one true friend more than I will ever know."

The magazine writer jotted a note on her pad. This story she was hearing wasn't anything like she had expected. No paeans to justice, no aggressive self-aggrandizement. It was all, to be truthful, just a little pathetic. When she looked up from the paper, the outlaw was staring at her.

"No, I'm not feeling sorry for myself," he said. "I'm just stating fact. I know exactly what I am; I'm determined that you see it clearly, too. That's the purpose of this interview, right? So breathe deeply: take in the fetid atmosphere of the only place I can now comfortably show my face. I want you to register how far I have fallen from the younger and still whole figure of Phillip Kubiak, standing on the far edge of the rooftop patio of that modernist house in Miami. If this sad and solitary wreck before you is the after, then he is the before, a man whose future is suddenly, and unexpectedly, infused with a great, if mysterious, promise.

"Picture him there, straight-backed, two-eyed, broad-shouldered and handsome, well dressed, well shod. Behind him there is music, laughter, the celebratory hum of wealth. He holds a glass of fine single malt and gazes across the glister of the wide canal, on which the house is sited, to the palm trees, the high-rise resorts, the perfect pale beach beyond. The ocean is so blue it had to have been put on earth just for him. Boaters that motor along the canal look up to see him standing by the rail on that roof and can't stop themselves from waving, hoping he will wave back. He doesn't give them the satisfaction. Instead he turns, and with eyes hard as the cut crystal of his Scotch glass he peers at the small claque of candidates that stand between him and his rightful place in this world.

"And already he is plotting."

***

There were twenty or so on that rooftop with me, along with those I already knew were with the firm. Behind the bar, Bert, lie-detector Bert, sweated in a plaid vest while he poured vodka and squeezed limes. Cassandra, in a shiny green sheath that matched her eyes, tossed her hair and smiled at me from a distance. As Mr. Maambong talked to a small group, he leaned on his cane and threw his head back in laughter. And I could tell that not all the others on that rooftop were candidates for the open position. A number seemed assured of their places in Mr. Maambong's scheme of things; they didn't have that edge of polite concentration and concentrated politeness that marks aspirants like a stain. That left seven or eight as competitors. I knew this game, and I knew the rules, which meant no rules. It was no longer about passing Mr. Maambong's tests; it was about playing the players.

This is the crux of it, so pay attention. Think of a game of chess. Each piece on the board controls its own territory and has its own quirks. The bishop attacks on a slant, the knight hops, the queen rules, and for that very reason she is always in danger. Pawns take mincing steps, yet can transmogrify into the most amazing things. But whatever the pieces arrayed before you, you never forget they are just knobs of wood to be maneuvered, or sacrificed, or utterly destroyed. That's the game I've played all my life, and it is as dispassionate as lunch. The rooftop patio was tiled in multicolored terracotta. I felt my cheeks twitch into a smile before I stepped onto the board.

"We want to thank you all for accepting our invitation for this weekend's festivities," speechified Mr. Maambong to the whole of the party. "We are in the business of servicing a very distinguished and powerful clientele and to that end we require from our employees the utmost loyalty, the utmost discretion, the utmost drive. That is what we will be looking for this weekend, along with your considerable individual skills, before we make our final decision as to whom we might hire. In return, if you obtain a position, we will be quite generous in your compensation and fringe benefits. That is why you are here, no?

For our outstanding medical and dental? In appreciation of your time and efforts in this tryout, we will be paying each of you one thousand dollars, payable upon the signing of a nondisclosure agreement insisted upon by our lawyers. Be aware that you may trifle with us, but you don't want to trifle with our lawyers. Tomorrow we will wake up with a bright morning jog and then the games will begin. Get your sleep, you'll need it. Now, my friends, please, let's enjoy our evening."

After the speech, the candidates congregated in wary huddles on the terra-cotta roof. With Scotch in hand, I made my way from grouping to grouping, taking the measure of my competition.

"Do you see that right there," said a man named Don, tall and beefy, with taut tendons framing his thick neck. Standing on the roof with me and another man, he was nodding and chuckling as he looked over at Cassandra. "Man, I need to hit that."

"You weren't here this afternoon by the pool," said the other man, Derrick. He was shorter and thinner than Don, with less arrogant features, but the resemblance was still close enough that they looked to be of the same gene pool. "She was sunbathing without her top. Man, they could use those beauties for marine recruitment. Put them on a poster above the words 'What we're fighting for.'"

"They'd be turning down enlistments," said Don, with another chuckle.

"Didn't you guys get Mr. Maambong's warning about Cassandra?" I said.

"Yeah, I did," said Derrick. "That's a bummer."

"But what's he going to do?" said Don, flexing. "Smack me with his cane?"

"Maybe you're right," I said. "It would be worth it anyway, wouldn't it?" I swallowed the rest of my Scotch, jiggled the ice. "I'm getting a refill. By the way, did you two know each other, I mean before you showed up here?"

"No, man," said Derrick. "Why?"

"You guys look like you pledged the same frat."

"We did," said big Don with a chuckle. "Phi fucka Sandra."

"Oh man," said Derrick. "That would be worth a paddling."

I joined in on their laughter before heading to order another couple of fingers of the good stuff from Bert. I leaned on the bar as he poured, looking around. A man and a woman came over and joined me. She grabbed a white wine; he ordered a rum and Coke.

"Don't you find this a little surreal?" said the woman, named Angela, tall and broad-shouldered, her mouth in a perpetual smirk. "In some fancy house, competing against each other to be the last person standing."

"Fighting for the final rose," I said.

"When I want a rose," she said, "I pick it myself, take a bite, and spit out the thorns."

"Remind me not to take you to the park."

She laughed. "Truth is, I always thought those shows were demeaning to everyone involved."

"Nothing demeaning about it," said the man, named Tom Preston. He was trim, and tightly coiled, and there was something cold about him, blank. He had a closely mown beard and a slight gap between his teeth that made him appear to be smiling all the time, but he wasn't smiling. "It's just the way it is. Life's a competition."

"But usually we know what we're competing for," said Angela.

"You don't know what you're competing for?" said Tom Preston.

"I mean what do they do here?" said Angela. "What will the job entail? Mr. Maambong still hasn't told us."

"Doesn't much matter, does it?" said Tom Preston. "We'll do what he tells us, at least at the beginning. What matters is what it gets us."

"Smile," I said. "He's looking over here. Where's he from anyway, do you know?"

"I went to school with a boy named Maambong from Manila," said Angela.

"Nice kid?"

"No," she said.

The frat-boy twins were now standing with Maambong, laughing at something he said. "Don and Derrick are sneaking in some extra face time with our potential boss," I said.

"Maybe we should join them," said Tom Preston. "Maybe we should make our presence felt." He looked at Angela and me like we were all plotting something together. "You coming?"

"I'll make an appearance," said Angela. "Give a little curtsy."

"Go ahead without me," I said. "I'll stay back and enjoy my drink."

I watched as they joined the group around Maambong. Interesting competition. Don and Derrick were idiots, I wasn't worried about them, but Angela was independent and quick—maybe too independent for my purposes. I couldn't get a read on Tom Preston, but there was something about him, something fierce and cold at the core. And he had been trying to build a team of the three of us, a move I respected. It was time to maybe build a team of my own.

"You think it matters how loud we hoot at Mr. Maambong's jokes?" said a woman named Riley with a twang in her voice. I had joined a cluster of three others, watching Mr. Maambong from a distance as our competitors listened to his stories and laughed at his wit. This Riley had a potato face, a short mop of pink hair, and a silver ring dripping out the bottom of her nose. "Because fake laughter is not in my toolbox."

"Nothing succeeds like sucking up," said a young man named Kief, short and wiry, with a loose-jawed slurry of a voice.

"Then why aren't you yukking it up with the rest of them?" said Riley.

"Pride."

"That and a fiver will get you a sandwich," said a handsome man named Gordon, oversize in every way, with a mop of short dreads. He wore a dark suit with an open white shirt, and his hands were huge. His hands were like great black crabs.

"I don't see you over there hanging on Mr. Maambong's every word," said Kief.

"They're so tight around him, it's like being closed out of a craps table," said Gordon.

"A man your size," said Riley, "you could just pick up one of them, toss him like a horseshoe, and take his place."

"It is tempting," said Gordon. "But I have enough enemies to last me. Tonight I believe I'll behave myself."

"Everything in life, when you get to the bone of it, is just high school," I said. "It's like we're in the back row again, smoking cigarettes and passing notes while they're in the front row, laughing at the teacher's jokes and studying every night for the SAT. I guess that makes them the A team."

"*A* as in aberrantly ambitious?" said Riley.

"*A* as in abnormally abased?" said Gordon.

"*A* as in apparent imbeciles?" said Kief.

"That has an *I*," said Gordon.

"It can't; my math teacher always told us there is no *I* in *imbecile*."

"I suppose Teach was wrong about that," said Riley.

"*A* as in fucking asswipes," I said.

Our laughter drew satisfyingly suspicious glances from the crew around Mr. Maambong.

It wasn't long until Mr. Maambong and his people made their way off the roof, leaving the eight candidates to congregate in a large pile of bland smiles and polite chatter. But already it seemed sides had been drawn. One by one the A team yawned and stretched and headed to the hotel to grab some sleep before the next day's sport, until it was just Riley and Kief and Gordon and myself on the roof patio, along with

Bert, of course, who stood dumbly behind the bar in his red vest, ever ready to mix our drinks and refill our nut bowls. We arranged some chairs in a circle and lit some cigarettes—only Gordon didn't smoke—and talked about this weird competition we had somehow volunteered to be part of.

"Does anyone know anything about this outfit we're prancing around like fools for?" said Gordon.

"No one I asked knew," said Kief. "It's a mystery."

"I maybe found something," said Riley. "I went into this darknet I have access to and put out a request for information on Maambong and this address. I set it up so that none of the traffic could be linked back to me, and then I sat back like a rockfish waiting for a school of minnows to swim by. I hit a lot of rumors, warnings, the usual bullshit stuff that floats around onionland, but one thing came back enough times to hook my attention."

"Go ahead," I said.

"Wait a second," said Kief. He stubbed out his butt, slipped a spindled joint from a pants pocket, and sparked it up. "Anyone want to get baked?" he said, as he held the first drag in his lungs.

"Man, we got ourselves a competition tomorrow," said Gordon.

"Exactly," said Kief. "A good night's sleep is not just optional, but imperative."

"Go ahead, Riley," I said. "What did you snag?"

"Just a name, but it gives you an idea of what they might have in mind for us. Among those that say they know, they say Maambong is the front man for something called the Hyena Squad."

We all stayed silent for a moment to let that sink in. Kief took a long drag from his joint.

"They want a pack of hyenas," said Gordon, finally.

"What the hell have we gotten ourselves into?" said Kief, before letting loose a smoke-filled cackle.

And the rest of us joined him, if not in the drug, at least in the laughter, because it sounded so right. The Hyena Squad. Which meant we all were now aspiring to turn ourselves into vicious little scavengers with sniveling laughs. That knowledge seemed to burn away any pretenses we might have had with each other. And in that atmosphere of openness, with the sweet smoke of Kief's reefer swirling around us, I volunteered my tale of how I became mixed up with the mysterious Mr. Maambong. I started it off by describing my failed careers as lawyer and gold salesman, before detailing how I got the boot from Joey Mitts, and how he slipped me Maambong's name and number. I tried to keep it light, and didn't stint on my description of Shelly Levalle's breasts, but I told it all. It was not a history of which I was particularly proud, but the perception of candor is always more important than candor itself, and I couldn't be sure what Mr. Maambong had told anyone else about my somewhat sordid past.

The move seemed to work, because after my confession, one by one my fellow competitors made confessions of their own.

7

THE LAST CHANCE CREW

Riley: "Kuta Beach. It was all about Kuta Beach. Man, I've never been, but I see it in my mind's eye like I was born there—the white sand, the laid-back beach bars, the long symmetrical break of the waves. I don't surf, but I would have on Kuta Beach. Cowabunga, bitches. Okay, I'll be honest. There was also a girl.

"Isn't that how all these stories begin? There was a girl. In a bar. Crap, is there a more clichéd cliché? But that night, in that Austin dive, it was like Terry was looking for me, the way she zeroed in. Hell yes we hooked right up, and I can tell you, it was like all my life I had been looking for her. She was tall, almost a foot taller than me, with shoulders and hips and a feline smile with a little pink tongue. Terry bowed her head to me and lapped like a leopard and all my defenses unspooled. After one night with her I was lost.

"Is there a problem, Kief? My God, if you saw her, you would have melted into a puddle of want.

"It didn't take but a week before, along with the confessing and the laughing and the screwing, we were planning. It's sort of a girl thing, you know, to be so quick on the draw. First a place together maybe, so we could keep our crappy jobs. Or what about just packing up a van and going all Kerouac on America's ass? Or better yet, what about a trip to Bali? Yeah. Bali. That was the ticket. There was a beach she told me about where the surfers hung and Bintang was cheap and nobody cared about anything but that evening's sunset. Kuta Beach. It sounds sexual, doesn't it? Kuta Beach. My Kuta got wet just thinking about it.

"The only issue, of course, was money. I was working in some tragically hip coffee shop, and she was an office manager, and between the two of us we were barely cranking out enough to get by, better yet to jet off to some Asian paradise to live out our lives barefoot and free. But then Terry came up with an idea.

"See, I was only pulling espresso shots because I was on probation for a hack on a government database that I still can't talk about or, I have been informed, I will be immediately shot. The case, though, got a fair amount of publicity at the time and I was a celebrity in the hacker world for a minute and a half. But my probation kept me from getting work in the technical sector, or even from going online—though I fudged that because, hell, it was too easy not to—thus the crappy indie coffee shop. Terry said she didn't know any of this until I told her the whole sad story, but in the telling it gave her an idea.

"There was a small customer who paid her company electronically. The amounts weren't large enough to really matter, no specific person was keeping tabs on the account. And best of all, the customer's system was antiquated. If we could break into their system, we could divert the payments to an account of our choosing. It wouldn't be much, we might be able to divert twenty, twenty-five thou before the missing payments would be discovered, but by then we could be halfway around the world, with enough to get a start on a new life on the sandy edge of the Indian Ocean. Terry told me all this with her lips on my neck and her hand a butterfly inside of me, and let me tell you, in that position it made perfect sense.

"Yeah, yeah, I know. It's as obvious as rain now, but that doesn't mean I wasn't shocked when the FBI showed up at my door. And it wasn't twenty or twenty-five thousand, it was more than half a million. And it was gone, all of it, along with Terry, who I later learned actually made it to Kuta Beach with her boyfriend, a surfer dude named Flap Top. In a way, I think that hurt the most. Flap Top? Really?

"When I got out of jail, there was no one waiting for me, not my mother, or my brother, or the friends who had never visited, or any Silicon Valley giant anxious to use and abuse my slick talents. I was a two-time loser and I was alone, and lost, and wondering what the hell to do with the rest of my sad, pitiful life.

"Three days out of prison I got a text message about a lucrative employment opportunity. The only requirement was absolute discretion. If I was interested I was to show up at an interview the very next day in Chicago. I was given a time and the name of a hotel and nothing else. I was in Austin, but I drove fifteen hours straight, showed up when told, and that was when Cassandra brought me up to the presidential suite to meet Mr. Maambong."

Kief: "Maambong got hold of me when I was out of work, too. But my unemployment, unlike Riley's and Phil's, wasn't my fault. At the time I was being considered by the cops as, get this, a person of interest in an arson investigation. Let me tell you, that sure as hell puts a crimp in your employment possibilities. No top-paying company would even glance at my résumé. There were some possibilities at this start-up or that start-up, all with pay less than my unemployment, but I decided I'd rather sit home all day with Netflix and my bong than put in with another damn start-up. The hell with slaving for a group of preening weenies desperately trying to crank their earnings by underpaying their engineers. And, in all honesty, my track record with start-ups wasn't so sizzling.

"Out of school I scored a primo job with GE, and I didn't know how good I had it, the pay, the lunches—ripping lunches at a reasonable price; they had veal every Tuesday. Veal! But I ditched that for a bioengineering start-up on its second round of financing. They said they were hot on a cure for Crohn's Disease, for arthritis, for cancer, for God's sake. Cancer.

"You want to make a bundle in this world, dudes? Cure cancer.

"The company's founders had hit on some way to genetically engineer these things called monoclonal antibodies that target diseases like a bullet. I could give you all the bio mumbo jumbo, but who cares, really. The pay was only okay, but the stock options were rich, and if it panned out like we all expected, I'd be done by thirty.

"I was on the team in charge of evaluating the experimental treatments. We killed enough mice to feed a third-world country if they didn't mind picking tumors out of their teeth. My job was to keep the diagnostic machines running. We had everything from spectroscopes to electron microscopes. I wrote the machines' programs, performed mechanical repairs when necessary, compiled the results—basic mechanical engineering stuff—while the bio-brains engineered the antibodies.

"And this is what we found as we cranked in the numbers and tallied the results: nothing. Not a damn thing. One experiment after another, all failures.

"Trust me when I tell you I know what failure tastes like: it's like sucking the wrong end of a dead goat. Our funding was drying up, we were graduating people left and right—that's what the managers called layoffs, graduations, which tells you all you need to know about those assholes—we were bleeding money and the results showed nothing. We weren't going to get a third round of financing, and surely not an IPO. My stock options had turned into toilet paper. My father died on his construction job. He worked and he died. It's enough to get you thinking, if you're not blowing dope every night to chase away the anxiety.

"Then a miracle. Hallelujah, brothers. Correlations started linking up. Progress was being proven with every graph spit out by the machines. We were on to something. The attitude around the place pinked right up. It was like we had all just popped the perfect pill, something like Molly cut with coke. I even started dating a lab tech from the third floor with pale-blue eyes. And the good vibrations weren't restricted to the company. The venture boys started circling again, throwing their money at us. A letter of intent to sell out to one of the big pharma firms was signed, and as the due diligence began, we were, all of us, promised ginormous bonuses. I was too excited about the future to be concerned about the hired guns sent in to check on our results.

"The fire wiped out everything. The building went up like a bale of hay, man. The company was renting three floors of a six-story building and everything we had was fried, along with the deli on the first floor and the offices above us. The cops suspected arson and one of the law firms on the fifth floor represented criminals and so that seemed to explain that: disappointed defendants, angry victims, the world turns, and fire cleanses, right? But what it meant for the company was a quick, sad death. All their lab samples, their technology, everything that could prove up the glowing numbers we had produced were gone in the blaze.

"Luckily for me, I had already removed all my stuff in a cardboard box. The guards had given me a few minutes to do that, at least, before they marched me out of the building. It was still standing then, the building, though my dates with the lab tech on the third floor no longer were. But even before the fire, the sale with the pharma firm, the sale that would make me rich as a king, that was as good as torched. It seemed that, quote, irregularities, unquote, in the findings had been discovered by the hired guns. The corporate assholes needed a scapegoat and decided I was it. So they graduated me, and marched me right out the doors. I remained under suspicion even though any evidence of how the irregularities got into the results was destroyed in the fire along with everything else.

"It was during my period of forced unemployment that one of the lawyers for the pharma firm showed up at my apartment. He was wearing a suit; I was wearing a pair of boxers and a ratty robe. He was clean shaven; I wasn't. He had showered that week, probably more than once. I had gone through so much weed I couldn't remember if I had showered that month.

"With two fingers, the pharma lawyer lifted a sock from the couch before sitting down. He leaned back, spread his arms wide, smirked like the kind of asshole who told everyone he met he had gone to Harvard, which he had, and he did. He said how impressed he had been by my efforts to bring about the sale. He said everything I had done was so clean, that the slight alterations I had made in the code and the equipment were virtually undetectable. It would have been the perfect scam, he said, except for a certain piece of information that had slipped out of a certain third-floor lab tech during a night of rather prodigious sex. His smile let me know that a Harvard man had done the investigative work personally.

"I asked him if he had come to gloat and he said yeah, a little, but then he gave me a card with a phone number on it. It was the number of somebody he had done business with in the past and would do business with in the future and could put my skills to good use. And then he told me to make sure that Mr. Maambong sent the referral fee."

Gordon: "When I was growing up in Fountain Park in Saint Louis, was a cat on the corner name of Nomar, just a few years older than me, who ran a pack of young boys selling drugs to those suburban cars driving by. The boys would take the orders, take the drugs from beneath the rock where they stashed it, take the money to Nomar, and take the arrests when they inevitably came on down. 'They just boys,' Nomar would say when confronted by this mother or that brother, 'a few months in juvie will do them good.' Every morning when I walked by that corner on my way to school, Nomar would call out, 'I'm a get you, Gordo. Yes I am.'

"But my mother was strong, and damn, she knew how to hit. There was no way she was going to let me become the tool of some lowlife, low-level dealer man. After school she had her hooks in me, taking me to art classes, to sporting leagues, to swimming lessons. Swimming lessons. My mother. But whatever she did, it worked, and I stayed on the mostly straight and somewhat narrow. 'You got a future,' she would tell me over and again, and after a while it looked like I did.

"I was a star on the field, the can't-miss kid. I was good in the classroom, too, my mother made sure of that, but on the field I was big and I was fast and I hit harder than even my mother could. By my junior year I was fielding offers from Maryland, Florida, Florida State. All through my high school career, as I ran onto the field, I'd see Nomar standing in a place of honor on the sidelines. He was now levels higher than that corner, he was a man with an aura of power, a man heading ever higher, heading right to the moon. And as I passed he'd yell out, 'I'm a still get you, Gordo. Don't you doubt it.' Nomar, man.

"I went away to college, Miami, majored in football, the can't-miss kid, feared all across the ACC, violence personified on the field, yeah. Until I busted up my knee junior year. By the time I came back I was a step slower, and let me tell you, that step made all the difference. I could still play, but I had been projected for the second round and ended up in the seventh to the Browns. I made the Cleveland practice squad my first year, the Indy practice squad my second. Hopes were high that I'd make an active squad, finally, my third year, but in camp with Indy the knee went again and that was that.

"Okay, it happens. I got a few checks, a few thrills, I came close, no tragedy, right? But you see I was the can't-miss kid, and I had been prepping my life for the can't-miss kind of success. My mother died when I was still in school and after that I went a little crazy. I had a son with one girl, a daughter with another. I married a third and we lived like I was earning those sweet game checks even before the damn draft. I had an agent's moneyman slipping me loans to pay my child support and my car payments and my party expenses as we waited for that first big contract, loans that were still due, and the moneyman wasn't being so patient anymore. I could keep the balls juggling with the practice-squad money—six, seven thou a week in season—but even so I was always falling further behind. My time in the Colts camp wasn't so much about finally letting my dream come alive, it was about needing the money, man, to keep my life spinning. There was nothing joyful about it and I pushed it too damn far. My knee didn't go because of a hit. I was just running and it went, no one near me. Pop went that weasel.

"After the second operation I felt my life slipping away. Drip, drip. I watched television, I drank, I closed down to anyone who cared even a damn for me. All I had was the alcohol and the gym. I worked out, I worked out fierce, that's what I knew, and I rehabbed the knee like a demon, but it was over. My wife divorced me, the mothers of my children sued for the child support I wasn't paying, I had nothing left, no money, no future. The can't-miss kid was dead. A gun in the mouth didn't seem desperate so much as a sensible move.

"That's when I found myself back in front of Nomar, in his office, surrounded by a pack of his guards. He was living in some grotesque party mansion out in la-di-da Ladue. He had rings on his fingers and sunglasses rimmed in gold, a harem servicing him, an entourage filling his glasses and laughing at his jokes. He had everything I thought had been destined for me. Tell me crime doesn't pay.

"After my brush with suicide I knew I needed a plan. I had almost finished college, I could have gotten my degree and started as the new man in a company, the intern, the clerk, I could have risen up like every other slob, but there was still a vestige of the can't-miss kid in me, and I didn't want to start at the bottom, I wanted to start high up with somebody who knew what I was when I was somebody. With Nomar I didn't have to say anything, my presence was enough. He had gotten me, just like he told me he would. He was my inevitability and all he had to do was open his arms to bring me into the fold.

"'Can't use you, Gordo,' he said. 'Ain't no room for you.'

"What the hell was that? I might not have been pro football material anymore, but I was big enough and could still hit, I was my mother's son after all. He had been chasing me from my childhood and now, when I needed the gig, he was pushing me away? That was bullshit and I told him so. And I must have told him with more than a touch of passion because the room suddenly bristled with heat, guns appearing like rabbits in a room full of magicians.

"'You are one sorry-assed fucker,' he said. 'Shit. You was the one I was never going to get. That was the point. The whole neighborhood heard me calling out to you. Them other boys they came to me because they couldn't be you. You were proof of their weakness, you were my control. If I bring you in, it's like the world shifts and their weakness disappears. Then what do I have? A bullet in the head? Can't use you, Gordo. But maybe I got something you could use.'

"That's when he scrawled a number and a name on a card, tossed it across his big empty desktop.

"'This ain't for you, mind you, because I truly don't give a shit about you—nothing more common in this world than an arrogant asshole athlete with a bum knee—but your mother, she was a hell of a lady. I'm doing this for her. You call this number, you ask for Mr. Maambong, you tell him Nomar sent you. And when you make his team, you make sure he pays me my cut. I need a get something out of the mess you made of your life.'"

"And so here I sit," said Gordon, "with one last chance to make it right. I need this gig, but then it looks like we all need this gig."

"We're all last chancers," I said. "That's why we're here, auditioning to be Hyenas."

"How many jobs with the squad you think are waiting on us?" said Riley.

"More than one for sure," said Kief. "We all have different skills. Athlete, engineer, hacker, lawyer. The only one of us sort of useless to them is the lawyer."

"Thanks for the encouragement," I said. "It will be a nice little spur as we compete against each other."

"Maybe we should work together," said Gordon. "Edge out the others before we go head-to-head."

"Is that even allowed?" said Riley, glancing over at Bert.

"Everything is allowed as long as you don't ask for permission first," I said. "Joey Mitts taught me that."

"Sounds right to me," said Kief after blowing out a line of smoke. "I like rolling with a crew."

"Riley?" I said.

"Sure, why not. Let's grind them other suckers into the dirt."

"That's it, then," said Gordon. "We'll be the Last Chance Crew."

"It's got a ring to it, doesn't it?" said Riley.

"Yes it does," I said.

See, it wasn't so complicated. I had surveyed the chessboard and made my first move. Having an antagonist is how you build a team, so I had built an antagonism between us and them. And for some reason, listening to a confession always puts the confessor in your debt, which is why I had started our string of confessions. A team is a useful thing in any competition: something to support you when you need support; something to betray when the opportunity arises.

Hyena indeed.

8

MORNING EXERCISE

Cassandra, in a tight green bodysuit that glistened in the sun, led the morning run, ten miles on a flat course within some nature preserve full of marsh and reed and skittering bird, along with flocks of birders and their monstrous cameras. She set a mean pace, nothing Gordon, who ran with a predatory grace, or I couldn't handle, but which left Riley and Kief struggling to keep up. Churning in the lead with Cassandra was the A team, consisting of the frat-boy twins, Don and Derrick, Angela, whose black ponytail bounced as she sprinted forward, and Tom Preston, with his closely mown beard and distant eyes. He was never looking at you, Tom Preston, he was looking through you.

The Last Chance Crew ran together, falling progressively farther behind with each step. When Riley or Kief struggled for air in the humid morning, I would drop with them and gently bring them up to speed as the other two slowed to absorb us again. We formed a proud pack of laggards and spent the time tossing snark about the crew in the lead.

"You think they get extra credit for keeping up with Cassandra?"

"Only after they polish her sneakers."

"With their tongues."

"Did Mr. Maambong warn you guys against sleeping with her?"

"Quite specifically."

"Almost like a dare."

"Good thing, because she's just my type."

"Inaccessible?"

"That too."

"Is there a problem?" said Cassandra, who was waiting for us at a turnoff. "Any of you suffering cardiac arrest?"

"We're enjoying the scenery," I said.

"How is it?"

"Getting better all the time," said Kief.

Cassandra turned her still-pale face toward him. "Talk less and run more; we have a busy day," she said before sprinting off.

The run ended at a squat maintenance building near the entrance to the nature preserve. Mr. Maambong, in his white suit, leaned on his cane at the door, his dark round glasses following our progress.

"We've been waiting," he said.

"It wasn't a race, was it?" I said.

"Life is a race, Mr. Kubiak," said Mr. Maambong. "You know that better than anyone. The fit part of the group is inside. Let's join them, shall we."

In a dim space cleared in the center of the building, amidst a welter of workbenches and power machines, two tables had been set up with charming arrays of flowers, yellow blossoms with blue highlights. One of the tables was laden with bottled water, the other with a bounty of apples, bananas, protein bars, little plastic cups of yogurt. I rolled a cool bottle of water against the edge of my forehead as I watched the lead runners huddle together on the far side of the room, trying to hide their smirks.

In the middle of the floor, illuminated by the room's one bright light, stood a boxing ring. Two pairs of yellow boxing gloves were slung over the ropes. Bert stood in the middle of the ring in black trousers and a white business shirt.

"We thought we'd have a friendly competition," said Mr. Maambong to the assembly. "The positions for which you are applying do not require the martial arts per se, but one never knows when situations will spin out of control. Our deals are not always the most conventional and the sites we travel to are not always the safest, so we appreciate flexibility in all matters. Your opponents will be picked at random. You will each fight one three-minute round. We are merely trying to get a sense of your abilities. If you are fearful or on the edge of being hurt, call out the word 'submit' and Bert will ensure that the fight is stopped. Do we understand each other?"

"But you want us to win, right?" said Don, his chest like twin boulders stretching his T-shirt. He might as well have been cracking his knuckles in anticipation.

"We appreciate winners," said Mr. Maambong.

"What are the rules?" I said.

"We just told you the rules," said Mr. Maambong. "The fight will last three minutes and if you are afraid of being hurt, just call out 'submit.' What could be clearer?"

"No other rules?"

"Is my name Queensberry, Mr. Kubiak?"

There was laughter, which I joined in. Then Mr. Maambong took a bowl from the table and gave it a shake. He pulled a card and read it out loud. "Angela," he said and then walked the bowl to Angela. Angela reached in for a card of her own.

"Derrick," she said, and the smaller of the frat-boy twins raised his arms like he had just won the heavyweight championship.

Mr. Maambong pulled out another card. "Riley," he said, and brought her the bowl. She visibly winced as she read the name on her card out loud.

"Don."

Her opponent, with the body of a lumberjack and the broad, ugly face of a boar, said something to his twin and chuckled.

Mr. Maambong's hand swirled in the bowl for a moment. "Phil," he read from the card, before bringing the bowl to me.

"Kief," I said, without looking at Kief, short, thin, and weighing about forty pounds less than me, who was standing just a few feet away.

The final drawing was a formality, Tom Preston's name being called and his pulling out Gordon's card.

"Excellent. We're due a first-class entertainment. There is a box of rubber mouth guards by the yogurt. No need for chipped teeth or severed tongues. Now let us, as they say, get this show on the road. Angela and Derrick, you two are first."

Ding.

As soon as Cassandra rang the bell, Derrick waded forward like a young bull in a Pottery Barn, throwing out roundhouse rights and lefts, scaring the very air about him, but not his opponent. Angela backed away with what looked like practiced grace. Her arms were longer than Derrick's and she flicked a few jabs, just enough to show she knew the rudiments of the game. She had played field hockey in college, we later learned, and had been kicked off the team for incessant fighting. I would have liked to see her pop Derrick once but good in the teeth, and she could have done it, too, but she stayed away and let him frustrate himself. As he kept charging, she kept dancing, snapping his head back now and then. Jab, jab. Retreat, shift, retreat. Jab.

Ding.

"You ready?" I said to Riley as Bert helped the fighters off with their gloves.

"That damn bronco's going to kill me. I'm going to die."

"It's just a friendly boxing match," said Kief.

"Does fat face look friendly?"

I peered over at Don, who was already inside the ring, fitting his thick hands into the yellow gloves. There was something about him that pissed me off—his arrogance, his stupid smile, the way he chuckled. I've always thought chuckling was a mark of deranged arrogance; there ought to be a law against it, there ought to be chuckler's ward in the state hospital for the criminally insane.

"I'll trade you cards," I said.

"We can't do that."

"Of course we can. No rules, right? You and Kief are a better match anyway."

"I can handle you, dude," said Kief, his hands up in some fake karate position.

"Sure, and you're not standing in a puddle. Just do me a favor, Riley, and don't hurt him too badly."

"Are you certain about this?" she said.

"This whole fight-club thing is stupid," I said. "I'm a lawyer, you're a hacker, Kief's an engineer. Who the hell are they to require us to fight like this for a job? I'll just rope-a-dope the lug for three minutes and we'll go on to the next game, which might actually test our applicable skills. Trust me."

In the middle of the ring Don hopped from sneaker to sneaker and blasted combinations at his shadow, hook, hook, uppercut, hook. He purposely wasn't looking at Riley as he played at being a boxer, and so he was a bit surprised when he looked up and saw me climbing through the ropes.

"Huh?" said Don.

"What are you doing, Phil?" said Cassandra. "This isn't your match."

I lifted the little card with Don's name on it and waved it in the air.

Cassandra looked at Bert, who looked at Mr. Maambong, who stared at me for a moment through his beetle-eye glasses before nodding ever so slightly.

Ding.

Don charged out of his corner and socked me in the side so sharply I nearly buckled.

I backed away and raised my hands and he started slugging at my arms, left right left, each blow like a sledge to the bone.

He slugged my side again and I fell onto a knee as a hook grazed the top of my head.

I looked at Bert, who stood still as a statue while Don loaded up once again. So I quick-punched him in the balls. Twice. Bada bing.

Don staggered back. I leaped up, stepped forward, jammed a sneaker atop his lead foot, and elbowed the sumbitch in the nose, which gave in with a squish, like Silly Putty smacked by a baseball bat.

I jumped back, danced to the left, to the right. Big Don was bent over, his arms forming an *X* over his stomach, and he looked up at me with confusion in his eyes, his nose now a mashed melon, gushing blood.

I spread my arms wide. "I submit," I said.

Before Don could take a step forward, Bert was between us, arms out to keep us apart.

I hopped like I was jumping rope, banged my gloves together, spit the rubber guard onto the canvas to get the bitter taste of copper out of my mouth.

***

"That was a nice thing you did for Riley," said Cassandra. "Taking on Don in her stead. Almost noble."

We were standing by the edge of the pool, set between the house and the canal. The whole crew was taking a break after a morning of running and fighting and an afternoon of test taking and puzzle solving, where each movement we made was noted and evaluated. Well, almost the whole crew.

Cassandra's red hair was loose, the pieces of her bathing suit were pink and white and small, her glistening lips held the barest hint of a smile. She was as luscious as a ripe plum. I turned from her and looked at Tom Preston, lying on a chaise, his dark chest bared to the sun. On the next chaise over was Don, whose eyes were drugged and whose face was covered with gauze and swaths of tape. Tom Preston was talking softly, and Don, no longer chuckling, was nodding along.

"I'm neither nice nor noble," I said.

"Mr. Maambong will be pleased to hear that."

"And you know how much we all want to please Mr. Maambong."

"It pays to please Mr. Maambong."

I turned my gaze to her. "What about pleasing you?"

She reached down and with her cool touch gently caressed the growing bruise on my side, before she pressed it. Pain slithered through my ribs like a shiv. "I don't please easy," she said.

The first fight after I'd smashed Don's ugly face with my elbow had gone as expected. Riley and Kief, both relieved to be facing each other, danced and flailed, each getting in enough shots to show that they were trying while avoiding any heavy combat that could have resulted in something decisive. But it was the second fight that I'd found as illuminating as a slap to the face.

When the bell dinged, Gordon, broad-chested and quick on his feet, his mop of hair bouncing with each step, shuffled forward and clocked Tom Preston but good right on the jaw. Tom Preston was half a foot shorter and a good fifty pounds lighter than his opponent, who moved with the solid assurance of a natural athlete, despite the long scars on his right knee. Bam: another shot to Tom Preston's face. A hook to the ribs, a straight that barely missed as Tom Preston ducked and back away, shaking his head to get the cotton out of his brain. Gordon rolled forward with the inevitability of a bulldozer.

And then Gordon stopped, hopped back, spread his arms, and smiled. It wasn't an expression of mercy so much as one of solidarity. They gave us three minutes; let's play. And Tom Preston, after a moment's hesitation, stepped forward and put his hands up. They looked like fighters, they danced like fighters, they fired off jabs and hooks, each giving as good as he got, but there was something of the exhibition in it. An agreement had been reached and a bond created. It was almost sweet, and it pissed me off because I recognized that there were skills at work that I hadn't noticed in my teammate before. Gordon, giving his soulful confession and running with the last chancers, yet bonding with Tom Preston in the ring, playing all sides like a champion. Gordon. Damn.

There is a moment in every fierce competition when the realization dawns that you are competing against more than you expected and you better step up your game or be annihilated. In Mr. Maambong's competition that realization dawned during that fight, when Gordon flicked out a friendly left jab and Tom Preston ducked down, leaned to the left, lifted his right foot, and slammed it with all his power into the side of Gordon's knee, the one with the long surgical scars. The knee snapped with an audible crack, like a rotted branch giving way to an ax, followed by a howl as Gordon tumbled to the canvas and grabbed at his flopping leg.

Tom Preston now stood over him, his fists still up, his face as impassive as a raw piece of rib eye.

I turned from the scene to look at Mr. Maambong, to get a sense of his thoughts on Tom Preston's brutal piece of betrayal. I wondered if I would see a pucker of disappointment, a smile of satisfaction, a flat sneer of indifference. But what I saw was more frightening than all those possibilities. Maambong's impassive beetle eyes weren't trained on the carnage in the ring; instead they were trained on me.

This was not an open competition between me and the other seven for a position in Mr. Maambong's operation. Riley and Kief, Gordon and Angela, even the frat-boy twins, all of them might be in the midst of their own competitions, but the only opponent I was facing was Tom Preston, with his bland handsomeness and gapped teeth and the instincts of an assassin. Mr. Maambong had set up a one-on-one, and I wasn't sure the loser would end up in one piece.

Gordon certainly hadn't.

9

THE BIG GAME

"I'll never get over that scream," said Riley. "He sounded like a gut-shot bear."

"Do you hunt?" said Kief.

"No, I don't hunt. It's inhumane. Those sweet little deer with their wide brown eyes. But I did grow up in Texas."

"Lot of bear in Texas?"

"Some in the hill country, but I never saw one."

"Then if you don't hunt, and you never saw a bear, how do you know what a gut-shot bear sounds like?"

"It sounds like Gordon with his leg waving in the wind," I said. "Maybe we'll visit if we have time tomorrow."

"Hospitals give me the willies," said Kief.

"You know what gives me the willies?" I said. "Tom Fucking Preston."

"What he did was cold," said Riley. "What he did was ice."

"It was like we were playing Chutes and Ladders," said Kief, "and Tom was playing *Grand Theft Auto*."

The three remaining members of the Last Chance Crew were huddled together on the rooftop patio, preparing for our evening's competition, which we had been assured would go a long way in determining who Mr. Maambong would end up hiring. The other team, the A team, Tom Preston's team, was drinking Bert's drinks, laughing, bonding. Even Don, with the tape on his face, was chuckling away. They had all been invigorated by the morning's butchery. Tom Preston stood off to the side, a drink in his hand, staring blandly through us.

"He's not going to stop at Gordon," I said. "He's going to take us out one by one if we don't take him out first."

"How on earth do we do that?" said Riley.

"Set his bed on fire and kill him in his sleep," said Kief.

"Snakes sleep with their eyes open," I said.

"That just means we have to be ninja quiet and ninja quick when we light the match."

"What do you know about being a ninja, Kief?" said Riley.

"I've played as Scorpion on *Mortal Kombat.*"

"You two can have it out on the Xbox later," I said, "but right now I think I have a better idea for killing that snake."

"All of you are wondering what exactly is this job for which you are competing," Mr. Maambong had said just a few moments before our huddle. We had been assembled on the rooftop for instructions. Mr. Maambong's white suit and dark glasses glowed orange in the setting sun. "It's time to let you in on your possible futures. We are what you might call problem solvers. We solve serious problems for a very specialized clientele. It is a service, as you can imagine, that is much in demand.

"Our clients will tell us that money is no object, but of course as soon as we raise a figure they object. And so we must negotiate a fee high enough to make them gulp but not high enough for them to gallop away. And then there are the parties who have the keys to solving our clients' problems, and who always seem to use the word 'priceless,' as if there were ever such a thing. Another negotiation. It would be tiresome if it weren't so lucrative. The key to our profit, then, as you can see, is our ability to negotiate.

"So this is what we shall do this evening, a simple little exercise. You will each enter a negotiation with the other candidates. Since seven of you are left, that means each will negotiate six times. There will be ten one-hundred-dollar bills at stake in each negotiation and you will have ten minutes to decide who gets how many of the bills. You keep what you agree to, but if no deal is made before the buzzer, then you each get nothing and the bills go back into our pockets. So for each of you, six thousand dollars is in play. Grab as much as you can. After the hour, whoever has the most money wins, and whoever has the least loses. We, in the firm, do not appreciate losers, as Gordon has already discovered. Do we understand each other? Good. We have set up three bargaining locations, which we will be monitoring at all times. There will be seven sessions, and you each will sit out one session. Good luck, though luck, under these conditions, will have nothing to do with it."

My first negotiation was with Angela, tall, sharp-eyed, whip smart, and smirking. We sat on either side of the granite island in the modern kitchen with sleek black counters and windows overlooking a garden. A stack of ten bills sat in front of us; Ben Franklin stared up at us with bemusement.

"So, Angela," I said. "What's your strategy?"

"Ask for everything."

"Mine too."

"Except I mean it."

"Me too."

"I don't think you do."

"Maybe we can come to an accommodation," I said.

"See, I was right."

"Just give me six hundred and we'll call it a deal."

"Perhaps you didn't understand."

"Oh, I understood. Make the wild offer, bicker back and forth, act tough as the clock ticks, then split the difference. The old high-low."

"No low, just high."

"We're going to go back and forth and back and forth and bore each other to tears, but we'll end up at fifty-fifty."

"Is that the way it will work?"

"Sure it will, because I won't accept anything less and I trust that neither will you."

"But I won't accept fifty-fifty."

"Five hundred dollars is better than nothing."

"But not better than a thousand," she said.

"In this kind of negotiation, the one thing you can't ever get is everything. Nothing, yes, but not everything."

"We'll see," she said.

I took a moment to sort the ten bills into stacks of five each. I pushed one of the stacks in front of Angela, removed a bill from her stack and put it on mine, and sat back to let the time tick away, tick tock. The clock was wielding its power. Make a deal by the deadline or lose everything. Tock tick. I had made an offer, it was just a matter of waiting for the inevitable counter. Tick tock.

But then her face betrayed her.

There was the little lip curl of power—the same curl I assumed she flashed before decking an opposing midfielder on the field-hockey pitch—and I knew. Just to be sure I took three bills from my pile and placed them on hers, offering her seven hundred dollars to make a deal. She didn't flinch, she didn't show surprise, she wasn't going to negotiate, she was going to watch me squirm until the buzzer sounded and Mr. Maambong pocketed our money. I did the calculation once and then twice and each time the numbers added up all wrong.

I felt a moment of panic, a moment of coppery rage, a moment where I wanted to strike out savagely at anything close. Control is everything and having lost it I had lost everything. That son of a bitch. I breathed deep and faked a smile, which wasn't as difficult as it might seem in the circumstances, since all my smiles are fake.

"So that's the way it's going to be," I said with as much calm as I could muster.

"That's the way it's going to be."

"He's playing you, you know."

"From here it looks like we're playing you."

"There's no *we* when it comes to him. He doesn't have it in him to look out for anyone but himself. He's playing us all, that's what he does. But you're the one doing his bidding."

"The way I see it, for this game at least we're in it together."

I gave my head a kindly shake, as if her gullibility would have been cute if it weren't so foolish. "Whose idea was this strategy?"

"What does it matter?"

"I guess that's my answer. How does it feel to be his pawn?"

"Right now it feels fine. But I'm nobody's pawn. I'll have my moment."

"Don't bet on that. I'd rather lose than be used, but that's just me. Some people are happier as serfs. Some people like to be kept in their places, sowing fields of wheat for the lord of the manor, until it's their turn to be buried in those same fields."

"Bitter are we, Phil?"

"Resigned maybe, but not bitter. I've seen it before. His turning on you is as inevitable as the dawn. And when he comes for you—and he will come, just ask Gordon if you have any doubt—if I'm still around, give me a heads-up and I'll do what I can to help."

She tilted her head at my reasonableness, my composed generosity.

"But my advice would be to take action before that happens," I said. "My advice would be to run the bastard over with a car while you're still able."

She laughed, and then in the shadow of that laughter she looked down at the stack of bills before her. I could see her considering the implications of going off Tom Preston's reservation, taking the seven hundred, raising her stock on her own. The thought washed across her face like a revelation. The move would satisfy the streak of independence I'd noticed in her the first time we talked, and seven hundred dollars is not nothing. You could buy a whole lot of—

Buzz.

Too late.

My last negotiation of the exercise, if you could call it a negotiation, was with Tom Preston.

We sat across from each other in the soaring living room with a round steel coffee table between our gray chairs. Above us was a camera on the wall, recording our interaction. Beside us was a two-story wall of windows that looked out at the pool, with its tile surround, and the palm trees, and the dark of the water reflecting the resorts across the way bright with light: the stakes, so to speak. On the table, along with a stack of hundred-dollar bills, was a blue glass ashtray.

Tom Preston was handsome, compact. His eyes were like marbles, cold and inhuman; you sensed that if you tapped them with a nail, they would give off a clink. He leaned to the side in his chair, his legs crossed, his gaze not meeting mine, but instead seemingly fixed on the ashtray, as if contemplating the effort it would take to grab hold of it and bury it in my skull. We were minutes into our negotiation and still neither of us had said a word.

The five prior negotiations had been full of language. I learned from Riley that Don had agreed to a fifty-fifty split with her, which meant

I was the only target of their ploy, which kind of pissed me off since denying Tom Preston any money in our negotiation had been exactly my plan. I told her, and later Kief, that the jig was up and that she and Kief should make what deals they could with Tom Preston and the others. With each of the frat-boy twins I had made a speech similar to the one I gave Angela, complete with the recommendation of running Tom Preston over with a car, even as they refused to make any deal that would end up with me netting a single hundred of the split. Don, behind the swatch of bandages on his face, merely chuckled at my situation, but Derrick's face expressed the same inklings of doubt as had Angela's. Something of what I had said had gotten through.

But with Tom Preston there was only silence, and that seemed fitting. What was there to say?

I speak to plot, to plan, to earn, to cajole, to confuse, to seduce, to handle, to employ. Others maybe speak to release the spark of their inner lives into the world, but I could not imagine anything more useless. In college I read Whitman waxing on—and on—about sounding his barbaric yawp over the rooftops of the world, and it was but jabbering nonsense to me. "For every atom belonging to me, as good belongs to you." Go tell it to the rock crushing your skull. If there is anything that is true in this world, it is our separateness. The only time there is a connection between me and you is when you have something I want. I speak to manipulate, that is all.

And with one look into Tom Preston's hard glass eyes I knew my words would fall upon him as upon a rock. There was something familiar and cruel in those eyes, like a mirror in a mirror. It was in the calm he showed when shattering Gordon's leg, in the way he stared through me just a moment into our negotiation before turning his attention to the blue glass ashtray. I mattered to him no more than the inanimate object on the stainless steel between us, and therefore merited not a word. He might as well induce the ashtray to turn into a swan as use his words to control me. I might as well try to convince the opposing king on a chessboard to take its own life as use my words to influence him. Anything either of us said would only be used against us by the other. So we sat silently, waiting out our time together. Three minutes. Five minutes. Seven minutes. The thousand dollars beside the ashtray moved ever closer to Mr. Maambong's pocket.

"Make an offer," I said, finally, as if the thought of losing even part of that money had forced me to speak.

"Everything," he said, as I knew he would.

"Done."

I stood immediately, before he could change his mind, and without another word headed up the stairs, toward the roof, where Bert would be standing behind the bar, wearing his red plaid vest, ever ready to build a drink.

I sure as hell needed one.

10

PHI FUCKA SANDRA

I stood off to the side as the party on Mr. Maambong's roof flowed on. I was already into my fourth Scotch of the night. The good stuff, I kept telling Bert, figuring it would be my last taste of it for a while. I wasn't surprised when Cassandra appeared at my side.

"Mr. Maambong would like to speak to you," she said.

"I bet he would."

"He's in the second-floor office."

"I'll just finish my drink."

"He doesn't like to be kept waiting."

"Doesn't much matter anymore, does it?" I said. "I'm a loser and there is no room for losers on the Hyena Squad."

"Where did you hear that name?"

"Oh, it's floating around the ether."

"Mr. Maambong doesn't like it."

"Every scavenger dreams himself to be a predator, but then a dead carcass presents itself and in he goes. Do you know what I'm going to miss the most around here?"

"The Scotch?"

"You."

"Now who's kidding whom?"

"What did you do before this?"

"I was in health care."

"What happened?"

"Let's just say it didn't fit my inclinations."

"I'm surprised, Cassandra, because I sense in you a great kindness."

"How many have you had?"

"Enough to see the true measure of your compassion."

"That's funny, because I sense in you no compassion at all."

"And you find that ruggedly attractive."

"Surprisingly, yes."

"Then we are the perfect pair, because I was lying."

I downed the rest of my drink and handed her the glass before heading through the doorway in the wall at the far side of the roof and then down the outdoor circular stairs to Mr. Maambong's office and my fate.

"What an illuminating display," Mr. Maambong had said a half hour before when we had all reconvened on the roof in our party clothes. "Thank you all for your wonderful work today. I can't tell you how much I am looking forward to tomorrow, our final day of testing." And then, with great formality and much aplomb, he gave the results of the negotiation game we had just played. In second place were Riley and Kief, with thirty-two hundred dollars each, which included the extra two hundred I had tossed each of them in our so-called negotiations. Behind them were Don and Derrick and Angela, who had sacrificed themselves to kick me to the curb, which they did with utter success. I came in dead last, as I knew I would, with a measly six hundred dollars in my pocket. Barely a pillow to break my fall; a week at a luxurious Days Inn if I stretched it. "Quite the disappointing number, I must say," had said Mr. Maambong, and I couldn't have agreed more.

"And finally in first place," he had announced, "with an impressive total of thirty-five hundred dollars is Tom Preston. Stand up,

Mr. Preston. Let's all give the winner a round of applause. We can all now understand, I believe, that Mr. Preston is more than just another candidate. He is, in fact, the man to beat. Keep that in mind, the rest of you, as you prepare for our next contest. Those of you who remain will be going on a scavenger hunt of the most unusual sort. The position you are applying for is very often about recovery and acquisition; we'll see how well you acquire. Now, drink up. This is a night of unraveling the tensions. As the prophet says, tomorrow will come what may, so tonight we might as well dance."

Standing off to the side, my back turned just slightly in feigned unconcern, I had kept my eyes on the six remaining candidates as Mr. Maambong declared the results. Riley and Kief were pleased with their placing—Riley lifted her glass in my direction, acknowledging the gifts that had boosted her and Kief's totals—but it was the reaction of the other three that had gratified me the most. When Tom Preston was announced as the winner with his impressive dollar amount, when Tom Preston stood to receive his applause and be coronated as the front-runner by Mr. Maambong, twitches of consternation marred their features. Angela even glanced my way and I shrugged as if to say, *What else could you have expected?* The doubts I had placed like earwigs in their brains were starting to do their work, even though it was too late to do me any good.

"We are disappointed, Mr. Kubiak," said Mr. Maambong, sitting behind a great glass-topped desk in the second-floor office after I had made my way down the circular steps. "We had expected a more robust showing from you."

"You're not as disappointed as I am," I said. The office overlooked the canal and the glittering resorts on the other side. It was minimalist in design, filled with sharp edges and blank walls and glass. It fit my eye.

He patted an envelope as he pushed a document toward me. "This is the thousand dollars we promised you. But to receive it, you'll need to sign a basic nondisclosure agreement."

I took hold of the document, gave it a cursory glance, grabbed a pen from the stand, and starting executing the thing.

"With your lawyering experience we expected you would take a more careful look at the precise language."

"It says I can't talk about you or this weekend."

"That is correct."

"Fine then," I said. "I'm not a big talker."

"There's a penalty section you might want to review."

"What will you do if I talk, hack out my tongue?"

"Excellent. You must read quite quickly. Any regrets, Mr. Kubiak?"

"Only that I didn't smash Don's nose all the way into his brainpan when I had the chance."

"Yes, that would have evened up the sides and taken away the advantage Tom Preston used for his win. So, why didn't you?"

I looked up from the document. Mr. Maambong's beetle eyes were staring at me intently. "That could have killed him," I said. "That would have been murder."

"Surely you might have found a way to take the lummox out without committing a homicide. Mr. Preston found a way with Mr. Johnstone. Taking out his leg gave Mr. Preston the numbers he needed to push you out the door. You could have done the same by breaking your opponent's jaw, for instance. That would have neatly done the trick. What was it that stopped you?"

I turned my attention back to the release. "It would have been counterproductive."

"How so?"

I finished dating and signing, put down the pen, took hold of the envelope, leaned back in my chair.

"I can tell when I go too far from the looks I get. It's as if, in that moment, they see the truth about me and it horrifies them."

"So you were anxious to keep up appearances."

"I don't get anxious and I don't give a damn about appearances. But when I see those looks I know that I'm no longer trusted, which means I can't fully trust either. Trust is a valuable tool; it's not profitable to squander it. In those circumstances, I've learned to hold back."

"Are you telling us it wasn't a matter of conscience?"

"It's an election year, Mr. Maambong. Since when is anything a matter of conscience?"

He laughed with a touch too much determination. "Tell me then why it wasn't counterproductive for Mr. Preston to take out his opponent like he did?"

"Don't pretend you weren't watching the reactions as Tom Preston stood and received your benediction as the top negotiator. That's why you made him stand, wasn't it? So you could get a better gauge. You know exactly what you saw."

"Yes, maybe we do."

"Tom Preston should never have made any kind of offer to me, even an offer he assumed I would reject. His fight with Gordon had already weakened the trust his so-called teammates felt for him. And then he let me maneuver him into taking the whole thousand from our negotiation, weakening that trust even further. By winning the negotiation game he showed quite clearly he isn't smart enough. We'll see how he fares through the rest of your little competition, but it doesn't concern me. I'll just take the cash and be gone."

"Oh, Mr. Kubiak, don't be in such a rush. Spend another night at the hotel, please. On us. Relax by the house pool tomorrow as the others are scavenging, get some sun, enjoy yourself. We're having a party in the evening to celebrate the end of the contest. Caviar, champagne, all kinds of delicious entertainments. You won't want to miss it."

***

I was in bed with Cassandra the next day when Mr. Maambong and Bert barged into her room.

It had been waiting to happen, Cassandra and me. When the candidates went off on their scavenger hunt, we played our little games of seduction, first in the kitchen, then by the pool. But it didn't take much playing from either of us, since we both knew where it would end and were both ready and willing to end there. At first we had gone at it hard and fast, with the due violence of untapped desire, and then, a second time slowly and coldly, with one of my hands bracing her arm above her head and the other around her neck. The first bout felt like a couple of horny teenagers playacting sex, the second felt like truth itself. We were sitting up in her bed after, sharing a cigarette, when the two men entered.

Mr. Maambong took a chair from the vanity, placed it at the foot of the bed, and sat. Bert stood behind him. There was a gun in Bert's hand. Cassandra's breasts were bared and she made no effort to cover them. I extracted the cigarette from between her fingers and took a drag.

"What did we tell you, Mr. Kubiak, about sleeping with Cassandra?" said Mr. Maambong.

"Oops," I said.

Cassandra took the cigarette back from me and placed it between her lips, bruised and smeared red.

"It wasn't a jealous possessiveness that prompted our warning," said Mr. Maambong. "We don't have relations with employees—it is bad form. As shocking as it may seem, our warning was for your own benefit. You see, Cassandra, due to some childhood trauma, has serious issues with intimacy. There is a mantis quality to her lovemaking, if you catch our drift. Those who sleep with her invariably end up dead, one way or the other. Sometimes it is her way."

"I can take care of myself," I said.

"Others have thought the very same thing. Still, around here she is known as the black widow. Where is it, Cassandra?"

Cassandra shrugged and smoked and then petulantly reached beneath her pillow, pulling out a buck knife, shiny and fat. She offered it handle first, and Bert, gun in hand, stepped from behind the chair to take hold of it.

"It's for protection," she said to me.

"If I had only known," I said to her, "I would have brought a piece of wood and we could have whittled a duck."

Cassandra laughed out a couple gulps of smoke.

"We have been thinking over what you said about holding back in your fight to save the trust of others," said Mr. Maambong. "And about why you gave Mr. Preston a free thousand dollars in your negotiation. We wondered if everything you told us was merely a rationalization for weakness, and if giving Mr. Preston the extra thousand was a flailing piece of frustration just to take money from our pockets. But something happened that has changed our opinion of you."

"It happened twice," I said.

Cassandra laughed again.

"There was an accident today," said Mr. Maambong. "A hit-and-run in the streets of Miami. Imagine that. There are no suspects. The police are baffled. We'll save you the suspense. It was Mr. Preston. He was off on his own to get hold of the most valuable piece on the scavenger hunt. We would have suspected you of being the driver, Mr. Kubiak, except you were here risking life and limb with dear Cassandra. But still, it makes one wonder."

"I trust he'll be all right."

"He is currently in the hospital. The same hospital, it turns out, that is caring for your Mr. Johnstone."

"Maybe they'll visit each other's rooms, play patty-cake together."

"It might be difficult for Mr. Preston. So many of his bones are broken he is like a bowl of Jell-O."

"I'll send him a spoon," I said.

"You made him a target."

"He made himself a target."

"His recovery will take quite a while. In such circumstances we will not be able to offer him an immediate position with our firm."

"Forget about the frat-boy twins, they're both chumps, but I'm sure Riley or Kief or even Angela will do a fine job."

"We're not looking for fine. We have had fine before and as Cassandra could tell you, all it brought us was grief. Instead we are looking for a unique talent. What do you think, Cassandra?"

"He's a talent all right," she said.

"You're making me blush," I said.

"We think you, Mr. Kubiak, provided you can survive Cassandra on this sunny afternoon, are exactly what we are looking for. We thought so from our first meeting in Las Vegas, and your performance here, though unorthodox, has confirmed our suspicions. It will require much work, complete obedience, and mutual trust. How do you like that? Trust. You seem to have a talent for gaining it, less a talent for deserving it, if your past is any indication. But you appear to be worth the gamble of a probationary period. What do you say, Mr. Kubiak? Are you ready to take your rightful place in the new economy?"

"Suit me up."

"Excellent," said Mr. Maambong, a broad smile breaking out across his cold face. Even his glasses seemed to glint with promise. "Welcome aboard. It is time to build your team."

II. Henchman

11

A Japanese Scotch

The magazine writer looked nervously into the outlaw's eye. His physical condition had been a rude shock to her when he first came into the bar, but that was no longer the most disconcerting aspect of his presence. She had driven to this desert shack to find a hero; she had seen enough movies to know what that word meant. Even the most world-weary of heroes had something inside that you could latch on to, some sense of higher purpose. But the outlaw's story so far had given no such sense at all. The disappointment she was feeling was palpable.

Or was that just dehydration?

"You've barely touched your beer," said the outlaw. "Not thirsty even in this heat, or a stickler for quality? I would guess the latter. Good for you. Then why don't we try something else?"

He pushed himself out of his chair and limped toward the bar, speaking softly to the grizzled barkeep. When he dragged his useless leg back to the table, he was smiling.

"I keep a rare bottle of Scotch under the counter here. I asked Ginsberg to bring it out, along with two glasses and some ice. Believe it or not, Ginsberg has some ice squirreled away in this rat hole, mostly frozen urine just to keep the squirrel meat cold. But he also has a batch of ice made from branch water I bring up from Kentucky. This whiskey is good enough to deserve the best."

The barkeep walked slowly toward the table carrying a dusty black box and two glasses, each with one large cube of ice. He put down the box and the two glasses, pulled a rag from his back pocket, and proceeded to smear the small puddles of spat and spilled beer across the tabletop. As the outlaw examined the box, the magazine writer asked the barkeep for some water.

"And nothing from the well," said the outlaw. "Her stomach couldn't handle that radioactive sludge. Something bottled, and cold."

Ginsberg stopped his wiping and stared at the outlaw for a moment before walking slowly back to the bar. When he returned, he brought a small plastic water bottle, not quite cold, but colder than the hot air being pushed to and fro by the fans. The magazine writer thanked him and twisted the top. The cool felt like a kiss to the inside of her throat. She downed the bottle with a just a few quick gulps, but when she looked up to ask for another, Ginsberg was already behind the bar with his back turned.

"Ta-da," said the outlaw as he opened the black box with a ceremonial flourish. Inside was a glass bottle, a third full, with a sketch of a Japanese man holding a sword on the label. The outlaw took the bottle out of the box, pulled off the top with a thwack, and tipped a bit of the Scotch over the ice in each of the glasses.

"Look at the color in your glass," he said as he handed her one of the drinks. "Like an exquisite piece of amber. Now I'll have you know this is not just any run-of-the-mill Scotch, but a Japanese-crafted whiskey that is older than you and quite rare. I first came across this Scotch in Cabo San Lucas, of all places, and I've been hooked on it ever since.

"Cheers."

As the outlaw stared expectantly, the magazine writer took a sip. The liquor was dark and sweet, a thing made of tangerine and smoke that filled her mouth with the flavor of an extravagant life so distant from this desert shack it seemed to belong on another planet. A life of grace and ease and money. The life she had always wanted and, to be honest, expected. She couldn't help but smile.

"Nice, right?" said the outlaw. "I could tell you that you're drinking it all wrong, but then I'd be like those assholes who tell me not to use ice in my Scotch. I like ice in my Scotch, so they can suck it. Anyway, try swirling it in your glass and taking a sniff before you swallow. Notes of toffee, bacon rind, flint. Yum. Good enough to gulp. One added benefit is that the distiller went out of business years ago, and so there's an ever-dwindling supply. That makes it obscenely expensive, true, but it also doubles the delight. Every sip we take is one sip less available to the other sons of bitches who want it for their own. These days even my joys are heartless.

"Sorry for all the blabbing. Me, me, me. It's enough to drive anyone crazy, with or without a psychiatrist in the room. So for a moment, let's talk about you.

"You're quite the writer. Oh, don't be modest, I've read some of your work. Let me see, there was 'Turn Him on from across the Room.' And then, the brilliantly titled 'Orgasm Virgins: How They Went from "Um, Not Yet" to "OMG Yes!"' But my favorite, I have to say, and the one I've been following assiduously ever since I read it in the magazine, was 'Best Foundations for a Natural You.' Doesn't my skin look natural? Oh my God, yes."

The magazine writer felt a blush rise. She had been caught out in something. She didn't belong here, in this bar, with this man; she was out of her depth. And she thought, suddenly, of the gun in her bag.

"But here's the thing that I found most peculiar about your oeuvre," continued the outlaw. "You're a writer of puff pieces, of lifestyle tips and celebrity gossip, yet for some reason you braved desert and danger to find me even though there is no way in hell a story about the likes of me would ever be assigned to you by one of the glossies you write for."

She began to speak, trying to defend her interest in the interview as her heart started racing, trying to deny any ulterior motive, even though she knew the outlaw would see right through her denial to the lie. But he took her off the hook.

"Don't bother," he said with a smile. "It doesn't matter. The one thing we know about every encounter with the press is there is always a hidden agenda. We'll get to all your reasons for being here eventually, and the roots of the disappointment that flooded your eyes when you saw me drag my crippled carcass into the room, but first you need to hear the story you came for. When I'm done, you might decide the best course of action is to stand up and step out that door and run, to run away as if running from damnation itself. And I wouldn't blame you one bit.

"I'd run the hell away from myself, too, if I still could—but you've seen my leg.

"So back to Mr. Maambong, back to the Hyena Squad. I had passed the tests, survived the contests. I was in. You would think what would follow would be an intensive bout of training. Cue the music, build the montage. Phil Kubiak skipping rope, Phil Kubiak working the heavy bag, Phil Kubiak running in gray sweats through the Italian market. Well, sister, let me tell you: wrong movie. You weren't hired for the Hyena Squad with the hope that you could be turned into the kind of predator they needed. You were hired because you were a fully formed specimen, ready to be turned loose. All you needed was an overlord to wave the greenbacks in front of your nose and then yell fetch."

12

THE CASE OF THE MISSING HEIRESS

The motel was a desolate little structure in the middle of a desert. It might seem like I was back where I started before I first heard the name Maambong, but it wasn't the same at all.

I was a new man, with new prospects, wearing a new blue suit, tight around the chest and leg, the pants short enough to flash a shock of red sock. My polka-dot tie was fastened to my dark shirt with a gold clip. Brown shoes? You bet. Brown to match the briefcase I was holding with the documents and the cash. With my hair brushed insolently high, I looked like a hip young man fresh out of Brooklyn, trying to sell real estate. When I Skyped him that morning, Mr. Maambong approved the getup with a spurt of hearty laughter. In my new business, appearances mattered, and sometimes it helped to appear a little ridiculous.

Room 232, upper level, door facing northeast. The air conditioner sticking out above the door growled into the still, hot air. It was only morning, but already the sun was a burning eye staring over my shoulder. I slid to the side of the door, putting cinder block between me and the room's inhabitants, sucked my teeth to ready my mind, and then knocked loudly, once, twice.

"Who the hell?" came the response, guttural and slow with a Texas twist.

"Management," I said.

"What you want?"

"There was a problem with your reservation, sir."

"Reservation?" I heard footsteps, bare feet on bare wood, the turning of the bolt. "What the hell you talking about reser—"

Before he could finish I kicked open the door.

Gordon ducked slightly as he stiff-legged his way through the doorway, his sunglasses on, his scowl firm enough on its own to tone down any danger. He wore a black suit, white shirt, thin black tie—he had purposely gone all Tarantino for this play—and he pointed the long barrel of his black gun down at the face of the man now sprawled naked on the floor.

"Don't," Gordon said in his startlingly deep voice.

Whatever the man on the floor was thinking, he stopped thinking it.

I slipped a shit-eating grin onto my face and strode into the room like I had paid for it. The man on the floor was lean and hard, with the requisite thug tattoos on his chest: a skull with a pirate bandanna on one breast, a bottle of Colt 45 and a pistol on the other. Not bad, actually. The face behind the beard was handsome in a long-jawed way, and his pale-gray eyes were fixated on Gordon's gun. I walked right past him to the woman propped up by pillows on the bed.

"Miss Gilbert, I presume," I said.

She looked at me with a studied unconcern. She was naked atop a swelter of mussed sheets, one knee raised. From my vantage I could see her legs were heavy and her blonde hair was bleached. Her arms lay languidly across her torso, not deigning to cover breasts that were slight and pale. She was young and she was pretty because she was young, but already you could tell she wouldn't be a beauty, and I suppose she could tell, too.

"I figured someone would get here sooner or later," she said. "This is just sooner than I expected. But you can go right back and tell him I'm not coming home. Tell him I'm in love."

I turned to look at the man on the floor. "With that?"

"Jimmy's the love of my life."

"I guess it hasn't been much of a life."

"Don't let him push you around, Bree darling," said the man on the floor. He was a good decade older and was taking things much more seriously, but then again he had the gun in his face. "Love will keep us together for now and for always."

"You found yourself a charmer, Miss Gilbert, I'll give you that," I said. "You call him the Captain, or is he Tennille?"

"Run back to my daddy like a good little servant boy," said the heiress, "and tell him to leave me alone."

"Oh, don't worry. He has every intention of leaving you alone. Both of you. In fact, Miss Gilbert, I just came here to get both your signatures on a few documents."

"What the hell are you talking about?" said the man on the floor. "She don't sign nothing without my say-so."

I looked up at Gordon; he nodded his head sadly and then slugged Jimmy in the jaw with the barrel of the gun. There was blood and a spit tooth and a gratifying volume of shouts and curses, all of it coming from him, none of it coming from her. When I turned back to the girl, she was looking at me with a fine impassivity.

"You're not one of his usual goons," she said.

"That's because I'm not a goon," I said cheerfully. "I'm a lawyer."

"God help us, then. What kind of documents are you talking about?"

"Well, for you an emancipation declaration." I put the briefcase on the table, opened it so that Jimmy could see a flash of money, and took out a multipage document with an official-looking legal-blue backing. "You want to be free to live your life with that fellow on the ground there, undisturbed, for all of eternity. Your father is determined not to stand in your way. I've no doubt he's told you over and again how he made it on his own, rising from nothing with just his wits and his wiles and how that made all the difference in his life."

"My God he goes on, which is funny because his own father started the business."

"Well, he wants you to have the same experience."

"Fuck that," said Jimmy.

"Here you go, Miss Gilbert," I said, offering her the document. "You're still only seventeen, so you can't really be independent without an official emancipation. But this will do it. Sign on the line and you're free to live your life without your father's interference."

She sat up in the bed, pulled her legs beneath her, took hold of the papers. I drew a pen from my pocket and held it out as she scanned the document, her face twisting in confusion. I had drafted it with enough legalese that it would take a team of Latin majors from Notre Dame to figure out that it meant absolutely nothing.

"Freedom," I said. "With just the stroke of a pen. Sign the document and the rest of your life is yours. How many would jump at such an offer?"

"And if I don't sign this thing?"

"Then, because of your age, I would have the legal authority to forcibly take you away from this motel, from this state, and from the love of your life. I would have the legal authority to take you to your father. He'll probably whisk you off to the house on Molokai so you can recuperate from this whole ordeal. You'd end up back in his clutches, back to being dependent on his money, a virtual prisoner. On Molokai."

"I do like the house on Molokai."

"Don't do nothing, honey," said Jimmy as he climbed onto his knees. "They can't do nothing to us."

"Sweet ring," I said, looking down at him.

"It was a gift."

"Is that a Super Bowl ring? It couldn't be a Super Bowl ring, could it?"

"It's mine."

"It's on your finger, that's for sure."

"And that's where it's staying."

"Go ahead, Miss Gilbert," I said. "Just sign on the dotted line and this wonderful font of grammar and dignity is yours forever."

"I'm hers forever anyways. What about her money? What about her trust funds?"

"Freedom and money," I said. "Sometimes you can't have both. You'd be poor, yes. But think of this, Miss Gilbert: you'd have Johnny."

"Jimmy," said Jimmy.

"Right. Jimmy. At your side. Forever and ever. Through all eternity. Jimmy, Jimmy, Jimmy. What could be sweeter?"

"Are you really a lawyer?" she said.

"Bar certified and everything."

"I hate lawyers."

"That's okay, we hate ourselves."

She laughed and then climbed off the bed, stooped beside the still-bleeding man. She caressed his face while she said, "Maybe I should talk to him, Boodles."

"No, baby, stay with me. We'll do this together."

"Maybe I should talk to him just to sort things out."

"There's a limo outside waiting for you," I said.

"I'll go, too," said the man.

"Just for Miss Gilbert. And there's a picnic lunch in the backseat. Some of Estela's fried chicken."

"Estela's chicken?" she said, her eyes brightening.

"Don't listen to him," said Jimmy. "Stay with me, baby."

"I need to talk to my father, Jimmy, sweetie, or he'll never let us alone." She kissed his bruised lips, his forehead, his ear, and then lifted her face to me. "Did Estela pack iced tea with the chicken?"

"With the limes how you like it," I said.

"I'll come with you," said Jimmy, "and make sure he don't do nothing funny." But she was no longer listening.

"It's best if I go alone, Boodles." She straightened. "You wait here, I'll be back." As she passed me on the way to the bathroom, she said, "Just give me a minute to clean up." She grabbed a suitcase and closed the bathroom door behind her.

Jimmy tried to scramble to his feet but Gordon knocked him down again, and that was that. Still on the floor, still with the gun pointed at his face, he leaned against the wall, poked at his missing tooth with his tongue, and stared at the briefcase. Whatever he wanted to do in the name of violence and greed, the money in the briefcase was stilling his hand, as I knew it would.

She came out of the bathroom in jeans and a T-shirt, her face scrubbed, her hair wet and loose. She looked wholesome and fresh and totally out of place in that shithole. Her posture was straight and haughty; she handed me the suitcase as one would hand it to a bellboy. She barely glanced at Jimmy on the floor as she walked out the door. Carrying her suitcase, I followed her to the parking lot, where Kief, in full chauffeur's getup, cap included, waited at the limousine's open door.

"It's tougher than you think being his daughter," she said.

"I couldn't imagine," I said.

"That's right, you couldn't. But at least now he's paying attention. Sometimes all we want is to be looked at the right way."

"I understand."

"You have nice eyes."

"I don't get that much."

"Don't hurt him."

"I'm a lawyer."

"I know Daddy's lawyers."

"Enjoy Molokai."

"Do you want to come? I think I'd like you to come. I could arrange it."

"Hawaii's not for me," I said. "Lawyers burn easily."

"The afterlife must be tough on you guys, huh?"

"Enjoy the ride."

After she was inside and the door slammed shut, Kief looked up at the still-open door of the motel room.

"That seemed easy enough," he said.

"It helps having Gordon along, especially Gordon with a gun. But in truth, she wanted out. If Riley hadn't found her when she did, the girl would have sent out a homing signal on her own."

"Desert motel, two kids on the lam. I'm assuming they had some pretty impressive pharmaceuticals up there."

"Take her right home," I said. "No detours."

"No problem."

"And no partying with the passenger."

"Really, boss? I thought we were a service industry."

"We're not servicing her. Take her home and take the next flight out."

"I might as well be working for Uber."

I watched the limousine pull out of the parking lot, turn onto the road, and start heading to the father's mansion high in the hills above LA. Then I walked over to our rental SUV, where Riley was leaning against the back bumper, her sunglasses on, her arms crossed.

"Now comes the fun part," she said. "How's our boy Jimmy doing?"

"Not so well. Gordon had to work him over a bit. There's a tooth on the floor."

"You find the jewels?"

"Not yet."

"What about the ring?"

"Oh, the ring is there."

"The old man, he seemed pretty hepped up about that damn ring."

"It's a collector's item."

"Will Jimmy boy give it up?"

"One way or the other." I opened the rear door of the vehicle, reached to the seat, and pulled out a large-handled wire cutter with the price sticker still attached. "It's all just another negotiation, right?"

Mr. Gilbert was in a silk robe, hunched gnomishly at a round table covered by a white cloth, eating a grapefruit. While I stood to the side, he sprinkled sugar onto the citrus with his shaking hand and then one by one scooped pink wedges and slipped them between bleached dentures. His skin had the pale, glossy brittleness of parchment, his hair was dark and full of false, a rivulet of juice rolled down his chin. On a chaise by the pool a woman not much older than his daughter, but breathtakingly more beautiful, sunned while topless. The house was a dated monstrosity on Mulholland Drive, but the pool was bluer than the sky and the city spread out beyond it like a carpet to be stepped on. It was ten in the morning.

"You took longer than I expected," said Gilbert without looking up from his grapefruit. His voice held the arrogance rich men get working in their fathers' businesses.

"They made themselves invisible," I said. "She turned off her phone and used the cash they had gotten from the pawnshops instead of the credit card."

"I don't like excuses, and I don't like being kept waiting. Where are the jewels she stole?"

"We're in the process of retrieving them."

"That sounds less than promising."

"Don't worry. It turns out he kept the pawn slips."

"And he just gave them to you?"

"Toward the end of our discussion he became quite reasonable."

"She does know how to pick them, doesn't she? There was a boxer from Fresno before this. Fresno. You know, I started with nothing. That made all the difference. I didn't have the luxury of screwing up my life. The money has ruined her and there's nothing I can do about it."

I sucked my teeth and looked at the breasts on display by the pool. The woman lifted one arm over her head. She did that for my benefit, I could tell. Her wrist was slender and bound with faded friendship bracelets.

"Nothing to say?" said the old man.

I said nothing.

"You're not the first I've sent to fetch my daughter out of a mess. I know how it goes. This is the part when you start telling me how to be a father. This is the part where you start telling me to show her some love."

"No," I said. "This is the part where I tell you because your daughter is safe in Molokai that it's time for us to get paid."

"You took longer than I expected. I don't pay for tardiness. And how do I know this baboon won't try to see her again."

"He signed an agreement."

"Oh, he signed an agreement. Wait, he signed an agreement?"

I took a document out of the briefcase and placed it beside his grapefruit. Four pages with a blue backer, signed by Jimmy boy and notarized by one Dick Triplett.

The old man barely glanced at it. "What is this worth? Less than toilet paper. What happens if he does see her again? What happens if he pursues her like an animal?"

"Pursuant to the agreement, you get to kill him."

He lifted his ugly, round head at that, finally, and gave me a full look, like I had suddenly become human. "And he signed it?"

"I told you he became quite reasonable."

"Is the agreement enforceable?"

"Not in a court of law."

"Too bad." He turned back to his breakfast, slipped out a wedge, let it shiver between his teeth before he bit it like it was a squirming salamander. "But I suppose it might have some deterrent effect. Now what about the ring? I told Maambong I especially wanted back the ring. It has sentimental value."

"Not to mention a diamond the size of a walnut."

"It's a Super Bowl ring. Those don't come cheap, and this one certainly didn't. Come back when you have the ring and we'll talk about the final payment."

"I have the ring."

"Where?"

"In my pocket."

"And let me guess, you're holding it as ransom? Pay up or the ring gets it."

"I wouldn't do that, Mr. Gilbert. That would be bad form." I took the box out of my pocket and placed it gently atop the document. "I happen to be responsible for ensuring you pay the full fee, yes, but Mr. Maambong told me you are a man of your word. I choose to believe him. And so consider this ring a token of our good faith."

He glanced up at me, turned his attention back to the grapefruit, above which he let the spoon hover shakily for a moment before he dropped it carelessly onto the table and opened the box.

"Oh, you are awful," said Cassandra.

"I try," I said.

"But that's the point, Phil. You don't have to try, you just are. That's exactly why you're here."

"I thought Mr. Maambong hired me for my especial talents."

"He did. That's what I'm saying. You're an improvement on what we had before. You are next generation, team leader two point oh. That's a good thing. Don't overthink this."

We were lounging in our bathing suits by the pool at the house in Miami, sipping frothy umbrella drinks prepared by Bert, letting the beat pumping out of the sound system slip into our slack muscles like a massage. This was just a normal Tuesday for my crew. So far, in addition to the case of the missing heiress, we had been assigned to steal back a stolen painting, to evict a renter from a million-dollar mansion he had refused to leave, to convince a wife's lover that he should find other fields to plow, and to rob a warehouse and then burn it down before returning the stolen items to the owner. It was a dirty business, and sweetly profitable, and when we were on duty, the Last Chance Crew turned into an admirably taut team.

But on days we weren't out on a job, we reported to the house and leisured by the pool as we waited for a new assignment. One thing I could say about our early days in the Hyena Squad: in moments of calm, we were chill. Gordon was floating on a yellow raft, a beer resting on his cut gut, his thick black knee brace lying on a granite tile beside the pool. Kief was sleeping off a high within the shade of an umbrella. Riley was at a table, sipping one of Bert's famous mojitos and tapping on her computer, keeping up with the world. I didn't care a damn about keeping up with the world, it was enough for me to keep up with the Joneses.

"So what did Gilbert do when he opened the box?" said Cassandra.

"He swallowed his own vomit," I said.

She let out a spurt of laughter.

"It took him a moment to realize what it was. Nestled inside the velvet it looked pale and fake, rubbery even, like the exposed piece of bone was just a piece of chalk added for effect. He maybe thought it was a joke before he touched it. And that's when his body heaved involuntarily and he turned away from me. I was waiting for it to hit the tiles around the pool, but nothing. He was tougher than I gave him credit for. He swallowed his vomit, then turned and thanked me for returning the ring."

"You do know how to get paid."

"That's the name of the game," I said just before taking a sip of the drink to burn away the taste of copper. I didn't tell Cassandra about the look Mr. Gilbert gave me, a look full of loathing. The kind of look you give a rat pawing through a piece of feces. The kind of look I had seen before. And I didn't tell Cassandra what I had done about it the very next day.

"Who had this job before me?" I said.

"Rand. He was quite dashing; too bad it didn't work out."

"Did you have sex with Rand?"

"I told you he was dashing. Where do you think we dashed to?"

"Why didn't it work out?"

"It is better not to ask too many questions here," said Cassandra as her phone started buzzing. She picked it up, peered at it lazily through her sunglasses. "Fun time's over. Mr. Maambong wants to see you."

"You'll be gratified to know," said Mr. Maambong, sitting behind the glass-topped desk in his office, wearing his white suit, his dark glasses, "that our friend Mr. Gilbert has paid in full both our extravagant fee and all billed expenses."

"Good old Gilby," I said.

"We have added the requisite percentage of the fee to your account, minus the extra night's stay at the hotel in Los Angeles that you requested and the expenses from the minibar. You know how we feel about the minibar."

"But it's just so damn convenient."

"What was the purpose of your extra night's stay?"

"It was personal."

"We expect so. Mr. Gilbert was making troubling insinuations about you and his current wife."

"That was his wife? She certainly didn't act like it."

"His fourth wife, if you must know. Did you have relations with her?"

"Absolutely not."

"Are you sure, Mr. Kubiak? No relations, hmm? For you see, we tracked Mrs. Gilbert heading into your hotel the day after your meeting with her husband."

"I wouldn't call what we had relations," I said. "More like a collision."

"Mr. Gilbert made it clear that he never wants to see you again. You seem to have that effect on our clients. Assuming it is not happenstance, Mr. Kubiak, to what would you attribute your unpopularity?"

"If I were to make an offhand guess, maybe it's that our clients sense my resentment."

"What do you resent?"

"The way they look at me."

"And how do they look at you?"

"Like a servant."

"But that is what you are, Mr. Kubiak. That is what we all are. We service their needs and wants for a price. And the price is high, which has served you and your bank account quite well. We can't keep having you insulting our patrons, causing them distress, ravaging their wives."

"I wasn't the one doing the ravaging."

"We're not joking, Mr. Kubiak."

"Neither am I. Do you want to see the bite marks?"

"We are beginning to think that you might not emerge from your probationary period."

"I get results."

"Yes, you do. Just like you got results for Joey Mitts. But this is a business that depends on the continuing goodwill of our clients, and you are squandering that at an alarming rate. There are only so many who can afford our services. We cannot continue to lose their patronage."

There was a shard of ice in his tone that froze the next quip in my throat. As it lodged there it released a familiar taste. I had been here before; for me this place was as recurring as the dawn. No matter in what situation I found myself, no matter how advantageous—and working for Mr. Maambong was quite advantageous—I couldn't help but screw it up. My next move was typically defiance and anger and sometimes a sweet piece of violence, but I knew where that led and I was sick of the desert.

"I understand," I said. "It won't happen again."

"Make sure that it doesn't."

"Is that what happened to Rand?"

He hesitated for a moment, the gaze of those beetle eyes boring into my skull. "You should be less concerned with former employees," he said finally, "and more concerned with your own status in our enterprise. Now we have a new job for you. There is a boy. He is ill. We're going to save his life."

"How heartwarming."

"Yes, and whose heart could more use a little warming than yours? The client lives in Philadelphia, old money, old manners, old manor. That ridiculous hipster suit you wore in California won't go over in such rarefied environs. Wear something pin-striped and baggy, and maybe flake some coconut on your shoulders for dandruff. This type, they seem to take great pride in their dandruff. You are to listen and commiserate and be a comfort in this uncertain time. We'll take care of the fee, you'll take care of the boy. Is that understood?"

"Yes sir," I said with the alacrity of an intern.

"Consider this your final test before we either offer you full-time employment or terminate our relationship. You'll be flying up this evening for a meeting at the estate tomorrow morning. We'll send Cassandra along to keep an eye on you. She has our authority to use her knife if you get out of line again. We're sure Mr. Gilbert would be quite pleased to receive that box."

13

THE CASE OF THE WARMING HEART

The drive was lined with leprous rows of sycamores. The great lawn was groomed like a restricted golf course. A loose pack of purebred hounds quit their roughhousing to stand at point and stare, their heads swiveling to follow the route of the long black Lincoln.

James, in a navy-blue suit, was driving; I was alone in the backseat. Behind us were the stone wall and iron gate that separated the manicured lawn from the less-kempt environs of the universe; before us was the Wister manse. When he had held the car door open at the hotel, James made it clear to Cassandra that Mrs. Wister was expecting to have a private meeting with only me. My suit was baggy and pin-striped, my shirt was starched and white, my tie was preppy, my wingtips were shined, my jaw was locked, my hair was combed over as if I had a bald spot to hide. A crystal glass with the remnants of a very good Scotch was now resting in the handle of the door.

"Thank you so much for coming, Mr. Kubiak. I am just a wreck of worry. I haven't slept in weeks. I can't imagine how I'll be able to thank you when this is over, but I will try, I assure you."

The great stone house rested high on a hill, stretching out its wings, staring down at the expanse of the Wister property and the surrounding suburbs with the gaze of a predator. Even on a sunny morning there was something dark about the place. With its arched windows, its turret, the gargoyles sneering from the rainspouts, it was the set for a bad horror film, where blood poured down the walls. As the Town Car approached the house, the huge red door opened and a cadaverous man in butlerish garb took a step outside and clasped his white-gloved hands.

"It is about my grandson, my Edwin, the light of my life. He is such a dear boy, caring and kind. Special. If you would meet him, you would understand. It is difficult to watch him struggle, but he does, cheerfully and with unbelievable courage. He is the light of my life. My son, sadly, has been a disappointment. I believe the money ruined him—be careful of money, Mr. Kubiak, it can warp you in so many ways—but my son did do one thing of greatness for our family. He sired Edwin."

I followed the butler through the soaring center hall, its ceiling held aloft by the stone arches of a church. Our footfalls on the black-and-white marble floor resounded crisply. The hall was lined with somber old paintings of sharp-faced men in suits and thin, ethereal women swathed in chiffon. They stared down at me with glassy eyes, hard and familiar. Welcome to the club and watch your step, please, the hounds, like the Wisters, do their business everywhere.

"Your heart can't help but reach out to such a boy, such a special, loving boy. Edwin is currently attending a preparatory school. He is so brilliant, so popular. On the water polo team he is one of the team captains, even though his condition doesn't allow him to swim. During matches he sits on the side of the pool, handing out the towels and cheering. We are not the cheering sort, you understand, and so the sight of it breaks your heart."

Mrs. Wister waited for me in the drawing room. She was thin and powdered pale, with high gray hair and a twitchy mouth painted grotesquely red. In her eighties or so, she sat stiffly in some frouffy French love seat, a tartan blanket over her legs, a wheelchair placed strategically in view. It was a sweet tableau of helplessness laid out for my benefit. I was bade toward a frouffy French chair of my own. I sat just as stiffly as did she. The room had wood-paneled walls, paintings of cherubs, a piano, shelves of old books that hadn't been read in decades, an ornate dark wooden ceiling. The tall windows looked over a garden of rose and hedge, where a thin man in a straw hat dabbed color on a canvas.

"To see my Edwin hooked up to that machine is to know one must do everything within one's power to make him whole again," said Mrs. Wister. "No expense can be spared. Would you like to see a picture? Here, you must see a picture."

I oohed and aahed and clucked my tongue. The picture was of a particularly ugly boy. There was something wrong with his forehead, it was too something or other, and I wondered what exactly she meant when she called him special.

"He has so much promise, he is the future of the family, the future of the nation, and so he must be cured. Your Mr. Maambong came highly recommended. I didn't know where to turn, and someone in the know, someone quite powerful, told me to turn to him, and now here you are, Mr. Kubiak. Do you have children of your own?"

"No."

"But you have a mother."

"Fortunately."

"Tell me about her."

"Everything I am I owe to her. When my father died, she did all she could to care for me. When I look back, I realize whatever I know that is worth knowing, she taught to me. She lives in Louisiana now, working with disadvantaged women. She is just a pure piece of God's love."

There were vases, huge blue-and-white things from some Chinese dynasty. They were big enough to stand in, big enough to screw in. Ming, Qing, Tang, Han. Blue dragons slithered across the cracked surfaces. Priceless, I was sure. I would have given a thousand dollars just then for a hammer. This must have been the room where they wrote that song.

"With your having a mother so full of love, I'm sure you understand how I feel about Edwin. I wanted to meet privately because of the delicate nature of the task. I'm sure you understand. And I must say, it is so comforting to have you here. I sense that we are kindred souls, that I can trust you, utterly."

I smiled, and let my gaze linger on her eyes. They were blue, a startling sky blue, and with that twitchy mouth and the curve of her jaw, I could tell that she had been something in her day. I bet she catted plenty, I bet she slummed hard and fast with the working classes. I wondered what she would do if I sauntered over and licked the pasty red right off her lips.

"You must be some kind of a saint, Mr. Kubiak, to listen to my troubles and seek to help."

"I try to do my share, Mrs. Wister."

"Yes, I can see it in your eyes. The kindness there. The great love your mother gave you is still in your heart. I have perfect faith, Mr. Kubiak, that you will stop at nothing to help my boy. You are a shaft of light in the middle of my darkness."

"May I confess something to you, Mrs. Wister?"

"Oh, please," she said, a smile twitching onto those lips.

"That's the first time anyone has ever said that to me."

"She wants the acquisition done as quickly as possible," I said as I stabbed a thick piece of beef with my fork. "She doesn't want precious little Edwin to miss another water polo season."

"And I suppose it's not like you can order it online and then pick it up at a brick-and-mortar store on your way to lunch," said Cassandra.

"No, I suppose not, though that would be so much more convenient. And the wrinkled old invalid could sure as hell afford the price. There was a vase in the room where we met that was worth more than me. I had the vague urge to fuck it into shards."

Cassandra laughed as I stuck the meat in my maw. We were in a steakhouse in downtown Philadelphia. The walls were yellow-brown and covered with caricatures, fans spun beneath the pressed tin celling, fat people sawed at sirloins. On our table was wine, meat, bread, a vegetable for show. My filet was rare enough to drip blood; quite tender, quite delicious, with just the slightest tang of liver to let you know it had once been inside a living carcass. Cassandra was working on a pale glob of sweetbreads. If cow face had been on the menu, we would have ordered two for an appetizer.

"But fortunately for us there is no website to handle the acquisition," said Cassandra, after downing a bite of gland with a swallow of blood-red cabernet. "That's why we'll always be in demand. We are the true anything store. Whatever you want—a missing daughter, a painting you've been pining for—"

"A kidney for your grandson."

"Yes, a kidney for your grandson—and who doesn't want a kidney for the grandson, it's quite stylish these days to have three—whatever your wilted little heart desires, we will provide it, at our price."

"So long as the blood stays on our hands," I said. "You know the way their servants pick up the dogs' leavings in little blue bags? I've come to believe that's us."

"The servants?"

"The bags. I'm meeting with the doctor tomorrow evening. At a tavern on the wrong side of the tracks. I'm to stand at the bar, order a martini, and wait for him, which pleases me not at all because I don't care much for martinis."

"Poor boy."

"He's going to let me know what he requires on-site when he does the deed. Apparently, we'll be responsible for finding the right kidney."

"I'm sure the left would be just as good."

"Apparently, he also insists on meeting me alone."

"Of course," she said as she forked another piece of pancreas. "Fewer witnesses."

"Then explain something to me, Cassandra. I'm having all these meetings in which they insist on being seen by only me. And yet here you are."

Cassandra stuck the slivered gland into her mouth, chewed slowly.

"I suddenly have a pressing curiosity about the guy who sat in this seat before me. Tell me about Rand."

She waited a moment, drank more wine, shrugged. "There's not much to tell. He was a high-flying Wall Street jockey who had traded beyond his limits, going full bore for that huge bonus, and was caught just before the whole thing tumbled into the deep red. The bank sold off his positions to some of its customers, former customers now, and averted disaster, but that was the end of that job. Rand was too ruthless even for Wall Street. But Mr. Maambong had done a service for his boss, so when Rand got the old heave-ho, he also got a phone number. Mr. Maambong thought he'd be a natural."

"And?"

"He wasn't."

"What went wrong?"

She looked at the red of her wine, lit bright by the overhead pencil light. "It turns out," she said, "his was a sensitive soul."

There was a moment of quiet—as if in contemplation of some deep meaning in the mists, something the import of which we could grasp but not its boundaries—and then we both burst into ribald laughter. I laughed so hard it was the first time in ages I remember tears in my eyes. People from other tables glanced our way and we didn't give a damn. We were young and good-looking, bloated with wine and red meat, and later that night we'd be screwing like monkeys in our ritzy hotel suite and then raiding the minibar. Why shouldn't we laugh; why shouldn't they stare? Who the hell didn't want to be us at that moment?

"Oh man," I said as I wiped at my eyes with the thick white napkin. "That's rich. So you've come to make sure I don't go squishy."

"Just a precaution," said Cassandra. "Mr. Maambong likes to be sure."

"How am I doing?"

"Better than Rand."

"Are you Kubiak?" said the man who slipped onto the bar stool to my left, nearly shouting so he could be heard over the pounding of the music. He was middle-aged, graying, heavy and chinless, wearing a trench coat and a tie.

"That's right," I said.

"Did you tell anyone where you were going?"

"No."

"Not even the redhead you're with at the hotel?"

"No one."

"Good."

"You know, we could have met there."

"I've seen enough movies to know not to meet in hotel rooms," he said, before ordering an old-fashioned from the bartender. As the barkeep was building the drink, the doctor slipped a hand beneath my suit jacket. He rubbed it all across the front of my shirt and around the inside of my jacket, and I let him.

"Do you want to lick my ear while you're at it?" I said.

"I'm checking for a wire."

"Check away. Just don't get offended if my nipples pop."

As he performed his search, I kept my eyes on the go-go dancer in the corner of the little dive. My martini was cold and pretty good for a martini; the bartender had comfortingly showed not the least bit of interest in me; the early-evening crowd was a sparse mixture of hipsters and suits, mostly ignoring the show. The place was purposely ironic, and the dancer, tall and thick with high boots, fishnet stockings, and a leather bra, gyrated like a 1960s moon girl. But there was something real about her indifference that overcame the staginess of the place.

The doctor had finished the massage when the bartender brought his drink. It was squat and brown with an orange peel and cherry amidst the ice. The doctor sucked at it like it was a tit.

"Thirsty?"

"I dropped a thumb drive into your suit pocket. All the details of what I need are on it. When the time comes, I can be in and out in forty minutes. I'll be masked the whole time. No one will see me enter or exit, no one will be in there with me but you and the nurse."

"Nurse?"

"Your boss told the old lady he had one on call. After the job, I'll leave with the product and you'll never see me again. The rest will be up to you and the nurse."

"Fine."

"Your job is to find our donor and get her prepped."

"So it's a she."

"Is that a problem for you?"

"There are no problems for me."

"The information is all on the drive. We have a serial number from a marrow registry that matches our patient. We know her gender, but that's all. She could be anyone, anywhere."

"Do we have much time?"

"The sooner the better. You're the last resort. But here's the real trick: when it's over, she can't know what has been done to her."

"That's a hell of a trick."

"She has a rare combination that matches exactly what we need. But if we can make the match, so can the authorities. That's the real danger here, since our patient is on a registry, too. If they start searching the wait lists, they'll link her right back to the boy."

"Any ideas?"

"Drugs, I suppose. Something hallucinogenic, maybe. Acid, mush-rooms. You can probably buy what you need at the local middle school.

Recovery from the procedure will take a good few days. She'll need to be out and cared for during that time."

"Is it risky?"

"Not if no one sees my face."

"It's nice you have a sense of humor."

"Tell me something, could that dancer be more bored?"

Even as she swayed in those long leather boots, her face was bland and unfocused, as if she was doing something no more interesting than watching cable news. Nothing in the bar concerned her, certainly not the men who were stuffing the tip jar.

"Why do I have the innate urge," said the doctor, "to screw the indifference right out of her?"

"It's genetic. We don't like to be ignored. So what is it? Did you buy too much house? Do you have two kids in college? Did you for some deranged reason buy a boat?"

He sat hunched over his drink for a long moment and then said, "I have a mistress."

"Is she worth it?"

"She was. Now it's like having two wives, who each insist on telling me about their days."

"You should have bought the boat."

He downed the rest of his drink. "Do you believe in God, Kubiak?"

"I don't believe in anything," I said.

"That must help."

And then he burst into tears. He didn't make anything of it, didn't wave his arms or create a scene. His face just collapsed and his nose reddened and the tears flowed unabated. He was a middle-aged man crying over a glass of rye; what could be more common on this good green earth? Maybe the bartender had built his drink with Old Overholt.

As the doctor wiped his eyes with a sleeve of his trench coat, I signaled for another round.

14

THE RADIOGRAPH

I checked myself in the mirror. My white jacket was clean, but not too clean—I was modest enough to put a DO after the name in red thread—my tie was just slightly askew, the stethoscope was slung rakishly about my neck. I mussed my hair a bit, settled my glasses, sucked my teeth. I entered the room with a professional brusqueness, as if there were forty more rooms to visit before the end of my shift.

"Ms. Lieu, I'm Dr. Triplett," I said to the woman on the hospital bed. She was pretty, early twenties, slim limbed, wide eyed, wearing a hospital gown with a bland pattern. Machines set up in the room winked and chirped. An IV dripped into her slender arm. "I'll be the HMO internist during your stay. How long have you been with Medina Brothers?"

"Two weeks," she said, her voice soft and high, like a young bird.

I smiled. "Lucky you. I've worked with their employees a number of years. I'm sure you'll be pleased to know everything here is covered."

"Where is here?"

"You're in a small surgical center supported by the HMO. While you were out, and because of the potential emergency, we took the liberty of taking some X-rays. Why don't you tell me about your symptoms?"

Her name was Cindy Lieu. A child of immigrants living in Murfreesboro, Tennessee, she now worked as a bookkeeper-slash-receptionist for a small construction company called Medina Brothers in Memphis. She had moved to Memphis to be close to her boyfriend and had been working for another firm in the city, but the online records for some of the business accounts under her control showed strange fluctuations and certain unexplained withdrawals that concerned her employer. There wasn't any evidence of wrongdoing, but the firm had decided to outsource her work and so they let her go. To top it all off, her boyfriend had suddenly and mysteriously broken up with her. And so there she was, living alone in Memphis, away from family, without a job or any network of friends.

As luck would have it, shortly thereafter Medina Brothers flooded the Internet with a help-wanted ad that seemed to perfectly fit her background, even down to the request for some art history experience, which just happened to be her minor at UT. The ad flowed directly to her through a friend on Facebook, and the pay, well, the pay was quite high. There were of course many applicants—there was a line out the door on the day of her interview—and she expected that her previous work issues might ruin any chance, but after two meetings with Mr. Medina, a large man with a kind smile, she was hired. The office was quiet, usually just her and Mr. Medina, and the workload was light, but the pay was rich, and the benefits, yes, the benefits were wonderful. And Mr. Medina warned that her workload would increase once a few of the RFPs they had submitted were accepted, which she looked forward to.

But then, in the middle of a workday, just after lunch, a pain seemed to explode in her stomach, accompanied by violent cramping and intense nausea. She collapsed in a faint, and when she awoke she was in this hospital room, tended by the pretty red-haired nurse, waiting for the doctor.

"If you'll let me, I'd like to do a quick examination," I said. I put down my clipboard, rubbed my hands to warm them, and then placed them gently on her belly. As I pressed, she winced. I tapped a bit with my palms, I played a bit with the stethoscope. "Nurse Fletcher took your vitals already, and everything is in line with what we've discovered from the radiograph. Care to see?"

From a large envelope I extracted a piece of X-ray film with Cindy Lieu's name and the current date in the corner. I snapped it onto the viewer. "Could you turn on the light, please?" I said to an orderly.

Kief flipped the switch and the piece of X-ray film lit. Ribs, heart, viscera, the usual, except for one oblong thing on the right side glowing like it was radioactive.

"This is your appendix," I said, pointing to the ominous glow. "It's a vestigial organ, useless really, but every once in a while it gets infected. If it's not caught in time, it bursts like an overripe melon and spews the infection all through your body. The results can be catastrophic. Fortunately, the surgery is quite simple. A quick snip and it's gone, with absolutely no ill effect. There will be a slight scar, but we can make that below the bikini line. We do, however, need to move very quickly."

"Are you sure?" she said.

"Quite sure." I sat down on the side of her bed, put my hand on hers. "I don't think we should wait a minute. Of course, you're welcome to get a second opinion. Doing so would be out of network, so the cost would accrue to you. Normally I would say such a move might be prudent, but I'm worried about a delay here. I advise we move quickly before this bad boy bursts."

She tried to sit up again, but it all hit her, the pain, the nausea, and she lapsed down in weariness.

"What is that after your name on the jacket, that DO?" she said.

"I'm a doctor of osteopathic medicine."

"Is that real?"

"Oh yes, real as rain. But I won't be doing the surgery. The HMO has one of the finest surgeons in western Tennessee on call. Dr. Heigenmeister. He's an MD and he's on his way now. Afterward, we'll all be here to take care of you during recovery. But if you want a second opinion, that's your right. I'll call Dr. Heigenmeister and tell him to turn around."

"I don't know."

"You're not in a condition to drive. Do you have someone you could call to take you to another facility?"

"My mother is in Murfreesboro."

"No friends? No boyfriend?"

"We just broke up."

"I'm sorry." I adjusted my glasses, let a slight intimation of interest slip onto my lips.

"Some old girlfriend started up with him on Facebook out of nowhere. He said he owed it to us both to figure it out."

"Sounds to me like you're well rid of him. If you'd like, we could call you a cab. And as I said, the choice of getting a second opinion is up to you."

"How much is this going to cost me?"

"With us it's all covered," I said. "That's the way our HMO works. After the surgery, you'll be good as new, better than new, because that pesky appendix will be gone. It will knock a pound or so off your weight in addition."

"Doctor," said Cassandra, in her nurse's uniform with breasts starched and jutting, standing by the heart monitor, "her pulse is rising."

"Add a sedative to the IV, please," I said. "We need your decision now, Cindy."

Cindy Lieu looked at me, then at Cassandra, who slowly inserted a needle into the line that dived into her arm, and then back at me.

"I thought DOs only worked with bad backs?" she said, slowly now, dreamily.

"That's chiropractors. They're not really doctors."

Her eyes closed for a moment. "At least you're not a podiatrist."

I snapped my fingers. "Cindy, Cindy, open your eyes, please."

"Okay." Her eyes fluttered open. "You have a nice smile."

"We need a decision."

"Do you like bears?"

"Little ones," I said. "Preferably stuffed."

"Me too."

"Should we go ahead with the surgery, Cindy?"

"If you think I should."

"I do."

"Okay. Yes. If you say so."

"That's good to hear, you've made the right decision." I pulled up the clipboard. "You'll have to sign a consent form and then we're good to go."

I put the pen in her hand, drew it to the line at the bottom of the form I had drafted, and let her place the signature. The *C* for *Cindy* was clear enough, and the *L* for *Lieu*, but by the end of her surname the track of her pen trailed until it fell off the page.

This time Mrs. Wister made me wait.

Before the job they wait for you. Before the job you are one of them, a member of the tribe, you are as precious as family, and the paintings stare at you benignly as you walk down the hall. Before the job their needs tremble in their throats and you are their savior and no expense is to be spared. But afterward they make you wait while they crumble scones into their tea. Or disregard your presence as they carve out slivers of their grapefruit while in their robes. Afterward you are less valuable than the servant who dusts their vases. Afterward the paintings in the center hall don't even deign to look your way. And afterward the expenses are squawked over as if by a pack of chickens in need of frying.

"I have concerns about some of the costs," she said after the butler with the white gloves finally wheeled her into the drawing room, before backing out, closing the door, and leaving us alone. This time she stayed in the chair, this time her chin was raised, this time I wasn't bade to sit in the frouffy French chair across from her. "They seem excessive."

"How is your grandson doing?"

"Better, thank you. The yellow has left his eyes, but he still is not permitted to swim with the water polo team."

"We should have charged extra for keeping him out of the pool."

"The expenses, Mr. Kubiak. They seem inordinate. Intolerable, even. I don't understand these ridiculous costs."

I wondered for a moment what she would have thought if she knew the kidney that saved her grandson had come from a second-generation Asian immigrant from Murfreesboro, Tennessee. Would she be horrified at the race mingling? Just then I doubted it. She would have instead been gratified, I believed, to know that the kidney had been pilfered from the class whose purpose was to serve. To her, the wave of humanity that stretched like a great field of wheat across the whole of the American continent had only one raison d'être: to satisfy the whims and needs of her and her kind. And of course, I, too, was a stalk of that crop waiting to be reaped. If she felt the need to drain all my blood just to give a drop to her precious grandson, I had no doubt but that she would stick the knife in my neck without a second's hesitation. I supposed we had that in common.

"Your doctor gave me conditions to follow," I said. "Expensive conditions. We followed them to the letter. If you have a problem, talk to him."

"And what is this here?" she said slapping the page in her hand. "Seventy-five thousand dollars for what?"

"Severance."

"For whom?"

"Our donor. We told her it was in lieu of a possible workman's compensation claim."

"Did she have such a claim?"

"No."

"Then I don't understand. Was it merely a gift? Or more pathetically, was it a salve to your overactive conscience?"

"It was a prudent measure. At some point in her life, probably sooner rather than later, she'll get another X-ray or a CAT scan. And when she does, she is going to learn that she is missing a kidney. What happens at that point is a risk. Our job was to minimize such risks, and we did. The severance was wired to her account from a Mexican bank. The severance is fully recorded and unwarranted from the facts of the short employment we created for her. If she goes to the authorities, we will make sure the information about the payment is disclosed, along with the consent that she signed detailing the donation of a kidney. The authorities will suspect she sold her organ willingly, which is against American law, and be less concerned with where it went. Consider the payment an inexpensive insurance policy."

"Inexpensive for you, maybe."

"If you're short, sell a fucking vase."

"Excuse me, young man?"

"You heard me."

Those overpainted lips twitched into a smile. "Maybe I underestimated you. But don't underestimate me, dear. I have a vicious bite and I won't be crossed."

"That's not what we do," I said. "What we do is serve. Would you like something more, madame? Another crumpet perhaps?"

When I arrived at the Miami house fresh from Philadelphia, Gordon was sitting at the bar by the pool. There was a stack of money on the bar top and bourbon in Gordon's glass. As he rested his head on his hand, he rolled a set of white dice with black dots. Bert, standing behind the small counter in his red vest, periodically pulled bills from the stack and placed them in his pocket. Gordon's eyes were a bleary mess.

"Is Bert taking your money?" I said.

"Every damn cent, the thief."

"My bet is he's spiking your drink."

"Doesn't need to," said Gordon before downing the bourbon and rattling the ice. "I'm spiking it on my own."

"Why don't you get some sleep?"

"Too many dreams, man."

"Well, enjoy the celebration. I have a check in my briefcase."

"That's good to know," he said as Bert refilled the glass. "Wouldn't have wanted to pull that off for nothing."

He picked up the dice, shook his huge hand, skittered the bones across the bar top. Bert put another bill into his pocket.

I turned around and looked over to Kief, sitting in the sun, his pale skin bright and reddening. A cloud of smoke hovered over him; the tip of the reefer between his lips glowed bright. In the pool, Riley was swimming laps, slapping at the water, kicking wildly. Only Cassandra lay in a sea of calm, sunning herself, her top off, her skin covered with an oily sheen.

She lifted her head, stared at me through oversize sunglasses. "Welcome home. Fun meeting?"

"For once I'd like a simple thank-you instead of all the squawking about the bill."

"Go up to Boca and help the little old ladies cross the street. They know how to be grateful. You get it done?"

"Yes, I got it done. Have you noticed anything strange about my team?"

"Nothing strange," she said, her head dropping back onto the chaise. "The usual crack-up after a tough job. It happens. No one lasts too long working for Mr. Maambong."

"Except you."

"I'm different. And so are you, handsome. Be happy. Today is payday."

***

"How did you leave our dear Mrs. Wister?" said Mr. Maambong after I climbed the stairs to his glass-enclosed office and handed over the sealed envelope with the check. "Any problems we should know about?"

"None."

"Excellent. Once the funds are secured, there will be a bonus for you and your entire team. You outdid yourself, Mr. Kubiak. The acquisition went forward without a hitch, and such acquisitions rarely do. The Principal is uncommonly pleased."

"The Principal?"

"We are all cogs, Mr. Kubiak. I am your boss, the Principal is mine."

"I thought this was your show?"

Mr. Maambong smiled as if I were a child who had just discovered Santa wasn't real. "You'll be gratified to know that the Principal has authorized us to pull you out of probationary status and to raise you to the rank of associate."

"What does that mean?"

"It means more money, first of all."

"Bravo for that."

"It also means you are on a partnership track. Gaining a partnership in the enterprise is uncommonly rewarding. It won't be easy, we assure you, but the prizes will outstrip your dreams."

"I dream big."

"We hope so."

"When do I get to meet this Principal?"

"Sooner than you might expect. There is a plane waiting for you at the airport. It is gassed and ready to go."

"Another job?"

"No, something completely different. There is a house. On the west coast of Mexico. Overlooking the ocean. It is fully staffed, it is fully stocked. It is time, Mr. Kubiak, for you and your team to take a holiday."

15

HOLIDAY

The house sat white and wide and extravagant on a rise at the tip of the Baja. As we lay in a line on the wooden chaises with their thick white cushions, our sunglasses on, our skin bathed with lotion, tall orange drinks in our hands, it appeared that the water in the infinity pool reached straight out to the great stretch of sea beyond. We had begun seriously drinking on the plane ride west, had continued through the night, and were now collapsed, hungover, and drinking ever more, and not without reason.

There were four of us in the sunglasses and the swimsuits on the lounges, the whole of the Last Chance Crew. Cassandra hadn't made the trip, but Bert had come, ostensibly to fulfill our every whim, but also, I knew, to keep an eye on us all and report back to Mr. Maambong. Bert stood now in his red vest, behind a bar just inside the house's open wall of windows. On the pool deck the umbrellas had been maneuvered to maintain perfect shade for Kief, whose skin was already the color of boiled lobster and whose eyes were even redder. There were fresh fruits and pastries on the side tables, platters of bacon and eggs on the dining table, but we were mainly working the drinks Bert had prepared, a little bit of orange juice and a lot of champagne, garnished with strawberry and mint.

"Have you guys noticed this shack is eerily similar to the Miami property?" said Riley.

"Mr. Maambong sure does love his stark white walls," said Gordon.

"It's not Mr. Maambong," I said. "There's someone above Mr. Maambong."

"Who?"

"I don't know his name. But get this: he's called the Principal."

"Reefer all night, spiked orange juice in the morning, and a principal in charge of discipline," said Kief. "You were right, boss, when you said we were back in high school. I wonder what they give instead of detention."

"My guess on that, little Kief, is that you don't ever want to find out," said Gordon. "What do we know about this Principal person?"

"Nothing really," I said. "He's Mr. Maambong's boss. He likes modernist architecture with the personality of a cinder block. He prefers to stay unnamed and behind the scenes. He has a nice jet."

"That nice jet belongs to a corporate thingery called Jungle Dog, LLC," said Riley. "I checked the call number on the tail."

"How could you do that?" said Kief. "No computers, no phones; that was the rule for this little jaunt."

"Fuck the rule."

"Keep it down or Bert will hear you."

"Fuck Bert."

"Poor guy sure could use it," said Gordon.

"I just figured if I'm selling my soul, I ought to figure out who's doing the buying," said Riley. "That plane belongs to Jungle Dog, LLC. That house in Miami belongs to Jungle Dog, LLC."

"I'm seeing a pattern," said Kief.

"I'm having trouble getting into the Mexican real estate database, but I'd be surprised if this house isn't owned by the same company."

"What about the four of us?" said Gordon. "Are we owned by Jungle Dog, LLC?"

"Absolutely," I said. "From our noses to our spleens."

"Are we ever gonna talk about what we up and did in Memphis?" said Riley.

"No," said Gordon. "No we are not."

"Just take the money and pour ourselves another drink, is that it?"

"That's it exactly, except we got Bert to do the pouring."

"I didn't sign on for stealing kidneys."

"What did you sign on for?" said Kief.

"Money," said Riley. "Flash. A life with a bit of strut and style."

"And have you gotten paid?"

"I've gotten paid."

"Then quit your bellyaching," said Kief. "It beats the drive-through. Big Mac, large fries, supersize soda: the crap they push through those windows will kill you quicker than a missing kidney. And those suckers do it for minimum wage. We're not that different when you strip it down to basics; we satisfy whims. We just do it for a better clientele, and get paid better to do it. It's called capitalism."

"Thank you for that lesson in Economics 101," said Riley. "I suppose all I needed to assuage my girlish conscience was a man explaining the way the world works to me."

"Obviously, yes. There's a demand that's not being met by the supply. Blame it on the government. If there was a marketplace for these things, we wouldn't have a role, but due to America's tendency to overregulate, there's an inefficiency of which we, fortunately, can take advantage. We're like the traders on Wall Street making fortunes by mining the little blips of inefficiency between oil prices in Bengali and Beijing. The only difference is that we don't bring down entire economies."

"Which makes us heroes."

"Pretty much. You didn't have so many scruples when you were stocking up your bank account for your trip to Bali."

"That was just money."

"Nice excuse. As the old gent at the dinner party said, 'We've already determined what kind of woman you are, madame. Now we're just haggling over the bill.'"

"Fuck you, Kief."

"Don't take it so personally," said Gordon. "We're all just hookers on that gravy train. You know, Maambong didn't get hold of us at our peaks. Riley was just out of prison, Kief was out of work and under investigation, Phil lost his sales job, and I had nothing. Nothing. But then, there's a reason the Hyena Squad doesn't set up a table at Harvard."

"I can just imagine Mr. Maambong standing between Google and KPMG at the work fair," said Riley. "He'd have pictures of a pool and stark white houses."

"And Cassandra's breasts," I said.

"They wanted us to be desperate," said Gordon, "so we'd be willing to do anything, and that's exactly what we were when he found us. What we still are. So let's not kid ourselves. We can flap our wings and pretend that we're anything other than last chancers with no real outs, but we are last chancers with no real outs."

"Speak for yourself," said Kief.

"Oh, I've been listening to you, my perma-fried friend. When you feel compelled to twist yourself in knots to defend what you did, when you've got no choice but to go all Ayn Rand on our asses, then you know what you are. You can rationalize it for a month of Sundays but it doesn't make a bit of difference. You know exactly what you are."

There was a moment of quiet before I broke the silence. "Ayn Rand?"

"Yo, yo, yo," said Gordon over the laughter. "I almost graduated from Miami."

"What about you, Kubiak?" said Riley. "What says the fearless leader?"

I sat up on the chaise and stared through my dark glasses at the sun high off to the left. I knew what I wanted to say, what I had the strange urge to finally spill with all the spite in my soul: all those things they said they felt, those guilts and regrets that gnashed their teeth and twisted their consciences, all of them were fictions imposed by those who wanted to keep us down and docile. When you get to the root of it, we don't feel anything for anyone beyond what that anyone can do for us. Whatever anyone claims beyond that baseline is an excuse for failure. Cindy Lieu? All she had for me was a kidney. The rest of her, her supposed hopes and fears and loves and sadnesses, they didn't register in the least. She was a problem to be solved and I solved it. End of story. That's all life is. A problem to be solved. And that's all they were, each of them, Riley and Kief and Gordon, as well as Cassandra, Bert, Mr. Maambong, even the damn Principal—problems to be solved. The urge to tell it all rose like bile in my throat.

How would that little truth go over?

I stood, tossed my glasses onto the chaise, and dived like a knife into the water. The cool kissed every inch of me with its calming touch as I swam to the far edge without a breath and rolled into a neat kick turn. When I returned to the near edge I pulled myself out of the pool and stood before the three of them, water pouring off me like it was in flight.

"You want to know what I think?" I said. "I think it's time for the drugs and the whores."

I woke up in one of the second-floor bedrooms with my mouth dry as dirt and pain oozing like slime through my head. White walls, white bedding, a multihued selection of women naked as blue jays. There was a leg slung over my hip, there was a breast in my face, there were two women twined together like the strands of a rope by my side. The marble tops of the side tables were littered with glasses and ash, remnants of white powder lines, joints burned to the nub. A used condom dripped off a table edge like wax off a candle. Even with my nose seemingly scorched and stuffed with writhing worms, I could still catch the stink of sex and sweat and shit and smoke.

I sat up and looked around dazedly at the unholy mess and laughed.

As I went about extracting myself from the torsos and limbs, a hand reached out and pulled at my chest. *"Bebé, quédate, por favor."* I took hold of the hand and scratched my balls with it before tossing it aside and rising from the bed. I made my way around the tipped bottles and the strappy heels to the bathroom, where I pissed like a fire hose before blowing my nose clear in the sink, one side at a time. Not just worms, bloodworms.

The great white tub beckoned, but I brushed my teeth and scratched my stomach and headed down the stairs instead, looking for something wet to drink.

On the main floor naked bodies were flung haphazardly on the carpets and atop the white upholstered furniture, as if knocked about by a giant bowling ball of sex and drugs. The rock and roll of the night before had been turned off, and a quiet reigned, except for the sleep scratching, the ratchety snores, the dreamy moans. The slumbering body of Gordon, with his arms flung wide and his sunglasses on, took up one couch. Riley was in a pile of legs and breasts on the carpet by the fireplace. A woman lay facedown on the dining table, the wood beneath her open mouth slicked with drool. Two naked women sat on stools in the kitchen, drinking orange juice.

I was about to join them and beg in my bad Spanish for some coffee when I saw the tall, thin woman. Her hair was white and loose and shiny, and unlike every other woman in the house, she was clothed. The wall of glass that separated the main house from the pool had been left open through the night and she stood at the pool's edge, wearing black pants and a loose white silk shirt, her hip cocked in a youthful contrapposto, looking away from the debauchery and toward the sun rising over the Gulf of California.

I walked around the couch where Gordon was sprawled, pulled the pair of sunglasses off his face, and stepped through the open wall. With the sunglasses on, and nothing else, I stood beside the woman, who barely glanced at me before saying:

"Every time I see the sun rise, I think, *Carpe diem*."

"I think about my per diem," I said.

"Coffee?"

"Absolutely."

The woman snapped her fingers and quick as that Bert showed up in full red-vest regalia. He never showed up that quickly for me. "Two double espressos," said the woman. "Or would you like a cappuccino?"

"I'm not much for froth," I said.

"Good. No milk, Bert. And get the man a robe."

"Why?" I said.

She looked at me, looked down at me, looked at me again. Her face was sharp, angular, with deep creases about her eyes and mouth. It was the face of a woman who didn't give enough of a damn about what you thought to have her face worked on. And there was something in the way her mouth protruded that let you know she was hungry and would always be hungry. "Feed me," that mouth said, even before it spoke.

"No robe then, Bert, just the coffees."

Bert bowed and backed away, and in the way he backed away it became clear this wasn't just some Josephine in a silk shirt. This was *the* Josephine in a silk shirt.

"We were talking of evolution," said the Principal.

"Were we?"

"Life is simple. You're either evolving or devolving. The one thing you can't do is stay the same. Darwin taught us that."

"Pete Darwin? I played little league with Pete Darwin. He wasn't very evolved at all."

"I've heard good things about you, but I have my doubts. Lawyer, gold salesman, fixer, thief. You're a skitterer. Like those spidery bugs that skim the surface of a pond."

"It's important to have role models," I said.

"They skitter here and skitter there, but they don't get anywhere."

"They stay afloat."

"And that's a fine goal—for an accountant. The world is thick with floaters, but where do they end up? In the same pond, waiting for the frog to lap them up for breakfast. Look at the far edge of the pool."

"This pool?"

"Yes, this pool."

"It's a nice pool."

"A marvel of simple engineering, because it seems to go on forever. But its infinity is only an illusion. This pool is just as closed in as any other, just as much a prison. There's only one way to get beyond the edge."

"Climb out?"

"And then what? Skitter to the next? And then the next? I read a story about that once; it ended badly. When you get down to it, one pool is the same as the next. They're just holes in the ground. Ahh, the coffees. Thank you, Bert."

Bert shuffled silently forward with a tray on which sat two cups of espresso thick with butterscotch-colored crema and a small bowl of sugar cubes. The woman in the silk shirt took one of the cups and lifted two sugar cubes with the little silver tongs, dropped them in the espresso, swirled her coffee with a little silver spoon. She used the silver utensils like she had picked her teeth with silver toothpicks in her crib.

"Let's sit," she said, gesturing to an arrangement of white upholstered chairs under an arcade to the left. "I have a proposition for you."

"If you're going to proposition me, maybe I should get that robe after all."

"Evolution," she said. "We were talking of evolution."

We were now beneath the arcade, leaning back in our chairs, looking down at the villas on the narrow flat of land beneath us and the wide gulf beyond. In two fingers she held a neat silver tube, the tip of which glowed red each time she inhaled from the oboe-like mouthpiece. As she exhaled, vapor wreathed her head in a mist smelling of jasmine and clove. I was wrapped in a white robe that matched the cushions on the chairs, like I was just another piece of her furniture.

"I started this whole operation with one used limousine bought on credit. This was right after I landed in Miami. Things had gone sour in New York and I needed a new start, so I dragged my daughter to Miami, bought a piece-of-crap limousine and a uniform, and went into business for myself. It wasn't much, but I had plans. I thought I'd work long enough hours to buy a few more vehicles, hire some drivers, build a small fleet. That was the extent of my shallow little pool, and I was a bundle of nerves about it, waking every night in a sweat, worried about that loan. More coffee?"

"I'm fine."

"How about a bite of the hair of the dog? There's a Scotch that Bert keeps here just for me. Japanese distilled, only five hundred bottles ever made."

"That sounds right."

She snapped her fingers and a few moments later I had a Scotch on the rocks in my hand. The whiskey was brilliant enough to piss me off.

"Then my limo clients started asking for more than just a ride. 'Where can you get a good plate of *ropa vieja*?' they asked. 'What's the best night-club in South Beach?' 'Could you hook me up with a couple doses of ecstasy and some of your lady friends to share them with?' I realized there was a need out there that I could fill if I had the courage to be more than a limo driver. So I took the leap, went deeper into debt, hired a recent immigrant from Quezon City to man the car, and started a luxury concierge service.

"Whatever was desired, I could get it for a price. And once word got out among a certain . . . demimonde, shall we say, I had more business than I could handle. I was a one-stop shop for anyone coming into town: not just a limo but the best hotels, the best restaurants, the best shows, the purest drugs, the classiest whores, the darkest entertainments. By now I had four limos running, and the money, I have to tell you, the money was quite impressive. Still I had worries—an even bigger loan, cash flow issues—still I woke in the middle of the night riven with anxiety. It was like I had skittered from one pool to another, something bigger, warmer, with a waterfall and an attached Jacuzzi, sure, but it was just another hole in the ground.

"Then one of my clients, a very well-connected financier, told me a story. His daughter was being stalked by an old boyfriend. The boyfriend had been abusive. The police were doing nothing. The man was fearful that something terrible would happen. He didn't know what to do, he was lost. And in his helplessness I suddenly saw the possibility that I could be more than a mere concierge. I could be a problem solver, whatever the problem, whatever the solution. But I was worried that the doing would be beyond me. You see, I knew it would take a certain kind of person to play it out all the way. A certain kind of person with a certain kind of ruthlessness. I had never been that before, it was why I was forced to run from New York in the first place. Could I become that person now? Could I evolve?

"The answer came as I stood over that stalker with a baseball bat in my hands. Later, these kinds of jobs I would contract out—like your piece of work in the desert for Mr. Gilbert—but this I had to do myself. I had to see if I could be something new and ferocious, something utterly unlike what I had been. And that something new rose in me like the laughter that I barked out as I hit him and hit him again. The bat dripped blood and I hit him once more and I kept laughing. I wasn't laughing at his pain—I'm no sadist—I was laughing at how easy it was to cross the line. That's when I realized that nothing was impossible, that no pool could contain me. That's when I realized that infinity was within me, because I myself had no limits.

"I still have that first used limo. I still have the concierge service. I still solve impossible problems for the people who pay me. But I've evolved beyond each of those operations. I've built up an operation in Washington. The people who come to us for favors have a great deal of power and when we help them, they transfer that power to me. I no longer fall to my knees and pray for luck, I make my own luck and grow exponentially every day. And the funny thing is now I sleep through the night like a well-fucked dog."

Her voice stopped its flow for a moment, thank goodness. The house was starting to rise into wakefulness. Two naked women were cavorting in the pool. I sucked down the watery remnants of my Scotch. No matter how insane she might have been, she did deliver a good swig of Scotch. And, to be truthful, there was something about this woman's insanity that resonated in my chest.

"So, Mr. Kubiak, let's get down to it, shall we? Can you be more than a skitterer? Are you ready to cross the line into something grander? You puzzle me. There's an admirable coldness in you, and yet wherever you find yourself, whatever the opportunity being offered like a fresh piece of meat to a lion, you seem to find a way to turn it into shit. At these heights, that is something we can no longer afford. Darwin made it clear, the old ways must die and something new must rise. Can you be more than your wisecracking, gold-selling, wife-stealing self? Are you ready to evolve into someone truly fearsome? Someone worthy of being a partner in my organization?"

For a moment I watched the pretty women frolic in the pool. The taste of copper leached from my teeth and I had the urge to chew their faces off.

"I couldn't be more ready," I said.

"There is a cold case investigation under way by the DC police," she said. "A dead woman. Found by a dog in Rock Creek Park. I need the investigation squashed like a water bug."

And there it was. All of this, the plane, the house, the drugs, the whores, the long-winded speech, had been about one thing, which meant it was a big thing. Something about the case rang ill. There was too much byplay, too much sell. If Mr. Maambong had assigned this little matter from his desk in Miami, I would have thought nothing of it, but these circumstances gave me nothing but pause. Still, this woman had evolved into something close to a monster, and with it had come wealth and power and a ridiculously fine bottle of Scotch. I was already a monster; what could I evolve into and what would it get me? That was the question of the day.

"Consider it done," I said.

16

GEOMETRY

We were talking of evolution.

The office was warm, fragrant with incense, and there was a ceremonial drum beside one of the chairs. This was back on the East Coast now, but in Washington, not Miami. Miami was the land of Mr. Maambong, where his beetle eyes were everywhere; Washington, DC, was the land of reinvention, where the brazen turn themselves into national figures and national buffoons. I was ostensibly there to kill a murder investigation—what seemed then, despite my reservations, a simple enough task for someone with my skills—but I had a deeper purpose for my time in Washington, and so I found my way to that office with its drum. Three bonsai trees lined the windowsill. Set atop a leather ottoman was a wicker-covered box of tissues in the event I broke into sobs. The walls were green, the chair was chocolate brown, the couch was beige.

I was on the couch.

"So Mr. Triplett, how can I help you?" said Caroline Brooks, tall, thin, an elderly woman with kind eyes and hoops in her ears. Her face on the website seemed to have answers.

"I have a question, Doctor."

"Call me Caroline."

"Good, and you can call me Dick."

"See, we're making progress already." She leaned forward, gave me an empathetic gaze. "So, Dick, you have a question."

"It's been bothering me for a long while now, and lately it's become more imperative. That's why I've come to you."

"Let's see if I can help you come up with an answer."

"I need to know if people can truly change."

She laughed at that. "I hope so, or I'd be out of job."

"But from what I understand, therapy is not about deep change. People can learn to feel better about what they are. People can train themselves to react differently to difficult situations. People can turn more cheerful with the right drug taken in excess. Or, alternatively, people can learn ways to live healthier and alleviate stress."

"Yoga and yogurt," she said, nodding. "There's much that can be solved with yoga and yogurt."

"And people simply like talking about their mothers."

"Do you?"

"No."

"Any particular reason?"

"Because I know her. But all this is not what I'm trying to get at. I mean, when you cut past the manners, the habits, the learned responses, the drugged-up affect, when you peel back the layers and cut to the root of everything, what you would find is the core. And the question I have is can that core change."

"What do you think?"

"I think no," I said. "I think we are what we are and the rest is bullshit."

"But here you are, in my office, which tells me something."

"I guess I have doubts."

"Or hopes," she said, and she was dead right about that. The Principal had been talking of evolution at that infinity pool in Cabo and maybe, finally, I was ready.

The geometry of fate is often simple. In my case, there is a rectangle, two points, and a line. The rectangle is a cheap motel room in New Orleans, the points are my mother and Jesse Duchamp, the line is the flight of the bullet that pierced his malignant little skull. The root of this neat composition is wearying in its utter banality: there wasn't enough money, there were too many drugs, there were other women. In truth, I believed it was this final factor that ultimately caused my mother to pull the trigger, though she continued to insist the impetus was love and only love. But whatever the true reason, the very geometry of that death haunted me.

In so many ways Jesse Duchamp was my brother. We had both suckled at the same breasts; we both suffered, I had no doubt, from the same flaw. With every job I lost, with every chance I chumped, with every disaster I brought down upon myself, Jesse Duchamp and I were becoming ever closer. He must have felt a bright-green bitterness fill his soul as the copper-jacketed round he had loaded into his handgun expanded to the size of a penny in his brain, and so I couldn't shake the sense that with every coppery piece of failure I was tasting my own death. Jesse Duchamp's ultimate fate was hurtling toward me with the unerring trajectory of a bullet, unless . . .

We were talking about evolution, and was I wrong to believe that this opportunity, in the swamp that was Washington, DC, could also be my opportunity to change, to grow, to evolve out of Jesse Duchamp's fate and into a brighter one of my own? The Principal wanted me to evolve into something that wouldn't screw up as I had multiple times before, something that would be worthy of a partnership in her enterprise. I didn't yet know if it was in me to become this new and brighter thing, but I believed I needed all the help I could get to find out.

"I will say first of all," said Caroline Brooks, "that you shouldn't discount the power of what you call manners and habits and learned responses. Behavioral therapy can be quite effective. Our actions very much define us."

"But a lot of it is just happenstance, don't you think? I won't cheat on my wife if the right woman with stiletto heels doesn't come along to tempt me."

"Are you married, Dick?"

"Not anymore. Let's just say that those stiletto heels did come along. And I won't steal a bar of gold if I never happen to see one lying around. But I could still, at heart, be a cheater or a thief just waiting for my moment."

"Are you?"

"Do you want an honest answer?"

"Nothing of worth can happen here if it doesn't come from honesty."

"Then yes, absolutely, I am both a cheater and a thief. You also should know it's not easy for me to be honest. Lying is more than second nature. It is my nature."

"But you're here, of your own free will."

"And I guess, in the spirit of honesty, I need to tell you my name is not Dick Triplett."

"So the very first words you said to me were a lie."

"The hello was genuine."

"Why didn't you want me to know your real name?"

"I thought it would be safer for everybody."

"You must have some terrible secrets." She laughed at that, laughed with just a touch of nervousness. "But as you know, whatever we say here is privileged; I can't reveal it or be forced to reveal it. So you can trust my confidentiality. What is your real name?"

"Phil."

"Just Phil?"

"Let's leave it at just Phil."

"I suppose then you'll be paying me in cash."

We both laughed at that.

"Okay, good," she said. "Now we might really be getting some-where. Your name is Phil and you want to know if people can change because you want to be someone other than who you are."

"I didn't say that."

"No, but it's certainly implied. What is it you do for a living, Phil?"

"I fix things."

"You're an engineer?"

"Of a sort. I fix situations. If our clients have a problem, no mat-ter how difficult or unseemly, I engineer a solution for them. It is very specialized, very lucrative."

"I suppose in the fixer business it helps to be a liar and a thief."

"It's a prerequisite."

"But something about it troubles you?"

"Only that it may not last."

"What is it you want to become?"

"Something different than what I am," I said. "Something that doesn't screw up every opportunity that comes his way. Something that doesn't end up dead on the floor of a New Orleans motel."

"That's quite a specific fear. We'll have to get into that at some point. But first I couldn't help but note that you used an interesting construction. Not someone, but something. And you believe you've screwed up your life at every opportunity?"

"Yes."

"How so?"

"I screwed up the good job I had at the firm that hired me out of law school. I had a sales job that I screwed up by being too good a salesman. I was married once and I pulled that apart like a kid pulling the wings off a fly. And every disaster tastes the same, if you know what I mean."

"No, I don't."

"Bitter and metallic, like I'm sucking a penny."

"And now you've got this new position and you're afraid if you can't change what you are, you're going to mess up everything again."

"Yes."

"You've told me you want to be something new. So tell me, Phil, what is the something you believe you are now?"

I hesitated. I'm not one to hesitate—a salesman who hesitates is lost—but I hesitated just then as Caroline Brooks's eyes shined with an almost indecent expectation. Some words have an incantatory power. Some words once spoken change everything, like the calling forth of a demon. The sky darkens, the air crackles with power, the word creates its own truth within you. But we were talking about evolution. Time to make the call.

"What I believe," I said, "is that I'm a psychopath."

17

THE CASE OF THE DEAD BLONDE

"Whoa," said the outlaw after the magazine writer downed what remained of her Scotch so forcefully the cube of ice bounced off her teeth. "You bolted that last bit like it was antacid. If you knew how expensive this Scotch actually was, you'd throw it up and drink it again just to get my money's worth."

The magazine writer closed her eyes for a moment and let the alcohol burn away the sudden spurt of fear that had choked her throat. When she opened them again, she was staring into the outlaw's hard, scarred face. She tried to see something in his eye that would reassure her, something in the line of his jaw, something of the higher purpose she had expected to find. What she saw, she realized, was a cipher. Every magazine interview was a dance of artifice; the subject presented an attractive facade and she grabbed hold of whichever shard of that facade created the juiciest story. It was all about words on the page instead of truth, because in the magazines she wrote for no one wanted the naked truth. No one wanted it ever, really. But now, after years of accepting faces at face value, when she desperately needed to know the truth of this specific subject, she was lost.

Was this man what he had thought he was? And if so, how could she have come to this place and trusted him with her life? But if he was what he had thought he was, who else would be better equipped to do this dark thing she needed done? She pushed her glass toward the bottle, as if the answer might be somewhere in there, beyond the sketch of the Japanese warrior.

"More?" said the outlaw. He poured another finger's worth of the precious Scotch. "I understand your sudden thirst. I've already told you my background, my work, my way of seeing the world, and in just the telling you could get a sense of my superficial charm, which is one of the telltales. You must have at least considered the possibility. And yet, still, when I accused myself out loud you couldn't help yourself from dashing the last swallow down your throat all at once. Though I sense in you it wasn't only fear but also hope. Hmm?"

With a sudden shriek of the door hinges, a shaft of light pierced the interior of the bar and slammed directly into the magazine writer's face.

She threw up a hand to shield her eyes and squinted. This was a private meeting, the outlaw was a wanted man; was the intruder someone coming after him, someone who wouldn't care about collateral damage in the quest for the bounty? Through her squint she could just make out a silhouette, short and slight—a boy's figure?

And then the door thumped shut and she saw him clearly, wild hair, scruffy beard, staring at the two of them. And, my God, those hands. The outlaw, who had twisted to see the intruder, turned back to the magazine writer with concern on his face.

"Stop staring, and we need to keep our voices down," he said. "The lost soul who has just entered is one of the gang of pathetic regulars that kill whatever ambience might actually exist in this joint. He's a glad-hander, despite having hands like the wrinkled claws of some prehistoric crab. If he sees an opening, he might want to join our little party and bore us to tears with his inane chatter. Put your head down and I'll whisper something and it'll appear like we're having a private moment and maybe we'll shame him into minding his own damn business. Laugh."

The magazine writer laughed, as if the outlaw had offered the most delightful bon mot, and the outlaw laughed with her and in the sound of their laughter the man turned toward the bar. The outlaw took a careful glance over.

"That's a relief," he said. "The word among the cactuses is that his mutilated hands were the result of a mishap in a meth lab. But I like to believe he grew up in a Catholic orphanage where the nuns who prowled the bathrooms carried torches and swords.

"So where were we? Oh yes, the psychiatrist and my little piece of self-diagnosis. I bet you're wondering if the skies did in fact darken and the air did in fact crackle with power when I said it out loud. Sadly, no. The only crackle of power was the way Caroline Brooks's eyes lit with fascination as she leaned toward me. I had just disclosed the secret that circled my heart like a ring of thorns and the woman to whom I had chosen to bear this brutal truth reacted like a hungry Parisian watching a snail slither across her plate."

"Interesting," Caroline Brooks said. "Why would you think such a thing?"

"Because of what I feel."

"And what is that?"

"Very little."

"Do you not get angry?"

"Oh, I get angry."

"Do you have envy, sexual desire, do you ever want to rip someone's face off?"

"Constantly."

"Then you do feel."

"But I don't feel awe, or love, or any of the things other people claim to feel. I can't look into your eyes and feel what you feel. I can fake it as well as you can, but it's not there."

"And you believe this is why you keep failing?"

"Don't you?"

"What do you want from our sessions together, Phil?"

"To be repaired."

"Like a car."

"Exactly."

"To what end? To become a better fixer? To become, maybe, a better psychopath?"

"I wouldn't put it that way."

"No, I suppose you wouldn't. But that's the sense I'm getting. And I must say, I believe you'll be disappointed. In all probability you are not a psychopath."

"And how can you know so soon?" I said.

"You're here," she said. "It's common for patients to dwell on their deficits when they diagnose themselves. Many come to the conclusion that they must be psychopathic. But the one thing we know about psychopaths is that they don't seek help for their condition. In fact, they don't even believe they have a condition. You think you're one, ergo you're not."

An interesting piece of logic from the good doctor, no? If you follow it to its logical conclusion, Descartes suddenly vanishes into thin air.

"Still, if you'd like," she said, "a few protocols exist that would help me make a more considered diagnosis. I could simply ask you some questions, and if your answers are honest, we could have a pretty decent idea of what we're looking at."

"A psychopath test?" I said.

"Of a sort."

"I think I took one already."

"How did you do?"

"Pretty damn well."

"Let me try my own," she said. "It might be instructive." And so that's we did. Over the next few sessions, Caroline Brooks probed into the inner recesses of my psyche. Think of a janitor poking around the hidden chambers of a high tower, collecting guano as rats scutter and pigeons take awkward flight. I didn't envy her the task, but I didn't dwell on it either. I had something else to keep me occupied, the job that had brought me to Washington in the first place. I had a murder to deal with, and nothing focuses the mind, if not the narrative, more than a murder.

It didn't matter who the dead woman was, only that she was dead. That's not cold, that's fact. If she had still been alive, you would have edged your way in front of her in line at the megaplex and not given her a second's thought. But in her dying she was worthy of a story. In her dying she suddenly mattered to someone with money, which meant she mattered to me.

The dead woman's name was Scarlett Gould. She was only a couple years out of University of Maryland, blonde, petite, one of the army who make their post-collegiate way to Washington to forge a career in the belly of the beast. In college, while majoring in communications, she had interned at a wildlife advocacy foundation and after graduating had settled in full-time, working to protect the seals and the whales and the ivory-billed woodpecker, so endangered, she liked to say, that it might already be extinct. She had dumped her college boyfriend a few months after moving to the District and switched her Facebook status to single. She tacked batik on the wall of her small apartment in Adams Morgan just above an Ethiopian restaurant. She doted on her baby nephews and had a cat named Didi. She maybe drank too much. She liked to dance. She bought boots that were too expensive. She read romance novels and played Ramones songs badly on her acoustic guitar. She was all hopped up and ready to go, ready to go now, until she was found by a neighborhood teenager who was walking her dog in Rock Creek Park.

The girl and the dog, a large black Labrador on a retractable leash, were on the southern end of the Western Ridge Trail, just below the tennis courts, when the dog's head suddenly perked. The dog raced away from the trail and down a hill toward the river. The leash fully extended, the dog kept yanking, the teenager followed. The dog stuck its nose in a patch of snow between two bristly shrubs, rummaging. When it finally looked back at the teenager, there was a cold blue hand in its mouth.

That image—the screaming teenager, the maroon-flecked snow, the blue hand in the black dog's mouth—all of it sparked a conflagration of public interest. But that had happened a year and a half before we arrived in Washington, and the police investigation into Scarlett Gould's murder had gotten exactly nowhere. The main suspect was Bradley Beamon, Scarlett Gould's college boyfriend, who had taken their breakup badly. Beamon had sent the victim a series of threatening text messages and Facebook posts, calling her all manner of misogynistic slander, and had threatened to ram an ivory-billed woodpecker up her . . . yeah. The boy remained under suspicion but also remained uncharged. The press had stopped reporting, the public had turned to more pressing scandals, the case had gone cold.

Our job was to make sure it stayed that way.

"They've gone and reassigned the investigation," said Riley, staring at the computer screen. "That's why we're here. They grabbed it away from the original detectives and handed it to a pair from the cold case division with orders to examine everything with new eyes. The head cop must be getting pressure to solve this."

"We need to find out where the pressure's coming from," I said. "Who are the new detectives?"

"Pickering and Booth, according to the reports. Experienced, successful, but not without issues. They got some press last year for closing a ten-year-old murder and dragging the suspect back from Mississippi. Before that there was a scandal involving Pickering. It was front page of the local for a few days and then died."

"Find out everything you can about the two of them," I said. "Their family situations, their finances, whatever shortcuts they may have taken in the past."

"You looking for dirt, chief?"

"Piles of it," I said. "We're here to bury a landfill. But they can't know we're looking into them."

"Got it," said Riley.

"Kief will give you whatever help you need."

"I think I can manage."

"I'm here if you need me," said Kief. "Right here, on the couch, if you need me."

Mr. Maambong had rented us a suite, along with three additional rooms on the same floor of a venerable downtown hotel. The suite was large and a little shabby, with wide sofas and brown easy chairs and a long dining room table. From the windows we had a sterling view of the White House with the Washington Monument rising behind it. Riley had set up two laptops, a monitor, and a laser printer on the dining table to serve as our command post. Gordon was standing by the counter that served as the kitchen, peeling an orange. Kief was sprawled on one of the sofas, with a bottle of beer resting on his belt buckle.

"The girls here don't smile at you, have you noticed that?" said Kief.

"They're just not smiling at you," said Riley.

"They smile at me in Miami. Even the pretty ones way out of my league."

"Pity smile," said Gordon. "It's a sad state when the only action you're getting is a pity smile. Where'd you find the beer?"

"Minibar. In Miami there's a friendliness. It's the culture."

"Culture?" said Riley. "In Miami?"

"But here," continued Kief, "everyone is so damn serious, with their oh-so-important jobs working for their oh-so-important dickhead politicians. They can't be bothered to smile at someone who might be less important than they are."

"You must be feeling rich, little Kief, raiding the minibar," said Gordon.

"I took it from Phil's minibar," said Kief, raising the bottle. "What? I mean he gets the sweet suite and all we have are those crappy rooms."

"The suite's where we work, dumbass," said Riley. "It's for all of us."

"Until there's a sock on the door."

"Yeah, yeah, yeah," I said into their laughter. "Kief, I also need you to find out what kind of forensic evidence they have and where they store it. I want a plan in place to contaminate what they have so that it's unusable in furthering the investigation or at trial."

"Fire will do the trick. Fire always does the trick. Do you want me just to go ahead and light the sucker?"

"Not until I say so. We might want to contaminate it in a specific way."

"Messing with state's evidence, man," said Gordon. "That's a thing."

"We've done worse," said Riley. "While Kief and I are digging up dirt on the cops and scouting their evidence, what are you and Gordon going to be up to?"

"We're here to divert the police investigation," I said. "The one thing we don't want to do is divert the damn thing to the truth. That means we have to shadow the official investigation with one of our own. Gordon and I will start taking care of that."

"How are we going to tromp around the same territory as the new detectives without getting our asses handed to us?" said Gordon.

"Leave that to me," I said. "Tomorrow I'll pick us up a shade."

The sky was bright, the day was filled with promise, and the bar was a dive. Pretty damn perfect all the way around. Sometimes, when the stakes are too high you have to lay both sides of a bet to keep yourself whole. This was that kind of play. I wore my tight-suit, gelled-hair getup with the brown briefcase. I wanted to look young in the eyes of the aged, I wanted to be underestimated. People will often debase themselves to help a fool.

The Raven Grill was a dark, narrow room in the northern part of the city, wedged between a Laundromat and a dry cleaner. The grill portion of the name was an inside joke. The pale wooden bar was long and worn, the leather on the mismatched stools was cracked. Four old-timers played cards in a booth; a man with a mustache and a worn suit huddled over some foul brown concoction at the bar. I sat one stool over and ordered a beer. The barkeep didn't give me a second look, which was the best thing about the place, that and the picture of Jimi Hendrix on the wall behind me.

"I have just enough time for a quick swallow," I said to no one in particular. I drummed the bar top. "You've got to take your moments when you can, am I right?"

The man one stool over didn't respond, but a slight shrug let me know he was listening. He was thin, balding, on the wrong side of sixty. There was something dignified in the way he held himself, as dignified as one can be drinking alone in a bar like that in the middle of the day.

When the bottle of beer was slapped down before me, I took a long pull like I needed it. "Cheers," I said.

"Customarily, one says that before one drinks," said the man with a Latin accent.

"I was thirsty."

He didn't smile or look at me, just stared forward, like some answer to the universe was on the other side of the bar top, maybe in the bags of chips and pretzels hanging from the rack on the wall. That was about it for food in that place; I supposed the pretzels were grilled. I finished the beer, motioned to the barkeep to bring me another, and indicated she should supply the man one stool over with another of whatever crap he was drinking as well.

"I guess I have time for one more," I said, "but then I've got to go. Got to go. Cheers."

"Proper form that time," said the man, lifting his freshly poured brown sludge in thanks while still not shifting his posture.

I took a long pull. "I'm just going to finish this, and maybe have one more, but then I've got to, got to, got to find myself a lawyer."

He turned at that, the man one seat over, his body opened up to me like a flower and the thin lips beneath the mustache spread into a wary smile even as his eyes stayed mysteriously sad. "Are you, perhaps, my young friend, searching for an attorney?"

"Not just any attorney," I said. "The right attorney. One who recognizes opportunity, because I have opportunity in my back pocket for a mouthpiece sharp enough to recognize it."

"Ah, I see. Opportunity you say. For an attorney. Which is a coincidence, I must say, because by mere happenstance I just so happen, myself, to be an attorney."

"No."

He lifted his hands and spread them wide as he bowed his head into the gap. "Just so happen."

"Well then," I said, "this might be both our lucky days. The name's Triplett, Dick Triplett."

"Alberto Menendez, attorney at law, and at your service."

"Al?"

"Alberto."

"Not Al? Al is so friendly."

"Alberto."

"Okay, so much for friendliness. Alberto, why don't you grab us a booth and I'll order us another couple of rounds."

We seated ourselves on either side of a white Formica table beneath a photograph of Dylan. There was a tabletop jukebox that we ignored, and a mess of drinks I brought over that we didn't. Oh, and I sprang for a bag of pretzels to serve as lunch. I didn't want Al to think me a cheapskate.

"What kind of lawyer do you happen to be there, Alberto?"

"Oh, I am what they call a jack-of-all-trades," he said in his courtly voice. He had the face of a benevolent landowner, with scores of peasants toiling in his fields, but with a family that had imploded. A leopard of the high hills of Mexico. "I have learned not to limit myself in service to my clients' interests. You want a will, I will make you a will. You have an immigration issue, I can work with ICE to solve it, if it is solvable. Sadly, not everything is solvable. You have a DUI, I know whom to talk to."

"Who?"

"That, my friend, must remain my secret. Not all the dark arts of the law can be given away over a cheap glass of bourbon."

"Maybe I should have bought you something top-shelf."

"This place only has bottom shelves, and sadly, they have become the shelves for me."

"What about PI?" I said. "Any experience? Do you do good old-fashioned plaintiff's work?"

"I have done some in the past, yes? Life is full of uncertainties. Negligence is everywhere, not to mention unspeakable violence. I would be a poor servant if I didn't protect my clients' interests when the worst occurs."

"And how did that work out for you, bottom line?"

"Let me ask you something, Mr. Triplett."

"Dick."

"Yes. Are you, perhaps, an attorney yourself?"

"As a matter of fact."

"Where did you attend law school?"

"Pacific McGeorge."

"Never heard of it."

"No one has."

"And so that leads me to conclude this was not a chance encounter."

"Don't get too clever on me, Alberto, you might make me nervous. I am looking for local counsel. I need someone discreet enough to remain quiet about the peculiarities of the case, someone desperate enough to take it with my conditions attached, and someone sturdy enough to handle the pushback that will surely come. I asked around and your name came up as fitting the criteria. Especially regarding the desperate part."

"And you thought it necessary to meet me here, in this unfortunate place, under false pretenses?"

"Showing up in your office in the middle of the day wouldn't do much good, would it, Alberto? And the pretense, as you can understand, was all about evaluating you before I made my offer."

"Did I pass your precious evaluation?"

"I liked that you didn't let me call you Al. Every Al I've ever known has been an asshole. And you seem to have discretion."

"Perhaps, before you go any further, I should—"

"If you are trying to tell me about that unfortunate matter in the Patel case, I already know."

"I would think that information, and the Bar Association's swift reaction, would have dissuaded you." He lifted his drink, swirled it a bit before knocking down a stiff gulp. "It seems to have dissuaded everyone else."

"On the contrary, it is what brought me here. I believe in second chances. And I believe in desperation. I think you'll do, Alberto, if you agree to my conditions."

"These days there are always conditions. And what are yours, pray tell?"

"Here's the story," I said, before leaning forward and lowering my voice. "I have a lead on a wrongful death. The case would have to be brought here, but I'm not licensed in DC. In any event, I don't want my name attached to the case in any way, shape, or form. That's the first requirement. Whatever heat comes down, you have to handle it without getting me involved."

"What kind of heat are we talking about?"

"I don't know exactly, but I expect pushback. So I need someone who can take care of himself when pushed."

"If you know about the Patel case, then you know the answer to that."

"You ask me, he had it coming. You were going to put the money back, of course you were. Look, what I'll need you to do is sign up the clients on your own and handle any inquiries from the authorities while leaving my team free to do the investigation in your name."

"And then I will handle the litigation?"

"I don't expect there will be litigation."

"Then I will handle the settlement negotiations."

"I don't expect there to be any settlement negotiations."

"Then I don't understand."

"All I expect there to be is an investigation and pushback. The police may even be involved. It could get messy. My guess is you're the man to handle the messy. But if, by chance, things turn in unanticipated ways and there is a case to move forward, then you will handle the litigation and any settlement discussions, and when the proceeds pour in, your firm will pay me a substantial referral fee."

"How substantial?"

"Fifty percent."

"It is usually a third. In my experience, it has always been a third."

"That's where the desperation comes in."

"Forty."

"We're not negotiating, Alberto. Whatever settlement or verdict you get, you will transfer, quite quietly, fifty percent of your firm's fee to an account I designate."

"After expenses?"

"No. The expenses are your problem. Fifty percent flat. I will, however, as consideration for all your trouble, and all the possible mess, pay you a nonrefundable retainer. Say five thousand dollars."

"I suppose we're not negotiating that either."

"Would seven make you happier?"

"Not happier, but less hungry. Up front?"

"That goes without saying."

"It sounds, how should I say, all of it, a trifle shady, my friend."

"More than a trifle, Alberto, but that is why I didn't go to Williams & Connolly, or Willkie, Farr. That is why I came to you."

He sat hunched over his drink, spinning the glass back and forth between his palms, thinking for a moment. "You know, it could have happened to anyone."

"But it didn't happen to anyone."

"And now here I am, deep in the shady." He stopped spinning his drink and took a swallow, winced. "The bourbon in this place is a crime, but at least it's a petty crime. There was a time I drank only the best. When only the best was good enough."

"We all have our sob stories."

"When would the retainer payment be made?"

"As soon as you sign the referral agreement and then get the requisite signatures on a contingency fee agreement. I drafted both." I opened the briefcase, pulled out two documents with blue backing, and slid them across the table. He took a pair of glasses out of his jacket and put them low on his nose as he looked over the documents. After a moment he raised his gaze above the lenses to peer at me.

"Gould? The Scarlett Gould case?"

"That's it exactly."

"You have a lead?"

"I know something no one else knows."

"Yet you're not expecting litigation or a settlement. And there is no place for the client's signature on the referral agreement."

"We will not be informing the client of our arrangement."

"You must not be so careful a lawyer, Mr. Triplett. The rules are clear. Without the client's consent this agreement is not enforceable."

"Not by a court, if you get my drift. But I don't want you thinking that you could screw me with a loophole, Alberto. That would be a dangerous thought, do you understand?"

"What am I supposed to understand?"

"I am here in good faith. I'm assuming the same from you. But you won't want to disappoint me as you disappointed the Patels. I have no scruples."

"Everyone has some scruples."

"I am the exception."

"Shady, shady, shady. I am beginning to have serious reservations."

"Good. That only goes to show your shining intelligence. If you agree, I'll set up an appointment and tomorrow we'll drive up together to Baltimore where the Goulds live. You'll be meeting them without me."

"And they'll agree?"

"That's the trick. But you'll convince them, Alberto, I have faith. I'll brief you on what to say on the drive. By now, what they want more than anything are answers, and you will promise to get them. Then, with signatures in tow, you'll hand a copy of the contingency fee agreement to me and return to your seat at the bar top. I'll take it from there."

"There was a time when my reputation was impeccable, beyond impeccable, when speeches were given in my honor. In those days I would have thrown you from my office with my own two hands."

"Time's a bitch."

"Seven thousand?"

"As soon as the family signs."

He stared at me for a moment and then shook his head with a weary sadness. As he scrawled *Alberto Menendez* on the referral agreement, he said, *"La necesidad tiene cara de perro."*

"Excuse me?"

"It's from García Márquez," said Alberto. "It is what I have learned to be truth ever since the incident with Patel. 'Necessity has the face of a dog.'"

18

INTERROGATIONS

"I was planning to go to law school," said Bradley Beamon, Scarlett Gould's ex-boyfriend. He was the most obvious suspect; isn't it always the ex-boyfriend with blood on his hands? We were in the living room of his parents' brick split-level just north of the northern curve of the Beltway. The house smelled of onions, the couch sagged beneath a plaid throw, a side table was populated with a corps of porcelain figurines: children and ballerinas and dogs.

"I was working as a paralegal at one of the best firms in the city. I had my own place, I was building a life. And then . . ."

As Bradley's voice trailed off into a sad reverie over lost opportunity, his mother bustled in with tea service on a silver-plated tray. "All I had was Lipton, I hope that's all right," she said.

"Mom."

"I'm just being polite." His mother, a chunky block of worry, had dressed for the occasion. Her print dress was faded, she had put on stockings, her shoes were so sensible they had become accountants. "It pays to be polite even in difficult circumstances. Isn't that right, Mr. Johnstone?"

"I've always thought so, ma'am," said Gordon.

"Sugar, Mr. Triplett?"

"Oh yes, thank you. And I must say, Mrs. Beamon, I love the figurines. Lladró?"

"A few yes," she said, brightening. "How fine of you to notice. And do you see the cute little boy reading the newspaper on the toilet? That's a Hummel."

"Ooh," I said. "Hummel."

"He always reminded me of Bradley."

"Mom."

"Except Bradley wasn't reading the newspaper."

"Mom, for Chrissakes, we're talking here."

"Let me pour and then I'll be out of your hair. I can keep myself busy in the kitchen. You really think you can help my son, Mr. Johnstone?"

"That's the hope," said Gordon. "The lawyer we work for, Alberto Menendez, represents the Gould family. The family is convinced that the police department's early obsession with Bradley allowed other possible avenues of investigation to wither. We're out to rectify that."

"It's about time someone took an interest in Bradley's well-being," said Mrs. Beamon. "The new police detectives were here just the other day. I don't think they care one whit about Bradley, or that girl if you ask me."

"What is it you think they care about?" I said.

"Clearing their docket, getting their faces in the paper, writing their names in the sky while pissing on the back of my son."

"Mom."

"That's just the way I feel. I'll be in the kitchen if you need me."

We waited quietly as Mrs. Beamon and her church shoes made their exit, along with any possibility that her son had killed Scarlett Gould. It was in the looseness of Mrs. Beamon's stockings, in the sensible height of her shoes, in the plaid throw on the couch, in the Lladrós and the Hummels and the scent of onions. The fact that we were involved meant that someone had spent an obscene amount of money to protect a killer, and no one would spend that kind of money to save the likes of that woman's son.

Bradley Beamon was fair, with pale eyes that were focused on his nervous hands. He wasn't that much younger than me, but it was if we were of different generations entirely, what with his lost-boyishness and the way he squirmed when his mother was in the room. He wore a T-shirt, jeans, sandals, really. On his jaw were the weak beginnings of an attempted beard. Whatever confidence he had carried as a Phi Gamma Delta at Maryland had been stepped on like a toad.

"We appreciate you meeting with us today, Bradley," I said. "There's a lot to discuss, I know, but for now we just want to talk about one aspect of the case, if that's all right."

"I have plenty of time. There's not too much job demand for a paralegal suspected in a murder investigation."

"From what we understand, you and Scarlett broke up at the beginning of November. But the shaming and threats coming from you in social media didn't happen until January, shortly before her murder. Why the gap?"

"I guess I didn't believe we were done at the start. It was sort of a mutual thing at first, but I figured after each of us played around some, we'd just start it over again. I always expected Scarlett and I would end up together. The breakup wasn't like the papers made it seem, all angry and bitter, at least at the beginning. It was just sad."

"Then what happened?" said Gordon.

"Something changed. We were talking more and more, on the edge of maybe giving it another try, and then suddenly her attitude changed. And I knew without a doubt what had happened."

"What was that?"

"She had started screwing someone else."

"She told you this?"

"No, but I could tell."

"Did you have any idea who it was?"

"None. I still don't."

"There was no indication of a new relationship on any of her social media accounts. And apparently none of her friends were aware of any new boyfriend."

"I know that. When I told this to the cops right off, they came back and told me there wasn't anyone, as far as they could tell. But there was someone, I'm sure of it."

"How are you so sure, Bradley?"

"I knew Scarlett. I could read her. It was in her voice, a sort of upswing at the end of all her words, as if there was someone there with her while she talked to me, breathing on her neck as she blew me off."

"And that's why you called her the names you did on Facebook and in the text messages? And that's why you posted that threat?"

"I didn't react well. I reacted terribly. I regret that every day, and not just for the trouble I caused myself. The last emotions she ever got from me were bitterness and hate."

"The thing with the ivory-billed woodpecker might have been a mite much," said Gordon.

"You think? Christ. I've been off social media for a year. Some people just can't handle it. But I didn't kill her. I loved her. I still do."

"I believe you," I said, and this was where I put a hand on his knee and gave him my version of Caroline Brook's empathetic gaze. "We're going to help you, Bradley. We're going to get this monkey off your back. We just have one more question. If you don't know who she was sleeping with, of all her friends, who would?"

From the digital recording:

Q: This is a session between Caroline Brooks, MD, and a patient we will refer to only as Phil. I'll be recording my questions and your answers, if that's okay with you, Phil. I'm going to need a verbal response.

A: Fine. Record away.

Q: All right, let's begin. On a scale of one to five, with five being total agreement, where would you put the following statement: Even if I were trying very hard to sell something, I wouldn't lie about it.

[Laughter]

Q: What's so funny?"

A: I thought this would be difficult. Let's give it a zero.

Q: The lowest allowed is one.

A: The reason I lost my sales job was that I was too good a liar.

Q: Was that the only reason?

A: Well, the lying, and also that I slept with the boss's girlfriend.

Q: Did you know that would cause a problem?

A: He specifically told me not to sleep with her when he hired me.

Q: But still you did it.

A: Well, we didn't exactly sleep. And her breasts were legendary. If you had seen them, you would know I didn't have much choice in the matter.

Q: It wasn't your fault, it was her fault.

A: Well, the fault of her breasts, I suppose. Joey had spent a lot of money on them and it was all well spent. If he had spent a little less, maybe I would have thought twice.

Q: So now it was this Joey's fault.

A: Joey Mitts. He was sort of like a father to me.

"What did that creep say about me?" said Denise Brucker, leaning against a wall outside the coffee shop, squinting into the sun as she spoke to me and Riley. She was a thick girl in a green smock with a ponytail and a pout.

"Only good things," I said.

"I bet." Her tattooed hands fumbled a bit as she lit a cigarette.

"You seem to have had a sorry history with Bradley?" said Riley.

"Let's just say we had a conflict of interest," said Denise.

"And the interest was Scarlett?"

"Who are you again?"

"I'm Riley. Hi."

She looked at Riley, at me, and then again at Riley. "And why are you here?"

"We represent Scarlett's family," I said, taking a copy of the contingency fee agreement from my jacket pocket and handing it to her to examine. "The family is trying to learn what really happened to Scarlett. Bradley sensed that she was seeing someone new at the time of her murder. He said if anyone would have known the truth, it would have been you."

"He's a worm," she said as she looked over the document. "He always has been. That thing with the woodpecker? Typical sexist troll stuff. With men, somehow or other it always comes back to violence. Are you Menendez?"

"We work for Menendez," I said. "I'm Dick, this is Riley, you're Denise. And you know as well as we do that Bradley might be an asshole, but he doesn't have the stones to have killed her."

She handed back the document, took a long drag, looked down the street.

"So what's the story between the three of you?" said Riley.

"There is no story. Scarlett and I were friends and he was screwing her. That's the end of that."

"But according to him," I said, "you were screwing her first."

"It wasn't like that." She ruefully laughed out some smoke. "Well, maybe it was exactly like that. We were all at College Park together. She was a sorority girl, I was a GDI."

"GDI?"

"Goddamned independent. It's what the Greek assholes called those who chose not to join their little clusterfucks. But then one night Scarlett and I hooked up and we kept at it for a bit. She was experimenting, so she said. That's always a good word to convince yourself that it isn't real. Like I'm really an artist but I'm experimenting at being a barista. When the experiment got a little too heated, she got scared and broke it off. And then, when she was at her most confused, Bradley the frat asshole swooped in. So that was the end of that little affair. But we still hung out a lot."

"I bet that was a boatload of laughs," said Riley.

"How do you mean?"

"Well, you were still in love with the girl, right?"

Denise took another drag of her cigarette.

"Are you denying it?"

Denise shrugged before exhaling.

"Still in love," said Riley, "but you could only be a friend, a confidante. It's what we do in middle school. Pajama parties, brushing each other's hair as a substitute for brushing something else. But you were a little old for that role, weren't you?"

"I've got to get back to my shift."

"What's that tattooed on your wrist?" I said.

"Nothing."

I reached out and gently took hold of her hand, turned it over. "Gabba Gabba Hey," I read. "And Scarlett named her cat Didi. What is it with you guys and the Ramones?"

She pulled her hand away, looked at Riley, looked away. "Whenever a Ramones song came on, wherever we were, even after we stopped screwing, we used to slam-dance like crazy. The floor would clear in self-defense as the two bat-shit crazy girls went at it. It was our bit."

"That must have been something," said Riley.

"It kept us together. But the Ramones are all dead now."

"And so is Scarlett," said Riley. "Was she seeing anyone new just before she was killed?"

"I already told this to the cops," said Denise. "She told me pretty much everything, and she never told me about anyone serious, anyone that mattered."

"But I'm sure there were some things she wouldn't tell you."

"Like what?"

"You tell me," said Riley.

"Did the lawyer send you over here thinking that I'd open up to you in a way I wouldn't open up to your friend with the ridiculous hair?"

"Too much gel?" I said.

"Do you buy it by the keg? Look, I've got to get back before my manager starts giving me the stink eye."

"Maybe we could talk more a little later," said Riley. "After your shift? When do you get off?"

"What are you going to do? Take me out, souse me up, put your hand on my leg, and pump me for information?"

"I don't know about you," said Riley, "but that sounds like a night to me."

Denise's pout twitched.

From the digital recording:

Q: Let's continue, Phil. One to five, with complete agreement being a five: I often admire a really clever scam.

A: Five. When I hear something that went over like gangbusters, the only thing I feel, other than admiration, is resentment that I didn't think of it myself.

Q: Even if it involved cheating other people.

A: Especially that. The way things are today, the way the economy's tilted against anyone who didn't end up on the right side of that silver spoon, I think we're justified in doing anything we can to succeed. Behind every great fortune is a crime. Who said that?

Q: Balzac?

A: No, maybe that was Joey Mitts, too. What's right is whatever we can get away with. People who are stupid enough to get ripped off usually deserve it, anyway. Losers are losers because they want to lose.

Q: And you're a winner.

A: You said it, not me.

Q: You know, Phil, you're sounding a bit defensive. Your voice has an edge to it.

A: This is why I lie. I tell people what they want to hear and they like me better.

Q: And you want to be liked.

A: I want people to like me, sure. If I ever let them see what was really inside, they'd run away screaming, and then where would I be?

Q: What is it that is really inside?

A: Ice.

Q: Does it get lonely?

A: Never.

Q: On a scale of one to five, with total agreement a five: Love is overrated.

A: Really, that's your question?

Q: What's your answer?

A: The only things not overrated are a good crap and a boatload of money.

Q: Why is money not overrated?

A: Because it doesn't give a damn about who holds it. It doesn't want to peer into your soul. It doesn't judge you because it doesn't care about you. It caresses your cheek or rips out your heart and it is the same either way. It just is. And what it is is perfect.

The next morning, in shorts and sweat-soaked T-shirt, I rode the elevator up from the gym. When the doors opened at my floor, I found Denise Brucker waiting for a ride down. She glanced up from her phone, blinked at me, and then looked down again.

"Good workout?" she said flatly as she walked past me into the elevator.

"Yes, thank you," I said as I walked out. "And you?"

After my shower, I found Riley in the suite, sitting at the dining table, staring at one of the computers, her face as impassive as the screen.

"Anything interesting?" I said.

"I'm looking at some ritzy apartment building in the District. The lap of luxury on Connecticut Avenue, surrounded by all the fancy embassies. Seven stories, twenty-six units, all co-op, starting at about a cool mil."

"Are you buying?"

"I'm searching. Trying to get a residence list at the time of Scarlett Gould's murder. Our victim was spending a suspicious amount of time there before her death."

"You learned that from Denise?"

"After much interrogation."

"So it was all business last night."

"It always is, chief," she said.

"You're getting as bad as me."

"After Scarlett broke up with Bradley boy, she had a few dates here and there, nothing special. But she always confided in her dear friend Denise. And then, suddenly she clammed. Nothing going on, she told Denise. But Denise suspected something, especially when Scarlett suddenly vanished from her Find Friends app. That's always the tell, right? And still being in love with her college fling, one night, after one of their after-work drinks, Denise followed Scarlett until she disappeared into the lobby of this apartment building, which happens to be not a stone's throw from Rock Creek Park. And Denise got the sense, by the way Scarlett greeted the doorman and strode into the building, that she had been there before."

"Did Denise tell this to the police?"

"That she was still so romantically unhinged over her ex-lover that she had been stalking her before the murder? No, she did not."

"But she told you."

"I have skills."

"I assume all the residents have some money, but this is about more than money. When you get the list, try to match it up with a database of political heavyweights. See if we can come up with a name."

"Will do."

"Then get me photographs."

"What is it with you and photographs?"

"You know those bulletin boards you see in the cop shows with all the photographs and articles and the crazy pieces of yarn to show the connections, the one that makes all the detectives look a bit unhinged?"

"Yeah, so?"

"I want one."

From the digital recording:

Q: When was the first time you got drunk?

A: I don't know. I was eleven or something. I stole the liquor from my father.

Q: When was the first time you set something on fire?

A: How do you know I did?

Q: You didn't?

A: There was a job site on our block in New Jersey. They were building a house. I thought it would be this wild, exciting thing, but it was just a few burned timbers and a bit of smoke. Disappointing, actually.

Q: How old were you?

A: I don't know. Grade school.

Q: When did you lose your virginity?

A: Eleven.

Q: It was a busy year.

A: Why do you think I stole the liquor? She was fifteen. She was only with me for the booze.

Q: Did you ever hurt an animal as a boy?

A: Next question.

Q: Okay, Phil. Agree or disagree: I make a point of trying not to hurt others in pursuit of my goals.

A: Actually, I agree with that. I have found that making everyone happy is the best way to run off with everything. You make enemies, you make problems. I'm pretty good at manipulating other people's feelings, and the most profitable way to manipulate them is to make them like you.

Q: Agree or disagree: I would be upset if my success came at someone else's expense.

A: Now you're making a joke.

"Hello. Is this Dick, Dick Triplett?"

"Alberto, it's good to hear from you," I said into my cell phone. I was in the living room of our suite, taping photographs and maps onto the wall. "I just didn't expect to hear from you so soon."

"I didn't expect to be calling you so soon myself, but it has begun."

"What has begun?"

"You said there would be pushback."

"Yes I did."

"First I need to warn you. There will be an article in the newspaper."

"Oh man, Alberto. Is this you ginning up business?"

"Heavens no, I tried to stop it. It is nothing that I wanted, but it is unavoidable. The Goulds, our clients, called the press. They have a lot of anger, which I unfortunately had to stoke to get their signatures. I specifically asked them to stay quiet about our arrangement, but they felt the need to talk. A reporter called me and asked about my plans. I had no choice but to speak to her."

"Did you mention me?"

"No, of course not. I just mentioned that the family had some new information we intended to pursue. It was a brief conversation, but shortly afterward the police called. A Detective Pickering. The detective asked about this new information."

"The reporter must have called the police asking for comment. I bet the cop wasn't pleased."

"Not at all, my friend. I tried to calm the situation. First I told the detective not to talk to my clients. Then I promised that if we found anything definitive, we would certainly turn it over. In the course of our conversation my unfortunate history was brought up and I was threatened with obstruction of justice. Imagine that, someone in my position, an officer of the court being threatened with obstruction of justice. Imagine how that made me feel."

"And how did that make you feel, Alberto?"

"Alive."

"Good. Hold on a second, please."

Riley had come over with a handful of papers. "I found something," she said.

I put the phone on mute. "Go ahead."

"I've been riffling through the DC Recorder of Deeds website, trying to find the condo owners on the relevant date, and this came up. Rufus and Melissa Davenport. Penthouse. Four point five mil."

"Sweet."

"They're still there. It turns out rich little Rufus is the son of Jules Davenport, the senior senator from Rhode Island and chairman of the Committee on Banking, Housing, and Urban Affairs."

"Banking?" I said, my eyes brightening.

"Banking, Housing, and Urban Affairs."

"Funny, I don't think it's a concern for urban affairs that pays for the son's four-point-five-million-dollar penthouse. Photographs?"

She handed me a photo of suits and smiles, with three figures circled. An older man with a rock jaw and leonine hair, a much younger man, squat with rodent eyes, and a woman quite attractive with dark hair and white teeth, holding a champagne flute with a slender hand. One of them, I assumed, was the face of the murderer I had been assigned to protect.

I pulled off a strip of tape and stuck the photograph to the wall, between photographs of Denise Brucker and Scarlett Gould. Then I unmuted the phone and put it back to my ear.

"Thank you for telling me about the article and the police, Alberto. If we keep quiet for a bit, this all will pass. No more talking, all right?"

"Of course. But the phone call from the detective is not the pushback I was referring to. A call from the police is simply to be expected. No, the pushback was a bit more alarming."

"Go ahead, Alberto."

"A man came to the office and sat down without being invited and began talking about football."

"Football?"

"About football, Dick. I have been in this country more than forty years and still I care not a whit about American football. But he spoke about the back and forth, the strategy, the violence. And as he talked of the danger, he mentioned some names. I wrote them down as soon as he left. Mike Webster. Andre Waters. Junior Seau. Who are these men, Dick?"

"Just players."

"My sense was that they are not in such good shape anymore."

"Your sense is correct, Alberto."

"So it was a threat."

"Yes, it was a threat."

"Then he asked who brought me in."

"What did you tell him?"

"The Goulds, I said. The family of the dead girl. But all he did was laugh. He said, and I wrote this down to get it exact, he said, 'You

tell Phil to hurry up because I am right behind and I owe him one.'
Alarming, no?"

"Alarming, yes, Alberto, but nothing I can't handle."

"Who is Phil, Dick?"

"Someone not to be messed with." I stepped away from the wall,
turned to a window that faced the White House, with the Washington
Monument sticking out behind it like a spike that had been driven
though its heart. "Did this visitor, perhaps, leave a name?"

"Oh yes. I wrote this down, too. He said his name was Preston,
Tom Preston."

From the digital recording:

Q: *Have you ever killed anyone, Phil?*

A: *No.*

Q: *Why not?*

A: *You know.*

Q: *No, I don't know.*

A: *Because, my God, to take someone's life is the ultimate act of savagery. There are lines, Caroline. What do you think I am?*

Q: *There is something in your voice that sounds disingenuous, like you
are making a joke of murder. We often joke about our fears. Are you afraid
of killing someone?*

A: *It's amazing what we can get away with in this world. I can swindle
you, steal your car, screw your wife, and then beat you to a pulp behind a
bar because you complain about it all, and I'm looked at as something of
a hero. But suddenly, if I kill you, everything changes. My mother killed a
man. She ran off with him and then shot him through the head. It sounds
like a country and western song, I know, but she's in jail, and will be for
decades.*

Q: *Do you visit her?*

A: *When I have to. There's a peculiar stink to her prison. When I visit my mother in her blue-and-white uniform, the stink sits in my stomach like a frog.*

Q. *What does it smell like?*

A. *Boiled green beans, ammonia, cheap perfume, fate.*

Q. *Whose fate, Phil?*

A. *Mine.*

Q. *What fate is that? Prison?*

A. *Something worse. Something that comes at me hard and fast in a motel room in New Orleans. It's why I set limits on myself.*

Q. *Limits like refusing to kill.*

A. *And other things. Steps I refuse to take.*

Q. *Are you upset about having these limits, Phil?*

A. *A little bit, sure. I think it's why I haven't achieved all I deserve to achieve.*

Q: *Is that why you came to me, to try to find a way to succeed despite these limits?*

A. *That would be good, yeah.*

Q. *Or are you here, instead, maybe to eradicate your limits altogether?*

A. *No limits? That would be a filthy piece of business, Caroline. You wouldn't want to see me without limits, trust me. Your eyes would bleed.*

19

PRESSURE POINTS

I flew into Miami the morning after Alberto's call. I traveled light with just a briefcase. I wasn't planning to be there long.

I Ubered to a hardware store and then to the white modern palace on the seaward side of Biscayne Bay. I had the car let me out before the iron gate. FISI. I stood there for a moment in my suit, sucked my teeth, and felt the beat of the music coming from the far side of the house. Then I pressed the button on the speaker. I didn't answer the request for identification, I didn't recite the purpose of my visit, I didn't wave. I just stood there, my legs spread, my sunglasses on, the briefcase heavy in my grip. A moment later the gate slowly slid open.

On my way up to the office, I stopped by the pool. The music was deathly loud now, as a crowd of good-looking strangers made themselves at home, lounging in the sun, dancing on the deck, swilling booze, and swimming naked. Bert in his red vest was behind the bar, shaking a cocktail. When he noticed me he tilted his head in puzzlement even as he kept working the Boston shaker. I turned away from him and surveyed the scene. Flesh, youth, alcohol. I hadn't seen a party like this at the house since our competition.

Cassandra was lying facedown on one of the lounges, the strings of her bikini top untied and her cheek resting on her folded arms while a man with pectorals and a tight Speedo massaged lotion into her back and shoulders. Her eyes were closed, her lips were curled in satisfaction.

"Has she shown you her knife yet?" I said to massage boy.

She opened her eyes. "Phil," she said in a slow, satisfied voice, "what a pleasant surprise. Is Mr. Maambong expecting you?"

"I'm sure he is."

"Bobo, this is Phil. Phil is one of our most valued employees, at least for the moment. Phil, this is Bobo. He's a hard charger. Now be a dear, Bobo, and leave us for a minute."

As Bobo stood and walked away, glancing back at me with a cruel curl on his lips, Cassandra turned onto her side and slid her long legs beneath her so she was now sitting on the edge of the chaise, one arm modestly holding the small top against her breasts.

"Don't mind me," I said.

"Oh, I don't mind you at all," she said as she tied the strings of her bikini top behind her back. "How's Washington?"

"Lousy with politicians and whores."

"What's the difference?"

"Heck of a party."

"Mr. Maambong has been told to step up recruiting. We need two more teams to handle the workload."

"I guess Bert's lie detector has been busy."

"They're looking for new leaders, too. How's the job?"

"Fine."

"They think Riley might be ready to step into management."

"Riley's crackerjack. I wouldn't want to lose her."

"The big decisions are beyond us. It helps to remember that. Drink?"

"I'm not in the mood."

"I can tell. You're wearing a suit. In Miami."

"I wanted to impress him with the seriousness of my visit."

She stood. "Come on, dear, have a drink with me. It will lighten your mood."

"I don't want it to lighten. I want it to be dark as midnight. Is he in?"

"Yes, he's in."

I looked up at his office window. Through the glare I imagined him in the swivel chair behind his glass desk, looking down at me. "What have you heard, Cassandra?"

"Oh, this and that."

"What about this and who about that?"

"They've been comparing you to Rand."

"My predecessor."

"It's not a good comparison."

"What ever happened to good old Rand?"

"Be careful, Phil. You have such promise, let's not waste it. I had hopes you and I would burn down this town together."

"And now you're afraid you'll be left with nothing but Bobo."

"He can be enormously consoling."

"Not from what I saw in the Speedo."

"It's the steroids," she said. "Will you have time to play before you leave? Just a drink someplace private? The Eden Rock maybe? We could get a room."

"I have to get back," I said. "I'll leave you in Bobo's capable, if tiny, hands."

"It's good to see you again, Phil, even if only for a few minutes."

"If I find myself in trouble, would you stand up for me?"

"If you have to ask, then you already know the answer."

I reached a hand to her red hair and fingered it as I leaned over and kissed her. She tasted of mint and coconut milk. In the distance Bobo was looking on.

"You've always been the most honest one in this whole damn crap-shoot," I said. "Sweet dreams."

I started toward the spiral stairs leading to Mr. Maambong's office, then I stopped and turned back to her. She was staring at me, her porcelain features inscrutable.

"I won't disappear as easily as Rand," I said.

"I'd be disappointed if you did."

I walked past Bert without a word and climbed the circular stairway. At the office doorway I looked around. Beneath me were the goings-on at the pool. Beyond that was the canal and then the palm trees fronting the line of hotels and then the beach and then the ocean and then the world. This was bright and sunny and rich. I had earned my spot in the Hyena Squad, I had earned this. So why the hell had they set Tom Preston on my tail?

"Mr. Kubiak, welcome back," said Mr. Maambong, greeting me warmly in his office, grabbing my shoulder like we were former frat brothers, friends yesterday, tomorrow, always. "We're surprised to see you back so soon."

I didn't return the smile.

"Sit down."

"I'll stand."

"As you wish." He took his seat behind the sleek glass desk that was empty as always, leaned back in his chair, trained his beetle-eyed glasses on me. "Have we completed our project in the nation's capital?"

"Not yet."

"But you are here, nonetheless. Do you have good news for us, then?"

"A demand," I said. "Call off the dogs."

"Dogs? We have no dogs."

"You have Tom Preston. I thought we had gotten rid of that vile creature, but suddenly he's sniffing my tail, mucking up my work, and making threats."

"Threats? Oh my. That is unfortunate. Threats."

"Why is he there?"

"He is insurance, Mr. Kubiak. Perhaps you have not appreciated the seriousness of this task we have given to you. Perhaps you thought you could take your time and play your old tricks and hope for the best. But this is nothing so simple as obtaining a kidney."

"I have this under control. I am making progress."

"Bringing in some third-rate attorney with a questionable past and a weakness for cheap bourbon is not quite the progress we had hoped for."

"Menendez is the cover we need to do what we have to do."

"And what is it that you need to do, blunder around the case, stirring up dead waters? There is a reporter sniffing around the case now, and the police have redoubled their efforts. The detectives are being pressured to find the truth before your Mr. Menendez makes them look like fools. Instead of squashing the investigation quickly, you have excited it."

"How were you able to connect Menendez with me?"

"We fear you have not appreciated the seriousness of this task, so let us make it clear for you. You saw the jolly group by the pool. They are applicants to fill new positions. As the rich get richer, our services are ever more in demand. We are growing faster than we ever expected, becoming a force far beyond even our rosiest hopes. And the new teams will need new handlers. Never has there been such room for advancement in our ranks. It is a boon for us all. But if we cannot complete this one task, this one simple task, it could all go awry. Perhaps of all the things you did not appreciate, the most telling was the honor the Principal bestowed when she gave this crucial task to you."

"I'll get it done."

"What else would you say? But if you don't get it done as quickly and as surely as we require, then our Mr. Preston will have no choice but to take matters into his own hands. We chose you, Mr. Kubiak, you are our man, but Mr. Preston has recovered from his wounds and seems to have talents you lack. We're sure you have what it takes to develop just those talents; we are less sure you will develop them in time. The question, Mr. Kubiak, as the Principal told you, concerns evolution. Are you ready to take the next step in your journey?"

"I'm ready to do what I have to do, but not with Tom Preston trailing behind me like I'm a bitch in heat."

"His path is laid out. If you want to defeat him, beat him to the punch."

"I sense, Mr. Maambong, a lack of trust. If we're going to continue to work together, if we're going to be partners in this growing enterprise, we need to trust one another. I have something to show you."

I turned and put my briefcase on the chair behind me, clicked it open, grabbed hold of my hardware purchase, then turned around again and raised my arm. I had thought about this many times in the past months; it was time to make the thought a reality.

"There you sit," I said, "in this house of windows, presiding over a desk of glass. And here I stand with a hammer in my hand."

There was a moment when disconcertment flooded his cold features and it was as if his beetle-eyed glasses seemed themselves to flinch, but then his face broke into a wide smile. "A good one, Mr. Kubiak. One thing we've always admired about you was your dry wit. It undoubtedly helps you get through the most trying times."

He was still smiling when I slammed down the hammer, not onto the surface of the tempered glass, where it would have bounced futilely, but smack into its edge. The glass turned instantly pale before it crackled into irregular shards that hovered in the air for the barest moment before crashing down.

"If Preston stays," I said, "there is going to be blood."

"Blood you say?" said Mr. Maambong, who had impressively kept his composure even as the glass rained upon his white suit pants and shiny black shoes. "Excellent. That's exactly the spirit we hoped to see."

***

When I arrived at Reagan National, back from Miami, I didn't head straight to the hotel. Instead I took the Metro to Union Station and then I hit a bar just down Massachusetts for a quick drink. The joint was beneath street level, the lights were low, the power crowd was flush faced and well suited, the Scotch in my glass was rich and peaty. And somewhere out there, stalking me like a panther, looking to make his mark at my expense, was Tom Preston. I had to figure out how to squash the Scarlett Gould investigation speedily enough so that I could then go about squashing him.

It was enough to drive a man to drink.

"Can I ask you something?" I said to the woman two stools down from me at the bar.

"Only if you want an answer," she said without looking at me. Her voice had an undertone of rough in it that exposed an inner fault line of misery. She was pretty enough, blonde hair glossy and just kissing her shoulders, blue eyes, thin waist, not young but not yet broken by life, although she was bending. I had noticed her legs as I took my place at the bar. The skirt of her suit was long enough so that she wasn't drawing attention to them, but they were good enough to draw it on their own.

"What are you drinking?" I said.

"Is that your question?"

"That's just me being polite."

"Skip the polite," she said. "I'm not in the mood."

"Tough day?"

"Is that your question?"

"That's not my question."

"I like a man who gets right to it. Too bad I don't see anyone like that around here."

"Maybe I'll keep the question to myself."

"Good idea," she said.

"Are you always so difficult?"

"Is that your question?"

173

"So you're still interested," I said as I scooted over to the stool next to hers. "Good. So here it is. You ready."

"I sit here with bated breath."

"What does that mean, anyway? Is it a fishing metaphor?"

"Do you want me to answer that?"

"No. This. Is love overrated?"

For the first time she turned and looked at me. It wasn't a casual glance; her cold blue eyes stared at me like they were knives and she was flaying my surface to get a better look. And then she laughed, and her laughter was soft and bright, like she meant it.

"Where the hell did that question come from?" she said.

"Someone asked me it recently and since then it's been on my mind."

"Someone blowing you off?"

"I don't get blown off."

"Then tonight will be a first."

"The night's still young."

"Not that young. No night in the history of the world has ever been that young."

She turned back to her drink, something clear in a martini glass with two olives on a little plastic sword, and took a sip and then another. As she did, I motioned to the bartender for another round for the two of us.

"Romantic love, you're talking about," she said after she had finished her drink and snatched down the olives, "because I have a daughter, and that love is definitely not overrated."

"And I love bacon."

She laughed again. "As for romantic love," she said, "I'd like to think it's not overrated. I'd like to think there's some huge thing waiting for us out there. But the truth is, it's not. That kind of love is nothing but hype."

"Hype," I said. "That's exactly the right word. They make their movies and write their songs and we pay our good money to want what they're selling. Along with the diamonds. But it feels like a fantasy being peddled to the masses. Like a light saber, or a time machine, or—"

Just then the bartender brought us another round. "Anything else I can get you two?" he said.

I shook my head.

"Or a bartender who dispenses the wisdom of the ages," she said after he left.

"Or a transporter."

"Or mind-blowing sex."

"No," I said. "That really exists."

"Mind-blowing?" she said, expanding the words of if they described some fantasy monster.

"Oh yes."

"Really? Truly? Like your mind is truly blown?"

"The universe shifts on it axis."

"I doubt that. It sounds as fantastical as a hover board."

"Hover boards. Yes. We were all promised hover boards by now, but the closest things they have for us don't float and spontaneously combust."

"Talk about comedowns."

"Popular culture just exists to make us feel like we're missing out."

"Facebook," she said. "It's funny how no one ever shows the dust balls on the stairs or the dishes in the sink or the tantrums and tears over the divorce."

"Whenever I see someone so goddamned happy on Facebook, so thrilled with their wonderful god-awful life, I'm just thankful that we all end up dead."

She laughed again and then trained her gaze back onto me. "Mind-blowing?"

"I guess the night's younger than you thought."

"What do you do for a living, if I may ask?"

"I'm a lawyer," I said.

"That's too bad. The night just got older. What kind?" She gave my suit the once-over. "Corporate?"

"Heavens no. I have standards. All-around troubleshooter. Of a sort. You have a problem, I'll solve it."

"You're a fixer?" she said.

"I can solve any problem but disappointment in love, because love, as we both agree, is overrated."

She smiled warmly. I reached out a hand and she took hold.

"My name's Phil. Phil Kubiak."

"Linda," she said, her smile attractively cockeyed. "Linda Pickering."

20

Pork Chops

"She's a lush who sleeps around, at least that's her reputation," said Riley. "Pickering's husband divorced her after an affair with her captain was made public in a tabloid scandal. It's why she was shunted from Homicide to the cold case division. One child, a daughter. Her husband currently has custody based on the publicized infidelity and the demands of her job; Pickering has her every other weekend when the job permits."

I was still in my suit the next morning as I breakfasted with my team. I purposely hadn't yet been back to the suite Mr. Maambong had arranged for us. Now we were in a booth at a greasy spoon on Florida Avenue. There were rows of photographs above the counter, pink plastic plates, fried pork chops and spiced stewed apples with our eggs. I had texted Riley the time and place and she had brought the others. The waitress kept filling our coffee cups.

"Any romantic relationship we should know about?" I said.

"Nothing that matters," said Gordon. "But they do tend to talk about her at her apartment building. Say there's a steady stream flowing in and out."

"I love neighbors. What about her finances?"

"A mess," said Riley. "She's been late on her child support. She owes some taxes. Her checking account is an embarrassment and the custody case is draining her retirement accounts. But she lives mostly within the limits of her salary, and there are no unexpected deposits."

"So she's honest."

"Apparently."

"That's always such a disappointment."

"And she's pretty good-looking, too," said Kief. "Man, I'd crush that."

"She'd crush you," said Gordon.

"What about her phone?" I said. "Any calls related to our case?"

"She has a home phone and a work phone, and I've been checking those records, but I'm having a difficult time getting hold of her cell. It's seriously unlisted."

I pulled a piece a paper from my shirt pocket, slid it past the dirty dishes to Riley. "Try these digits."

Riley didn't say anything, just raised an eyebrow.

"Weren't you due to come home last night?" said Kief.

"I got delayed."

"And weren't you wearing that suit yesterday?"

"It was a serious delay." I turned and gave a Kief a cold look as I said, "What about her partner?"

"Detective Booth's story has a bit more meat on its bones for our purposes," said Gordon. "He's living higher than his salary, there are some deposits that look suspicious, and he seems to have a role in a club of sorts that has a reputation."

"As what?"

"A purveyor of pleasures. More like a bordello."

"Bordello," I said, emphasizing the vowels. "Such a sophisticated word. Bordello."

"A sophisticated word for a sophisticated joint," said Gordon. "The Chadwick Club, it's called. They meet every month or so, lately at an exclusive Georgetown address. It's got itself a high-toned clientele: lobbyists and the marks they lobby. Very la-di-da, very protected. Actually, a little too high class for an MPD detective sergeant."

"I guess that's where the protection comes in. Is there a club meeting coming up?"

"In a few days, actually, according to our sources," said Riley.

"Good. Let's visit him there. Who can get me in?"

"I might know someone who knows someone," said Gordon.

"And let's try to put a squeeze on the detective's finances. Riley, see if you can alter his mortgage records so it seems like he missed a payment. I'd like an overdue notice sent as soon as possible. And Kief, I think Detective Booth's car is ready for an expensive repair. Timing belts are surprisingly expensive to replace. And it's perfectly okay if it looks like the belt was cut. Let's get him a little hungry. Now what about the Davenports in their swanky Connecticut Avenue penthouse? Any link between either of them and our detectives?"

"Nothing yet," said Riley. "Maybe there's something in the number you gave me. But I got the dope you wanted on the wife. She's been married to Rufus Davenport for seven years. They have one child, Jason, four years old. It must be nice to have a grandpop who's the senior senator of the great state of Rhode Island."

"Is that a great state, really?" said Kief. "It's kind of small. They should call it the petite state of Rhode Island. And what kind of parents name their kid Rufus?"

"Maybe he was named for an old family dog," I said.

"Rufus," said Kief.

"Melissa Davenport works for some fancy foundation, handing out funds to worthwhile nonprofits," said Riley. "Her husband works for a lobbying firm, pretty much getting paid so he can have lunch with his daddy."

"Rufus."

"He's got the usual vices," said Gordon. "Porn, strip bars, whores."

"In this town that's almost wholesome," I said.

"And he hits his wife now and then."

"Oh, Rufus," said Kief.

"Melissa has an old college friend named Adele she confides in," said Riley. "I was able to access Adele's e-mails. Adele was quite original with her password."

"Password?" I said.

"Close. In the e-mails Mrs. Davenport is pretty damn frank about the marriage being in ruins. At this point she's staying with Rufus because of the kid."

"Just the kid?" said Kief.

"Well, that and the prenup."

"At least her priorities are in order," said Kief.

"Did she say anything to this old college friend about Scarlett Gould?" said Gordon.

"Nothing in the e-mails."

"Anything at all about the murder?"

"No, which I found a bit puzzling, because it was big news. But this is interesting. You'll like this. Right after the murder, Melissa started writing about how terrified she was in the marriage. Afraid for her life. Adele urged her to leave, said she would have a place for her and the kid if she needed one. Melissa wanted to run but couldn't. She feared if she went up against the Davenports, she'd lose custody."

"And the money," said Kief.

"What's Adele's story?" I said.

"Divorced. Living in Seattle. Two kids of her own."

"Anything specific about the relationship with this friend?" I said. "You get any vibes."

"They're close," said Riley. "They used to be closer."

"Because I'm wondering what Scarlett Gould's involvement was with the Davenports. Was she a nanny? Was she screwing Rufus? My guess is neither. What's the one thing Scarlett Gould wouldn't have shared with her dear friend Denise?"

"An affair with another woman," said Riley. "For Denise that would have been crushing."

"And maybe that's the same reason why Melissa wasn't sharing the news with her old friend Adele," I said.

"Lot of vagina action going on," said Kief.

"If you know where to look, there always is," said Riley.

"I think the thing to do," I said, "is to check and see if the foundation Melissa Davenport works for ever gave money to Scarlett's wildlife nonprofit. Maybe they had lunch, maybe they had drinks, maybe they had some late nights, just one nonprofit working out the funding with another nonprofit, until it became something else. Maybe when Bradley thought there was a lover breathing down Scarlett's neck as she spoke to him, that lover was Melissa Davenport. And maybe Rufus found out, and maybe Rufus, with his violent temper, did something about it."

"Bad Rufus," said Kief.

"Let's go with the assumption that Senator Davenport hired the Hyenas a year and a half ago to kill the investigation because he feared it would end up pointing at his son. With the case having gone cold, his vote was owned by the Principal, but then someone pushed the police commissioner to send the file to Pickering and Booth and give it new life and here we are."

"Who's pushing?" said Gordon.

"If my guesses are correct, the pressure is—" I stopped speaking and waited as a waitress refilled our coffee cups, and then I leaned forward and lowered my voice. "I think the pressure is coming from Senator Davenport's daughter-in-law. She also thinks Rufus did it, but unlike the senator, she wants him found out. It would let her run into Adele's welcoming arms safe from Rufus, and still with her son and the Davenport cash."

"So what do we do?" said Gordon.

"Follow her," I said. "Discover her routine. Find a button to push. We need her to back off. And we still need to protect Rufus. Kief, did you figure out how to mess with the DNA?"

"I have a plan if we need it," said Kief. "It will be expensive, but if you get me the sample you want in there, it should work. Of course, fire is always a neater option. There is something so cleansing about a nice little fire. How was the trip?"

"Smashing," I said.

"I miss Miami," said Kief. "The house, the bikinis, Bert making me mojitos. He makes a good mojito. Not too sweet and he never bruises the mint, that's the key."

"I have one more thing I need to bring up," I said. "The reason, actually, that I went down to Miami. And the reason we're talking here and not at the hotel."

"I thought it was the pork chops," said Gordon.

"Remember Tom Preston?" I said.

"That piece of gnarl?" said Gordon.

"Well, he's back on his feet after his unfortunate accident, and he's now working for Maambong. Worst of all, Maambong brought him in to make sure we get this done quickly and right."

"Crap," said Kief.

"Mr. Maambong doesn't trust us?" said Riley.

"Maybe he sensed your squirmy little qualms," said Kief.

"It's not that," I said. "Apparently this is such an important job the Principal sent Tom Preston to cover her bets."

"I get my hands on that sumbitch," said Gordon, "he won't get up so easy."

"Hopefully you'll get your chance," I said. "But somehow he learned that Menendez is linked to us."

"How?" said Kief.

"I don't know, but we're not holding meetings in the hotel rooms that Maambong rents for us anymore. And that thing on the wall with all the photos and yarn. I'm taking that down as soon as I get back. Here on out we don't trust anyone."

"Except each other," said Kief.

"Yes, Kief, that's right," I said, giving him a stare like a power drill. "Except each other."

21

DIAGNOSIS

I didn't like the way Caroline Brooks was looking at me as I sat on the couch of her green-walled office with the bonsai trees and the box of tissues. She was leaning solicitously forward in her chair, her face filled with sympathy, as if I was about to learn of the cancer that was riddling my brain.

"I guess the news is bad," I said.

"Not bad, just interesting," said Caroline. "How honest were you being when I asked you those questions?"

"As honest as I could be."

"Even though you admit to being a liar."

"That's the rub, yes, but I lie for a purpose. I don't see any purpose in lying to you."

"Patients often give doctors the symptoms they believe will get them the treatment they seek. Some want drugs, some want sympathy, some just want affirmation that they are special. I already told you that the strongest indication that you are not a psychopath was that you came to me in the first place. When I add to that the consistency of your answers, I find myself on the horns of a dilemma. If you were lying, then the truth probably wouldn't fit the diagnosis, and if you were being truthful, the very truthfulness is a mitigation."

"So you think I'm not. Good. That's a relief."

"Is that what you wanted to hear?"

"Isn't that what anyone would want to hear? I mean, Caroline, who the hell wants to be a fucking psychopath?"

"Your mother is in jail for killing someone. Is that why you're here, Phil, so you don't end up in jail like her?"

"I don't want to end up like her, certainly. She mucked up everything she ever touched, including me. But her presence in that jail is only a reminder of what I really fear: ending up like the man she shot in the head."

"Who was he, Phil?"

"His name was Jesse Duchamp."

"And he's the one who died in the motel room in New Orleans?"

"That's right."

"Maybe you should tell me the story."

"Maybe we should just let it go."

"If you need a tissue while you tell it to me, there are plenty in the box."

You've heard it already, the whole sordid tale—I couldn't wait to pathetically blab it to you at the first opportunity—but at that point I had never told it to anyone, not a friend, not a lover, not my erstwhile wife. I could have used it to garner some sympathy—*Oh, you poor boy, it must have been such a trial*—but I never wanted any damn sympathy. The story wasn't about what had been done to me, it was about what I was and where I was headed; if any of them had glimpsed that truth I would have transformed in their eyes to something low and vile, something less than human. They would have seen me slithering about them like a snake. And they would have been right. So it had remained my secret touchstone, my secret chain.

But Caroline Brooks had glimpsed the absence within me and hadn't pulled away in horror. Instead she had leaned forward and smiled. I was curious to see how she would react when I bared to her the root of my affliction, and so I did. I told her the story of my mother and my father and the murderer Jesse Duchamp. It took a while to get it right, with all the hesitations, the detours, and restatements that happen in a first telling. By the time you got hold of it, the story had been sanded down and polished. In the first telling it was jagged, but it was out.

The interesting thing was that as she listened to it all without judgment creasing her features, I began to listen to it the same way. It didn't change the facts of the story, and it didn't weaken the chain the story had wrapped around my fate, but it did, I must admit, lessen the dismay it caused in my gut, and maybe that was the start of something new.

When it was over and the quiet at the end of any telling passed, I waited for some reaction from the one person who seemed to matter in that moment.

"So that's why you came," she said finally.

"Kind of sad, isn't it?"

"For Jesse."

"So let's get down to it. What do you think? Am I him?"

"No, you're not Jesse Duchamp."

"Is this an official diagnosis?"

"I'm not in a position to diagnose Jesse Duchamp, Phil."

"He was a killer, a thief, he destroyed my family without a second's thought. He was a psychopath. Am I one, too?"

"It's not as simple as a yes or no. There is a spectrum to any disorder. Part of that spectrum would be considered totally normal. We all have moments where our empathy fails and our behavior becomes problematic. There is also a part of the scale that is abnormal, and another, smaller part, that is pathological."

"All very enlightening but beside the point. What am I?"

"In light of the protocols, and your professed honesty, balanced with your reasons for seeing me and my sense of you from our discussions . . ."

"You're hesitating. That's not good."

"I think you are what you think you are," she said in a voice soft as a whisper.

There it was. I winced slightly, I rubbed my neck as if to salve the dagger wound, I let my eyes go out of focus. I played it subtly, letting her see me struggle not to make a big moment out of it, but I played it. For her sake. She had been so reluctant to say it outright, I wanted her to have her payoff before I got to the meat of what I was there for.

"So what do we do about it?" I said.

"What do you mean?"

"Is there a pill?"

"There's no pill. Sometimes drugs are prescribed to mildly tranquilize or deal with outgrowths of the condition, such as depression, but there is no drug to treat the condition itself."

"An operation? A procedure? Is there a form of therapy that will snap me to normal? Electroshock?"

"It has been tried, but it doesn't work."

"So what do I do now?"

"It depends on what you want."

"What does anyone want when they're diagnosed with a disease? I want to be cured."

"It's not that simple, Phil. First, it is not considered a disease so much as a condition. And it's not clear what causes it. There is a theory that it derives from a defect in parts of the brain called the amygdalae, possibly in the way they interact with the orbitofrontal cortex."

"So stick an electrode in my brain and fire it up."

"That's not going to happen. Operations are sometimes used where psychopathy was acquired through a brain injury, but that is certainly not your case, and I wouldn't approve of it in any event. We don't experiment with functioning human brains anymore. About eighty years ago there was a doctor who went around the country sticking an ice pick in the brains of some seriously ill patients."

"Do you have his number? Maybe I'll give him a call."

"It wasn't psychiatry, it was butchery, and it turned out very badly for all, including him. Since then we've been more prudent."

"So there's nothing you can do."

"There is no physical solution that I would recommend."

"I guess that's that," I said, standing and slapping my thighs. "I've got a diagnosis without a cure. Thanks for everything. But at least I have an answer to my question."

"Which question, Phil?"

"Whether someone can really change. Apparently not."

"Oh, it's not that bleak," she said. "There are therapies we can try. Intense behavioral therapy over many years has shown beneficial effects."

"Over many years."

"It would take a commitment."

"And what kind of effects are we talking about?"

"Less destructive behavior, at the least. It is a demanding road, but there have been positive results if the patient really wants to do the work. You can be trained to treat people as individuals of worth instead of things to maneuver. You can be trained to help instead of exploit."

"So if I had the years to put into it, I could maybe learn to better fool everyone as to what I really am, but the core of me will always be me. You see that bonsai tree on the windowsill?" I walked over, picked up one of the trees, and contemplated it like it was Yorick's skull. "When you look at it, Caroline, do you sense its hopes and its dreams? Can you feel what it feels?"

"Is that what you want, Phil? I thought you just wanted to keep your job."

"I want everything. Anything anyone else can get, I want in spades. Money, sex, power, even love, if it's not a myth." I hefted the plant in my hand and felt a familiar anger begin to rise. "Do you think you could create a mutual and loving relationship with this beautiful specimen?"

"Of course not."

"The way you feel about the tree is the way I feel about you and every other person in the world. In the end you're each just a piece of wood, to be used while useful and tossed aside when the time is right. And sitting around talking about my feelings is not going to change that one whit."

"But I know what that plant needs, Phil. It needs sun, water, and food. It needs to be cared for in a certain way. To learn how to care for it, actually, I took a course. Think of our work as a course in caring for other human beings."

"But next week when you tire of your tragic earth-mother decor and decide to go modern and sleek like that really special office you see in *Psychiatry Digest*, you'll toss that tree into the garbage right next to the sagging gray couch and that stupid drum."

"You are not Jesse Duchamp, Phil. There is more in you than you know. We can find it, together. You don't have to be alone in this."

"That's where you're wrong." I hefted the bonsai in my hand. My mouth filled with a thick green tang, metallic and electric. "In everything I've ever done, in everything I'll ever do, you've just told me I'll be nothing but alone."

And then I tossed it. Well, maybe I threw it. Maybe I hurled the son of a bitch like a speedball at the wall behind her, where the pot shattered, and the dirt flew every which way as if it were blood from my wound, and the tree landed like a splayed corpse on the floor.

22

Behavioral Therapy

"You want to top off your drink?" said the outlaw. "I'm guessing you do. My mouth sure as hell got suddenly dry. And with what's coming we're both going to need another belt."

He pulled the top off the bottle, poured a splash of Scotch into the magazine writer's glass and then into his own. When he replaced the top there was less than an eighth of a bottle's worth of the precious liquor remaining. He lifted his glass, took a swallow, and winked at her. With just the one eye it looked like a grimace of pain.

As she downed a lovely swallow and let the richness flow through her, she felt a sense of relief. She had carried into the desert a dark purpose and heavy doubts, but somehow these last moments of the story, ending with the throwing of the tree, had erased the doubts once and for all.

She had made a decision.

She liked her lazy Sunday brunches, nights out with friends, kissing shallow, good-looking men on the couch while watching Netflix. She liked all the smooth appurtenances of her life, including the work, writing fluff so she didn't have to think about more ferocious things.

But this kidney-stealing, bonsai-hurling, one-eyed psychopath was living proof that she couldn't have her life and satisfy the purpose she'd come here for at the same time. Once you linked arms with someone like him, there was no way to turn back.

All she had to do was look around at the wasteland of this bar to be certain it was not a future she wanted or could handle. So she would give up on her darker hopes; she wasn't hard enough to see them through anyhow, she knew that now. Instead she would finish the interview and write the article. Already she was wondering if she could maybe jump a few journalistic levels and hawk it to the *New York Times*. What kind of new and wonderful job would that lead to? Then again there was already so much detail on the recorder, it wouldn't take much to stretch it all out into three hundred pages of true-crime sensation, just the thing to land her on the nonfiction bestseller list. The press, the speeches, the glamour of the bookstore signings. She took another sip of Scotch and tasted the lush possibilities. She was looking beyond the outlaw, seeing her future unspool in brilliantly surprising ways, when the bar door squealed open and a blast of the afternoon sun spilled upon the floor.

"Christ," said the outlaw. "Another one of Ginsberg's mutants has joined the party."

This time the shaft was dimmer because so much of it was blocked by the colossal silhouette in the door frame. When the door slammed shut, the magazine writer could see the hulking man clearly. As he entered, he ducked down so as not to bang the crown of his great bald head into the stuffed big horn set over the door. The behemoth wore a leather motorcycle vest with no shirt beneath and boots he had wrestled off the feet of Frankenstein's monster. He stood for a moment with his legs spread, his massive fists opening and closing, glaring at the two of them with no good intent on his face. She would have thought he was one of the bounty hunters after the outlaw's hide, yet the outlaw himself, after a quick glance, seemed not alarmed.

"Look at that piece of gristle with hands like wrecking balls," said the outlaw calmly. "There's a tribe of them out here, a plague of leather-clad ogres roaming the desert, living in mobile homes, cooking meth and snorting tumbleweeds. They ride the range on Harleys the size of oxen and leave trails of broken beer bottles and fractured bones. And this one I know, this one's a prime specimen, a prince of the wasteland, with all the bile and twice the size."

The giant stretched his neck to the left, to the right, cracking bones with each twist, and then spat a great glob onto the floor right next to the outlaw's chair. He turned to the bar, taking a seat a stool away from the thin man with the three-fingered hands. On the back of the giant's vest was a flat, grinning face with sharp teeth and the ears of a bat.

"They make quite a pair, don't they," said the outlaw. "Maybe the exploding meth that Crab Hands was cooking he was cooking for this beast. Oh, and look, Ginsberg has entered the conversation. Next thing you know the meerkat will join in; he'd be the wit of the group, tossing snark as he snapped scorpions between his teeth. I swear, sometimes this joint is like the cantina in *Star Wars*, without the charm.

"Look at the three losers in their little huddle, a dyspeptic barkeep moving with the alacrity of sludge, a bald giant with the visage of death on his vest, and a crab-handed freak with barely six fingers to his name. Oh, how I envy them. Their lives might be as dry and static as the landscape outside this desert shack, yet someday they could be inspired by a sunset, their spirits could be sent soaring by a piece of music or the lines of a sonnet, someday one of these sons of bitches could even fall in love. Imagine that; I can't.

"After receiving my diagnosis I went to a bar, anonymous and brown, and sucked down a row of shot glasses filled with a rye just as anonymous and just as brown. The liquor was so rough it scorched my throat with every gulp. I was trying to burn the taste of what I was out of my mouth; this was not a moment for a fine sipping whiskey, this was a moment for something harsh and painful. Something more painful, actually, than when Caroline Brooks had delivered her verdict.

"'I think you are what you think you are,' she had said.

"Despite my little playacting in the psychiatrist's office, that little declaration didn't come down like a hammer's blow because I had known. From the earliest days I had known, with every tear I hadn't shed and every rending of emotion I hadn't felt, I had known. It was in the way the beauty of the world never called to me, in the way cheating on my wife was as easy as cheating on a crossword puzzle, and discarding her was as poignant as discarding the morning trash. It would have been worse, in its way, to not have been what she said I was. Then I would have had no explanation and my monstrousness might have been too much to bear.

"So it wasn't her diagnosis that had me pouring the rye down my gullet. It was that other thing, the gift she delivered like a shiv along with the diagnosis, when she had made it clear there was nothing to be done, no drug, no operation, no way out. It wasn't just that I was this thing, it was that I would always be this thing.

"But we were talking of evolution.

"The whole time I was feeling sorry for myself in that brown little bar, something Caroline Brooks had said was chewing through my brain. 'I know what that plant needs, Phil,' she said. 'It needs sun, water, and food. It needs to be cared for in a certain way.' Evolution was my point in coming to Caroline Brooks in the first place, to be something that could not just find success but keep it, too, something more than the skittering water bug I had been my whole life. Could I transcend the limitations of my blighted soul? Could I be different even if my core didn't change? Maybe there was a way. I took out my phone.

"'Tonight?' I texted.

"'Sure,' was the reply.

"'Tell me when,' I texted back, 'and I'll be there.'"

***

After I left the bar I bought a bouquet of flowers because I thought she would like a bouquet of flowers. I had the flower shop place the flowers in crystal because in her mess of an apartment I hadn't detected anything so ordered and useful as a vase. When I rang the bell, I put on my most ingratiating smile because I assumed that was what she wanted to see.

"Okay?" said Linda Pickering. Her pretty face tightened with concern as she took the vase. Her lips pressed one against the other. "Thank you?"

"I figured I'd do something nice."

"Well, that's so . . . so nice of you, Phil." She fluffed the flowers a bit. "Nice." Her face had a forced smile on it as if instead of saying "nice" she was saying "tubercular."

"I hope you're hungry. I made a reservation at Del Frisco's."

"Isn't it a bit late for a belly full of meat?"

"Order the fish then."

"Phil?"

"We'll have fun. Maybe we'll go dancing later."

"Dancing?"

"Who doesn't love dancing?"

"Me."

"You just haven't danced with the right partner."

"It's a Wednesday night."

"Are there Wednesday rules? Is it written somewhere in stone by Hammurabi? No steak, no wine, no dancing?"

"Wine's allowed," she said.

"Thank heaven for that. Let's show a little spontaneity, Linda. Let's go wild. Let's eat meat and dance like fools."

"I thought we were going to just, I don't know—"

"Get drunk and fuck?"

She laughed, her rough, sexy laugh. "That sounds good."

"Is that all you want?"

"I thought that's all we were."

"And you don't want to try something a little—"

"This is sweet and all, Phil, but when I met you I didn't take you for sweet."

"I'm not usually."

"But now you're trying, and that is so nice."

"You say it like it's an affliction."

"Here's the thing. I have so much going on right now with my job and my daughter and my situation with that bastard who used to be my husband that, truth is, I don't really have room in my life for nice."

"You want me to be an asshole? Because I can do that, too. I can put on any mask you want. That's what I fucking do."

"Oh God, okay. Phil, calm down."

"I'm calm as dirt."

"We need to talk."

That's when I laughed. The whole thing was too perfectly pathetic. My failure was manifest in the way she held the flowers, the way her pretty face was suddenly suffused with pity. She thought she was going to crush my feelings, she thought she was going to cut me to the core. If only she knew.

"What's funny?" she said.

"Me. I think I'm not doing something right. Let me see the flowers for a moment." When she handed me the vase, I took it to the kitchen, yanked out the flowers, and tossed them into the garbage pail. Then I dumped out the water and hoisted the vase like it was a great glass stein. "Do you have anything here to drink?"

She looked at me like I had grown another head. "Vodka?"

"That will do," I said. "Fill 'er up."

I know what that plant needs, Phil. It needs sun, water, and food. And maybe vodka, too.

Caroline Brooks had implied that I could become someone new and better simply by giving the pieces of wood what they wanted. By pretending I cared I might actually learn to care; by being selfless I would perhaps become another self. She intended that I do it under her supervision with years of therapy, and that little boondoggle wasn't going to happen. But why should I look to a guild professional to change me when I had the wherewithal to do it on my own. If giving someone like Linda Pickering exactly what she wanted for no reason other than the fact that she wanted it could spark my evolution, then I could surely play that game. Isn't that what sales was all about? In my bleary rye-fueled funk, I had figured it was worth a try, though I was beginning to learn that figuring out what Linda wanted wouldn't be as easy as I had hoped.

"Do you want a cigarette?" I said as I reached from her bed for my jacket, tossed over a chair.

"No. But go ahead. I have enough disgusting habits of my own."

"Like what?"

"Have you ever tweezed your eyebrows?"

I laughed as I pulled a pack and my lighter from the inside pocket. This was after a too-long bout of ragged sex, made hard by some secret anger on both sides and soft by drink. It was strangely satisfying even if not quite mind-blowing. I liked that when things went off the rails, Linda Pickering offered up that laugh of hers, sexy and true. And I was surprised to find that I liked Linda Pickering, too. Was that evolutionary?

"A cigarette after sex is not a disgusting habit," I said. "It's a primal pleasure. The heat, the flavor, the little hit of nicotine that lifts the brain amidst the smoky perfume of burning leaves. I can imagine the first humans, huddling around the fire after making like their monkey forebears, bonding as sparks and smoke twine about them."

"After sex the only thing I want to bond with is a pillow."

"So I guess that means no cuddling."

"Really, who the hell are you?"

"Just a guy trying to figure you out."

"Trust me, it's not worth it."

"You sure you don't want one? Another thing about the after-sex cigarette: it is so beautifully self-destructive that it becomes the natural exclamation point on the whole act. *La petite mort* and then, bam, a coffin nail."

"All right, you convinced me. Spark one up."

"Now you're talking." I did the two-cigarettes-in-the-mouth trick from the movies. It was a calculated gesture that always seemed to go over. I pulled the same trick on my wife when we just started. Linda took the one I proffered, looked at it for a long moment, and then greedily sucked at it with such assurance that I couldn't help but laugh.

"I used to smoke incessantly," she said. "It was a cop thing. But then I had my daughter."

"I suppose nothing ruins a good healthy vice like a kid."

"Do you have one?"

"A healthy vice?"

"A kid."

"No, my wife and I ended our marriage before we made a mistake."

"My daughter wasn't a mistake. The marriage was, but not her. The first thing a cop is taught is to compartmentalize and I learned my lesson."

"When you talk about her you get all sincere, but everything else about you is crust, which makes it tough to figure you out."

"Then stop trying. I don't want to be figured out. Is that what that whole meat-and-dance absurdity was all about?"

"I thought I'd be a little nice."

"I've seen enough nice to last me. My husband was nice when I married him. Our divorce was going to be nice before the lawyer convinced my husband to take out the knives. And I've learned it's always the nice neighbor who ends up hacking off the head after he's done with the rape. Don't be nice, Phil. Be hard, maybe a little harder than you were tonight."

"I had a few drinks before the vodka."

"I don't want excuses, I want performance. But you were right about the cigarette. Now I'd like to cuddle with my pillow."

"You're kicking me out."

"You catch on quick."

"You don't want to finish our cigarettes and talk about our days."

"How was your day?"

"Not so good."

"Fascinating." She reached over and dropped her still-smoking cigarette in the dregs of one of her drinks. "Are we done now?"

"Yes," I said, rising from the bed, reaching down to grab my underwear and pants before heading toward the bathroom. "We're done."

"Good. Tomorrow night?"

"I'm busy tomorrow night."

"Oh, I've hurt your feelings. Did I hurt your feelings, Phil?"

I stopped and turned, facing her naked as a bear. "Did you want to hurt my feelings?"

"I didn't know I could."

"Whatever you want, that's what I want, too. So go ahead, consider them hurt."

"You think I'm a bitch."

"Do you want me to think you're a bitch?"

"What a fun night," she said. "Wasn't this a fun night?"

23

THE CHADWICK CLUB

There are moments deep within the murk of uncertainty when a flash of insight illuminates the darkest of mysteries. And what you discover is usually a truth so obvious as to be wearying. Such a moment struck me during the bimonthly meeting of the Chadwick Club.

Ah, the Chadwick Club, convening on the plutocratic edge of Georgetown, beyond the fine townhouses cheek by jowl on well-lit streets, houses inhabited by lobbyists and lawyers and secretaries of the state. You wove this way, you wove that way, you turned onto a dark, leafy street and glimpsed, on the other side of a row of hedges, the brick walls of a great winged thing. A black limousine pulling out of the drive signaled that you were at the right place at the right time as long as you were the right person. Fortunately, Gordon had placed a call to one of his Missouri contacts, actually the drug dealer who had directed him to Mr. Maambong in the first place, who got in touch with a congressman, who got in touch with a lobbyist, who was able, for a vote on some obscure appropriations rider, to put Dick Triplett on the list.

"This property abuts Rock Creek Park," said Riley, as we sat in the car on the road outside the mansion, "not very far from where they found Scarlett Gould's body."

"Who owns the house?"

"It's not a house, Phil. It's a mansion. And not a McMansion but the full-out real thing. Owned by some shell corporation. It's rented out for parties and weddings and such."

"Not to mention wild, lascivious orgies."

"I just said they rented it out to weddings. You don't get out much, do you?"

"What's Detective Booth's role in all this?"

"He moonlights as security. Either he'll be at the door, checking names and searching for weapons, or wandering around, making sure the girls don't start pickpocketing wallets."

"Whores have such loose morals."

"That's why we love them so. Be aware that when he moonlights, Booth wears himself a toupee."

"Really?"

"And a bad one, too. From the dead marmoset collection."

"Thanks for the warning. Pointing at his head and bursting out in laughter won't help me grease his wheels. While I'm inside, crack the shell and find out who owns this place. I also want to know who's running the Chadwick Club. Somebody's hiring Booth to keep things under control, which means somebody's got control of Booth. We could use an ally."

"Will do. And just so you know, it turns out that there have been calls back and forth between the other detective and Melissa Davenport. A number of calls, as if Detective Pickering and Mrs. Davenport are almost working together."

"I'll take care of that." I took another long look at the mansion on the other side of the hedges. "When I was in Miami, there was another competition going on at the house. Another bunch of wannabes looking for the high life, just like we were."

"The hyena business must be rocking."

"They're building more teams, and they're looking for more team leaders. Your name was mentioned. Are you ready to rise?"

"I'm ready to quit," she said. "I'm not cut out for this kind of work. Stealing kidneys, squashing police investigations."

"But you're so good at it," I said.

"That's the problem."

"Think about the money. Think about that beach of yours in Bali. You'll be able to buy it."

"We stole a kidney, Phil."

"She had two. If you're so torn up about it all, what are you still doing here?"

"I don't know. Loyalty maybe?"

"To Maambong?"

"No, God no. To you, and Gordon, and even to Kief, believe it or not."

"Let me tell you something true, Riley. Loyalty is for saps. My loyalty ends on the far side of my teeth."

"You just say that."

"I live it, and you should, too. But you should also know, it might not be so easy to leave. I get the sense you can't just give Maambong notice and waltz away. When you decide to bolt, don't make any big announcement, in fact don't tell anyone, not even me. Just disappear."

"Jesus, Phil, what have we gotten ourselves into?"

"A gravy train heading straight downtown. Don't wait, I'll find my own way back to the hotel."

"Try not to have too much fun."

"You know what I think about drugs and drink and whores," I said as I opened the door. "Work, work, work."

The house was a big Georgian thing from a distant century, wide and regal, sitting like a swaddled prince on a rise overlooking the federal city. A man and woman in tight black suits stood on either side of the front door. I knew their type, I was their type. Henchmen.

"Dick Triplett," I said. For the occasion my suit was loosely tailored, something name brand and stupidly expensive that didn't call attention to itself, something better than a corporate lawyer would wear, but that cost less than an investment banker would pay. That was the sweet spot for my play that night.

The woman smiled at me with a noted lack of interest before taking out her phone and typing in the name.

"Of course, Mr. Triplett," she said, stepping aside after she received a return text. "Enjoy your night."

Inside the front door, another man stood in his black suit, hands clasped together. "Good evening, Mr. Triplett," he said, a smooth maître d' smile plastered on his rough-hewn face. "Since this is your first time, we need to cover some business matters before you join the other guests. Will you accompany me to the office, please? Skye will take care of you."

There was already a crowd in the large salon to the right, but I was led to the left, down a hallway to a small cloakroom, where, among mostly empty racks, a woman with the exaggerated lips and false breasts of an aging stripper sat behind a desk. "Can I have your card, please, Mr. Triplett?"

"Business card?"

"Business or personal," said Skye. "Whichever you choose for payment is fine. Most members use a business card."

"Got you," I said, pulling out a Dick Triplett American Express Platinum that Maambong arranged for use in my Hyena cases.

"Excellent. Are you here with a client tonight, or are you alone?"

"I thought I'd check it out before I brought a client, but if it is as ripe as I've been led to believe, I'll be back."

"Very good. You'll be charged a membership fee, an entrance fee, and entertainment fees depending on the amusements you choose. Drinks, as always, are complimentary. Now I will need some information. Your birth date and Social Security number, please."

"Birth date and Social Security number?"

"Yes, along with some personal information such as your mother's maiden name and the name of your first pet."

"For the credit card company when they decline payment."

"It often happens at these amounts, especially with newer members."

I gave her the details of my false identity while she typed the answers onto her tablet. She ran the card through a little white reader sticking out the top and returned it to me, along with the tablet for me to sign. I rubbed my finger across the screen in an approximation of Dick Triplett's signature.

"This is your number," said Skye, handing me a plastic card imprinted with a large blue 348. "Just show it to the hosts if there is anything you desire. They'll take care of the rest. Henry will escort you to the salon. Welcome to the Chadwick Club, Mr. Triplett."

The salon was paneled in wood and littered with too many men in dark suits. Couches were pushed against the walls and largely ignored. A man in a tuxedo tickled the ivories of a grand piano in the corner, which gave the room the charm of a Nordstrom. There were a few women in the room, older women with hair plastered and long, sheathy dresses, looking about with nervous mouths, but this was mostly a men's club, some of the men slick, some of them doddering, some overfed with ruddy necks stuffed like blood sausages into the tight collars of their custom-made shirts. I recognized a few, a secretary of something over here, a White House staffer with a flag in his lapel over there, a slew of elected representatives scattered about like cow pies in a pasture. Others owned the unmistakable bearing of military officers, though they scrupulously were devoid of their military uniforms. I searched the faces for Booth as I headed to one of the bars.

"Would you like the Macallan or the Balblair?" said the barkeep after I had asked for a Scotch with ice.

"Have the Balblair," said a short, thick man leaning on the bar with his back to me. "They're serving the '89, third release. It's a treat."

"The Balblair, then," I said.

"Good choice," said the short man. When he turned to look at me I was startled for a moment. His face was wide, his rodent eyes were small and too close together, his nose was pugged like a pig's.

"Rufus Davenport," he said as he reached out a hand.

"Dick Triplett."

"You'll like the Balblair, Dick. Nice caramel color, a little sweet, a little spice."

"Sounds like my wife," I said.

"Then why are you wasting your time here?"

"Ex-wife."

"Ah. My wife would be a white zinfandel, thin and cheap and avoided at all costs."

"Ex?"

"Sadly no."

I reached past him to get hold of my drink.

"What's your game, Dick?" said Rufus.

"Acquisitions."

"Interesting. Companies? People? Art?"

"All of the above."

"Did you come with a buyer or a seller?"

"I'm a new member so I came alone. I didn't want to bring anyone without first seeing what the Chadwick Club was all about."

"Lucky you, you can leave when you choose. I'm here until the fat lady finally pulls herself off the carcass of a congressman from Oklahoma."

"So you're a lobbyist."

"Most of the members are lobbyists of one sort or another. The guests are either clients in from Omaha or assholes with a whiff of power. The members pay, the guests play, and everything gets written off. That, my friend, is how legislation is baked in the real world."

"You sound quite cynical there, Rufus."

"I've been doing this too long. I should have been a high school teacher like I set out to be a long time ago."

"That sure sounds rich," I said. "Banging all those nubile high school girls with stars in their eyes."

"What? No. Jesus. How creepy is that? I just wanted to teach English. Gatsby and Hamlet." He gave me a stare from those beady little eyes that would have frozen the heart of a man with a heart, and then smiled thinly. "At least you're in the right place, Dick. Drink up."

As he waddled off to find his guest, I took a sip of the liquor. A little sweet, a little spice, yes, but with a line of bitterness running through it. Whatever Rufus Davenport knew about Fitzgerald or the Bard, he didn't know his Scotch. I took a moment to scan the crowd. There was something thrilling about the scene, this conglomeration of money and power discussing how to sell the American people down the toilet before the whores arrived. The very sight was enough to renew your faith in the genius of democracy.

And then I saw him, standing like a sentry in the corner, tall and mournful with a marmoset on his head. Detective Booth. I took another sip of the Scotch and headed over. This was what I had planned for, this was why I had come. I would casually chat with him, flatter him when I could, mention an opportunity that might fit his unique talents, and set up a meeting in which I would buy his soul. It would be as easy as eating pie. I was making my way toward him through the crowd when a bell tinkled in my brain and the room quieted.

"Ladies and gentlemen," said Skye, standing now at the door of the salon, her breasts almost spilling out of her top, her wide, puffy lips smiling, a triangle dangling from one hand and a silver wand held delicately in the other. "If you'll please make your way to the ballroom, the festivities are about to begin."

The crowd surged to the far end of the salon, where a great set of double doors were suddenly flung open. I wanted still to have my moment with Detective Booth, but something had dulled my purpose and I found myself swept along with the tide. The chatter had dimmed, as if we were about to witness a spectacle of sorts, the hush broken only by a bout of senseless laughter. I took another sip of my Scotch and felt my head fill with bitter cotton as the crowd carried me through the doors and along a portico toward the entrance to a great room thrumming with music and brightly colored lights. When we were all inside, a row of spotlights flashed on.

And suddenly there they were, all in a line, up against windows curtained shut from the night, women, young and younger, with long hair and red lipstick, dressed in tight dresses that showed off leg and breast, smiling with bright-white teeth. There were men, too, young and thin in tuxedos, but it was the women who stole the applause and drew out another bout of insane laughter. And after a moment and a few words from Skye that I couldn't decipher, the neat line broke up as the women made their way about the room, smiling like hostesses out to ensure the comfort of the guests. Thank you for flying Chadwick Air.

"Hi there," said a blonde who had taken hold of my arm. I don't know how she got from the far side of the room to my side, but it seemed to have happened in a skip. "My name is Mandy. You look happy."

I laughed, and realized the strange manic laughter I had been hearing was my own.

"Would you like another drink, Dick?" said Mandy.

I looked down at the Scotch: two ice cubes stranded in a shallow puddle with a hint of blue. "You know my name."

"I've been told to take special care of you."

The other women who'd been in the line had made their way among the members and their guests. The women were clutching arms, talking with bright eyes. The men's faces were flushed, they had their arms possessively around the women's waists and were leaning forward while they talked as if they were making points during an intense discussion of moral philosophy. I looked at Mandy and realized she might have been the most beautiful woman I had ever seen.

"You might be the most beautiful woman I have ever sheen," I said.

"Do you want another drink?"

"Not like the lasht one. How young are you?"

"Old enough. Do you want to go somewhere, Dick? Somewhere private? There are rooms upstairs."

"I don't feel so shpunky."

"Maybe another drink would help."

"Maybe. But not the Scotch. No more Scotch."

"We could rustle up some cocaine or weed if you want?"

"The dynamic duo."

"But first I need your card."

I patted my jacket and then pulled out a white card. She took it and waved it in the air and suddenly Skye was in front of us.

"Three four eight," said Mandy.

"That's me," I said.

"We'll need a room and some refreshments," said Mandy. "Along with a blue twist."

"Got it," said Skye, handing over a key. "Two F."

"Are you ready, Dick?" said Mandy.

"Ready weddy meddy."

"Let's go upstairs."

"Lovely."

And so we did, though I don't remember climbing the steps. But I do remember that as she pulled my nearly paralytic frame out of the ballroom, we passed a stolid, mournful figure with a furry little monkey on his head.

"Look who it ish," I said. "Detective Booth."

Detective Booth said nothing.

24

BLOOD

Blood.

25

Cain & Cain

I bolted upright, stark naked except for a plastic tube sticking straight out of my chest. In that moment the world burst upon me with all its sordidness and morbidity, and what had been the silvery hum of angels in my ears exploded into an uproar. Bright light was raw pain in my eyes, washing out all the color of the room except for the red on my hands, on my legs, spattered upon the walls and across the sodden bed upon which now I sat. The wild array of red against a bleached backdrop was a crimson Rorschach pattern, two roosters humping a butterfly during the apocalypse.

I grabbed hold of the tube and yanked it from my body. More red swelled along the needle and rolled down my chest. The room swayed, I began to fall—until something as rough as iron clutched my shoulders and pulled me back to sitting.

"Mr. Triplett, stay with us." A woman leaned over and slapped me; I barely felt it and slap! she did it again. "We need to get you up and out." A pair of grotesque swollen lips danced over rows of bleached teeth forming something like words. "Mr. Triplett, do you hear?"

"Where?"

"Wherever you tell us to take you."

"What?"

"You need to wake up. You need to get on your way. Breathe this in, it will help."

A pile of white powder was pressed to my nose and I inhaled out of reflex. My head jerked back from a pain shooting like fire up the inside of my face even as the cap of my skull lifted and a trumpet sounded to start the derby. My heart took off, galloping like a speed horse.

"Mr. Triplett. We need to get you out of here. Lift him up, Henry, and take him to the shower."

"What did you do to me?" I said as I felt the iron grips leave my shoulders and grab me beneath the arms.

"Henry is taking you into the shower. You need to be cleaned off. Do you know what you've done?"

"Done?"

"Clean him up."

I was hauled from a great mess smeared upon the bed and lugged out of the room, my feet leaving a trail of red as they dragged across the wooden floor. Lying on the boards, beside the trail, was a pocketknife, drenched in blood, marked with prints.

I sat in the shower stall as barbs of heat struck my flesh. The water swirling around me before heading to the drain was stained crimson. My memory of the night was like that swirling water, mostly clear except for discrete lines of shocking color.

I remembered Mandy with her long, blonde hair and lithe body pulling me past Detective Booth and up the stairs.

I remembered her undressing me like an invalid, cutting off my shirt with a pocketknife when I fumbled with the buttons, and then her own clothes falling from her body like leaves from an autumn tree, revealing something so perfect as to almost be proof of God's existence.

I remembered Mandy slowly laying her naked body upon mine like a gentle kiss.

I remembered the cocaine, chopped and lined with a knife's blade, becoming a dart of pain shooting through me.

I remembered banging away at Mandy from behind, working like a piston as she looked back with something dead on her face, and me carrying on, banging and banging, feeling nothing but anger.

I remembered wandering the hallway, naked and dazed, glimpsing images of bodies twining, of limbs being devoured by mouths, of boots and breasts and whips and ball gags until it all became in my mind a whirlpool of naked body parts and old men with teeth stained crimson sucking youth from long, perfect bodies.

I remember Mandy pulling me back, forming a line with the knife, something blue now mixed with the white, and my "Wallahoo!" as I sucked it up through nostrils already scorched.

I remembered pounding away with her legs over my shoulders and my hands about her throat.

I remembered waking from the dead with a needle in my chest, the whole of my body baptized in blood.

And now, in the shower, with the water beating against me and the speed coursing through my veins, I felt a panic rise. I needed to get out of the shower, out of this room. What had happened and why was a mystery that didn't need to be immediately solved; what needed to be solved was my presence in that house, with these people, in this weakened state.

I reached up to the water knob and tried to pull myself to standing. The knob spun out of my grip and I fell back, even as the water turned to scalding. I writhed on the tiles, my skin being flayed by the heat, before scrabbling to my knees and pulling at the knob until the water shut off completely. I sat on my haunches for a moment, futilely trying to slow my breath and my heart.

I pushed open the door and crawled out of the shower, and collapsed upon the tile, noticing only after a few desperate breaths that my clothes were in a heap by the toilet.

When I staggered out of the bathroom, a mournful Detective Booth was waiting for me. My suit was creased, my shirt in tatters, my socks were somehow missing, but my cuff links, watch, and wallet were in the suit jacket, which surprised me a bit before I remembered that I had already signed for any charges the Chadwick Club chose to place upon my card.

"This way please, Mr. Triplett," said the detective, grabbing my arm as I tottered. "A car is waiting."

Now was not the time to give Detective Booth my spiel or to ask what crimes I might have committed under the influence of their drugs. Now was the time to get the hell out of there. So I silently let the detective pull me along the hallway, now empty of reveler and whore, down a back stairway, and out a rear door into the dying night, where a black limousine waited on a wide asphalt lot, its engine purring.

As I started walking toward the car, the detective kept his grip on my arm. "You knew my name."

I turned and gave him a good look. His eyes were brown and as flat as a calculator. He was adding up something and I had a pretty good idea what it was.

"You were pointed out to me," I said.

"By who?"

"One of the club members. Rufus Davenport?"

"Mr. Davenport is quite active."

"He said you were the man to see if I ever got into trouble."

"There's blood on your right cuff."

I looked down. One dark splatter lay on the fold.

"Who runs the club?"

The detective let the slightest smile crease his mournful face. "I expect I'll be seeing you again quite soon, Mr. Triplett."

I was a little dazed at just how conveniently this had worked out when the car's driver stepped out from behind the wheel. He was beefy and tall, one of those steroid boys whose ears sprouted right from their necks, and I wondered for a moment if I recognized him. He opened the passenger door and stood there waiting. I staggered forward, thinking of the name Jojo or Robo, and slammed my head into the car roof. When I bent over in pain, I found myself facing the interior of the black car, where a man sat calmly on the rear-facing bench seat, a manila envelope resting on one thigh. His hair was short, his beard was trimmed tight, there was a gap between his two front teeth. I could feel the cold coming off him as he gave me his best approximation of a smile.

"Tough night?" said Tom Preston.

We sat across from each other in silence, Tom Preston and I, as the limousine prowled through the darkness. Where Bobo was driving us—I now recognized the driver as the hulk in Miami who had been lathering Cassandra with lotion—I had not a clue, but the silence wasn't a surprise. What would we discuss? The weather? Our feelings? Would I make a little joke to put him at ease? Would he put a hand on my shoulder and look into my eyes and tell me he cared? Each possibility was an absurdity. We shared the same condition, that had been clear the moment he shattered Gordon's leg, but instead of solidarity our brotherhood spurred a murderous rivalry. Cain and Cain. What do two sticks of wood talk about? Nothing, they just scrape one against the other until they combust.

"You know I owe you," said Tom Preston, finally, his marble eyes frosted with ice, his voice a calm piece of violence. "You might not have driven the car that whacked me in Miami, but you made me a target."

"It wasn't personal."

He looked at me for a moment, his face creasing with bemusement before he laughed. Both of us understood that when it came to the two of us, nothing was personal, not even a private conversation. I had been surprised that he had spoken at all, but I knew immediately what it meant. He wanted something from me other than my demise, which was one thing more than I wanted from him.

"We don't need to be enemies," said Tom Preston.

"We sure as hell won't be friends."

"Do you want a friend? I don't want a friend. Who the hell ever needs a friend? I was given a goldfish when I was young. Swimmy the fish. He was going to be my friend. I thought I'd be a good boy and fill his bowl with fresh water from the tap. The next morning I found him floating. For some reason I kept buying a new Swimmy, ten at least, one at a time, a few pennies at the store, and filling his bowl with tap water. I seemed never to learn my lesson. Or maybe that was the lesson. Swimmy was my last friend. How did you find the Chadwick Club?"

"Not especially amusing."

"You couldn't tell by the photographs." He lifted the manila envelope, slid out a stack of eight-by-tens, and cocked an eyebrow as he peered at the top photo. "Young breasts. They should name a tequila Young Breasts. Forget Jose Cuervo or Don Julio. Who wants to drink something named after an old Mexican dude? Call it Young Breasts and they'd make a mint. What was she, seventeen maybe?"

"She said she was old enough."

"That always goes over in front of a judge. But from this it looks like it was worth the risk. And from this one, too. And . . . oh my." He turned the photograph this way and that for effect and then flipped it to show me. "Is that even legal in Washington?"

"It's not only legal," I said, "it's mandatory."

Tom Preston laughed. "What a great town. I don't think we could have done a better job of inventing a place for ourselves if we started from scratch. A town that runs on money, sex, and power is the town for the likes of you and me. Mr. Maambong told me of your strategy in our little contest down in Miami. He told me how you held back your true nature so as to maintain trust with the others. Mr. Maambong says that's a restraint I need to learn. But he also told me there are things I can teach you. Like how to lose all restraint to get a job done right."

"I'm getting this job done right."

"By bringing in an old drunk lawyer to be your shill? By banging an alcoholic cop? By letting yourself get drugged by some baby-faced bartender? It's weakness not to get straight to the heart of things. So let's get to the heart of things."

He thumbed through his stack of photographs, found what he was looking for, and tossed it at me. It hit my chest and fell on the floor. I kept my eyes on him as I reached down to pick it up. I tried to keep my face stone as I examined it, a grainy black and white of me naked and passed out over a corpse, blood everywhere and a knife in my hand.

"Convincing, no?" he said.

"No."

"Maybe you're right. Maybe the wounds on her chest and neck were drawn in Halloween makeup. Maybe the deadness in the girl's open eyes is just a remarkable piece of acting for such a young whore. Maybe the blood is from a decapitated chicken and that knife was carefully placed in your drugged-out fingers. Maybe a club that will take photographs of orgy sex for purposes of blackmail might also be in the business of staging horrific scenes of mayhem and murder just to up the ante."

"Exactly."

"Or maybe in a drug- and sex-fueled state of rage and lust you grabbed the first thing you could lay your hands on and stabbed that girl to death even as you finished inside her because that's what you wanted to do, had always wanted to do, and the drugs had merely taken away your genteel reticence."

"Not that."

"I'll take your word for it. But here's the thing: the truth of the way it went down doesn't really matter."

"It does to me."

"One morning I woke up and found one of my Swimmys still alive, doing happy figure eights in his little bowl. I looked at him and he swam into position to look at me and we were looking at each other. There was a strange equality in our stares. Like we understood each other. And we did; I cared just as much about him as he cared about me. Feel familiar? I reached my whole hand into the bowl and pulled Swimmy out and felt him squirm in my palm. I liked the feeling, like an itch I didn't know I had was being scratched. I opened a gap in my fist and his little gold head squiggled out. He was a beautiful color. A rainbow danced on his golden surface. And there was a little plea in his eye. 'Put me back. We're friends.' I gently brushed his head with my thumb and then rubbed a little harder and then squeezed his head with my thumb until the sweet pleading eye popped. Afterward I cried. I was young and I cried."

"Am I supposed to be touched?"

"You're not supposed to be anything other than what you are. Mr. Maambong and the Principal asked me to speed your development. I think the specific word they used, actually, was 'evolution.'"

He smiled, and in that smile I saw it all, not just the truth about the Chadwick Club, and who it belonged to, but the truth about what they had wanted from me all along. The revelation must have shown on my face.

"What did you think?" said Tom Preston, laughing at my expression. "That they wanted you to stop raiding the minibar?"

"And so you set me up to send me on my way."

"I only arranged the theater, you gave the performance."

"Well, fuck you and fuck them," I said.

"I'll pass it on."

"Just so you know, if I do decide to evolve in the way they want, you'll be the first to know."

"At least you're catching on."

"So the Principal owns and operates the Chadwick Club."

"It's one of her bases of power. Maambong's operation is another. And she's got a lobbying firm that plays as her cover and handles the transfers of money. Massive transfers. It's quite a racket, perfect for this town, because it's all about money, sex, and power."

"And that's what you're after, too? Money, sex, and power?"

"That's what everybody is after. But you and me, we're not everybody. We two want all that, absolutely, but we want more."

"I don't."

"Sure you do. One thing you want in addition is acceptance. That's a weakness I'm here to stamp out. You think you have lines you won't cross, but they're not lines of conscience. Men like you and me, we are free of the burden of conscience. Which can only mean the lines are external. You care about the way they look at you. You let them draw your lines. And that's why it doesn't matter whether what happened in that room with that whore was real or not. The pictures are enough to change the way they look at you. With the pictures out there, you'll never get acceptance. But why you care about their acceptance is beyond me. I mean, who the hell are they and what the hell do they know about us?"

There was a touch of anger now in his voice. He looked out the window and his lips curled in a way so that the gap in his front teeth grew fearsome. I bent the bloody photograph and tucked it into my jacket pocket.

"Take it," he said, noticing. "Jack off to it in the middle of the night to keep yourself primed. Truth is, the only time they truly appreciate all that we are is when our guns are at their heads. The only time they look at us with the proper amount of respect is when our hands are around their throats. The only time they understand the true order of things is when their blood is gushing over our knives."

"Not my gun," I said. "Not my hands."

"But it sure as hell was your hand on the knife. The fingerprints prove that. And let me tell you what you might not remember from your drugged-out odyssey. Watching the life drain from their sad little eyes while we stand over them, in all our glory, is the truest satisfaction we can achieve in this world. It's better than money and power, better than sex. And when you blend it with sex like you did last night—oh man, it makes everything they want as pallid as soup."

I should have been horrified. I should have shrunk away as if from an alien creature with red scales and shark's teeth, oozing goo all over the limousine's leather. I had been given a glimpse of the bright, molten iron at the core of this man's soul and it should have scorched my eyes. But all the should-haves disappeared in an abyss of my own. I understood Tom Preston, I was Tom Preston. What was dead in him was dead within me, what lived in him called to me with a seductive tongue.

"Was it really chicken blood?" I said.

He thought about it for a moment and then chuckled, yeah, he chuckled, and you know how I feel about chuckling. The son of a bitch chuckled. "This has been good. This has been refreshing. Who else could I confide in like this? Instead of threatening and fighting, we should be working together."

Ah, there it was. I tilted my head like he had started talking French.

"They recruited us because we have talents they can't muster on their own," he said. "Then why are we taking orders from them? You can do things I can't. I can do things you won't. Together we can go further than they ever could. It wouldn't take much of a scheme to pull the money, sex, and power from their tiny, tired hands. Think of how all the little senators will quake when we walk into a room."

"You want us to team up against Mr. Maambong and the Principal?"

"They can't handle what they've got. That fact that they need you and me here, now, proves it. But we don't need anybody. Nothing can stop a psychopath who knows no bounds."

"You want to take over their business?"

"For a start."

"And then?"

"I want to take over the world."

"Yeah," I said, "you and every other asshole in this town."

26

DARWIN'S DREAM

"All this gab about blood and gore is making me hungry," said the outlaw, rubbing his hands together. "How about you? What do you say to a bone-in rib eye, ribboned with fat, grilled to perfection over mesquite, served with a pile of Chateau potatoes and a plate of asparagus with hollandaise? Is that the ticket or what?"

Before the magazine writer could respond, the outlaw yelled to the barkeep, "Ginsberg, two rib eyes, burnt, with the works, pronto, tonto. We're famished here."

The barkeep, huddled with the two customers at the bar, looked up for a moment, shook his head as if at a clown, and then lowered his head back to the conversation.

"He's not moving so fast," said the outlaw. "In fact, he's not moving at all, the lazy bastard. But he has a point. I fear I might have oversold the menu. See the jars on either side of the meerkat on the counter? One is filled with pickled eggs, the other with pickled eyeballs of lamb. Both are about as tender as a thumb. Do you have a preference?"

When she chose the egg over the eyeball, the outlaw gave a shrug of disappointment before he rose from the table and dragged his leg to the bar. He stood next to the behemoth in the leather vest, spoke softly to the bartender. There was a bout of gruff laughter before he limped back to the table.

"Don't expect too much," said the outlaw. "They're so sour your cheeks will contract until the vessels burst. But on the positive side, you'll stagger out of here looking like a model.

"You're wondering, perhaps, as we wait for our repast, how I responded to Tom Preston's offer. You're wondering if I linked arms with my brother Cain and marched ever forward toward the holy grail of money, sex, and power. I was sorely tempted. Yet while the offer certainly fit my proclivities, I could still figure the odds. We'd be battling not just Mr. Maambong and the Principal, but all the henchmen at their disposal. And even if that worked out, there'd be no telling when Tom Preston would turn around and go after me. I mean, that guy was a fucking psychopath.

"But there was another, stronger reason to turn down his offer of a collaboration. My night at the Chadwick Club had made three things clear. First, Rufus Davenport hadn't killed Scarlett Gould, though I suddenly strongly suspected who had. Second, I discovered that cocaine and Viagra mixed in a neat line is really quite sparkly. And finally, I knew now, without any doubt, what the Principal had wanted when she had talked to me about evolution, and I couldn't blame her for wanting it.

"What good is a triggerman who won't pull the trigger; what good is a henchman who won't hench?

"Ahh, the eggs."

Ginsberg made his slow way from the bar to the table, carrying two mugs of beer and two plates, each topped by a pair of hard-boiled eggs, slimy and sickly purple. He slammed the mugs onto the table next to the others, then slammed the plates. The sharp scent of dirty socks swirled.

"I know the beer is bad," said the outlaw as Ginsberg returned to the bar, "but let's not waste what's left of our brilliant Scotch as we wash down these gelatinous balls of muck. Are you sure you don't want the lamb eyes? The trailing tendrils sliding down the throat give a unique sensation, along with a piquant aftertaste. Too bad. Now the procedure for the eggs is quite precise; failure to adhere to the exact steps could be disastrous to your health as well as to the decor. Hold your nose, put the whole thing in your mouth at once like Cool Hand Luke, two quick chews, a fast swallow, and then a gush of the skunked beer before the full taste of Ginsberg's pickling explodes. Like this."

She watched in horror and fascination as the outlaw followed his directions to the letter. While he chewed, his one eye bulged; when he swallowed, a tear rolled from beneath his patch. As the magazine writer gagged, the outlaw chugged the beer like he was in a fraternity house.

"Whoa," he said, slapping the table as he gasped for breath. "That's abominable. Yow. I can't imagine anything more disgusting. It's like swallowing a sour aspic filled with shit. If you don't mind, I think I'll have another. Go ahead. It won't bite back, at least it shouldn't, though I wouldn't be surprised if you found a beak inside."

If this was the outlaw's idea of a test, she had already failed. The mere thought of putting one of those vile eggs in her mouth brought up an empty retch. She had no doubt that the end result of an attempt to eat such a thing would be a slick of vomit across the table. How quick would Ginsberg move to clean that? Not very, she was sure. She pushed the putrid thing away from her.

But then she remembered her brother's smile that summer night when she was seven and they were catching fireflies and he put the insects in a jar with a lid pocked through with holes, and how the jar spun with magic as he held it up against the stars. And she remembered the way he'd hugged her close during their mother's funeral before he went up and spoke for them both in a choked voice because she was too broken apart to rise from her chair. And she remembered the sight of her brother's body in the morgue, a sight that now plagued her whenever she closed her eyes.

He still lay there, pale and punctured with buckshot, dead and unavenged, as she protected her overpriced brunches, her tepid nights of Netflix and chill, her pieces of fluff that filled the pages of the vapid press. He lay there on that metal slab with half his face obliterated while she deigned not to mar her breath with pickling juice. She had sworn she would do everything necessary to find her brother the justice the system had denied him, but what she really meant was she would do anything so long as it wouldn't upset her fragile little tummy. She had come looking for a henchman and now, face-to-face with exactly what she had sought, she was unwilling to pay the price, any price, because he wasn't the right kind of henchman.

Her weakness made her sicker than the egg ever could. She was acting exactly like the coward she had feared herself to be. And that realization steeled her determination. She held her nose, popped a slime-ridden ovoid in her mouth, chewed twice, swallowed, and then drowned the thing with gulps of beer that washed it straight into her stomach like a hissing chunk of hot steel. And in so doing, she felt suddenly different, stronger, larger in a way, as if written on the egg had been the words "Eat me." She opened her mouth to prove it was down and let out a deep belch, tasting the pickled thing again.

And verily it was good.

"I'm just grateful only air came up," said the outlaw. "Ginsberg's eggs have been known to cause ejectments of all kinds. But now I know you're desperate enough to swallow a Ginsberg-pickled egg, which is something. I suppose a dead brother will obliterate even the most commonsense lines, hmm? Not unlike what the Principal wanted to obliterate within me."

***

Here's some physics for you. When stars form in the utter emptiness of the universe, the fusion going on at their brilliant centers turns hydrogen into all manner of element. We are children of these huge burning monsters, creatures formed of the dust churned from the fire at their hearts. Stars burn on and on, for billions of years, creating heat and life and ever more elements, until they create, finally, iron. And once that happens, once iron finally appears, these stars are doomed. Iron cannot fuse into another element, iron is a cancer at the core, a star killer.

There was the molten iron of murder in the depths of Tom Preston's soul and it glowed ever so brightly, but ultimately, I had no doubt, it would destroy him. There was the same molten iron in Jesse Duchamp, and he had shown me the toll of allowing it to form and glow. When the Principal spoke of evolution, she was speaking about me embracing that murderous element, but no Hyena, not Tom Preston, not Mr. Maambong, not the goddamned Principal was going to punch my ticket to New Orleans.

Yet that didn't mean I was doomed to failure in the Hyena universe. In fact, my night at the Chadwick Club and my meeting with Tom Preston had given an entirely new impetus to my time in Washington. Maybe the very stink of the place had infected my liver, but suddenly I had an ambition grander than the mere squelching of an investigation. Tom Preston wanted me to make a move with him, and I wanted nothing whatsoever to do with Tom Preston, but that didn't mean it wasn't time to make a move.

"Jungle Dog, LLC, is registered in the Cayman Islands," said Alberto Menendez. "Information about it is quite thin. The funds to pay taxes on its properties in this country are paid from an account held by CIBC Caymans. CIBC discloses very little about its account holders and nothing about the individuals or organizations behind the corporate veil. Your friend Riley, however, is quite relentless. She was able to find an attorney in Miami who handled a real estate issue for the Jungle Dog company, a Ms. Secada."

"I assume there's a reason you asked me to meet you here at this overpriced coffeehouse," I said. We were just off K Street, with its tall, ritzy buildings, and swarms of parasites sucking their sustenance from the body politic. Parasites like me.

"They make quite a fine brew here," said Alberto.

"Nicely bitter, yes."

"I thought you would like it. It is as if you and it were made for each other. But also, from this window, there is a capital view of that building right there."

"And that building has some relevance to Jungle Dog, I assume."

"Indeed," said Menendez. "I happened to contact Ms. Secada down in Miami. She was not interested in being of help—she was almost rude, imagine that—but when I mentioned we had a serious criminal issue with the Georgetown property where this so-called Chadwick Club of yours met, she referred me to a real estate lawyer in the District, a Mr. Cooper."

"And he's in that building across the street?"

"No," said Menendez. "He is in Georgetown. Now when I contacted Mr. Cooper, he was remarkably unhelpful. Even after I mentioned the potentially serious criminal issue, he still refused to meet with me. It wasn't until I had a friend of mine in the police department give him a call and ask some embarrassing questions about the Chadwick Club that he immediately rang me back up."

"It is nice to have friends in the police department."

"I was told to meet someone named Portofoy in that building right across the street. My appointment is for fifteen minutes from now. It was this Portofoy who referred the real estate cases to Ms. Secada and Mr. Cooper. I've been asking around. Portofoy, it turns out, is not a corporate lawyer as one would expect."

"Portofoy is a lobbyist," I said.

"Very good. But not just a lobbyist, a lobbyist's lobbyist, the head of a small shop with a great deal of power. When one of the more traditional firms has trouble making headway on a crucial issue, they go to Portofoy. And the fees are quite extravagant."

"Do you have a photograph?"

Menendez showed me an image on his phone. A beefy figure in a pin-striped suit, short, squat, thinning hair, well bejowled.

"In the last few years Portofoy has become something of a legend with the legislative victories he has pulled out of his rear pocket," said Alberto. "Other firms have tried to poach him, but he is apparently happy where he is. They say he is quite ferocious."

"And you are meeting him in fifteen minutes."

"Thirteen, now. And I'm afraid I will need something a little more definite than a vague threat about a criminal matter to rattle Mr. Portofoy's cage."

"Show him this," I said, taking a padded manila envelope out of my briefcase. Inside was the photograph of me and Mandy and the blood and the knife. "You can leave it with him. Tell him the photograph was snapped inside the Chadwick Club. That will be enough. I'll take it from there."

"Should I mention the Scarlett Gould case?"

"You won't have to. He already knows who you are; he wouldn't have agreed to meet with you if he didn't. I haven't yet learned who did the actual wet work, but if you ever ended up filing the Scarlett Gould complaint, Portofoy's name would be among those on the caption. But this isn't about him, it's about the woman Portofoy is fronting for. Once you show the lobbyist what is inside the envelope, he'll want to get it right into the hands of his boss. No scanning and e-mailing—he wouldn't want an electronic record—this will be a hand delivery. Either Portofoy will do it himself or he'll send a messenger."

"And you'll follow."

"I'll try."

"Why was she killed, Dick? Scarlett Gould. What had she done?"

"Nothing at all. I thought she was murdered out of rank jealousy by the son of a senator, but then I met the son and I realized he didn't care enough about his wife to raise that kind of passion. But if you need a senator's vote badly enough, and you need it right away, maybe you don't have time to wait for a crime to occur before you reap the rewards of covering it up. Sometimes you have to make your own luck."

"I'm not sure I follow."

"It's all a matter of evolution. Give him the envelope, I'll take care of the rest. And that, I expect, will be the end of our relationship, Alberto. It was a pleasure working with you. You exceeded my expectations."

"Maybe so," he said. "But I don't think that was so very difficult."

"Not really, no."

"I'm sorry it is ending. I would have liked to filet the sons of bitches who killed Ms. Gould."

"Who knows," I said. "If things go really south on me, you might get that chance."

You could say I lost Portofoy's trail, but that wouldn't be quite true. I never caught his trail to begin with. I had expected him to leave by the building's front door, to hightail it along the wide sidewalks to another high, shiny building in that high, shiny section of the city, or to one of the restaurants that fed the capital's insatiable desire for meat: Ruth's Chris, Charlie Palmer, Annie's, Claudia's, Bobby Van's. But even after Menendez stepped out of the building, gave me a nod from across the street, and made his way to the Metro, our boy Portofoy never showed.

But it didn't much matter. Within the stuffing of the padded envelope was a tracking device the size of a credit card, and it wasn't long after Menendez left that the envelope was on the move. I ordered another coffee and waited in the shop as Kief did the tracking. When he gave me the call, I caught a cab and took it south to the river.

Kief, in shorts and a T-shirt, was sitting on the hood of a car in a parking lot overlooking a crowded marina. I leaned beside him, sunglasses on, wearing a snug suit with no tie, and surveyed the scene. To the right was the Jefferson Memorial, on the far side of the inlet was a golf course, and before us a wide collection of pleasure craft. The Capital Yacht Club. Bully for them.

"Do you see that sweet yacht parked on the tee of the third dock down?" said Kief. "With the orange canvas stretched over the third level?"

"It's big, isn't it?"

"It's like the perfect crash pad. When you run chronically low you can just motor on down to Mexico and top off the tank."

"What's it called?"

"Darwin's Dream."

I laughed. "That would be the one. Anyone getting on or off?"

"Some fire hydrant with a briefcase just left. Fiftyish, walked like he was angry. Drove a Mercedes."

"Portofoy. Any idea of the boat's owner?"

"It's not a boat," said Kief. "It's a yacht. I took a saunter and copped the registration number. Riley ran it for me. It's based in Miami, so she went into the Florida website. We figured it would be that Jungle Dog outfit, but we copped a surprise. There was an individual owner. The boat—sorry, the yacht—is registered to one Yvonne Quarry."

"What do we have on her?"

"Nada much. Her profile is low. There's a daughter stashed at some school in Paris, there's a bit of charity stuff. She's known as a business shark, got started with a limousine company. She's not mentioned as a political player, but there are pictures of her with politicians, congressmen, a few senators."

"Our Senator Davenport?"

"At a fund-raiser in Newport. But generally she stays on the down low."

"She feels more comfortable with fronts."

"So, boss," said Kief, "who is she and why do we care?"

"She's the Principal," I said.

"Oh man, what the fuck?" said Kief. "Riley was right and I hate it when she's right. Don't you think it's stupid as shit to be busting in on the head boss uninvited?"

"I think I've been invited, Kief," I said. "I think from the moment she put Tom Preston on our asses she's been waiting for my visit."

"You're going to get us all fired."

"If that's all it is, we're lucky."

"Are you going to stand with us if things go bad?"

"Maybe I'll run with you," I said. "How about that?"

"As long as we stay together, man. When Tom Preston comes after me, I don't want to be standing alone with just a bong in my hand."

"At least you'll die relaxed."

"You're killing us here, Phil."

"Lately I've taken on a new tack: I'm trying to give everyone what they want. That's all I'm going to do with the Principal. Things work out, you might end up getting promoted. Now, while I'm in there, go back to the suite and tell everyone to do what we have to do so we can get this job finished. Riley and Gordon should finish up their work on our Detective Booth. And I want you on the trail of Melissa Davenport; I need to meet up with her and soon."

"You still want me to mess with the DNA results?"

"Forget about that. If push comes to shove, and my suspicions are right, we might need them just as they are. But let's get everything tied up that needs tying so we can get the hell out of this burg."

"Whatever you do, do me a favor and don't give her my regards."

I looked at the boat, sitting fat and arrogant at the end of the dock. *Darwin's Dream*. The question, I suppose, was whether I was fit enough.

"If you don't hear from me in a couple of hours," I said, before pushing myself off the car's front and heading to the yacht club, "drag the river."

27

THE PROPOSAL

If I thought I could slip onto the boat unobtrusively and surprise the Principal in her waterborne lair, the man in the crisp white blazer standing at the entrance of the Yacht Club dissuaded me of that notion immediately.

"Mr. Kubiak?"

"Guilty," I said.

"Could you come this way, please? We've been waiting for you."

"Not too long I hope."

"No, not too long," he said, blond and as officious as his blazer. "The docks can be slippery, so please watch your step."

I figured that was good advice as I followed him through the gate, down to the water, and then along one of the weathered cement walkways set between two rows of heavy-breasted boats. At the end of the pier, *Darwin's Dream* was lashed fore and aft to the abutment. He stepped down onto a low platform at the stern of the yacht and I stepped behind him.

I was led up a short flight of exterior stairs, across a deck, and up more stairs. I smelled her before I saw her, that vapor scent of jasmine and clove. Atop the second flight of stairs was a large covered deck with a table set for lunch, an L-shaped couch, and a bar. The Principal, in a red kimono tied tight, was sitting on the couch, inhaling from her vapor pen as she stared at a laptop on the cocktail table. A man in white shorts and a tight polo shirt kneeled on the deck beside her, rubbing one of her calves. On the table, beside the laptop, was the manila envelope with the photograph, the padding ripped open to show the tracking device.

"Mr. Kubiak has arrived," said the man in the blazer, before heading through a set of dark glass doors and disappearing into the boat's interior.

"Something to drink?" said the Principal without looking up from her screen. "Water, perhaps?"

"I liked that Scotch," I said.

"Of course you did. Two waters please, Jeremy," she said, waving her vapor pen in the general direction of the bar. "Sparkling. With lime." The man in the polo stopped his kneading and rose to make up the drinks. "The Scotch I save for invited guests, otherwise people would barge in like boors. There's a reason I try to remain difficult to find."

"Good job on that," I said. "It took me almost forty minutes."

She snapped closed her laptop, inhaled. The tip of her pen glowed as she looked up at me blandly with those sharp, pale eyes. Mist floated from her nose. "Did you think the photograph would please me?"

I sat down on the facing stretch of couch, leaned back, crossed my legs, pulled an imaginary piece of lint off my suit pants. "I assumed you had already seen it. But I also assumed Portofoy hadn't. I hope I didn't terrify the poor man. He looked quite put out as he left the boat. A tender soul, no doubt."

"He has his uses. All my employees have their uses or they don't remain employees."

"Tom Preston, too?"

"Yes, Tom Preston, too. Good employees are hard to find, but finding employees like Tom Preston is even harder. I was hoping you would be one of those. It can be quite disappointing when hope dies. Ah, thank you Jeremy. Now leave us be for a time. We won't be long."

After handing us our waters, Jeremy disappeared through the dark doors. She took a vape.

"How's that evolution going?" said the Principal.

"I'm working on it."

"Work faster."

"Tom Preston wants to take over your organization."

"He's ambitious. I prize ambition."

"He's a savage."

"I also prize a certain level of savagery. You should see Portofoy laying into a junior congressman who is bucking our position. He can be positively barbaric."

"Tom Preston is a little more savage than that. There you sit, sucking in scented vapors to avoid the dangers of tobacco when you have let into your organization something ever more deadly. There is no telling what Tom Preston is capable of in pursuing his goals."

"He is capable," said the Principal, "of everything. That is why he is such a valuable employee."

"He wants me to join him in a plot to kill you and Maambong."

"And you came to warn me, as if I'm not aware of everything that goes on in my houses, or my limousines, or even in the hotel rooms I rent for my employees. It is gratifying that you care so much about my welfare, but everything is very much under control."

"You can't control Tom Preston, you can only kill him."

"I'll do whatever must be done. What about you? Can you say the same? For example, have you done what must be done to conclude your task here?"

"Not quite yet, but three simple conversations will finish it off."

"Three conversations? That's all? Are you certain?"

"It's called working with tact and brains. I should wrap the whole thing up in a day or two. But let me ask you: How much is the firm getting paid for this operation of ours in Washington?"

"Is that what you came to learn?"

"I didn't come to learn anything, I came to propose."

"The details of the payments on this case are none of your business. But have no doubt you will be paid, and handsomely, when the task is completed."

"It's not my bank account I'm worried about. I think the firm is getting nothing, nada, zilch. I think my team is up here at premium rates just to clean up the mess left by someone else in the organization. I think instead of sending Tom Preston to spread chicken blood over a young girl's body in order to gain some power over me, you should be dealing with whoever made the mess in the first place."

"If you have a proposal, get on with it."

I took a sip of sparkling water and looked around calmly. The snap in her voice was encouraging. The sun was bright off the river, the golf course glowed in the light, a breeze stirred the water and slipped up and over the deck, caressing our cheeks.

"Gosh, this is beautiful, isn't it? What could be better, Yvonne? You don't mind if I call you Yvonne, do you? Ms. Quarry is so formal. And to call you the Principal, well, it makes me feel like I'm in grade school. So Yvonne it is. Do you know what could be better than this, Yvonne? More of this. More crew like the man in the crisp white jacket with his oh-so-officious manner or Jeremy in the tight polo shirt who is undoubtedly so adept at rubbing and pressing and soothing and telling you to turn around please; more stark white architectural monstrosities like Fisi to call home; more rare Japanese Scotches to guzzle. This is a nice boat, absolutely, a hundred-footer I'm guessing, some would even call it a yacht. But wouldn't more be better? Let's say a one-fifty-five, or even a two-twenty. Do you know the size of Larry Ellison's yacht? I do. Bigger."

"Get to your point, Mr. Kubiak."

"Call me Phil. In my time as a gold salesman, I found pitches worked so much better on a first-name basis. Let me put it straight out there, Yvonne, straight because you're a discerning woman and anything else you'd see right through. You want a boat that would make this look like a rubber ducky bobbing in the bathtub? Then put me behind the desk in Miami."

She stared at me for a moment before her cold eyes warmed and she broke into laughter. "You want Maambong's job?"

"That's your route to more, Yvonne. See, I won't make the same mistakes Maambong is making."

"And what mistakes are they?"

"I wouldn't have saddled you with a potential murder rap just to pocket a senator's vote, for one. It's a neat trick killing a girl and then convincing a senator that his son is the culprit and only you can cover it up, but at what price? And I wouldn't have saddled you with Tom Preston, for another. You told me I needed to evolve, but what I think, Yvonne, after looking at everything clearly, is that the Hyena Squad is the thing that needs evolution. You need to be nimble, smart, and most of all aggressive, but only in the right way. You need to step into a new realm, where homicide detectives aren't on your ass and you don't have to hide behind fat shades like Portofoy."

"Check your fly, Mr. Kubiak, your weakness is showing."

"All I'm showing is the reason I was hired in the first place. Murder is easy—bang bang, any idiot can do it—but then what? This whole town is about bribery, theft, prostitution, blackmail, crimes that are not only common as dirt here, but positively encouraged. If you can't blackmail a congressman, bribe a general, and get rich on a bogus government contract all while riding Jeremy there, then you're not trying hard enough. But as soon as you step over a certain line, everything you worked for is at risk, and you spend more and more of your time and resources keeping your head out of the noose. That's not a recipe for more, Yvonne, that's not even a recipe for less. That's a recipe for annihilation. And over that line is where Maambong has put you."

"And you can step the firm back?"

"I will."

"And still be effective?"

"Try me."

"Let's say I do try you, Mr. Kubiak. What do I do with Maambong? He won't take kindly to losing his position."

"Promote him," I said. "Send him to LA to concentrate on West Coast client development. We should be working for the studios. Talk about a bunch of thieving bastards who need our help. There's a fortune waiting out there and Maambong could mine it for you."

"And what do I do with Tom Preston?"

"Fire him."

"He won't take kindly to that."

"Here's a tip, Yvonne. Don't ever hire anyone you have to kill to get rid of. Put Maambong on it. They deserve each other."

"Even if I agreed with you about the direction of the firm, what makes you think you're the person for the job? What makes you think you can be as effective for me as Maambong has been?"

"Try me. Or fire me, either one. I won't stay around while you self-destruct. No one knows more about self-destruction than me. But I'm done with that. I've taken your advice and evolved."

"Three conversations?"

"That's all it will take."

"Do it and then I'll consider your proposal."

"Good. This has been quite pleasant." I put my empty glass on the cocktail table, slapped my leg, and stood. "I could get used to this. I believe we'll have many fruitful discussions on this boat, and the bigger one you'll buy in a few short years. It would be best if Tom Preston was taken care of as soon as possible. We won't have any use for him as we walk arm in arm into the future."

"You're afraid of him."

"We're brothers, he and I. I know what's in his heart because it's the same as what is in my heart. And so I can tell you with complete confidence, Yvonne, that if you're not afraid of Tom Preston, then you deserve everything he's going to do to you."

28

THREE CONVERSATIONS

Three conversations to kill the cold case Scarlett Gould investigation, stuff it full of horsehair like Ginsberg's meerkat, and mount it on a wall. Three conversations to prove that there was another way to play fixer in this fixed-up town. Three conversations to raise me to the top of the Hyena heap.

The first conversation was the easiest, a little give-and-take setup over a burner cell with Detective Booth. I identified myself as Dick Triplett and arranged a meeting so my associate could give the good detective a token of my appreciation for his help in spiriting me away from the Chadwick Club. The detective was agreeable, especially after I mentioned that the amount should cover the difficulties he had been having with his mortgage. He didn't like that I knew the status of his mortgage arrears, but he appreciated the amount. I tasked Gordon and Riley with handling the rendezvous at the naval yard. Gordon would carry the envelope; Riley would carry a camera with a long zoom lens.

"Why am I stuck making the handoff?" said Gordon. "Why am I hanging out there like a sacrificial lamb with an envelope full of money and a cop being bribed? You set it up, you finish it off."

"If things go south, you can just say you're a delivery man who didn't know what was in the envelope or who you were giving it to."

"Oh, the SWAT team bearing down on me with AKs bristling will buy that for sure."

"Since when was risk not part of this gig?"

"I accept risk, but I won't be doing the scut work for this team."

"He's right," said Riley. "That's why we have Kief."

"Riley, when you set up for the photograph, grab an angle where Gordon's face is hidden while the detective's bald head and mournful face are clear."

"I'll try."

"They'll have enough on me anyway," said Gordon. "They'll have more than enough. You need to treat me with more respect. Read your Coates, man. The black body is always being put at risk."

"That's what you think this is?"

"That's what it sure as hell looks like. I'm not taking a fall for anybody."

"It's not for anybody," I said. "It's for the rest of us."

That at least got a laugh out of Riley.

"Truth is, Gordon," I said, "you know so little about me you should be embarrassed. All I see in this world is me and everyone else. You're one of everyone else. And out of the everyone elses we have working for us, you're the best qualified to keep this from getting out of hand. Your size alone is enough to keep Booth from getting ideas about playing hero. Quit the squawking and get it done."

That he did.

The second conversation was with Melissa Davenport, Rufus's dissatisfied wife. I braced her in a Starbucks as she picked up her regular Grande Nonfat Latte Macchiato. I identified myself as Dick Triplett, that friend of Adele's she met at that party in that place. When she pretended to remember me and tried to blow me off at the same time, I mentioned Scarlett Gould and that got her attention. We settled at one of the small round tables with the tall chairs for a chat. I have found that a small round table at a Starbucks is the perfect place for a private conversation: no one ever listens in because nothing is rarer in the world than something of interest being said at a small round table at a Starbucks.

Melissa tried to avoid talking about Scarlett. Instead we talked about our families—I lied about mine—we talked about Adele—I lied about her, too—and then I showed her the contingency fee agreement signed by the Goulds and Alberto Menendez. When she asked how I knew she had any connection with Scarlett, I just looked at her. It took only a few seconds before the stern cast of her face collapsed into desolation.

"I still can't get over it," she said. "Scarlett was so sweet and strong and independent. She cared so much about the world and with one act of violence all that caring is gone. We met when our foundation was looking to contribute to her nonprofit. We talked about the animals and life and we just hit it off. We had coffee, we met for drinks, I felt sort of like a mentor. And with my advice her organization was picking up steam, and not just from our funding. She was in discussions to go international. Her organization was negotiating to join forces with a wildlife sanctuary to help save the endangered Visayan warty pig."

"The Visayan warty pig?"

"It's a cute little animal with striped sides and warts on its face. It lives on only two small islands in the Philippines, very endangered, and right up Scarlett's alley. It was all so exciting. She was just bursting with enthusiasm, bursting with life. And then . . ."

I asked the expected questions about whether she had any information about the murder itself and she said she didn't. And then I asked why she had contacted the police commissioner about the case, and why she had placed a series of calls to Detective Pickering's cell phone, and when I did that a line of fear crept into her expression, which was good.

"How would you know such things?" she said.

"Maybe you should have used a pay phone when you made the calls," I said.

"Who the hell are you?"

"Dick Triplett," I said. "I work for the lawyer who is representing the Goulds. And our clients have made it clear that they want the memory of their daughter to remain pristine. They don't want it soiled by publicity about a torrid sexual affair with an older married woman. They want you out of the picture, and out of pushing the investigation for your own purposes."

There was a flash of anger, something truly fierce in her eyes, and then it went out of her like a balloon deflating. "I didn't like that Scarlett just disappeared and nothing was being done," she said. "I wanted them to do more. I couldn't bear that she'd be forgotten. That's all it was."

"Maybe the time has come for forgetting. Maybe you should stay away from the police and spend more time with little Jason. Maybe volunteer at his preschool on Wisconsin Avenue. Maybe take him to the zoo on sunny afternoons instead of dumping him on the nanny. Heaven knows you would regret missing those special moments if something happened to the dear, sweet boy down the road."

That look, there, yes, that's the look you get when they see you torturing the hamster. That's the look you get when they finally realize exactly what you are. I used to hate that look, but not so much anymore. Now I find it a bracing bit of truth. But that day, when I got the look, I knew the job was done. Melissa Davenport would no longer be pushing the investigation, which meant that with the third and final conversation I could pretty much wrap up the case.

I had set it up with a text, and she was sitting at the bar when I arrived, a martini in front of her, double olive. Her blonde hair was newscaster glossy, her dress was black and short. Pearls. Bright-red lips and blue high heels. Yeah. It seemed like she had something on her mind.

"You look great," I said. "You meeting someone?"

"I wanted you to pine."

"I'm sweating Pine-Sol."

"Good. You hungry?"

"Yes, please."

"I made a reservation. Let's have a drink and then we'll Uber there."

"That sounds right."

She turned to the bartender. "Scotch, over ice, and make it something good. This is a man who knows the difference."

It wasn't much of a surprise, the way she was acting over drinks, that we ended up at Del Frisco's for dinner. Del Frisco's, of course, was the same steakhouse I had tried to take her to the last time we were together. That night, instead of the date I thought she would want, she got me drunk and screwed me and sent me packing. Now, at this silken high-toned restaurant, after she ordered the sea bass with spinach, and I ordered the twenty-two-ounce bone-in rib eye, with Chateau potatoes and a plate of asparagus with hollandaise, she asked for a bottle of champagne.

The bottle opened with a satisfying pop; the bubbles rose like laughter in our glasses. We clinked, we drank, the wine went down our throats like soft kisses.

"You might be wondering what this is all about," she said.

"I'm just enjoying seeing you happy."

"I'm not quite happy. I don't get happy. For me, Jefferson's pursuit is destined to end in failure, but I'm trying."

"Champagne always helps."

"Martinis, too. And sex."

"And money."

"I don't know about that," she said. "Are rich people really happy?"

"They're at least happy that we're not as rich as they are."

"True. But by the cut of your suit, you're doing okay."

"What does okay have to do with it? Since when does okay fit the bill? What do you want to be, little Johnny, when you grow up? I want to be okay."

"But from this end of the conversation, okay seems pretty damn sweet."

"So, Linda, what's this really all about? Champagne and steak? Are you breaking up with me?"

"I wanted to apologize."

"Why? Did you get sober behind my back?"

"I've been through a lot the last couple of years. The way the marriage fell apart, and the divorce, and the fight over our daughter. And then there's the job. It's a great job and I love it but it turns you cynical. Everyone's lying, everyone's guilty, even if not of the crime you're investigating. Life has jaundiced me. And then you appeared and picked me up in a bar and I thought I knew exactly what this was, which was all I thought I could handle. All I wanted to handle."

She traced a finger across the rim of her flute. Her finger was slender, her nail short, her polish natural. She was looking down at the table and so I could stare. She was quite pretty, not young but pretty with a sense of substance in her cheekbones, in the tight skin around her mouth, and an appealing sadness in her eyes. My wife had been bouncy and young and game for anything and I thought that was what I wanted. But just then, in that restaurant, I sensed that Linda Pickering, with her toughness and her sadness and the way she laughed through her pain, might be just the thing. We meshed in a way I didn't understand. And I did like looking at her.

"So when you came in with your flowers and your romantic plans," she said, "I wanted nothing to do with it. It was so sweet, sweeter than anyone's been to me in a long while, except I just wasn't able to deal with sweetness right then. It was easier to get drunk and screw and roll over to go to sleep than to actually try. It was easier to stay in a fog. But when you stormed out—"

"Did I storm? I thought it was like a drizzle."

"Maybe a squall."

"Heavy drizzle."

"But when you left in a heavy drizzle, carrying your hurt feelings with you, I began to think. You were sweet and I was a bitch and I just wanted to apologize, and not just for that night. I wanted to apologize for not treating you, or this, like it mattered. I don't know where it's going, maybe nowhere and that's fine, but it matters enough to take it seriously. At least a bit. So there it is."

"There it is."

"You want to run? I wouldn't blame you."

I didn't run just then. What I did was stand, walk around the table, and lean forward and kiss her. And she reached a hand up to my cheek. And I put my hand over hers. And I thought again that maybe she was just the right match for this thing that I was. That she was the one who could maybe save me from myself. But of course, there was no saving me from myself.

"Are we going dancing after this?" I said when I was back in my seat.

"God, I hope not."

I was famished from my day of conversations and so I smartly waited until we were finished eating to get down to business. The steak was marbled and fat and burnt like I like it, the potatoes creamy, the asparagus snappy as a lounge singer under its cape of butter and egg yolk and lemon. We kept up with the champagne, and the bubbles tickled the roof of my mouth as Linda Pickering twittered on about this and that in a voice as appealing as apple sauce. I gazed at her while she picked at her bass and felt a wave of happiness. It gave me hope, the whole evening, like even with my condition I could create something sustaining in my life. But not with her.

"I have something for you," I said, finally getting down to it after the waiter cleared the plates from our tabletop.

She looked at me and then looked down and her smile glowed in the light of the candle, like I had a gift for her, and I suppose I did.

"I told you I was a fixer of sorts," I continued, "and in the course of that work I came across something that I thought might interest you. I shouldn't be sharing, but because I care about you, I'm going to anyway."

She tilted her head in confusion as I took a thin envelope from my pocket, placed it on the table, and slid it to her. As she picked it up, her hands slightly shaking, I told her that inside the envelope were photographs of her partner, Detective Booth, taking a bribe. Also inside were financial documents that showed Detective Booth with high debts and an income that exceeded his salary.

"And why are you giving this to me?" she said, her voice taking on the rhythm of an old-fashioned typewriter being hunted and pecked.

"If this information got out, it wouldn't just impact your partner, it would impact your department, your division, and, most troublingly, you. It could even impact your custody fight."

"My custody fight? You're talking about my custody fight?"

"There's more that we found," I said. "Some of it quite ugly, involving an after-hours sex club in Georgetown for politicians and people of power. If Detective Booth's involvement with such a club was spread across the media, it could be the worst kind of scandal."

"I still don't understand what you're doing."

"I'm trying to protect you. Which is why it is important that you know that there are concerns about the way the Scarlett Gould investigation is progressing."

"Scarlett Gould? This is about Scarlett Gould?"

"Somehow the investigation is turning away from the obvious suspect into a direction that is overtly political, driven by a woman with an ulterior motive. That is a problem. Some would like the emphasis turned back where it belongs."

"Oh God," she said, trying to force out a laugh even as her face finished its collapse from happiness to wariness to misery. "Now I see. Sometimes I am such a fool."

"The pressure from Melissa Davenport will disappear; my associate has already taken care of that."

"You're a fixer, and I'm the one that needed fixing."

"And these photographs and documents will be fully buried, I promise you."

"Sometimes I want to just shoot myself in the face."

"But we think Bradley Beamon really should remain the prime focus of the investigation. I mean, who else threatened the victim in such an overt fashion? Who else had such a brutal motive? And really, with Bradley around, you wouldn't be able to convict anyone else anyway. They'd just point the finger and put the infamous woodpecker Facebook post on the screen before the jury and that would be that."

"You don't mind if I take more champagne for myself, do you, Phil?" Even as she asked this she turned over the bottle and poured gulps into her flute until the wine splashed over onto the table and then she swallowed what remained in the glass like water.

"But if the whole investigation just slows down and gets buried beneath the other files on your desk," I said, "that wouldn't concern us at all. And it would give you plenty of time with your daughter, which is preferable to what would happen if all of this got out."

"The thing was I liked you," she said. "That is what's so laughable."

"And I liked you, too, truly. But now I have to run, I'm sorry. You can keep those, they're just copies." I pulled out my wallet, took out a short stack of hundreds, and dropped them on the table. "This should cover the tab. Keep what's left over. I actually had a wonderful time. I'm going to miss you."

"What's amazing is that you did all this as breezily as if you were discussing the weather. I don't know if I've ever been so appalled and impressed at the same time. It is surely more impressive than your technique in bed. I suppose you're mixed up with that Dick Triplett fellow we've been hearing about. Is he as cold as you?"

"Colder," I said as I stood. "He wouldn't have cut short the evening like this. With those blue heels of yours, he would have fucked you first."

"It's nice to know," she said with eyes appealingly wet, "that chivalry isn't dead after all."

III. Samurai

29

IDYLL

When the magazine writer returned through the shack's back door, her hand was clasped over nose and mouth. The outlaw had warned her that Ginsberg's eggs had been known to cause ejectments of all kinds, and he hadn't been wrong. She was embarrassed enough to have run out like she did; her mortification was only made worse by the way the outlaw laughed as she sheepishly slunk back to her seat. His mockery was a fitting price for her self-righteous impulsivity. As if a single pickled egg could lend her the courage she so desperately sought.

"I'm sorry," the outlaw said after trying and failing to cut short his laughter, "but the disgust on your face is thick enough to carve. I should have warned you before you visited the outhouse. It's almost better to crap on a rock and wipe yourself on a cactus than to enter that vile little hut. Here, try this."

He pushed her Scotch glass toward her, a fresh cube of ice inside, and poured another dram. The noxious fumes still in her nose and mouth were burned away by the smoky brilliance of the whiskey. And yet, it wasn't only the lingering stink that was the cause of her distress. It was the man across from her, too.

"Nothing cuts the tang of Ginsberg's outhouse better than an epic Scotch," said the outlaw, "and this one is indeed epic, even in its name." He leaned forward and injected into his hushed voice all the false portent of a movie trailer:

"Samurai.

"It really is ridiculously priced," he continued, without the movie-trailer voice, "but what else can I spend my cash on. It's not like I can waltz into the Four Seasons and blow a wad on the Royal Suite, though the price of this bottle itself could keep me comfortably ensconced for a week or more, meals included. Assuming I don't order another bottle from room service.

"Samurai.

"Funny, even after a few desperate gulps, your expression remains just as jolting. Maybe I overassumed, maybe the disgust on your face is not from Ginsberg's outhouse but from my presence across from you. Oh, don't demur. I'd disgust myself, too, if I wasn't, you know . . . yeah.

"Samurai."

He laughed, but she didn't laugh with him, and his laughter after a moment choked in his throat. She looked down, embarrassed by the single searching eye. It was uncanny how he seemed to see right through her, as if he could grab with his fist the thoughts flickering like moths through her consciousness. He was either reading her or leading her, and she began to believe it was the latter, as if he had mapped every twist and turn of his story to pull the desired emotions. Just like a psychopath would.

"It's easy to judge, isn't it?" said the outlaw. "It's easy to look in my eye and let revulsion fill your soul. That slug oozing down the fence post, that cockroach crawling across your shoe, that psychopath sitting across from you, swilling priceless Scotch. Well, whatever disgust you feel, don't forget that you came to me. Did you ever wonder why of all the reporters who sent an interview request to my lawyer, you're the one I chose to tell my story to?

"Let's get to it, shall we? Your brother was blowing the whistle on an oil company poisoning half of Pennsylvania and someone blew off half his face before he could lay his facts in front of the United States Attorney. You want vengeance and you thought I was the Ronin who could exact it for you. You came to the monster to beg for his help, and the disappointment you felt when you first laid eyes on my sorry condition arose from the fear that the monster could no longer do what you wanted done. Am I far off?"

For the magazine writer to hear it spoken so simply, to have the facts laid out so clearly, filled her with something more than pain and hope. There was shame, too. The perfidy of this long-sought interview had been fully exposed as if to the desert sun, along with her uneasiness about him, and she didn't know what to say to make it better, to make the truth sound less squalid, so she said nothing.

"Don't worry, I don't want to hear from you—yet. Let your disgust marinate a bit. You'll have your chance to choose between journalism and vengeance. Just know that when you do, it will be one or the other. If you choose vengeance, then nothing I say to you will ever go beyond the walls of this shack, that's the deal. And trust me, you don't want to break a deal with someone like me. But I promised you the whole sorry story, and that's what you're going to get before you choose. So hold on, this is where it turns.

"When I returned to Miami after my sojourn in the nation's capital, I was feeling more than a little self-satisfied. I had gone to Washington with the goal of squashing a murder investigation and I had done just that, killing the investigation without being pushed into killing. I believed then that I was a brilliant enough henchman not to need such an untidy tool as murder. But even better, I had made my move and expected I would be rewarded, shortly, with a position presiding over the operations of the vast Hyena organization from that white house on the water in Miami."

***

"The accounts we have gotten on your progress are quite interesting," said Mr. Maambong from behind a new tempered-glass desktop. I couldn't help but rub a finger across the sharp edge of what would soon be my desk. "Are you sure this matter is completely taken care of?"

This was the very day after my dinner with Linda Pickering; once I had shown my true colors to her, I thought it prudent for all of us to get the hell out of Dodge. Upon arriving at the Miami house in my leisure wear, I went straight up to the office to render my report.

"It is taken care of," I said. "The woman who had been pushing to revive the investigation has been quieted, and the lead detective has been given every reason to slow her pursuit of an answer. Not to mention that you already have your claws into her partner."

"We do?"

"Don't kid a kidder, Mr. Maambong. You wouldn't even have needed us if Booth had been named lead and wasn't already under suspicion. Pickering was the key and I took care of her."

"If things are as you say they are, Mr. Kubiak, this then is excellent news," said Mr. Maambong. "You should be proud of your accomplishment. Excepting the horrid abuse of the minibar, for which you will be docked, everything seems to have gone swimmingly. Take a few days off, go on vacation. You've earned it."

"When do I get paid?"

"When we are sure of your success. We have kept Tom Preston in place to monitor things."

"That's disappointing. He's a fiend who will only muck things up."

"He is our fiend and the Principal insisted. The Principal is observing the situation with a rare intensity, as if fates hang in the balance. Let us give you some advice, Mr. Kubiak. It doesn't pay to disappoint the Principal, or to barge in on her uninvited and use her first name. She has earned a certain formality."

The beetle eyes of his dark glasses stared. I had gotten to the point where I could read the lenses as one would read the eyes of a naïf. He was projecting steel, our Mr. Maambong, and an intimate knowledge of everything that had happened on the Principal's boat, but there was also worry.

"You're going to like the West Coast," I said.

"We could get used to it, yes, the Hollywood parties, the California vineyards. There is a house high in the hills that is owned by the organization."

"All white walls and glass, I suppose, with an infinity pool overlooking the city."

"It almost sounds like you've been there. If that is where we are sent, we will make the best of it. It might be a challenge to find a good *ropa vieja* out there, but it can be difficult to find an authentic sour *pinangat* down here, so it balances out."

"You're taking this well."

"Do you think you are the first associate to want this seat, Mr. Kubiak? You are not even the first this week. We would not have hired you if you had not the ambition to climb. But wanting and getting are two very different things. We are willing to serve wherever the Principal believes it most efficient for us to serve. We trust you, too, will continue to carry out your assignments, whatever they might be. Especially considering the disturbing photographs we have now on file."

"Chicken blood, as you well know," I said.

"You mentioned chicken blood to the Principal, too. She had no idea of what you were talking about. It is charming the fictions we tell ourselves to make it through the day. And, pray tell, how is sweet Mandy holding up? Have you kept in touch with the dear girl? No? We thought not. But you can trust that we will not let Tom Preston muck things up, as you say. Your success in Washington would be a benefit to us all."

"Especially to you, let's not forget that."

"Whatever could you mean?"

"I had wondered which of your operatives had taken care of poor Scarlett Gould, but I don't wonder anymore. Tell me, Mr. Maambong, when did you become so concerned about the fate of the rare and endangered Visayan warty pig?"

Mr. Maambong laughed, it was a hearty laugh, big and forced, and gratifyingly threatening, the kind of laugh you put on when somebody just stomped on your foot and you don't want the pain to show.

"Take your vacation, Mr. Kubiak. Go someplace restful as we contemplate your future."

I stood on the stairwell outside his office and looked down at the pool. My team was lounging; other operatives were swimming and drinking. Bert was standing stiffly behind the bar. Cassandra was lying on a chaise facedown, her top untied, her perfect pale body staying just as perfectly pale under the pressure of the sun. Beyond was the inlet and the palm trees and the beach and the . . . yeah, yeah, I know, enough with the travelogue already. This was everything I had ever wanted just a few months before and now the scene was tinted with nostalgia, like the boiler room in Carson City before it, or the law firm in Sacramento, or my marriage bed. I had made my move and was ready to ascend, but there was something in Mr. Maambong's manner that put doubt in my mind. Just then, standing there on that stairwell, I sensed that this paradise would join the others that had been lost to me. But this time the loss didn't choke my throat. One benefit of learning the precise nature of my character was knowing I'd always find another spot to ply my deficits.

I climbed down the stairs and headed straight for Cassandra. I sat on the edge of her chaise, gently laid my hand in the sweet hollow formed by her scapulae, and started kneading. She didn't open her eyes as her mouth curled like a contented cat.

"Mr. Maambong told me to take a vacation," I said.

"Weren't you just in Cabo?"

"He wants me out of his hair for a while. Did he ever send my predecessor Rand on vacation?"

"He went off to Belize one day and was never heard from again."

"Must have been the crocodiles."

"Where are you going?"

"Not Belize, that's for sure. I thought Jamaica. Negril maybe. Red Stripe and reggae and seven miles of beach."

"Sounds dreamy."

"Come with me."

"I can't. I have things."

I looked up. Mr. Maambong was at his office window, his dark glasses staring down. "With the way things have been going, my guess is Mr. Maambong will want to keep track of me for a bit."

"Have you been a bad boy, Phil?"

"I can't help it. It's in my character. Why don't you volunteer to spy on me while we're getting stoned and staring at the sunset?"

"That sounds tempting."

"I'll make the reservations," I said.

There's a road in Negril that leads up to a cliff, and after nightfall you are climbing only by the light of the moon and stars until, in the distance, you see a dim glow and hear a soft driving beat from what turns out to be a candlelit shack serving jerk and Red Stripe. You sit at a brightly painted table and drink your beer and eat your dark, spicy chicken and fried plantains and talk over the music and then you move on through the darkness to the next shack, where you buy another beer and a joint already rolled and smoke with the proprietor and listen to the music until you're ready to climb some more. And at end of the road is a bar on the edge of the cliff with a band and a dance floor and you stay there dancing and drinking until the western sky turns a marvelous reddish gray and you stumble down the path past the now-shuttered shacks, back to your thatched hut, where you collapse in each other's arms until the sun is high and while still half-asleep you find yourself screwing to the rhythms of a steel drum playing from the beach.

Cassandra was a perfect companion for Jamaica. On rented mopeds we sped along narrow roads with shoulders overrun by greenery so lush it seemed not of this earth. With our scuba tanks we haunted reefs and waited for moray eels to dart from their holes and snap their teeth at us. On the white-sand beach, beneath our layers of lotion and mirrored glasses, with a bottle of beer on each of our bellies, we lay like slugs shriveling in the marvelous heat. In late afternoons we screwed and laughed and the sight of her red hair, her pale skin, the way her lips curled into a sly smile, all of it made me want to screw her some more. And yet, in the oddest moments, I caught myself thinking about Linda Pickering. Maybe that was just part of my affliction, the way no matter who I was with or how wonderful the moment I couldn't help but think of another. But there was something about Linda's strength, her shielded vulnerability, the effort she put out even as she expected only doom, her rueful laugh, all of it, that had sunk into my flesh like a barb.

"Are you okay?" said Cassandra.

"I'm great. Just great."

"You ready to go back."

"No."

It was the meat of the afternoon. We were naked inside our hut; the buzz of a fly circling the thatched roof matched the buzz in our heads as the scent of reefer floated around us like a sweet memory.

"Then we should stay," she said, rolling over until her chest was atop mine, and her lips inches from my lips. She kissed me and her tongue did tricks in my mouth, but somehow I was tasting Linda Pickering's olive breath after one too many martinis. "We should go on strike and hold out here until all our demands are met."

"And what are our demands?"

"A better espresso machine."

"And you know that golf course we pass on the way to the house," I said. "What is it, La Gorge or something? Let's become members."

"I didn't know you played golf."

"I don't, but I'd get a blazer with that shield on the breast and I'd stride through the place like Vlad the Impaler, fucking the wives and pissing on the greens. Or is it the other way around."

"What about a masseuse? Shouldn't there be a masseuse at the house?"

"Svea or Sven?"

"Sven, absolutely," she said. "With hands strong enough to strangle a horse."

"Doesn't sound very gentle."

"No it does not. He'll twist me like a Twizzler."

"Is that what you want?"

"From Sven."

"What do you want from me?"

"Nothing. That's why we get along so well. Neither of us wants anything from the other except what we can take." As she said this she took hold of my prick.

"Oh, Sven," I said, "you dirty boy."

Then she squeezed.

"Ow. Fuck." I tried to pull her hand away but she tightened her grip. "What the—"

"You're screwing up," she said, before letting go and rolling off me. We were lying now at an acute angle, our heads just touching. "If you're not careful, you're going to end up in Belize with Rand."

"You've been talking to Mr. Maambong."

"He wants us home. He has a new job for you, and a message."

"I don't know if I want either."

"It doesn't matter what you want, don't you understand that yet, Phil? You take your orders and do your jobs and do them the way they want and then you get to keep playing with me. It seems like a pretty fair trade, doesn't it?"

"What's the job?"

"The old woman in Philadelphia wants to see you again. You and she seemed to have hit it off."

"She likes it hard and fast from behind."

"Of course she does."

"And she's hoping I'll give it to her."

"Then do it. Bend her over the wheelchair and go full Sven on her bony ass. Do whatever she wants and then do it again."

"You sound worried, Cassandra. I'm surprised you have it in you. You must miss poor Rand?"

"Not as much as I'd miss you."

"But how much would you miss me, really?"

"I wouldn't weep, if that's what you're asking."

"Good girl. That's one thing we don't do. What's the message?"

"He told me to tell you that someone name Bradley Beamon just confessed to a murder on Facebook and then shot himself in the face."

Do you see him, do you see him there? In that moment he loomed over our two naked bodies like a ghost. And I knew, with all my certainties, that someday, somewhere, Tom Preston and I would finally have another moment together, and this time it would end in blood.

30

Brotherly Love

"You let us down in Washington, Mr. Kubiak," said Mr. Maambong in his office. He leaned back in his chair, his fingers thrummed the tempered desktop, the lenses of his glasses stared with a dark merriment.

"I had it under control."

"You may have thought so, but your lady detective was continuing on despite your maneuvers and threats. She strode into the offices of Senator Davenport with a badge and a series of embarrassing questions."

"Good for her. She was making a point."

"To whom?"

"To me. She knew enough to ruffle the right feathers so I would hear of it. But it would have ended there. She had nothing else to go on, no one to push her, and the costs of her continuing out on that limb were too high, I made sure of that. Her investigation would have died a quiet death."

"We couldn't take the chance. The senator was distressed and that distress was relayed with ringing clarity to Mr. Portofoy. Something needed to be done and so it was. The investigation is now quite neatly sealed in the way it should have been sealed from the first."

"Except everyone involved in the investigation knew that boy was innocent. So instead of a cold case going nowhere, your Tom Preston stirred the hornet's nest. It's a serial killing now—first Scarlett Gould, then Bradley Beamon—and my name is in the middle of it."

"We have every confidence you'll weather the storm."

"It's easy to have confidence when it is someone else's neck in the noose."

"This is so true, Mr. Kubiak, and it gives us great comfort. As you now no doubt realize, we won't be heading to the West Coast. Our place behind the desk remains secure. It was a nice try, and we all respect the effort, but it won't happen again. Once is expected; twice is bad form. And you should know that with our pronounced growth, we are still in need of another partner. The position would be quite lucrative in so many ways. Even with the glitch in Washington, the Principal was impressed with your efforts. She's decided to give you another chance, maybe a final chance at this opportunity. The organization is deciding between you and Mr. Preston."

"He'll ruin you."

"There are concerns about his temperament, but the man does get things done. Can you get things done, Mr. Kubiak?"

"You're sending me back to Philadelphia."

"Mrs. Wister has another task. She asked for you specifically."

"And if I succeed?"

"Congratulations."

"You know, it's me or him. We can't work together."

"There is only one partnership position available and we understand that it might be prickly for the person who doesn't achieve it to remain with the organization. What to do about that will be decided once you have satisfied the dear Mrs. Wister."

"Good," I said. "I just hope the son of a bitch enjoys Belize."

The mirth in Mr. Maambong's laugh lodged like an unchewed piece of meat in my throat.

***

I flew up alone to Philadelphia. The driver was waiting for me at baggage claim even though I had no baggage. He took me directly to the Wister estate. The long drive leading to the mansion was dense with shadows from the sycamores. The cadaverous butler met me at the door and informed me that Mrs. Wister was waiting in the drawing room.

As I followed the walking corpse through the high-ceilinged center hall, the lines of Wisters on the wall stared down at me with encouraging expressions on their paint-daubed faces. At my first visit they had arrogantly welcomed me into their heartless little club. Then they had ignored me, their eyes searching for more interesting specimens to follow, like the overfed rodent running like an escaped convict along the painted baseboards. But now they peered down with parental pride. *Look at our child all grown up, look at the man he has become.* In their presence I became a thirteen-year-old Jewish boy.

"It is so good to see you again, Mr. Kubiak," said the old lady when I finally stood before her. She was situated in her wheelchair, a blanket over her withered legs. Her lips, accordioned by age and painted a bright red, twitched into a suggestive smile. The butler stood behind her.

"Sit down, please," she said.

"I'll stand."

"As you wish. I wasn't happy with how our last meeting ended. I felt I came off ungrateful."

"A tad."

"It is a crime, I think, to be ungrateful for all God's gifts, and the way you saved my grandson's life was surely one. So I asked you here to apologize. I am sorry. And I thought it might cheer you to meet the darling boy."

"That's not necessary, Mrs. Wister. I hold no grudges and I need no cheering. It was all business."

"Nonsense. This wasn't business to us, it was much more . . . personal." She lifted her chin and called out, "Oh, Edwin. Could you come in please for a moment?"

On cue a side door opened and a boy in a blazer stepped confidently into the room. He was about twelve, blond and whippet thin, with hollow eyes and a forehead that bulged out grotesquely. I remembered him from the photo she had shown me on a previous visit. When he smiled, it was the smile of a starving albino ape.

"Edwin," said the old lady, "this is Mr. Kubiak. He wanted to meet you. He has been very helpful with your treatments. I brought him here so you could thank him."

"Thank you, Mr. Kubiak."

"You're welcome, Edwin," I said.

"I have a duty that won't wait," said the old lady. "I'll be back in a moment. Why don't you two get acquainted while I'm away."

She snapped her fingers and the butler immediately started wheeling her. The boy and I watched as her chair slowly crossed and then exited the room, the door closing behind her. I looked at the boy, he looked at me.

"I'm supposed to charm you," said Edwin.

"You probably weren't supposed to say that."

"Wasn't it a charming thing to say?"

"It was, actually."

"My grandmother said you helped me get my new kidney. Was it yours?"

"No."

"Whose was it?"

"How is school, Edwin? I hear you're on the water polo team."

"I hate water polo. When they're not looking I spit in the water bottles. You don't want to tell me whose kidney it was?"

"The kidney was from someone who was happy to help."

"Will he want it back?"

"No."

260

"Good. He can't have it. I like it. I like not having yellow skin. I like not having to be hooked up to that machine."

"What do you want to be when you grow up, Edwin?"

"I want to be a baseball player but I'm not very good. I'm not even good enough to play at school. Which is why I'm on the water polo team. We are required to do some sort of athletics."

"So if not baseball, then what?"

"My grandmother wants me to be president."

"That's something to strive for."

"It is not as much fun as being a baseball player."

"No."

"But at least you can order people to drop bombs when you get angry."

"There is that."

"Maybe I could bomb my prep school."

"That a boy," I said.

"What did you want to be when you grew up?"

"Rich."

"Are you?"

"I'm getting there."

"I already am there. Or I will be when my daddy dies. He has cancer. He stays outside and paints and hopes it will go away. I don't think it will. When he dies, I think I'll use my money and buy a bank. I'm already rich but it would be fun to be richer. Then I could really tell everyone else to suck it."

"By giving lollipops to all the little children, I suppose."

"Why would I do that?"

After Edwin shook my hand with great seriousness and then excused himself, I was left alone in the drawing room. I walked around, looking at the vases, at the old leather-bound books with their uncut pages, at the gilded furniture and paintings of horses on the walls. On the leather-topped desk was an ornate silver desk set, ink pot, blotter, and letter opener. The letter opener was a dagger with the figure of a young bare-breasted woman cast into the handle. I hefted it in my hand, it was heavier then it looked. I placed it in my breast pocket in case I needed to fight my way out of that house of zombies. Through the window I saw the man in the straw-hat painting. Poor cancerous sot, caught between his mother's murderous ambitions and his son's hollow eyes.

"What did you think of my grandson?" said Mrs. Wister after she was wheeled back into the room. The butler had creaked when he bowed before leaving us alone.

"Adorable," I said.

"He is quite special. His mother died young and his father dabbles, so much of his upbringing was left to me."

"You've done quite a job on him."

"Thank you. His future is unlimited."

"I got that sense."

"I wanted you to meet him. I wanted you to know just how special he is so you could feel good about what you had done."

"I feel terrific."

"I'm gratified, Mr. Kubiak. Because I've been thinking of what you said about how someday our donor would learn she only had one kidney. I was upset about the money at the time we talked, but later, I found myself dwelling on the inevitable moment when she discovers what has been done to her. And how easy it would be to trace her condition back to Edwin and threaten the legacy of our entire family. I find myself now to be haunted by this inevitability. The thought of it rises in me like a great wave of concern, ruining my sleep. I wasn't born a Wister, my husband married beneath him. I was a twice-married waitress when he met me, from a common family."

"My family was uncommonly common, too," I said.

"So you understand. But I would do things to Mr. Wister the precious debutantes who swarmed about him dared not dream of. Things that cut so deep he couldn't resist me. It was a scandal when we married, and my son was shunned by polite society. But know this, Mr. Kubiak, time gentrifies. Now I am an arbiter of polite society, imagine that, and the protector of all that the Wisters were and can become again. With my son's illness, that hope now resides within Edwin. And I won't have it jeopardized. I won't sleep easy until the threat is taken care of. Do you understand what I am getting at or must I be grossly specific?"

"No," I said. "I see it quite clearly."

"I knew you would. I talked to your Mr. Maambong. I told him money was no object and that got his attention. He suggested another of his employees, a Mr. Preston, take over the job, but I specifically asked for you, Mr. Kubiak. I didn't want to expose my family to another operative. And you best understand the situation, you already know the woman, and, if I may be so bold, you have almost as much to lose as we do if the truth gets out."

"You can count on me, Mrs. Wister."

"That is good to hear. The sooner this thing is done, the better. Every day has become torture with this expectation of discovery hanging like a sword over our heads. When do you think you could alleviate the threat?"

"Give me a week," I said.

"And there will be nothing left leading back to Edwin?"

"That goes without saying."

"Still, it's better to be said, don't you think?"

"I'll take care of everything."

"Splendid. And once it is taken care of, there will be a bonus for you over and above what I negotiated with Mr. Maambong. I am willing to pay for loyalty."

"Nothing breeds loyalty like a healthy bonus."

"I knew we would come to an understanding. Now that business is taken care of, would you like some tea, Mr. Kubiak? I could have some brought in. And cake. How about some cake? I always say in happy times all of us should eat a little cake."

31

ROOM 242

Picture a motel room with a sagging bed, an old television with a greenish tint, walls covered in fake wood, the bedspread and curtain a matching pattern of vomited-up color to hide whatever stains were left by previous residents. A stray splatter on the bathroom floor, crusty streaks on the walls, a carpet moist to the touch: room 242 of the lovely GrandView Motel in New Orleans, well west of the French Quarter, the grand view being of the beauteous Tulane Avenue, with its whores and passing trucks and whores giving road head in the passing trucks. There are cigarette butts in the ashtray—some of them mine—and crap floating in the john that barely flushes—some of it mine—and syringes in the drawer—none of them mine, although the night is still young. It is dark out, and thumping rhythms pour out of passing cars, and there is a hubbub about the motel as hustler and whore start going about their businesses.

Picture me naked and sweating in that room, with a spotted water glass, a bottle of Old Overholt, and a bucket of ice from the machine. I am holding the glass and bottle both, and ignoring the television that blathers on as I go through the karate moves I once learned in college after a drunken brawl at a frat house broke my jaw.

Stomp, wave, "Hah!"

Wave, stomp, "Hah!"

Why am I going full *Apocalypse Now*? Because it feels like the thing to do. Every now and then the light in my room and the drone from the television draw a neighborly knock on the door. "What you doing in there alone?"

Stomp, wave, wave, "Hah!"

"Listen up, I got just what you need."

Wave, stomp, stomp, wave, "Hah!"

"Open up the door, man, and let's party."

"Hah!"

"Hah!"

"Hah!"

I spill the rye on the carpet as I punch and kick and battle my singular demon, who stands before me with blood pouring down his face and dripping onto his hands, the ghost of Jesse Duchamp.

"Why do you want to know about Jesse?" said my mother in the visiting room of the Louisiana Correctional Institute for Women in lovely Saint Gabriel, Louisiana. Saint Gabriel, the patron saint of postal workers, was the archangel who told Mary that she would conceive a son born of the Holy Spirit. The irony would have been lost on my mother. After my meeting with Mrs. Wister, I flew right back to Miami, but upon Ubering home, instead of driving the gray Porsche to the Hyena house, I packed a bag, turned off my phone, and headed straight north and then west, pushing the car through the night so I'd make the morning visitation with my mother. It was time to get some perspective on the man whose fate was so entangled with my own.

"I've just been thinking about him, Mom," I said. "I seem linked to Jesse Duchamp somehow."

"Don't be silly. You're nothing like him. He was so romantic. His long hair, the way the cigarette bobbed in his mouth when he sang to the car radio."

"The way he killed those convenience-store clerks."

"A man is more than the worst moments in his life. Jesse only wanted what all of us want."

"And what was that, Mom?"

"Love."

"He wanted love."

"Oh yes he did. He craved it, that man. Needed it like a drug, because of his problem. That was what held us together in the dark times. He knew I loved him and I knew he needed my love. Your father may have loved me, Phil, but he never needed anything other than a bottle. There wasn't much I could give in this world, but Jesse needed them both."

"You said he had a problem."

"I don't want to speak about that. Did you get the job you were talking about last time you were here?"

"I did."

"And it pays all right."

"Yes, it pays all right."

"That's good, son, because I need some money for my account. I can't keep begging off Lana. And you never got that two thousand dollars to the man in Winn Parish like you promised."

"I never promised."

"Louis Boudin."

"Like the sausage."

"You not paying that debt cost me some additional time in this rat hole."

"How so?"

"Well, when the Boudin girl came at me I had to do something. I couldn't just let her slice me like a Sunday ham."

"I suppose you couldn't."

"There was blood on the floor. And some teeth, too, little Chiclet teeth, that's what she had. The meal trays here are sturdy, that's for sure. The men stamp them out up there in Cottonport."

"Didn't you tell the guards it was self-defense?"

"I did, in no uncertain terms, but somehow they don't believe anything we say. You'd be surprised, but they treat us in here like we are common criminals."

"What was Jesse Duchamp's problem, Mom?"

"Oh, Phil, why do you even care?"

"I just do."

"It was sad, the way he was. It was why he drank and whored and thieved, and why he could be so brutal to me at times. He did anything he could to get right up close to it, to try to feel its power, but it wasn't any good. He could never get close enough."

"Close to what?"

"To love. That was his flaw. He couldn't love. He just couldn't. And he wanted to, more than anything. That's why he needed to be loved so much, why he chased any skirt that would lift for him. Being loved was the closest he could come to loving. But there was something in him that was wrong. Something in him that killed the emotions. And it killed him, too."

"You killed him, Mom."

"He begged me to. He had been out whoring, that motel you only had to step outside your door to find them hanging around the parking lot like a herd of cats, and when he came back he was so angry at himself, and hurt, that he up and let me have it. And then he fell at my feet and hugged my knees and said he wanted to be sorry but he couldn't be sorry enough, he just couldn't, and while his tears washed my bare legs he begged me to kill him, begged me to put him out of his misery. Then he stood and gave me the gun and hit me again right across the face. Oh, Phil, what's the use of talking about it? I did him a kindness and I ended up in here."

"He just wanted to love?"

"Can you imagine such a thing? It was all he ever wanted. Money didn't matter to him, he just needed enough to keep looking for what he never found."

"But he found you."

"And I loved him, Phil. And he knew it. That's why he asked. And when I loved him most of all, that's when I killed him."

"It's funny how that works," I said.

After visiting my mother I drove down to the GrandView Motel, paid my fifty-three bucks, and was both thrilled and horrified that room 242 was available, the very room in which my mother pierced with love the head of Jesse Duchamp. The Duchamp blood had long ago been mopped up and painted over, but I could see the geography of the event as if a white outline of the corpse was painted on the rug. My mother stood here. Jesse Duchamp stood there. The bullet entered here. The blood spattered there. The body collapsed there. The blood pooled there. Exhausted from my bad karate, I took a swig of the Old Overholt and let myself fall where his body had fallen. The light of a passing truck washed across the ceiling. The carpet was wet as tears on my back.

I had gotten it wrong, all of it. I had thought Jesse Duchamp was a cautionary tale, and he was, truly, but the caution I had gotten was all wrong. His problem was not that he expressed in the real world the eternal darkness within and suffered the consequences, it was merely that he wanted the wrong damn thing. He had watched the treacly TV movies, read the greeting cards, let the cigarette bob in his lips as he sang along to the sappy love songs on the car radio. He had been fed the story that love was the highest and brightest of human emotions and he had swallowed it all, like a fool. Of course it had killed him; downing that much crap would have killed an elephant.

I tilted the bottle of Old Overholt and poured a gush into my mouth.

How much easier would his life have been if he had wanted only money? He might not have been so reckless with other men's wives. He might not have been so cavalier about shooting off that gun of his and going on the lam. He might have found a way to stuff his wallet without being killed in the process. I could imagine Jesse Duchamp in some New Orleans manse, sucking down French champagne and screwing lithe beauties. I could imagine him buying politicians so that he could soak the government and get ever richer. Why, I could imagine him in Congress himself. That was the ticket: Jesse Duchamp, man of the people. And it's not like they hadn't been hawking the splendor of money as ruthlessly as they hawked the magnificence of love.

His mistake was so damn simple it was a joke. So why wasn't I laughing?

I tried to imagine what it was like to be so desperate to feel some sort of love that I'd rather die than continue numb. I tried and failed; of course I failed. Yet I could admire the nobility in Jesse Duchamp's effort, a foolish nobility, yes, but maybe the only nobility available to our kind. Was there anything I wanted as much in this world?

I poured another bolt of my father's rye into my mouth. I swallowed some and coughed out the rest. It ran down my cheeks like tears.

I fell asleep on the floor, dead naked, arms and legs akimbo. I was exhausted from the drive, from the visit with my mother, my bizarre calisthenics, the drugging effects of the whiskey. I fell asleep but my mind whirred and my dreams were brutally vivid. I don't remember them all, one bled into the next before fading into the mists, leaving only the vaguest impressions, but when I woke with a start and a screaming bladder, the dream I was in the middle of at that moment somehow stayed with me. It has stayed with me still. And in its adhesion, I discovered something.

We were talking of evolution.

After my diagnosis I knew with an utter certainty that my inner core would always remain as it was, stunted, deformed, a heartless, soulless abomination. How could such an abomination ever evolve? Lying on the sodden carpet, still overcome by the dream, I realized I had received an answer from the most unlikely of sources: Jesse Duchamp.

And someone was going to pay the price.

I rolled onto my side, pushed myself somehow to standing, staggered into the bathroom, and loosed a hydrant into the brown, reeking toilet bowl. As I scratched at the bites on my neck I remembered the moment in Caroline Brooks's office after I'd smashed her bonsai tree against the wall.

Caroline had leaped to her feet, with dirt now sprinkled on hair and shoulder, but her voice remained calm and her face betrayed her pity. "You're doing it again, Phil, don't you see? Using violence to force an ending. Like with your law firm, and your wife. But our work here doesn't have to end. And you don't have to fall into the same tired patterns. You're better than this."

My fists were balled in anger, tensed so tightly I was shaking. "But you've just told me I'm not. And I never will be. The question now is how the hell do I live with myself?" The query had been rhetorical, I didn't want an answer, especially not from her, but she gave me one anyway.

"You just do," she said.

Slowly she turned away from me, stooped down, and gently took hold of the bonsai now sprawled on the floor. There was something brave in the motion, turning her back to me as I stood there with fury surging through my veins, brave enough to bleed my anger. "There's a shallow ceramic pot in the closet," she said, "along with some Akadama, gravel, and potting compost."

"Akadama?"

"A sort of Japanese clay. You have to repot the plants every couple of years or so to keep the roots strong, and this one was overdue."

She twisted her neck to look at me, her smile surprisingly warm. "Come on."

I had never before tried to repair something damaged in one of my fits of anger. Normally I just stormed out and bore the consequences— a broken jaw, a destroyed marriage, a lost career. But Caroline's calm smile was like a challenge. There was no bullshit discussion of my feelings or thoughts, we just worked. She cradled the damaged plant as she shook the roots free of any clinging soil. I mixed the clay and gravel and compost. She trimmed the roots with a small pair of shears until they lost the appearance of a ghastly dead spider and looked instead sturdy enough to support a life. While she held the little tree in a jade-colored piece of pottery, I spooned the soil mixture into place, tapping it here and there so that it made its way between the roots. In the end the tiny tree rested securely in a new pot, green and shiny. The tree was not all it had been—a main branch had snapped, many of the little green needles had fallen off—but it was still standing, a thing saved.

The morning after my dream I checked out of the GrandView Motel, scratching like a mangy dog at my side and shoulders, took all my available money out of the Chase bank branch on Metairie Road, and headed west on Interstate 10 to visit my mother in prison for the very last time.

32

MAKING SAUSAGE

I drowned my cell phone in the slow, black waters of the Saline Bayou, just outside Saint Maurice, Louisiana, in Winn Parish. Saint Maurice was west and north of New Orleans, and I thought killing the phone there might lead them in a different direction when they tracked the signal and started coming after me. But before I tossed it, standing on the banks of the river, I made one final call.

"Phil?"

"Can you talk?" I said.

"Hold on a sec and I'll go to the other room. Where are you? You were supposed to be back yesterday."

"I had a change in plans. Who is she?"

"Just someone."

"Do you care about her?"

"Yes, no, I don't know. What the hell, Phil?"

"Remember that beach in Bali you were talking about. What was it, Cootie or something?"

"Kuta. Kuta Beach."

"Well, now might be a good time to see it."

"I thought we had ourselves a job in Philadelphia."

"Maybe you could take your friend in the other room. And before you go, close out your bank account. I've already closed out mine."

"Phil?"

"Do me a favor and tell Gordon and Kief the same thing. Quietly, if you get me. The longer Mr. Maambong doesn't know anything's going on the easier it will be for the rest of you to get out of harm's way. Things are about to get messy, and you won't want to be in the middle."

"What happened?"

"I got a new pot."

"Hell, it must be killer stuff. Bring it back to Miami and Kief will bong it up."

"No, not that kind of pot, sorry. You know all those qualms you've been having about what we do? I don't have them, I never did, not like you. But I don't like being pushed to play someone else's game. If I'm going to become what they want me to become, it's going to be because of what I want, not what they want."

"And what you do you want, Phil?"

"I want to see all the assholes burn."

She laughed, but when I didn't laugh with her, she stopped. "You're serious."

"I'm heading west. I'm going to set up operations in the middle of the desert, well away from Maambong and the Principal."

"You want me to join you?"

"No. I want you just to get the hell out of there. I've got to go."

"Thanks for the warning."

"Don't thank me, Riley. The sad truth is, I don't care about you and I never did."

"I don't believe it."

"We all love our fairy tales."

273

"Maybe, but you told me when I decided to run that I shouldn't tell a soul, that I should just disappear. And yet here you are, Phil, warning me. What does that say about you?"

"Enjoy the beach," I said before killing the call and tossing the phone.

My car was parked behind me on a rutted dirt drive just north of a bridge. I left the car where it was and walked away from the main road, toward a mobile home about fifty yards away. The scrub had been cleared between the front door and the river. A blue wooden boat sat on an unhitched trailer. A faded red barn listed farther down the road.

I went up to the front door and knocked. When I heard nothing I knocked again. I was looking at the dark waters of the river when the door opened.

"Kay couyon tu?"

I turned around. The man was squat and bald and fat and ugly. His overalls were filthy, his face was a desiccated orange, his mouth collapsed around a sorry collection of ten or so scattered teeth. He kept on speaking some weird French mixture as he climbed down the wooden steps leading from the door, and it took me a moment to realize I had no idea what he was saying. I tried to slow his speech, I tried to get a grasp of the words flying out of his mouth, tried and failed and figured, the hell with it.

"Are you Mr. Boudin," I said. "Mr. Louis Boudin, like the sausage?"

He nodded as he spoke, which clued me that I had knocked on the right trailer door and that he could understand me fine enough.

"I believe you have a daughter in the Louisiana Correctional Institute for Women."

He kept nodding, kept talking, undoubtedly telling me the whole sad story of how his lovely girl had ended up in such a place, but I wouldn't have cared even if I could have understood him.

"My mother is in jail with your daughter," I said. "My mother's name is Madeline Kubiak, and she has told me that she owes your daughter two thousand dollars, and she has asked that I pay that amount to you."

A smile, wide and butt ugly. He yammered on and made some motions with his hand that at first looked like he was having a seizure but that I eventually deciphered as him offering me a drink.

"No sir," I said. "I don't have time for a drink. But I do have the two thousand dollars. If you'll permit me I'd like to pay that debt."

He kept yammering, even as I took a wad of hundreds out of my pocket and counted out twenty before handing them over. His smile broadened as he took hold of the bills, stuffing them into a pocket on the chest of his overalls. Then he laughed and snapped the shoulder straps and climbed back inside the mobile home, returning with an old bottle, something clear sloshing within. He pulled the cork out with what was left of his teeth and pushed the bottle at me, and it was all I could do to decline the honor. Instead I stripped off another ten bills from the wad.

"I also understand there was an unfortunate altercation in the prison between my mother and your daughter and there will be some necessary dental work and I hope this will cover that expense."

Louis Boudin spit the cork into his hand and talked some more and nodded with great seriousness and paused to take a swig and then kept talking. I held out the bills and he snatched at the stack like a crab snatching at a finger.

"Finally, Mr. Boudin, I worry about my mother, as you understand, and I was hoping we could come to some sort of arrangement." I slipped another stack bills off the wad. "If I give you two thousand dollars more, do you think your daughter could ensure that my mother remains safe during her time in prison?"

Boudin's whole face lit up, he stretched out his arms as in preparation for a great hug, and babbled on with some French-sounding words that I'm sure were designed to let me know I had become like a nephew to him, which meant my mother had become like a sister to him, and what kind of man would he be if he didn't do everything in his power to protect his sister in such difficult circumstances.

"Thank you, sir," I said after he took this final offering and put it into the front pocket of his overalls with the rest. "It warms my heart knowing that my mother will be so well taken care of."

He smiled and yabbered and took another swig of the bottle and nodded like he had just won some sort of lottery.

"Now as a favor I'd like you to look into my eyes."

He pulled back and tilted his head at me.

"Go ahead."

He smiled and shrugged and took another swill from the bottle and then stepped forward and raised himself on his tiptoes and peered deep into my eyes. The smell was rank, worse than my New Orleans motel room, and I had to fight not to stagger or blink. He looked for a long moment, into a darkness as black as the waters roiling past his trailer, and then stepped back, his face suddenly creased with concern.

"I just wanted you to know how serious I am, Mr. Boudin. And I want you to know I am now holding you responsible for my mother's welfare in that prison. I'm headed to the West Coast, to my home in Sacramento. But if anything happens to her, anything at all, have no doubt that I am going to come back to Winn Parish, and I am going to murder you in your sleep, and then I'm going to spread enough gasoline over your dead body so that when I light the match, the only thing your daughter will find to bury in that churchyard down the road will be the charred remnants of your thick skull. *Tu comprends* that, you fat tub of lard?"

My mother, I suppose, loved me in her way when I was a boy. Too bad her way was all about neglect and desertion. That I paid her back by threatening a fat old Cajun with murder and immolation seemed about right.

My last visit to the prison I had filled her account with as much cash as they would take and then told her I would never see her again. She cried—she is good at crying when she thinks she's supposed to—but despite her tears I have been true to my word. I expect they have someone keeping tabs on her visitors. I expect if I ever pulled into Saint Gabriel again, I'd never pull out of that town alive. My mother would appreciate the gesture, though, giving my life to see her one last time.

Two of a kind.

33

SHARK

All my life I thought I had known what I had wanted. Cash, baby, on the barrelhead, along with sharp clothes, fast cars, stuff, so much stuff, more stuff. I wanted sex and power, too—Tom Preston had used the right lures to get me on his board—along with the admiration of the multitudes, but in the end, when you got to the root, it all came down to cash. The world charged me rent, billed me for food, showed me that everything had a price and the prices of the best of things were sky high, including the reverence gained from speaking softly and carrying a big stack, and so what I always wanted most was money. Simple enough. I became a lawyer because I thought it was the road to riches. Talk about your punch lines. Then I sold gold because who couldn't make a killing selling gold? Then I joined the Hyena Squad because there was money to be made in selling my especial talents to those who had more than I did. Why do geeks bite the heads off chickens? Exactly. Money was the thing for me, for always and forever.

And then I had the dream.

***

After delivering my message to Louis Boudin, I drove along the bridge stretching across the black bayou and then wended my way to Natchitoches, half an hour distant. At the Walmart Supercenter I bought a couple of prepaid iPhones and six months' worth of unlimited service. At the Orange Leaf I bought a mango frozen yogurt that promised to be a luau in my tummy. Aloha. While spooning the yogurt, I used one of the phones to find myself a pawnshop.

I parked in front of the squat white building. Two cars on the wide asphalt lot, splotched paint on the wall, iron bars on the door. WE BUY GOLD & DIAMONDS. CASH LOANS. My kind of place.

Inside, I looked around a bit before heading for the guitars, a range of acoustics and well-shined electrics. I lifted a Gibson off the wall, black body, tan accents. I found a chair and strummed the thing badly as I watched the clerk behind the glass counter conclude a jewelry sale for a young man in low pants. A row of amplifiers was up against the wall and there were a couple of coiled chords looped over two of the boxes, but I left the guitar unplugged as I strummed.

"That's a Les Paul standard," said the clerk, who had ambled over when the young man left. In his sixties, he was tall and chesty, with an unshaven jaw. One cheek was distended, in his hand he held a tin can, on his hip was a gun. "It's a lovely thing."

"I don't really play."

"I can see that, but if you're going to learn, that's a nice thing to have sitting on your lap."

"I'd rather have a girl."

"One gets the other, if'n you know what I mean."

"In high school maybe. But truth is I didn't really come for a guitar," I said. "You got guns?"

"Do we got guns." He worked the wad in his cheek and then spit a brown line of sludge into the can. Slurp, smack. "Where'd you say you from? Not from here, I can tell."

"New Jersey, originally. But now I live in California."

"I don't know what you got up there in New Jersey, but down here we got guns. What you looking for exactly?"

"Just a pistol, with ammunition."

"Any type you got in mind?"

"The type where I don't have to fill out any federal paperwork."

He looked me up and down, squinted one eye. Slurp, smack. "We don't do that here, mister."

"I'd pay more."

"Sorry. Law's the law, whether I take to it or not. No paperwork required on the guitar, though."

"I'll pass on that. Thanks for your help."

I stood, and took a moment to put the guitar back on its prongs. "They're going to be coming for them sooner or later."

"They're going to try," said the clerk.

"It's going to be more than just a try. You see what they did out there in Oregon? I make it a practice not to put my name on their lists. If they're coming for mine, I'd rather it be later."

"I get you, I do, and I'm not saying I disagree."

"Usually I buy through the shows, or private. But I was just passing through and saw the sign and got an itch. Thanks for your time."

"You driving straight along to California?"

"I'll stop now and then," I said. "Sleep and eat, check out the gun shops. I usually find someone willing to sell on my terms. Lots of folks feel like we feel, less are willing to act on it, but enough."

"If you was buying," he said, "how'd you be paying?"

"Cash."

"And you mentioned something about a premium?"

"Thirty percent more than list."

"Cash, you say?"

"Unless you fellows don't take cash."

"What kind of pistol you thinking of?"

"You got Glocks?"

"Do we got Glocks." Slurp, smack. "Fourth-generation 17s are popular with the local folk, but you don't want to get caught with the big magazine out there in California."

"Who's getting caught?"

"Well, if you're not in no hurry, I could maybe let you see what we got."

"You got an AR-15 to show me for the heck of it?"

"Just so happens. I could let you see that, too. Only to look, you know."

"Sure," I said. "I know."

I am floating on my back in the ocean.

I was really in that motel room in New Orleans, naked, lying on my back on the sodden carpet as the mites snapped at my neck. I was sleeping uneasily—in such a place how else was one to sleep?

But now, in my dream I am floating on my back in the ocean, staring up at the stars. My mouth is dry and I am thirsty; I am ill from the rocking of the waves; there are sharks; I need to pee. I call out into the emptiness. Save me. Save me. So I can pee. Yet even as I wallow in my fear and need, the stars, the stars are like a blanket of loveliness, and in their cold beauty I begin to sense there may be some truth about myself up there in the heavens. But before I can wrestle that shimmering truth into words, a great shape blots out my sky.

It is a boat, a yacht really, big and arrogant, twice the size of the Principal's dinghy, brightly lit, with wide decks that stretch across the stern like gaping superior grins. There is a grand party whirling on the yacht, beautiful people, dancing and kissing, eating bits of roasted heart speared with toothpicks, drinking champagne from blue high heels. Laughter, the clinking of glasses, a steady rap beat strangely muffled. And I recognize some of the faces.

There is Joey Mitts and Shelly Levalle, there is Cassandra and Mr. Maambong, there is Mr. Boggs, the partner at the law firm I slugged, and Mrs. Boggs, the partner's wife I bagged, there is Tom Preston and Mr. Gilbert, and the Principal, and Jeremy with his tight polo shirt, and Mrs. Wister and her awful grandson, Edwin. All of them are having just the dandiest time. And suddenly, even more than needing to pee, I need to be with them. I need to drink champagne out of blue high heels.

I call out and wave my arms, hoping to be saved, and they all notice me, lost in the ocean, floating and calling out. They look down with something dead in their eyes, a deadness more cruel than the shark fin circling me in the water.

Save me, save me. There are sharks and I need to pee. Save me.

They look down with lifeless eyes as they chew their bits of heart. Then the Principal shouts something and Mr. Maambong goes to the rear of the boat and picks up a green ring buoy. I am saved, and relief spreads through me, until I realize Mr. Maambong is not holding a life buoy at all, instead he is holding a great wad of paper. One by one he peels sheaves off the wad and tosses them into the ocean. These sheaves are bills, hundred-dollar bills, and they float in a snaking line from the boat.

The shark swims by and grabs a mouthful. I reach for the bills, one after another, as if they will somehow keep me afloat. I trail after the boat, grabbing at the bills, punching the shark in the nose to keep him away as I grab at the bills. And the boat continues on, and the party continues on, and I fall farther behind.

Out of desperation, as the shark swims by, I grab that dangerous fin and hold on as he chases the boat. We chase the boat together, forgetting about the bills now as we chase that boat. And the partyers on the boat spy us coming, and the dead gazes become suddenly alive with fear. And as we get ever closer, I am becoming one with the shark. And their fear rips through me with a shiver of joy. And our teeth are razors.

***

I had a few hours to kill—it wouldn't do for me to get where I was going too early—so I found a range just off the highway in east Shreveport. There had been a shooting park on Route 50 outside Carson City, not far from the Gold Dog International sales office, and some of us used to go after work. Nothing calms the bile after a day of cold-calling like blasting an old television set with a pump-action Remington. One of the salesmen had a Glock, and I used to shoot bottles and cans full of beans with that little beast, but it had been a while, so I thought I'd get some work in before I relied on my new toy in something more than a target shoot.

I had never had much use for a firearm; a gun is a lousy way to chase after money. It may fill your pocket in the short run—John Dillinger and Jesse Duchamp proved that—but you're haunted by the act ever after and it will get you in the end—John Dillinger and Jesse Duchamp proved that, too. The smart guys take money with their law licenses, or their gift for gab, or the contacts they make at the golfing club. I always considered myself one of the smart guys—self-deception is one of the markers of my condition—so I never had much interest in guns. But after my shark dream in the Jesse Duchamp death room, it was time to armor up.

The woman on duty was familiar with the model. She showed me how to fill the big magazine, how to slap it in, how to rock the slide, how to hold the thing with two hands when firing. There was a safety on the trigger, but nowhere else, she told me, so I should keep my finger off the trigger until I was ready to shoot. After a few more safety tips, she wheeled the target downrange, had me shoot a few, and then left me to it.

Rippity bing.

It had a nice kick to it.

Rippity bong.

There's a predatory sense of direction when you're shooting off a gun. The gap between you and your target shrinks to a narrow cylinder even as you yourself expand with dangerous possibilities.

Rippity bing bong bing.

***

The last time I rocked across the country in my Porsche with nothing but burned bridges behind me and uncertainty ahead, desperation cleaved my heart and the taste of copper stained my tongue. But now, racing along similarly barren highways with the very same conditions both behind and ahead, I tasted not the sourness of copper but something strange and marvelous. I wasn't running from what I was anymore, I embraced it. I wasn't dancing to their tunes and begging for their rewards anymore, I was instead writing my own song according to the dictates of my own twisted psyche. What I was tasting now was freedom pure, and it was fresh as mint.

I played the radio loud. I lowered my window so the wind would whip. Even with my sunglasses in place, the verdant landscape zipping by on either side was almost too bright to bear. Shreveport, Texarkana, Hope, yes, Hope, on the way to Arkadelphia and Benton and Little Rock. It was about 9:00 p.m. when I crossed the Mississippi on I-40 and skirted the bright lights of downtown. I let the GPS lead me off the highway and onto the main road that ran east from the river. I turned this way, I turned that way, until I was on a narrow road, an apartment complex on one side, a fenced-in truck depot on the other. Beyond that, amidst the swelter of mature trees, was a row of tidy bungalows.

I drove by slowly, looking for anything of interest, anyone casing anything. The first floor of the bungalow I had aimed for, a squat green building, was lit. I drove past, saw nothing that worried me, turned left, and then left again. I parked on the street across from a house without a fence. I took the Glock from the case. One of the magazines was full. I slapped it in, loaded the chamber, and stuck the gun into the pocket of my jacket.

A dog barked as I made my way down the house's drive and across a lawn to the rear of the squat green bungalow. I leaned up against the wall on one side and listened. A television. That seemed innocent enough. I walked toward the front, looked around the street, and then went to the front door as if there was nothing to it.

I pushed the buzzer, I pushed it again. A moment later the front door opened and she was standing there, pretty, barefoot, wearing jeans and a T-shirt.

"Hello, Cindy," I said.

Cindy Lieu's face twisted in puzzlement before her eyes widened in recognition. "Dr. Triplett?"

"It's good to see you again. You're looking healthy."

"I'm feeling okay, yes. What are you doing here, Doctor?"

"I'm here to save your life," I said. "Again."

34

CINDY LIEU

"I'm glad you came," she said. She had offered tea, but I had suggested coffee instead, and so we both held a mug of a watery Keurig brew. Her living room was bright purple with a painted rainbow stretching across one of the walls. I was sitting on a wooden chair, my jacket still on; she was curled like a cat on the sofa. There was a stuffed bear sitting beside her, and a stuffed unicorn sitting beside the bear, and Cindy was exceedingly, painfully cheerful. "I've actually been looking for you. I wanted to thank you for all you did for me when I was sick."

"I was just doing my job," I said.

"Is being here, now, part of your job, too?"

"My new job. I'm here to make sure you're okay and continue to be okay."

"I didn't think doctors made house calls anymore."

"I'm not your normal doctor."

"I know that already," she said, taking a sip. "There was something about your eyes and your smile. And then I went to the Department of Health website. A number of Dr. Tripletts came up, but none of them matched."

"I'm not surprised."

"Why is that?"

"Do you want the tough truth or a comforting lie?" I said.

"Maybe the lie," she said, laughing, flirting. "You can always tell more from a lie than from the truth."

"The lie is that I came over from California, and my Tennessee license hasn't yet been issued. It also happens to be the truth."

"That's almost intriguing. So what are you doing here, really?"

"Like I said, I've come to save your life."

She laughed. "You are such the gentleman, aren't you?" She lifted a plate of chocolate-dipped sticks from the coffee table. "Pocky?"

"No thank you."

"It's like the greatest thing ever."

"I'll pass, really."

She put the plate down, took one, and snapped it suggestively in her teeth. "Don't you think," she said, "it's a little presumptuous in this day and age to assume I need saving? Maybe I don't need your help."

"Oh, you need my help." I looked around. "Nice place."

"I'm just renting, but I added my own touches. I assume the color will cost me my deposit. Do you like it?"

"It's very purple."

"Exactly. Are you living in Memphis now?"

"No."

"Good. I don't think I'm staying."

"Where would you go? Back home to Murfreesboro?"

"God, no."

"Why not?"

"Go on down to Murfreesboro for a couple of weeks, live with my mother, and then you tell me. I was thinking San Francisco, but it's so expensive."

"You'd fit in."

"Why thank you, Dr. Triplett. I'll take that as a compliment."

"I think we need to go somewhere, now."

"It's a little late, but there's a bar not too far away on Madison."

"I'm not thinking of a bar, I'm thinking out of town."

"Now you're being a little forward. What about getting to know each other first? Or is that too old-fashioned for a doctor practicing in Memphis without a license?"

"I apologize that I haven't been clear. I am not here to date you, I'm here to save your life, and to do that we need to get you out of town, now."

She sat up on the couch. "You're starting to scare me."

"Good."

Her eyes brightened. "I sort of like it."

"Not so good, but I admire your attitude."

"I suppose there's an explanation for all this."

"There is, but there isn't time to go into it all right now, and, frankly, your reaction to the truth won't be good. So I think I'm going to short-circuit the whole thing."

I took the gun out of my pocket and laid it on my thigh.

She looked at the gun, at my face, back at the gun. "You're taking it up a notch," she said. "Maybe I'll see your gun and raise you a pair of stilettos."

"You're not getting what's going on. This isn't a sex game. What I need you to do is to put on some shoes, sensible shoes, and pack up what you need in a small bag. Take your keys, but leave your cell phone, your laptop, and your tablet here so they can't track you."

"I don't have a tablet."

"We need to get you out of town, now." I picked up the gun and waved it in the air. "Let's go."

"I don't think you're going to shoot me."

"I'm not. This isn't for you. There's a man named Tom Preston from Miami who is coming to kill you. This is for him."

"Why would anyone from Miami want to kill me?"

"Because he's getting paid to, and he's the kind of killer who finds nobility in killing, not to mention a sexual charge. The safest thing for you and me both is to get out of this house as quickly as possible."

She looked at me, and for the first time a real concern creased her features. "Either you're totally insane," she said, "like crazy insane, which I kind of like, or I'm in trouble."

"One or the other, and maybe both. But it doesn't much matter, does it?"

While she packed, I went around the apartment, pulling shades and closing curtains. We would leave the lights on, but I didn't want anyone seeing inside. I kept the front porch light burning but turned off the light over the rear door. When Cindy appeared with sneakers on, a leather jacket, and a small black bag, I held out my hand.

"I'll turn it off," she said.

"It will be here when you get back."

"If I get back."

"You have to trust me."

"Why would I do that?"

"You trusted me with your appendix and that turned out okay. And you like my smile, right?"

"I do."

"And also, if you want, I'll give you the gun, but I know how to use it."

"Now you're really scaring me."

"That's the point. Let me have the phone."

She took it out of her bag, put it in my hand. I tossed it on the kitchen counter before turning out the kitchen lights.

"Follow me," I said.

Just then her phone rang. The sound track of an old Nintendo game. We both stopped, turned toward it. The game continued. She started walking to the phone but I put out an arm to stop her.

"It could be my mother," she said.

289

"It could be him."

"Who?"

"Tom Preston."

"The bogeyman."

"The bogeyman has nightmares that Tom Preston is in its closet." I walked to the phone and checked the caller. "A number with no name. Not one of your contacts. Let's go."

I stepped out the back door and crouched down as I looked all about. The gun was out, but my finger was off the trigger. Nothing seemed amiss. I stood and gestured for Cindy to follow me and quietly closed the door behind her. Together we slipped across her backyard and onto her neighbor's drive. We kept well within the shadows of the house as we moved toward the road. On the far side I could see the outline of my car.

And then a figure, a mere silhouette in the darkness, standing behind the car, examining it.

"Wait," I said softly, taking hold of Cindy's arm and pulling her up against the house. The figure by the car looked around. For a moment he appeared to gaze right down the driveway, past us to the back of Cindy's house, as if his confederates were already there, swarming. I slipped my finger into the trigger guard, tickled the protruding trigger safety, swiveled my head to see who was behind us.

No one.

I looked back to the car and the silhouette was now walking away, being pulled forward by a large dog on a leash. He wasn't a henchman, he was a guy walking his Labrador, wondering what a Porsche was doing parked on his crappy street.

"A little jumpy?" she said quietly.

"Sometimes it pays to be jumpy. Let's go."

Nothing stopped us from getting in the car, nothing stopped us from calmly pulling away from the curb. I imagined Tom Preston ripping after us in a car of his own, I imagined Tom Preston slamming into us from behind as we drove calmly to the end of the street and took a left. I feared we might have to fight our way out, but our exit was as smooth as the icing on a layer cake.

"That was surely the most dramatic walk to a car outside my house ever," said Cindy as we drove toward the highway. "What other fun games are we going to play?"

"Be happy it was anticlimactic," I said, "because the number that came up on your phone had a Miami area code. Let me get us on the interstate and then I'll tell you what this is all about."

"Does that mean you're not really a doctor?" she said.

This came after I told her the entire story, including a short review of my career as a henchman. This came after she yelped when I told her what we had really done to her during that operation. This came after a long bout of silence when she crossed her arms and closed her expression, even as her eyes wriggled back and forth like two of Tom Preston's goldfish in their small deadly bowl. Finally, her question came out of the darkness from the other bed in our motel room off the highway east of Nashville.

"That's right," I said. "But the man who operated on you was."

"Dr. Heigenmeister?"

"Well, not the name. I made that up."

"Nice touch."

The plan had been to not stop until we got out of Tennessee, but about four hours out of Memphis, weariness hit me like a frying pan. I was afraid of running the car into a ditch, either from exhaustion or out of despair over the country music on the radio, so I stopped at the first cheap motel I could find off the highway. I parked where the car couldn't be seen from the road and paid for a single room with twin beds. I had been trying to fall asleep—I had barely slept in the past three days—but somehow my very exhaustion was keeping me awake. So instead of sleeping I was going through all the necessary steps I would have to take on this journey to hell I had set myself upon, when Cindy broke the silence.

"If you're not a doctor, then what are you?"

"A lawyer, actually."

"I guess that explains the severance payment. I thought it was way high. Only a lawyer would insist on paying for a stolen kidney."

"It just seemed fair."

"Was it your money?"

"I made the old lady pay it."

"Good. What's he like, the kid who ended up with it?"

"He's just a kid, with too much money and a future he'll never live up to. He'll either be president or drink himself to death for falling short."

"Well, he has the kidney for it."

We both laughed a little at that.

"You're taking this better than I thought you would," I said.

"How should I have taken it?"

"I would be out for blood."

"Who says I'm not? I can be a sweet little thing until I'm crossed. Some of the girls found that out in high school. Why did you come back to save me? Why did you secret me out of my house? Why did you tell me that horrible story? Out of the goodness of your heart?"

"My heart has no goodness," I said.

"Then why?"

"I decided to stop being their well-paid servant."

"What are you now?"

"Their worst nightmare."

"That's what I want to be, too."

"You?"

"Right now I feel like I could strangle someone with my bare hands."

"Good girl."

"Except all we're doing is running."

"I have a plan."

"Oh, thank goodness, the man who stole my kidney has a plan."

"Maybe we should get some sleep."

"What's the plan, kidney thief?"

"We'll deal with it tomorrow."

"Why should I trust your plan?"

"Who else are you going to trust?"

"Well, I've got a plan, too."

"What's your plan?"

"Take me up to Philadelphia, give me a knife, point me in the direction of the little bastard," she said in that high, sweet voice. "I want my kidney back. Once I get that sucker bagged, all I'll need is someone to put it back in for me. Too bad you're not really a doctor."

"I was thinking something a little less bloody. And we won't be going to Philadelphia."

"Where are we going then?"

"DC," I said.

"How will I get me my kidney back in DC when it's wandering around like a ghost in Philadelphia?"

"I have a plan," I said. "It's not a sure thing, but at least in DC we can put the fear of God into their dark shrunken hearts, and at the same time maybe make you rich."

35

Maria Guadalupe

"There's a wee bit left of the Scotch," said the outlaw.

He grabbed the bottle, thwacked off the top, and poured the remainder evenly into the two glasses.

"Who said I couldn't kill? I just killed this bottle." He grinned. "Drink up."

To the magazine writer, the outlaw's ugly smile was just then filled with threat. From that horrible dream, and his reaction to it, it seemed the only thing burning behind his single dead eye was a brutal nihilism. Where would that lead her? She lifted her glass, peered into the color, not as bright as before, and took a swallow. Her tongue had numbed, and the whiskey no longer tasted rich with promise, just harsh and dark and slightly nauseating.

"Oh Christ," said the outlaw after the shack's door once again yelped open and the late-afternoon sun sliced through the dimness, before dying again when the door closed. "Another freak."

The woman now standing at the bar's entrance wore a cowboy hat, a denim jacket, boots. The hat left her face in shadow, and her jacket was bulky, and in the gloom of the bar there was something indistinct about her, lonely and lost. The magazine writer wondered for a moment if the woman was a specter of her own future.

"They call her Cactus Annie when they call her anything," said the outlaw softly. "Look at her in her cowgirl finery, like she's riding the range, when the only thing she rides is a Range Rover and the occasional drunk. She comes in about this time most every afternoon, sits with the other losers drinking herself sick, and staggers out with whatever piece of meat can put up with her smell. Let's just say when it comes to her priorities, hygiene takes a backseat to gin. One thing she's not short of is money, but even with her neat little nest egg, she chooses to drink here, which tells you all you need to know about her. An alcoholic's alcoholic."

Cactus Annie thumbed up her hat, nodded at their table as if she somehow knew the magazine writer, and then made her way to the bar, sitting to the left of the behemoth in the leather vest. There was no fuss made, no greeting. Without waiting for an order, Ginsberg started building her a drink.

"Is something wrong with the Scotch?" said the outlaw. "Enjoy it while you can. There are so few bottles of Samurai Scotch left in the world that I keep the empties in a cabinet beneath the bar as mementos, tombstones commemorating past glories. Visiting my little graveyard in this sad, stinking joint is a bitter little reminder of how empty my life has now become. Choices matter; the choice I made in that motel room in New Orleans led me straight to this hellhole. If you choose to bend your knee and beg for my help in finding justice for your precious brother, then that choice will matter, too.

"Listen up, sister. If you ever want the marriage, the kids, the house in the suburbs or the loft in the city, the dinner parties with old friends, the money to spend and the freedom to spend it, if all of that is what you might someday want, then when my story is told you will shake my hand, pocket your recorder, write your article, and move on.

"Because if I'm going to fight your battle, then you'll be fighting it, too, and all those American-dreamy things are as unlikely as a dance band at Ginsberg's. If you go after them, they'll come after you. And if you start looking behind the injustice done to your brother, you'll find a hundred other crimes, each graver than the last. And the louder you scream, the more you'll be ignored. And the closer you get to the truth, the more danger you'll be in. And in the end, when you're hiding out in some run-down motel from henchmen as brutal and indifferent as me, with nothing to show for your life but an empty bank account and a string of failures—because rightness in this world is thwarted every which way by the good as well as the depraved—you'll need to comfort yourself with the choice you made this day in this bar.

"And trust me when I tell you this: that comfort will be threadbare."

And she did, just then, trust that the outlaw was telling the truth. For his whole dreadful story seemed to be a taste of her future foretold: wild threats and seedy motels and frantic dashes through the night. It was all fear and waste, it was all blight. For an instant, when faced with the test of the pickled egg, she had screwed up her courage and taken the plunge. But now, when contemplating the future she would be stepping into, her reaction was utter weariness. She wasn't hard enough to live that life. She wasn't even hard enough to drink the outlaw's Scotch. She felt just then to be a failed thing, forlorn of purpose, devoid of any hope, and with no idea of where to find it.

"Look closely at the three wiseacres at the bar," said the outlaw. "Minnie, Moe, and Jackass, along with their pathetic barkeep. There's more intelligence and class in a chinchilla farm. Try to do one halfway-decent thing in the world, try to save one woman from a murderous thug, and this is where you end up, drinking in the worst saloon in America. Ginsberg's bar is the lesson of the moment. And there were more lessons to come in the muck pits of Washington."

"What if I don't like him?" said Cindy Lieu. We had arrived in DC and landed in a bar almost as grim this one.

"It doesn't matter."

"I don't get to choose?"

"We don't have time."

On her first visit to our nation's capital, Cindy had been in an adventurous mood. She wanted something fizzy and bright to match the neon champagne glass replete with bubbles on the window outside the bar, but I told her it was false advertising and that everything they served at the Raven Grill was as brown as the walls. I ordered a beer, she ordered a rum and Coke, we tried not to look at the door as we drank, pretending we weren't on the run.

"What about you?" she said. "Why can't you be my lawyer?"

"Because it's awkward getting legal things done when there's a bullet with your name on it in someone else's gun. They want to kill me as much as they want to kill you. They want to kill me more."

She shifted down a seat and pretended not to know me.

"Not funny," I said.

"I think it's funny."

"You seem a little cavalier, considering the circumstances."

"What am I supposed to do, sit and cry in the corner?"

"That's what I figured you'd do, what with your unicorns and teddy bears."

"You ever read manga?"

"What is that, the word for 'eat' in Italian?"

"Japanese comic books."

"But you're not Japanese."

"And you're not Italian, but you eat Italian food. Manga heroes don't sit in the corner and cry. They pull out their swords and start slicing. My favorite series is *Lone Wolf and Cub*, about this samurai who brings his little child along as he goes about seeking revenge for the murder of his wife."

"That's sounds about right," I said. "How does it end?"

"The samurai dies."

"Ouch."

"But then the cub ends up killing the bad guy, so it all works out. See, it's aspirational. Do they have food in this place?"

I gestured toward the chips and pretzels on the rack behind the bar.

"It's the Raven Grill," she said. "Where's the grill?"

"In the bartender's mouth. When the lawyer comes in, you let me talk to him first and then you can join us, okay?"

"Okay."

"I'm going to sit in a booth and wait. Pretend you don't know me."

"But I don't know you."

"Then it will be easy."

I slid off the stool and slipped into a booth—this time beneath a photograph of Elvis—sipped my beer, and waited.

Cindy and I had set up shop at a motel on New York Avenue, just south of the railroad tracks. The room was decent enough for a motel—low ceiling, two beds, checkerboard pattern on the rug, air freshener covering some foul scent that was almost alive, and there was a pool in the parking lot, a pool!—but even though it was a step up from the GrandView, it was still my third motel in three nights. And now here we were, in this downtrodden joint, a step up maybe from Ginsberg's, but only a step. There was no getting around the fact that my grand epiphany in New Orleans might have loosened the iron chains that constrained my soul, but it had also consigned me to a future of dive bars and cheap motels, the very landscape Jesse Duchamp moved through on his voyage to oblivion. I was contemplating the bitter irony when Alberto Menendez walked through the bar's door, and not alone.

"It is good to see you again, my friend," said Alberto, standing beside my booth. His suit was new and elegant, quite different from the rag he was wearing when I first spied him in that same bar. "I thought we were finished with each other. I'm glad I was mistaken. What are you drinking? I'll buy you another."

I didn't say anything, I merely looked at his companion, a young woman, shortish and squattish, dark hair, dark eyes, green jacket of her pantsuit tightly buttoned, and then I looked back at Alberto.

"I understand," said Alberto. "You are concerned, but you need not be. This is my new associate, and also my granddaughter, Maria Guadalupe Menendez. You can trust her implicitly, as do I. Now, another beer or something more festive?"

"A beer is fine," I said.

He spouted a line of Spanish to the woman, who then went to the bar as Alberto slid into the booth across from me. He shrugged off my stare.

"My son's daughter, a recent law school graduate. Not the prettiest, I admit, but I am suddenly busier than I have been in years. I needed some help."

"It's good to be busy."

"It is different, at least. And you look different, too, my friend."

"How do I look different?"

He tilted his head. "Somehow less frivolous, less pleased with yourself. It is as if you were diagnosed with some terminal illness."

"Something like that."

"It looks good on you. I have less urge to punch you in the face."

"Just as long as you pay me as you promised. Is your granddaughter aware of our arrangement?"

"I told her the details. She was not pleased. The young have such strong lines, but she was mollified when I informed her you were an attorney, and she will abide. It is a matter of family honor and respect. You took a chance on an old man. The whole family is grateful."

I removed a piece of paper from my pocket and slipped it across the bar. "This is the number and the details for an account in Belize where you'll send my share of the fees for the Gould case, and any other case I give to you."

He took the paper, looked at it before sticking it into a pocket. "I will keep this, but sadly, I don't think it will ever be used. We haven't talked since the unfortunate suicide of Scarlett Gould's former boy-friend. The publicity over our renewed interest was blamed for his act, which is a shame if true, but not a great shame, considering. I fear his suicide is the end of our involvement. Even if we bring a suit and win against his estate, there will be nothing to collect."

Just then Maria Guadalupe came back with a beer, a bourbon, and a glass of something clear and frizzy with a lime sticking out. She sat beside her grandfather and gave him the bourbon as she took a sip of the clear drink.

"Gin and tonic?" I said.

"Seltzer," said Alberto's granddaughter. "I don't drink."

"That's a shame. Your grandfather thinks the Scarlett Gould case is over as far as he is concerned. What do you think?"

"My grandfather is probably right. After the suicide, it would be difficult to win against another defendant. And Mr. Beamon's estate is judgment proof. But then again," she said, smiling, "his suicide seems a bit convenient, don't you think?"

"Where did you go to law school?" I said.

"Georgetown."

"I could never have afforded such an astute legal talent if I wasn't her grandfather," said Alberto, beaming.

"You're right, Maria," I said. "The suicide was damn convenient, except it wasn't a suicide. Bradley Beamon was murdered. You should sign his parents up as clients so they can be part of the suit along with the Goulds. It will be the same defendants. It's all part of the same conspiracy. We could maybe even RICO it."

"Treble damages," said Maria.

"Were two sweeter words ever coined?"

"And you can prove all this, my friend?" said Alberto.

"In time. But right now I have a related matter to discuss, one that must be taken care of immediately. Can you get a full medical examina-tion done right away? Today. With an MRI and a battery of blood tests."

"That could be difficult to arrange," said Alberto.

"I know someone at George Washington," said Maria. "She'll do it for me. It might cost, though."

"Cover it," I said.

"What do you have for us, friend?"

"A case worth millions, if you're brave enough to take it on. A rich old lady in Philadelphia hiring a firm from Miami to steal something of great value in Memphis."

"But that case is no good to us," said Alberto. "We can't file it here."

"You'll have to find local counsel in Tennessee, but it'll be your case because it'll be your plaintiff. And the pockets are as deep as you'll ever find. After I leave here I'm going to try to get the police involved, but whatever happens, you'll need to get it filed right away, before the same man who killed Bradley Beamon kills your plaintiff."

"What have you gotten us into?" said Alberto.

"The big time, Alberto." I reached into my jacket pocket, pulled out the thumb drive that had been given to me in the go-go bar in Philadelphia. "Show this to your doctor. She'll figure out what it means. This should link the whole thing back to the defendants."

"Where is the plaintiff?"

"In the city, waiting on you."

"And the plaintiff already agreed to have us represent him?"

"Just whip up a contingency fee agreement. It has already been arranged."

Maria Guadalupe turned her head to look at Cindy Lieu, still sitting at the bar, and then leaned forward, running a finger around the rim of her glass. "That's our plaintiff, isn't it?"

"It could be."

"So tell us, Mr. Triplett. What did the bastards steal from her?"

"A kidney," I said.

Alberto's eyes widened with alarm, but Maria Guadalupe's eyes glistened and she bared her teeth like a shark.

36

BONSAI

It was all going so smoothly. And why shouldn't it have been? The dream had shown me something with utter clarity—my life's true purpose—and in so doing had allowed me to short-circuit the reinforcing loop of self-sabotage that had heretofore always wrecked my prospects. Finally my talents for mendacity and rank manipulation were shining through. It seemed just then that I had found the answer to all of life's adversities. I had the urge to tell someone, to tell everyone. It was as if the secret of the universe had been whispered in my ear.

Can we meet?

Who is this? I don't recognize the number.

Phil.

Fuck yourself.

After sending Cindy off with Alberto and Maria Guadalupe for the requisite medical testing for our lawsuit, I drove over to a nondescript office building near a Metro stop on Connecticut Avenue. Inside the fifth-floor doors there was no receptionist, the waiting room was bland as fog, the door to the inner office was locked, as I knew it would be. I sat, and picked up a *People* magazine from three weeks prior, paged through the noxious photographs as I waited. My watch told me I wouldn't have to wait long.

I have something to tell you you'll want to hear.

Are you sick and dying a slow and painful death?

No.

Then there is nothing you can tell me that I want to hear.

When the door finally opened, a slight man with a bad toupee slunk through the gap. A latex fetishist with a masochistic wife, I guessed. I let him steal out the front door before I stuck my head into the office.

"Hello, Doctor," I said.

"Phil," said Caroline Brooks, a bit of startle in her voice. She stood abruptly behind her desk, fidgeted with something on the desktop. "Should I be expecting you?"

"No, and don't worry, I'm not here to throw a tree."

"That's good to know."

"I won't take long, I know you probably have an appointment in a few minutes, but I was in town and I thought I'd just pop in and say hello."

"That's nice. Thank you. How are you doing?"

"I'm doing okay. Actually, great. That's what I wanted to tell you."

"I'm so glad to hear that, Phil."

"I was a little upset the last time we were together. It was no easy thing being told I really was what I feared I was, and that I wouldn't ever be able to change."

"That wasn't what I actually said."

"But that was what you actually meant, I know, and in the end, I must say, it was liberating. I've learned to accept what I am, to even embrace it."

"I see."

"The question was how to move forward knowing what I now know. I decided to make a change."

"That sounds promising."

"At first I took your suggestion and tried to give other people what they wanted, tried to treat them like things of worth instead of just things that I could take advantage of. And, I have to say, that didn't work out too well."

"I'm sorry to hear that, but it's a long process. It can't be done in just days or weeks."

"But then I had this strange dream and out of it came the realization that the reason I kept on screwing up my life was because I wanted the wrong things. For me, it was all about money. I was a slave to the dollar bills they were waving before my eyes."

"I guess we all are in a way."

"But see, that's them putting their purpose into us. What I needed was to understand my own deeper purpose. And I have, and it has made all the difference. That's what I came to tell you, that's the solution to all our dilemmas. To find out why we each were put on this earth and then to act on it."

"And why were you put on this earth, Phil?"

This was the first time I actually tried to put the change into words. It had lived in my breast, imbuing my actions with a strange certainty, but somehow now, having to express it to another person, it suddenly became as easily lassoed as a cloud. Still, I lowered my chin slightly, a lawyer's move when making the crucial point to the jury, and gave it a shot: "To make the bastards tremble with fear."

"Who are the bastards, Phil?"

"People with money, with power. The people who control everything. I decided I wasn't going to be their pawn anymore. I wasn't going to be controlled with dollars, or with perfectly shaped breasts, or job titles with apparent clout that had no real power at all. I was going to play my own game. I'm not out for revenge, Caroline, don't worry. And I'm certainly not out to do good for my fellow man; you know better than anyone that would be all pretense for me, and pretense falls apart at the first thumb of pressure. But the time has come for all those who looked at me as no better than a servant as I did their bidding, for all those who failed to give me the proper deference, to pay a price for their slights."

You know how the face of a child lights up when she finally gets what you're trying to teach, how the sheer understanding shoots through her and she can't hide the joy? I expected to see that expression on Caroline Brooks's face, but that's not what I saw. Instead I saw deep concern, along with something else: horror.

"Maybe I didn't express it correctly," I said.

"If you want, we could talk about it some more," she said, stepping around her desk and toward me, one hand grasping the other. "I do have an appointment but I could cancel it. Let's talk some more, Phil."

"I'd like that, Caroline. But I can't, really. I have things."

"What kind of things?"

"Things. You know. I just came to thank you for your help."

"You still have limits, don't you, Phil? You're not going to resort to violence, are you?"

"Why would you think that?"

"There's something different about you. Colder."

"Well, I did buy a gun. Two, actually. These are not pleasant people, Caroline. You don't know them like I know them. Maybe I screwed their wives and got away with it, yeah, but that was just small-time grifting. This is something else entirely. Now if they make one wrong move, step one foot over the line, give me any excuse at all, they will know that their days of judgment are coming and that I am the Hellmouth."

"Stay and talk to me, Phil. Sit down. Let's talk this over."

"I can't. I'm only here to say thank you. In a way, you were right all along, I did originally come to you to get fixed, and somehow it worked. I am a better psychopath now."

"Phil?"

I looked over to the windowsill. Where there had been three bonsai trees, there were now only two.

"What happened to the bonsai I threw, the one we repotted together?"

"It didn't make it," she said. "The needles were turning brown, falling out."

"So you just tossed it?"

"It was dying, Phil."

"We're all dying."

"I want to help you, Phil. How can I help you?"

"Good-bye, Caroline. I'm sorry to have bothered you. I won't be back."

Well, that hadn't gone as I expected. Maybe the Hellmouth thing had been a bit much.

After I stepped outside the building I looked up to her office window. With the reflection of the sky playing across the glass I couldn't see inside, but I assumed she was looking down on me. I couldn't figure out if it was just a failure of language—if I had merely presented the new and improved vision of my life all wrong—or if there was some deeper problem with my altered direction. It had been such a peculiar moment that I wanted to talk it through with someone, but who could that someone be? I couldn't talk to Caroline Brooks anymore, that was clear. I took out my phone and typed.

Do you really think BB killed himself?

You don't?

Six o'clock, where I first met you.

Fuck yourself.

The drinks are on me.

You bet they are.

And keep it quiet.

When I turned off the phone I looked around. For some reason things had suddenly turned alarming. It felt as if there were guns pointed at me from every direction. The whole Caroline Brooks encounter had upset my equilibrium, but the thing that troubled me most was the fate of the tree. The repotting of the bonsai had been the metaphor on which I had based my new direction. Change the pot and even though the tree remains the same, it suddenly thrives. The metaphor was all too obvious and a little too cute, I admit now, but I had found it comforting until Caroline told me the repotted tree had been tossed out with yesterday's garbage.

37

THE SWITCH

I parked in a lot across the street from the bar and sat in my car watching the goings-on. I was ridiculously early, and not because I had time to kill. I was looking for patterns of strange in the street, anything that indicated I would be taken down as soon as I stepped toward the bar's entrance. I watched that woman in the orange vest, that cop car cruising, that pedestrian walking back and forth as if he had someplace to be, that guy sweeping up litter from the street. But even though I was still filled with the alarm I had felt after leaving Caroline Brooks, I saw nothing that definitively scared me off. And then, right at six, I spotted Linda Pickering making her way down Massachusetts Avenue.

She was dressed like a cop, no short skirt or plunging neckline, no blue heels with points sharp as a shiv. Her shiny blonde hair was tied into a short ponytail, her shoes were utterly sensible. I liked the look, surprisingly, but then I liked all her looks. I didn't feel regret seeing her, I don't feel regret, but I did remember the smell of her naked and on top of me, boozy and smoky and musky all at once, with the sharp smack of a perfume that was trying too hard. She looked around before climbing down the stairs to the entrance, and I had to determine whether it was just the natural carefulness of a cop or a furtive glance to make sure her operatives were in place. The scent of her still smoking through my memory convinced me all was clear.

The bar was quiet, not yet crowded, and so it didn't take me but a moment to spot her. She was waiting for me at a small table off the bar, seated on the bench seat with her back to the wall, facing an empty chair. She didn't smile when she saw me coming, and she positively cringed when I slid onto the bench seat beside her.

"There's an empty chair," she said.

"This is more romantic, don't you think? Like in those old French movies, sitting side by side, smoking cigarettes and sipping champagne."

"Except it's illegal to smoke cigarettes in here."

"And we don't have champagne."

"And I can't bear the rotten smell of you."

"It's my cologne," I said. "Eau de spoiled camembert. Drink?"

I looked around, made a quick judgment about everyone I could spy in the bar, and then kept watch on the entrance.

"I've been spending the last week wondering," she said, "why I didn't arrest you for obstruction of justice at our last meeting."

"Did you figure it out?"

"I was just so flustered, so appalled, and so fascinated at the same time. It was like I was watching a cockroach eat its own vomit."

"Do they do that?"

"You're the expert, you tell me."

A beefy man walked in alone and stood with a spread-legged stance, looking around, before he broke into a smile and joined a crew at the other side of the room. I signaled the waitress. When she came over to our table, I ordered a martini, double olives, and a Scotch with ice.

"Maybe I should arrest you now," said Linda after the waitress left.

"We should at least wait for the drinks. And from what I can tell, I didn't obstruct anything. You kept right on investigating. I heard about your meeting with Senator Davenport. How did that work out?"

"None of your business."

"It sure didn't work out well for Bradley Beamon. I give you a friendly warning, you are just enough of a hard-ass to ignore it, and then . . ."

"One had nothing to do with the other."

"Keep telling yourself that."

"What did you do?"

"Me? Nothing, I wasn't involved. I was actually sunning in Jamaica at the time. When I heard, I was as stunned as you undoubtedly were. But now that you've got Bradley's confession, I suppose you've already closed the Scarlett Gould case."

"They want me to."

"But you're fighting it. Good. I've missed you, Linda. I think about you at odd times. Your laugh, your scent, the way your hair tickled my cheek when you were riding me like a Harley."

"Can you lend me a bucket? I need to hurl. Or maybe I'll just do it right on your shoes. Do you have any idea how disgusting I find you right now?"

"I have a pretty good idea."

"And I suppose this is the moment you tell me how much you disgust yourself."

"But I don't, you see. I was just doing my job. I only regret that it happened on a night you looked so fetching."

She barked out a laugh at that, which was peculiar because I wasn't trying to be funny. The drinks came. We sat quietly for a bit. Even with her back hunched in tension, I liked being next to her.

"So," she said.

"So what?"

"You said you had something to tell me. What do you know, Phil?"

"I know enough to sit with my back to the wall." I gave the crowd another quick scan. There were two men in suits, barely talking, standing in the corner by a chalkboard with the names of wines listed. "I know enough to blow the lid off some pretty ugly stuff in this god-awful town. Did you tell anyone we were meeting?"

"I'd be too embarrassed."

"Do you know those guys in the corner?"

"Don't be so paranoid. If I was coming after you, you'd already be gotten. Let me have what you've got."

"Not yet."

"What a surprise, you were bullshitting me all along."

"It's not bullshit, but I need something from you first."

"I bet." She lifted up the martini, drained it, pulled out the plastic toothpick, and bit off one of the olives. "If I see you again, I will arrest you."

"I have a case for you," I said. "You'll want to move on it right away. There's a woman in Philadelphia. She's rich, and she's vile. Her name is Wister and she's put out a hit on a woman named Cindy Lieu who lives in Memphis. And the reason why will slay you."

"Doubtful."

"Because the old lady already stole Cindy Lieu's kidney for her grandson. How's that? And now she wants to destroy the evidence."

"You know the sweetest stories," she said, and then went quiet for a moment. "What can I do about it? Philadelphia, Memphis. I'm a cold case cop with no jurisdiction."

"It's a federal case, with all the crisscrossing of state lines. I figure you know someone in the FBI who could take this and run with it."

"I might," she said. "Yeah, I do. But why would I bring him in?"

"Because if he puts you on the task force and you work the case like it matters, it will wend its way right back to the Scarlett Gould murder and give you all the answers you could ever want."

"I'm listening."

"Because the son of a bitch who right now is trying to kill Cindy Lieu is the same son of a bitch who killed Bradley Beamon. And the organization he's working for is the organization that killed Scarlett Gould."

She took a moment, biting the second olive off her toothpick, and then she gave her verdict. "It sounds too cute."

"It does, yes."

"And I know you're a liar."

"I am."

"And you still want me to believe it."

"Absolutely."

"Why should I?"

"Because I was working for the same organization. But I'm not anymore. I'm trying something new." I gave her my most brilliant smile. "I've gone rogue."

"So that's it. You've gone rogue. That sounds so romantic it makes me want to punch you in the face. What it means is you found a new route to the money."

"There's money involved, sure, there always is. But the pursuit of other people's money isn't driving me anymore."

"Then what are you really after, Phil?"

I thought about it for a moment. I would have blurted out my line about making them tremble with fear to Linda Pickering, the same way I blurted it out to Caroline Brooks, but if Linda looked at me the same way Caroline did while I spoke about judgment day and my role as the Hellmouth, the game was over. I needed her to look at me with some understanding, at least. I needed her to believe I was different than I had been, led now by a nobler purpose. I not only needed this, I wanted it, too. From her. Especially from her. I wasn't going to lie to put it over, this new purpose was too fragile within me, too susceptible to my own words to taint it with deceit. What I needed instead was a way to repackage my new purpose in a spiffier box, to make it salable to this new audience. What would Linda Pickering be willing, even eager, to buy?

"Justice," I said. "I've decided to pursue justice."

"Bullshit." And she laughed when she said it, but something had lit in her eyes. The brightness seemed to contain, if only in nascent form, a newfound respect and admiration, along with a gratifying element of fear. "I don't believe you," she said, but she did believe me. She believed me because she wanted to believe me. You all want to believe I am more than I could ever be. That's your secret power. Your naive belief is what I ruthlessly take advantage of, but it also bears strange fruit.

"No," I said, "it's true," I said, and suddenly, in the very saying, I knew that it was. "I realized that everything I was doing for these rich assholes was for their little ribbons and bows. I don't want to be chasing those stinking ribbons anymore. I'm going to chase something else. I'm not even sure it matters what, just that it be something that is my own and will let whatever is true and hard in my gut have free rein. Justice fits the bill, so there it is. And, to be truthful, I knew you would like it."

"You changed for me?"

"Why not?"

"Jesus, you're an idiot."

"I don't blame you for not believing me. I wouldn't believe me either." The bar had grown dense with the red-faced and the thick-bellied. It was getting difficult now to keep track of who was who. "It's too crowded. Let's go."

"Where to?"

"Back to my motel room."

"Really? That's the best you've got? God, you are a rotten peach, Phil. A fake case, a promise of information later, this whole pursuit-of-justice crap, and then a backhanded invitation to the sack. Maybe I will arrest you now."

"It's not what you think, though neither of us would mind."

"You have the right to remain silent; exercise it. Anything you say can and will be used against you in a court of law; count on it."

"There's someone in my room you'll want to meet."

"Oh God, it only gets worse."

"The girl with the missing kidney."

"Wait, what? She's here? In DC?"

"I brought her here just for you."

"And she wants to talk?"

I stood, took out my wallet, dropped more than enough to cover the bill. "Let's get out of here."

With my hand lightly on her arm, we edged our way through the well-heeled crowd, women with that DC ambition stamped on their foreheads, men in suits or studiously dressed down to look start-up executive rather than hipster. Money and power. They all looked at me and saw nothing. That would change. I glanced left and right as we moved to the exit, on guard for some dangerous lunge.

"Where's your hotel?" said Linda over the babble of the crowd.

"Last time I was at a hotel," I said. "Now it's a cheap motel on New York Avenue."

"Going down in the world."

"My car's in the lot across the street."

She dipped her head as we pushed through the glass doors. When we stepped outside and started climbing the stairs to the street level, it was still light out, but there was the brisk sense of night coming, with all its quickening. As soon as we hit the sidewalk, I did a neck twist to take in the scene, and that's when I saw her.

Coming toward me. A white blouse, a tight black skirt, shiny high heels, green eyes bright, a tight smile on her gorgeous pale face. Looking just like she had looked the first time I saw her.

I was so surprised to see Cassandra outside the bar that first I marveled at the coincidence, and then felt a wave of embarrassment at being caught by one lover with another. It was only when, with that tight smile still on her face, she lifted her arm and pointed the gun at my face that I realized I was going to die. And then she fired. Twice.

Bam bam.

38

GHOSTS

How does it feel to be swilling Scotch with a dead man?

Every story is a ghost story when you get right down to it, and this is no exception. As Cassandra lifted her gun and aimed it in my direction, the stink of death filled my nostrils. I was as sure of my demise as a man on the gallows.

And what did I feel?

A coppery brew of acrid emotions twined around the twin poles of fear and anger—and have no doubt that I can surely taste my emotions even if I can't taste yours. But the strongest emotion I felt as the barrel of Cassandra's gun stared at me with its dark, deadly eye was disappointment. Something new had been birthed in me in just the last few hours, and I was disappointed I wouldn't be able to ride it like a surfer on a wild wave. It was as if just as I was entering a new and most interesting dream, the cold light of wakefulness slapped me in the face.

You are what you always were, that light told me, you are what you will always be, and nothing more now is possible. Such is the tragedy within every ghost story. What could be more disappointing?

And then something happened, something as quick and instinctual as a flinch. As Cassandra's finger tensed on the trigger, I reached for Linda Pickering and pulled at her just as the gun went off, twice, the retorts themselves a dagger of pain in my ear.

And even as I was searching the numbness that spread in a flash across my body for the killing wounds, the act of pulling at Linda Pickering had turned me enough so that I could see something in her face, some deep surprise, and then looking over her shoulder, I could see behind us a bald man with a gun in his hand, staggering as two buds of red blossomed on his chest.

And then he fell, Detective Booth, he fell in a heap, one leg shaking while he lay on the cement, while I, shockingly, was still up and alive. I swiveled my head to look at Cassandra.

"We have to go," said Cassandra as she came toward me.

"You told Booth we were meeting," I said to Linda Pickering.

"Just that I was, yes, but not where. He's my partner. How could I trust you after what you did?"

"We have to go, Phil," said Cassandra. "Now."

At that moment Linda suddenly remembered who she was, drawing her revolver, dropping into a stance. "Put down the gun."

I placed myself between Linda's police revolver and Cassandra. "I told you he was working for them," I said to Linda.

"Tell your friend to put the gun down."

"We have to go," said Cassandra.

"No one's going anywhere," said Linda.

"He came to kill me," I said. "He works for them and you led him right to me."

"Neither of you move," she said, but she looked up at me with something more than anger in her face.

"Wait, he's still breathing," I said.

Linda Pickering spun around to look at her fallen partner, and Cassandra and I took off, sprinting through traffic as we crossed the wide street while a crowd encircled Detective Booth and his partner, who was leaning over him to see if there was anything she could do to save his life.

There wasn't.

The Porsche roared out of the lot, charging through the exit farthest from the bar. I turned right toward Union Station, spun around the circle, and kept heading north along the tracks, weaving through slower cars. When we passed two black-and-whites coming the other way— lights flashing, sirens on, the whole emergency docket—I careered right and then left again. The tires squealed neatly.

"Do you have a cigarette?" said Cassandra with a brilliant calm as the car skittered and roared.

"In the glove compartment."

She opened the hatch, peered inside. "That gun's not doing you any good in there," she said as she pushed the Glock I had bought in Natchitoches to the side. She removed the pack of cigarettes, closed the hatch, and pressed in the car's lighter.

"I've got to tell you, Cassandra, when I saw you coming at me, I thought I was done for."

She slid out a cigarette, pulled the lighter, placed the cigarette's tip on the glowing spiral. As she took a long, deep inhale, her hands were steady as pillars. "How did it feel to die?"

"Disappointing."

She laughed clouds of smoke.

"Thank you for not killing me," I said.

"Don't get all emotional about it, darling. I probably would have if I wasn't going to be next anyway."

"Not you, Cassandra."

"You act like you don't understand what you've done. Like all is cookies and cake in the wake of your betrayal. When they finish with you, sweet, that doesn't mean it's finished. There will be a purge. They've done it before."

"But you've been their most loyal servant."

She took another inhale, looked out the window. "Ever since Rand, they've worried that I had been infected by his qualms. Which is a laugh, really. I brush my teeth with his qualms and spit them into the sink. But he had a certain charm, and the sex was good, so I missed him. When you smashed Mr. Maambong's desk and they were ready to get rid of you then and there, I held them off. I didn't want to lose you like I lost him."

"You went to bat for me?"

"I have a soft spot for the certified. That's why I went with you to Jamaica; I was trying to bring you back to your senses."

"I thought it was just a vacation."

"Nothing is just anything with them. When you went missing, it was clear I had failed. They don't appreciate failure."

"Tough crowd."

"Well, darling, you did smash his desk, try to take his job, and then steal away with kidney girl. They sent a team into Louisiana to scout out your last location. An old man living in a trailer by the creek said you had been there, had just left, and were now heading out to Sacramento."

"I knew that old Cajun was a sieve."

"They were searching for you on the road west when they learned about your meeting with the lady cop. They sent me up on a private plane to take care of you. Ostensibly I was to back up Booth, but I figure I was supposed to be next. Maybe right there, on the street. How neat would that have been? And with a gun in my hand, it would have been a righteous shooting; it would have made Booth a hero cop."

"Where's Tom Preston in all this?"

"On his way. He's been tasked with finding the girl. Where is she, by the way?"

"Here."

"You brought her here?"

"She had to meet with her new lawyer."

She laughed out a few wry puffs of smoke. "They'll love that."

"Nothing settles things down like a lawsuit."

"But you don't want to settle things down."

"No."

"You're going to burn it all to the ground."

"I'm going to try."

"Why?"

"To see the flames."

She took a final inhale, powered down the window, and flicked out the butt. "There was a plague of arsons in our neighborhood when I was growing up. This was a dying suburb outside Atlanta whose time had come and gone. At first just abandoned houses were being torched. But then, later, houses where people were merely on vacation. Everyone was frightened, including my folks. People moved away, the police were stumped. I was twelve when the wave started, fourteen when we moved. Funny, the fires stopped at the same time. The dead cats, too. We ended up in a small town in Texas."

"Nice place?"

"Lovely, unless you had to live there. I've been getting bored lying in the sun like a tick, doing their bidding. I'm ready again for something bright to singe my retinas. If you want to burn down the Hyena Squad, I'll bring the blowtorch."

"Welcome aboard," I said. "What do we do now?"

"For now we run," she said. "We run and keep running."

"I don't want to run."

"We run, until we stop and turn around. That's when the fun starts."

***

When we reached the motel, I parked the car tight behind the bushes so it couldn't be seen from the road. After killing the engine, I reached across Cassandra for the glove compartment and pulled out the Glock. Cassandra gave me a cat's smile.

"What?" I said.

"I never saw you with a gun before. It's a good look for you."

"I prefer less forceful means of persuasion."

"But the color of gunmetal matches your eyes."

With the Glock gripped in my pocket, I led Cassandra up the stairs to the second level and then along the outside passage to the room. I looked around to see who might be watching, who might be coming. I had given enough information to Linda Pickering so she could, in time, figure out where we were. It wouldn't be long before the sirens started rising in the distance as police cars burned their way toward us.

I banged twice. "It's me," I said, and then stepped out of the way, my grip tight on the gun, as the door opened.

It was Cindy who stood at the door; Alberto was inside. The lights were bright, the bed was made, the room smelled of Alberto's aftershave. I motioned Cassandra in ahead of me, gave a quick look around, and then followed, closing the door behind me.

"This is Cassandra," I said. "An old friend. We can trust her."

"Charmed," said Alberto.

"Cassandra, this is Alberto, our lawyer, and you know Cindy."

"Hello, Cindy," said Cassandra.

"Nurse Fletcher?"

"You're looking well. Any problems with your recovery?"

"No, everything's peachy except for what's missing. Are you really a nurse?"

"Yes, actually. At least I was."

"He's not a doctor, you know."

"I know," she said, "but he could play one on TV."

"Yes, exactly, with that cute jacket he had."

"I hate cutting the reunion short," I said, "but we don't have much time. How did it go with the doctor?"

"We have what we need," said Alberto. "It is all very interesting, including the fact of your involvement in the . . . extraction."

"Put Dick Triplett in the caption as a defendant, it doesn't matter, he's as judgment proof as they come. Cassandra has detailed information on all the other defendants, names, addresses. Can you stay with Alberto and give him what he needs?"

"What about you?" said Cassandra.

"I have to get Cindy out of here."

"Yes, I'll stay, of course. Actually, I can use a drink, Alberto."

"I know just the place," he said.

"Cindy, do you have somewhere safe you can go," I said, "somewhere you can hide out without anyone finding you?"

"I don't know. A relative?"

"A friend would be better, someone with a distant connection that would be difficult to trace."

"There's a high school friend in Denver."

"Pack up."

"I'm packed."

"Good. We need to leave here right away." I stepped toward Cassandra, took hold of her arm, said softly, "When Cindy's settled, we'll reconnect and light our torches."

She went to the desk and jotted down a number. "Don't wait too long," she said before kissing me.

Albert watched this with an amused smile. "You know, Dick, this could be a valuable lawsuit. While the doctor was working, I did research on your Mrs. Wister. She inherited quite the fortune."

"Let's decimate it," I said.

He stood, stepped toward me. "Thank you again for bringing Cindy's case to me. And the Gould case." He reached out his big old hand, which I took hold of. Leathery and warm, like a broken-in baseball mitt. "You should know, my friend, that in a way you saved my life."

"Don't thank me, Alberto. It was just business. Make us all rich."

Cindy was now standing by the bed, her pack hanging off one shoulder.

"We'll go first," I said. "You follow. Be safe, both of you. I'll be in touch."

And then we were out the door, Cindy gripping her bag, me gripping the gun still in my jacket pocket, skipping along the passage, down the stairs, across the lot to the car.

I kept on expecting to hear the sirens, the sound of gunfire, I kept on expecting something to crash our escape, but all I heard was the normal drone of traffic on New York Avenue. The car shuddered to life.

I pulled us out of the lot heading into the city before making the first left, not caring where it took us, just so it took us off that road. I wended the car this way and that through a warren of parkways and residential streets, just wanting to get away from whatever was going to happen in that motel. And something was going to happen in that motel, though not the something I had expected. And then, comfortably lost in the wilds of Washington, DC, I punched Denver, Colorado, into the GPS.

We were just beyond the Maryland border, traveling through the night on the old highway in the shadow of the interstate, headed toward the lovely metropolis of Morgantown, West Virginia, when a pair of headlights, like the eyes of fate, shot up behind us.

39

CABIN FEVER

So here we are, back at the beginning. In my Porsche, on the run, the red Pontiac charging from behind. It slam-banged right into our rear bumper, intending to ram us off the road. I guess they should have used a Dodge.

I gained just enough control to veer into the oncoming lane of traffic. The wide, fat headlights of a truck barreled headlong toward us. I stamped the brakes, let the Pontiac zoom ahead, downshifted, and just avoided the truck as I slipped behind our pursuer. I could have pulled the emergency brake and tried a U-turn skid that had just as much chance of hurtling us into the thick grove of trees off the shoulder as keeping us on the road, but even if I succeeded, they'd still be chasing. When the Pontiac shot past us as if from a slingshot, in the glare of the truck's headlights I got a clean look at the driver. Bobo, the steroid meathead who had been lathering up Cassandra at the Miami house. A hard charger indeed. You don't run from henchmen like that, you attack.

I slapped on my high beams and chased after the Pontiac. I gave it a tap on the bumper to speed it up. I slid to the left and accelerated to the right, slamming the car just behind its rear tire like a race-car driver taking out the machine of a rival team. I skidded onto the graveled shoulder, darted around the whirling hunk of metal, and jerked back onto the smooth asphalt. In my rearview mirror the Pontiac's lights revolved at a strange angle, as if the car had been picked up by some dark giant and set spinning like a top. A moment later, amidst a hurtling din that engulfed us along with the pitch of Cindy's shouts, the headlights jerked into stillness, aiming now deep into the woods, one stacked atop the other.

"Are you okay?" I said to Cindy as we raced on, a screeching following us as we powered away from the ruined Pontiac.

"Bang gang, what the hell was that?"

"They're onto us. They sent a team out to kill us both. I had to do something."

"Are they dead?"

"Hopefully. But the question, Cindy, is how are they onto us?"

With my gaze more aimed at the rearview mirror than on the road, I kept waiting for the leap of fire. In every movie where a car spins and crashes like that, there's always a leap of fire. But here, now there was nothing. I considered turning around, going back, and finishing the job, but what if there was a team behind them? Why wouldn't there be a team behind them?

"We have to get off this road."

The engine roared like an angry beast, still healthy in its rear compartment, but along with the roar was the screech of metal on metal, and a sour rubber smoke was leaking into the interior. We wouldn't get very far before something snapped or a tire blew. That's when I spotted in my high beams a rusted sign for a camp of tourist cabins.

"Hold on," I said.

I took the turn at speed.

The car limped onto the gravel drive of the old tourist camp. The beams of my headlights painted the lot haphazardly, like the gaze of two crossed eyes. I parked within the ambit of light in front of the far cabin, got out, and checked the car's condition. Something viscous and dark was dripping from the rear-mounted engine as a result of the first slam, and the left side of the front was entirely crumpled, with a metal edge pressing into the top of the tire that was now blown. In the morning light I might be able to bend back the metal, change the tire, fix the oil leak. In the morning light we might be able to get somewhere other than here, but what did it matter? They were onto us, and here was as good a place as any.

I pulled open Cindy's door. Metal creaked and bent with the pulling. "Wait," I said as I leaned in, opened the glove compartment, pulled out the gun. "I'll check us in."

"We're staying here?"

"We're not getting much farther with the car as it is."

"Who were they, the people in the car?"

"Just some hoods. There will probably be more."

"So what do we do now?"

"Get some sleep. Let me check us in."

"You'll come back, won't you, Dick?"

"Sure," I said. "I'll be back."

Her eyes were still wide with fear and hope when I shut the door and headed across the curve of cabins to where a neon "Vacancy" sign was lit in front of the largest of the cabins. I turned back and saw Cindy staring at me as I stepped into the office.

In the dimly lit log-cabin interior, alongside the counter, was a rack with pamphlets for all the local attractions: water slides, train rides, Fallingwater, Cooper's Rock. And ooh, golf. There was a bell on the desk and a door behind the desk, where the innkeeper would be sleeping, and a door on the far side of the cabin, where I could sneak out without being seen by Cindy Lieu.

They were onto us. They were tracking her, or me, or my car, but most likely her. There was something she brought, something in that bag, a phone she didn't give me, the tablet she said she didn't have, maybe a marker the good Dr. Heigenmeister stuck inside her when he took out the kidney. What it was didn't much matter. Out of Virginia I had gotten off the interstate. We were driving west on a dark local road when that Pontiac came after us like a guided missile. They were onto us, which meant they still were coming. And right now we were no match for them.

The smart thing was for me to get the hell away, alone, to take the gun and slip out the far door and head into the woods, alone, into the mountains, alone. I could roam the landscape, find a cabin here, some empty vacation home there, hide out in places where they would never find me, and regroup. Then, if there was going to be a fight, it would be on my terms, on my ground, where I had the advantage. There was nothing keeping me here that I cared about in the least, except maybe for the Porsche. I did like the Porsche. It would be a shame if something fatal happened to the Porsche. But something already near fatal had happened to the Porsche. And if Alberto came through, I could buy a fleet. Better yet, I'd still be alive to drive past the gaping suckers in their Hondas. The smart thing was to go.

But for the second time in a span of only a few hours, I didn't do the smart thing. (Did you catch the first time?) What I did instead was ring the bell and wake the kid sleeping in the room behind the desk. He was thin and tall, his dark hair mussed, his face a spilled glass of milk.

"You guys busy?" I said.

"It's midweek."

"Is the cabin at the far end available?"

"Pick whichever one you want," he said without looking out the window. "It doesn't matter. It's midweek."

"Two nights. Cash okay?"

"Yeah, sure. But I'll still need to see a card."

"All I have is cash, but I can add a hundred to cover expenses. You get to keep what's left."

"Cool."

"Yeah," I said.

After Cindy and I were set in the cabin, along with our bags, the guns, and the ammunition, I moved the car to the cabin in the middle of the row. On the way back, I kicked gravel over the pool of oil that had leaked from the Porsche's engine. I told Cindy to get some sleep, and then I pulled the easy chair around. I sat in the chair, looking out the opened window, with the Glock on the table and the AR-15 in my lap. They were onto us, which meant they were coming.

Well, let the bastards come, I welcomed them. They weren't just assassins to me anymore, they were opportunity.

I sat in that chair and stared at the darkness surrounding the poorly lighted gravel clearing in front of the cabins. The sounds of nature floated in through the window as I waited for them to come: a breeze slipping through the trees, the chirrups and buzzes of insects, the distant song of an insomniac bird. It was soothing and innocent, lulling, all of it, until I jerked awake from the slam of a car door.

A blue SUV had pulled behind the Porsche in the middle of the row of cabins. Behind the SUV, illuminated by the dim yellow light, looking around to get the lay of the land, stood Riley. She wore a leather jacket and she had a gun in her hand. Another car door slammed and there was Kief, slowly circling the Porsche, holding some device, shaking his head as he inspected the car's wounds. He walked up to the cabin and tried to peer into the window.

I could just barely make out his nasal voice floating above the insec-tile hum. "I don't think he's in there."

"Of course he's not in there," said Riley. "It would be suicide."

"And what he's done isn't?"

"Maybe he hiked off into the mountains."

"Phil ever seem much of a hikey guy to you? He probably stole another car, stopped to get a manicure, and is now heading west, like he said. I'll check in the office."

The shot kicked up gravel in front of the cabin. Kief dove to the side of the Porsche and lifted his head just above the crumpled hood. Riley turned toward me.

"I hope you missed on purpose," she said. "Because if you didn't, then you're a piss-poor shot, which doesn't bode well for your survival."

"Drop the gun and raise your hands, both of you," I said. The gun dropped, their hands rose. "Where are the rest of the Hyenas?"

"They're coming," said Riley. "But we're not with them. We both ran as soon as you told us to."

"Then why aren't you on that beach halfway across the world with that girl you were with?"

"It didn't quite work out," said Riley.

"Like it didn't work out last time?"

"You got a point to make?"

"I don't think you're ever getting to that beach."

"Tell me about it."

"Put the gun down, boss," called out Kief, his hands raised while he still was hiding behind the Porsche. "We're here to help."

"They didn't send us," said Riley.

"Then what are you doing here?"

"They're tracking your ass," said Kief.

"I figured they were, but you're the ones who showed up."

"Yeah, well, Riley broke into their server and found the signal specs they had sent off to their teams. At that point, all I had to do was reprogram the receiver that we used—"

"Where's the signaling device?"

"From what I can tell it's in your car. It seems to be coming from the glove compartment. Want me to get rid of it?"

"Leave it," I said. "I wouldn't want your pals to get lost."

"Who was in your car who could have planted the device?" said Riley.

"Just our kidney girl," I said, "and Cassandra."

"Cassandra?" said Kief.

"She saved my life in DC."

"So they could get to the girl."

"I suppose I know that now. And I guess our lawyer's dead, too. That's a shame. So why are you here again?"

"To warn you. To help you. To stand with you."

"Why would you want to stand with me?"

"You think they're going to leave us be?" said Kief. "They already came after us once."

"If they come after us again," said Riley, "we figured we'd rather be with you when they do."

"What about Gordon?" I said.

"He's with them. As soon as I warned him, like you said, the shit hit the fanny. Apparently he'd been keeping tabs on you for them from the start, playing a double game all along. He was the one who told Mr. Maambong about the lawyer in Washington."

"Gordon, huh. I knew someone was blabbing, but I thought the traitor was you, Kief."

"Me?"

"Are you saying you wouldn't have?"

"I'm saying that Gordon beat me to it."

"So, how do you propose to help?"

"First you put down the rifle," said Riley.

"Sure," I said, keeping the barrel trained their way. "How's that?"

"We could run, man," said Kief. "Your car's not going anywhere the way it is now, but we could get away in the SUV."

"Until they find us again."

"Or, since we know they're coming," said Riley, "we could wait here and plead our case."

"Like they would listen."

"I wasn't thinking about talking."

"How many guns you got?"

"There's the handgun you made me drop," said Riley. "And a shotgun in the car."

"That's not going to do much to stop Maambong's army."

"The shotgun's a twelve gauge," said Riley. "Pump action with a magazine extender. It can do some damage, trust me. And Kief brought along some of his toys."

"Toys?"

"Would it help," said Kief, "if one of the toys was a flamethrower?"

40

WATERLOO

The sun had not yet risen when they came. The treetops were barely visible in the lightening sky, and the drive into the tourist camp remained dark, impenetrable to my sight in a morning mist, but suddenly I knew they had come. The sounds of nature had gone abruptly quiet, as if a great speckled cat was moving swiftly through the woods, and I caught the scent of something rich with corruption and rot and inevitability. A moment later, through the hush, approaching footfalls tolled clearly on the gravel drive.

They emerged out of the mist in two rows, like a murder of crows perched on twin electric wires. There were six henchmen up front, including Bobo, whom I had run off the road the night before—the bandages about his head and neck giving me more than a little satisfaction—and Bert, good old Bert, checking my veracity, building my drinks, coming now to put a bullet in my brain. The henchmen wore armored vests festooned with magazines and carried assault rifles as big as tree trunks. Behind them came four Hyenas: Gordon and Tom Preston and Mr. Maambong and sweet Cassandra, my Cassandra. All but Mr. Maambong bore weapons: Cassandra gripped the automatic she used in Washington; Gordon held an assault rifle with both hands; Tom Preston carried a huge gun with what looked like another gun fixed on top.

Mr. Maambong in his white suit walked gingerly, leaning on his cane, his beetle-eyed glasses surveying the scene with that terrifying blankness. Sent here by the Principal, no doubt, to clean up his mess, which meant wiping me off the register of the organization as well as the face of the earth. I supposed that meant I wasn't getting the partnership.

When they were still a distance from the cabins, Tom Preston said something quietly and two of the henchmen broke off and headed to my right in order to flank the row of cabins. Another of the men headed to my left, entering the office. Then Bobo and a gunman from the front row walked right up to the Porsche parked before the middle cabin and raised their weapons. Only Bert now remained in front of the main hyenas. There was no attempt at negotiation, no call to wake me from my slumber and then entreat me to give up the girl without a fight. This wasn't about giving up without a fight. Instead, the two gunmen stood in silence behind the Porsche, rifles aimed at the cabin, as if waiting for a signal.

And then a shot rang out from inside the office.

And suddenly the two men behind the Porsche started firing in bursts of four or five shots each. Burst after burst. And they kept at it, reloading when necessary with the magazines hanging off their vests. Burst after burst after burst, in a rhythm steady and strangely beautiful. The smoke rising, the dead magazines littering the gravel, the crisp scent of gunpowder, the very coldness of it. Blasting through the thin walls of the cabin, raising spinning splinters of wood and shards of glass, along with apocalyptic dust, loosing a relentless fusillade that brought the merest of smiles to Mr. Maambong's face.

Until the Porsche blew all to hell.

The explosion bounced the car onto its side and unleashed an orange ball of flame and woe that flattened Bobo and the other gunman like a seven-eight spare.

And at the same time, amidst a chorus of howls off to my right, fire poured through the woods like a tilted oil gusher gone mad. One of the henchmen ran out of the trees and onto the gravel, fire rising from every part of him, along with a thick, noisome smoke. He twirled and howled and fell. No one rushed over to pat out the flames, no one gave succor to the fallen man. Fire continued to drench the woods, even in the face of gunfire. Mr. Maambong's glasses glinted blankly in the firelight.

Things were going peachy. Before they arrived I had given Cindy the Glock and sent her into the woods behind the cabins to wait for us in safety. We had set our positions in anticipation. Already my assumption was that there were five down—the shot in the office was most likely from Riley, who had sent the young clerk off and was waiting behind the desk—five henchmen lost in the first wave of the battle. It would seem like a crushing blow, losing half your force in a snap of time, but what were five down to Mr. Maambong? They were henchmen, after all, and who in this world is more disposable than a henchman?

As the Hyenas backed away, Bert firing haphazardly, I was confident enough to rise from behind the fortress of furniture and mattresses I had constructed to reinforce the wall of my cabin farthest from the office. I rested the barrel of the gun on the windowsill and was taking aim at Tom Preston himself, when I saw a puff of smoke rise from his position. Something like a small football spiraled through the air, coming right at me.

And in the time span of its arcing flight, I began to reconsider this whole make-a-stand-at-the-tourist-camp thing.

***

The explosion not only ripped a hole in the cabin and in my face, but in the very stream of time, creating a black hole that devoured memory. I have no recollection of the building disintegrating around me from the first grenade, or the incoming arc of the second grenade, or my dramatic bent-back flight through the air. All I know for sure is I landed faceup in the middle of the gravel lot, not far from the ruined hulk of my Porsche, both of us streaming smoke into the morning air.

When I came to, my pathetic little piece of resistance was over. I struggled to rise and finally did so, sitting up with my legs spread before me. I put a hand to my face and it came back bloody. My vision was spotty, unfocused, and one eye screamed with pain when I tried to wipe the blood away. Something was in it, something was sticking out of it. Kief was kneeling beside me, moaning. On the ground to his side was the whole flamethrower rig of tanks and nozzle torch he had whipped up from parts bought at a Home Depot, the nozzle gashed by a bullet and blackened. Kief's pants were singed, his hands were burned hunks of flesh.

Mr. Maambong stood before me, staring down with those blank beetle eyes. "You're awake, Mr. Kubiak. Finally. Now answer us quickly. Where is she?"

"Where is who?" I said, and it wasn't an idle question. At that moment I was still fighting to clear the smog of unknowing in my brain. I wasn't even sure who I was, where I was, whether or not this was reality or some brutal dream. Was I truly sitting on this gravel drive, or was I instead reclining on a chaise at the pool in Miami, the burns on my body from the sun, my brain fogged by a sweet stick of high-powered White Widow put into my lips by my lovely Cassandra? But as the fog lifted I realized that Cassandra wasn't lying beside me but standing behind Kief with a gun at his head, and the sweet popcorn scent wasn't reefer but the stink of Kief's burned flesh.

"The girl," said Mr. Maambong. "The one you were assigned to eliminate and who you instead spirited away from Memphis and introduced to your former lawyer. Ms. Lieu. Where is she?"

"I dropped her off on the road," I said. "She's on a bus somewhere."

"We don't believe you."

He took his stick and pressed the pulped mess that was my knee. The pain shot like a spike from my leg up my spine, detonating in the base of my brain. I fell back onto the gravel, my head hitting the stones so forcefully it actually felt like relief.

"Should Cassandra kill your associate?" said Maambong. "Would that jog your memory?"

"I told you what I know," I said, the gravel pressing daggers into my back. "Do whatever you want to him, I don't give a shit."

"Really, dude?" said Kief. "That's the best you've got?"

"What about you?" he said to Kief.

"I could use some pharmaceuticals. Tylenol, methadone, Oxy if you have it. Eighties would be good."

"Tell us where the girl is and we'll take care of you."

"I didn't see her," said Kief, which was a startling lie. "She wasn't here. Maybe Phil's telling the truth."

"We doubt that. Mr. Kubiak is incapable of telling the truth. Isn't that right, Mr. Kubiak? Isn't that a sad symptom of your condition?"

I struggled to sit up again on the gravel, my head weaving this way and that. "Then why the hell are you even asking me?"

"It seems the thing to do before we kill you both. We would offer to let your associate run free if you told us, but you know we would do no such thing, and in any event, the fate of another human being wouldn't matter to a specimen like you."

"You're right," I said. "It wouldn't matter."

"Again?" said Kief. "How many times are you throwing me under that bus, boss?"

"So, Cassandra," I said, "I see that once again you end up on the right side of the purge."

"I'm going to miss you, Phil. We were a nice match. But we always understood each other perfectly. Sentimentality is for saps."

"What really happened to Rand?"

"We had the most wonderful weekend in Belize. It was perfect, the sun, the wine, the sex, even the ending. In the rain forest, up against a tree. I slit his throat as he came."

"Maybe he was faking it."

"With me?"

"Everything's been checked," said Tom Preston, walking away from the line of cabins with Bert and Gordon trailing. "No one there, not even the clerk."

"What about our man?" said Mr. Maambong.

"Dead."

"Set up a perimeter," said Mr. Maambong. "Once these two are taken care of, we'll find the girl. She didn't get far."

"I told you she's not here," I said.

"Yes, you told us," said Mr. Maambong. "And we choose not to believe you. She is somewhere in these woods. And your other team member is probably with her. It would be quite convenient finding them together."

I looked over at Gordon, who was surveying the tourist camp, studiously avoiding my gaze. "I see you're still on that gravy train, Gordon?" I said.

"Man's got to eat," said Gordon without looking my way.

"Let's finish them now and get on with it," said Tom Preston. "The longer we wait the more lead they have."

"The perimeter, Mr. Preston," said Mr. Maambong. "You and Mr. Johnstone take the road. Don't let anyone pass, wave away any visitors. Bert will watch the area behind the cabins."

Tom Preston stared for a moment and then did as he was told, giving Gordon and Bert their orders.

"There is something we don't understand, Mr. Kubiak," said Mr. Maambong. "Maybe you could enlighten us." He braced both hands on his cane and leaned forward. "You were vetted most carefully. You passed all our tests with the highest scores we ever tabulated. You even bested Tom Preston at the games. You were a perfect specimen. But you went wrong, somehow. We want to know why."

"I didn't want to kill," I said. "My mother taught me better than that."

"You are making a joke," said Mr. Maambong, his face serious as death. "In time we will think back on this moment and laugh and laugh. But we all know with people like you there is no right or wrong, there just is. That is why we picked you. But even more troubling than not following our specific orders was the craziness of these last few days. Grabbing Miss Lieu, running all across the country, bringing in a lawyer, trying to fight us. Was it simple derangement, or is there a deeper flaw? See, Mr. Kubiak, there are more like you, this country is full of candidates for our positions. And when we find another specimen so pure—and we will keep on searching, it is what we do—how can we make sure that this new operative plies our trade without disappointing? What do you say, Mr. Kubiak? Tell us why a perfect specimen like yourself went so very wrong. Why, Mr. Kubiak? Why?"

"Why not?"

"Another joke. You must think you are in a comedy club. Let us put this starkly. If you would deign to help us, we could make your death as painless as possible. Otherwise . . . the problem with death is not the destination, it is the journey that takes you there. Tell us how you ended up here, lying like a corpse already on this gravel, outsmarted, outgunned, a mewling mess of bone and gristle with nothing to look forward to but nothingness."

That was the question, absolutely. What had happened to me? Why did I keep making all the wrong decisions, and how did I end up here, now, beneath this gaunt fiend staring down at me with death in his beetle eyes? In the ominous hours I waited for Maambong to appear, I had contemplated how I had chosen to be in that tourist camp, waiting for a pack of killers with the odds all against me. And in those hours an answer was becoming clear, but I would sooner have grabbed that sliver sticking in my eye and twisted it than told the answer to Maambong.

So what I did instead was let a little sob erupt in my throat, a pathetic little sob of fear to hide the sound of me hawking up a glob of phlegm, and then, with Mr. Maambong still waiting for my answer, I thrust my neck forward and expectorated.

The glob splattered nicely onto one of those cold, dark lenses. And the sight of it was cheering. As the man said, there is no fate that cannot be overcome by spit. Or is that spite?

Mr. Maambong didn't react as I expected. There was no anger or disgust, nothing really at all on his cruel face. He stayed bent forward, looking down at me coldly, and then, slowly, hands pressing on the knob of his cane, he stood straight again. He took a handkerchief from his pocket and removed the glasses, and as he wiped off my spit he looked about. His eyes were small and red and porcine, as if someone had grafted the eyes of a pink little pig onto his face. When the lens was clean, he put the glasses back on.

"Take them into one of the cabins and kill them," he said to Cassandra.

"We're not going anywhere," I said.

"Very well, then do it here, and do it slowly." Mr. Maambong smiled at us both before walking toward Gordon and Tom Preston at the mouth of the drive.

"Wait a second," shouted Kief. "What about the drugs, man? Medicate the hell out of me and I'll tell you what went wrong with him, I'll tell you anything you want to know about Phil. Is one fucking pill too much to ask?"

Maambong stopped and turned and looked at Kief. "Yes," he said. "Yes it is." And then he continued on his way.

"This is such a pity, Phil," said Cassandra. "And so unnecessary. But I suppose we'll always have Jamaica."

"Why don't you do it to me like you did to Rand?"

"Do you have any idea how difficult it is to get out bloodstains? But I really am going to miss you."

"You don't have to do this, you know. You said you wanted to see everything burn. Let me strap on Kief's flamethrower. The fire would be so beautiful."

"It's the purge. Rule number two is to always stay on the right side of the purge. Which means following orders, one thing you were never very good at."

"What's rule number one?"

"Don't let the strap of your top ruin a good tan."

"I'll remember that in hell."

"I'm sorry, darling, but Mr. Maambong told me to do it slowly."

She lowered her pistol from my face, to my chest, and then to my outstretched leg. But the thunder that came, came not from her gun.

41

POCKET CHANGE

Have you detected the incongruity at the core of my story?

I am incapable of caring about others, but I always schemed to make sure others cared about me. I had learned early, living in an alien world, that pretending friendship was a useful tool—a true friend would do anything to help you—and over the years I've convinced many that they were true friends of mine. I couldn't feel what they felt, but if they believed I felt what they felt, I could manipulate them all the same. The friendships never lasted, the truth would out eventually and my so-called friends would drift away with a vague sense of horror, but the approach proved useful over and again.

Take, for example, Riley. I had fought for her, joked with her, told her uncomfortable truths while repeatedly and annoyingly confessing my inability to care, all in order to build a bridge of trust and engender caring in her. Even that last call to her from Louisiana was only about keeping her on the hook in case I needed her help later on. And the fruit of that effort was her and Kief being willing to toss away their lives fighting with me at that ragged tourist camp. The same could be said for Cindy Lieu. Though I had deceived her enthusiastically and ripped a kidney from her torso, she had come to believe that my purpose now was to save her for her own sake. It all would have been worthy of a laugh if it wasn't so pathetic.

And yet all my manipulations ripened brilliantly as Cassandra aimed her gun at my leg. For when Cindy could have been running through the woods and searching for safety, she was instead driving a blue SUV right into the murderous heart of the tourist camp. And when Riley could have been running headlong to that beach of hers for real, she was instead riding shotgun with, well, a shotgun.

The SUV roared like a wild beast as it barreled forward along the road, spitting gravel behind it as Gordon and Tom Preston and Cassandra, too, trained their guns on the charging monster and started pumping bullets into its grill and windshield. But the van kept coming, kept coming, in a mad rush, seemingly impervious to the feeble attempts to stop its progress, kept gaining speed and coming, coming.

Until it leaped at Gordon, sending him flying even as Riley suddenly appeared out of the moon roof, quickly letting loose a blast from the shotgun that spun Tom Preston off his feet in a splatter of blood.

Until it veered straight for Mr. Maambong, who stood transfixed for just a moment before trying to leap out of the way, an attempt made futile by his lameness, and so he was still within the van's charge when it smacked him solidly enough to send his glasses flying as it slammed him forward before bounding over his body.

Until it careered toward our sad grouping as Cassandra emptied her gun into the windshield and Kief leaped over me to get out of its way. For a moment it seemed that Cassandra had altered the van's direction with her gun, before Riley again appeared out of the moonroof with her shotgun and not only riddled Cassandra's perfect body but hit Kief's flame-throwing rig, unleashing a tornado of fire that swirled around Cassandra like a plague of snakes.

Until it slammed into the remains of the Porsche still on its side, and both hunks of metal lurched forward before stopping dead.

But for a groan and a hiss, the assault was over. The whole thing had happened in just seconds, a magnificent vainglorious charge, which in its singular purpose and ruthlessness has become, at least for me, a model for the never-ending war against fate itself.

I was in too much pain from my shattered leg to do much but gape at the brutality of the run and the demolition it left behind. I turned after the crash to see no movement at all in the van's interior. I was struggling to rise as best I could on one leg so as to make my way to the ruined blue thing, when out of the corner of my eye I spied some horrid creature staggering toward me from the mouth of the road.

Tom Preston, bloodied and hunched with pain, but still with the massive rifle in his hands, was coming at me.

He didn't say anything as he approached, and neither did I. What was there to say? He was going to kill me and there was nothing I could say to stop him. We had gone through this before, Tom Preston and I. There was the slightest smirk on his bloodied face and I knew what that smirk was all about. He had told me his plans to take over the squad, and I had taken his cue and made my own move for Maambong's chair. But now his ascension was clear. After he killed me and Kief, he would no doubt kill what was left of Mr. Maambong. Then with great ceremony he, not I, would fill the seat behind the glass desk in the Miami house. He, not I, would control the teams and reap the rewards. And he, not I, would eventually move against the Principal herself, becoming the greatest Hyena of them all. It was all so easy, so obvious, and I had set it up as if just for him. He would win in the end, as he told me he would. Nothing can stop a psychopath who knows no bounds.

Except maybe a bullet in the brain.

I saw it before I heard it, the puff of gore that erupted from Tom Preston's skull. A beat later he keeled over with a stiff-bodied fall, the humped rifle clattering on the gravel. And through the gap where he had been, I could see Gordon about twenty yards back, standing awkwardly, blood rolling down his face, his rifle still aimed at where Tom Preston's head had been, which meant it was now aimed at me.

"Took you long enough," I said.

"I needed some time to figure things out," said Gordon, lowering the gun.

"And what did you figure?"

"I owed you both something, and now you both are paid."

"I guess he shouldn't have done what he did to your leg."

"Now he knows."

"It looks busted up again."

"Yes it does. You mind if I sit down a bit?"

"Be my guest," I said.

I watched Gordon collapse slowly to the ground. And then I heard something rattle on the ground behind me. I turned around and saw a blood-streaked Cindy with the Glock in her hand aiming it at Bert, who had dropped his rifle in response.

"What should I do with him?" she said.

"Leave him be," I said as I dragged my ruined leg toward them. "He makes a mean mojito. You're not going to cause any trouble, are you, Bert?"

"No sir, Mr. Kubiak," said Bert, which were the first words I ever heard him say.

"Who is Mr. Kubiak?" said Cindy.

"I'll tell you later. What's the story with Riley?"

"She slammed into something when we hit the Porsche and fell into the backseat. She wasn't moving when I left the car. There's no air bag in the moonroof."

"You guys shouldn't have come back."

"You came back for me."

"But not for why you think."

"What do I care about the why?" said Cindy Lieu. "The doing was enough."

I nodded and headed over to the SUV. The rear door had slammed open in the crash and Riley lay on her back upon the humped floor, one leg on the seat, the shotgun resting on her torso. The position of her neck was awkward; blood dripped from her mouth. I was staring at her, wondering idly if she was still alive, when I heard Mr. Maambong moan.

He had been leveled in the wild charge of the SUV and now there he lay, on the gravel, halfway to the road. I turned and watched as he struggled to crawl across the drive, using one hand to pull himself forward. His lower body was useless, which wasn't a surprise since the SUV had driven over his legs. Moving as he was, in that awkward, ruined way, he reminded me of a cockroach who had been stepped on once and was now trying to crawl away before it was stepped on again. I turned back to the SUV, leaned forward, and lifted the shotgun off Riley's body. I gave it a pump and a new shell filled the chamber.

Can people change?

That was the question I asked when Ginsberg gave us our first skunky beer, the question I asked the shrink in Washington, the question at the root of this story. And my guess is, having heard the sad litany of all my crimes and misdemeanors, you wouldn't still be suffering my presence if you weren't certain that change not only was possible, but that it had occurred like a miracle in my diseased brain. Why else would I have faced near-certain death to save Cindy Lieu if not because of my empathy and sense of responsibility for another human being? Cindy's wide, scared eyes must have finally shaken something loose in my soul.

You will think that I had changed for the better, and that thought will warm the chambers of your open heart, but you would be as much a chump as all the rest. You and your kind can look into the hearts of others, I can hear only my own singular beat, but I will tell you with my newfound honesty that it has changed not a whit. I still have no empathy, no sense of responsibility, no concern for anyone but my own ruined self. The world is still a chessboard, and in my dead eye all of you, every last one of you, are nothing more to me than pieces to be shuttled or sacrificed.

And if you, sitting prettily across from me with tears now in your eyes, are to me as nothing but a knob of wood, imagine what I felt about that bastard Maambong flopping like a stomped-upon arthropod on that gravel lot.

Holding on to the barrel of the shotgun and using it as a cane, I limped to his ruin of a carcass. When he saw me standing over him, he stopped the struggle and rolled with great effort onto his back. His little pink eyes blinked into the sky as they stared up at me. His lips juddered into a smile.

"You're still alive, Mr. Kubiak," he said.

"I'm as surprised about it as you."

"Well done. We would clap but we think our arm is broken. And our legs. What happened to our legs?"

"Kidney girl ran over them with the SUV."

"Resourceful, isn't she, though they were not of much use in any event. But we are most impressed with your skills. Once again you exceeded our expectations. You have indeed earned your partnership."

"You ordered Cassandra to kill me slowly."

"And you survived. Survival is the mark of a true champion. You cannot imagine how lucrative a partnership will prove to be. Where is Cassandra?"

"Dead."

"That is a shame. You and she were such good friends. And Tom Preston?"

"Dead."

"Of course. So you bested him again. You should be quite proud of yourself. But right now the blood is draining from your leg and we have broken bones. We should get ourselves to a hospital, don't you think?"

"What about the girl?"

"Ms. Lieu? Well, Mr. Kubiak, you know as well as we do that business is business. But don't worry, she will be well taken care of. From now on you can ply your trade as you best see fit and leave the ugly parts to us."

I lifted the shotgun, turned it around, and gripped the trigger as its muzzle hovered over his heart.

"Oh, let's not pretend to be something we're not," he said. "The explosion, the fire, the runaway SUV. All of that was someone else's doing. Under your sway, no doubt, but still. Tell us, who killed Tom Preston. You?"

"No."

"We are what we are, Mr. Kubiak. And you are not a killer. Some are warriors, some are figure skaters. That is the way of things, and you would look quite natural in gold lamé. But you have proven your case, you are worthy of a partnership in any event, and now we will adapt to you. But for the moment, a hospital is in order. Would you mind helping us to rise?"

The muzzle of the shotgun drifted back and forth over Mr. Maambong's heart, hovering like a bee over a flower. He was right, Mr. Maambong, all the carnage that surrounded us was of my doing, but not of my doing, do you understand? I had brought it to be but had left it to others to execute the violence. I imagined what it would feel like to finally step over the Jesse Duchamp line and become the thing I was born to be. I tried conjuring the emotions that might well up when I terminated the life of another human being, and what I felt was nothing. Nothing. I felt nothing then, like I feel nothing now. Like I will always only feel nothing. For good or for ill that is my fate. And in the space of that nothingness, which remains the one great truth of my existence, I slowly squeezed the trigger.

The gun kicked loudly. My wrist jammed with pain. The future blossomed red like the most gorgeous of roses.

Is that the change you were looking for?

42

Decision Time

I don't expect this was the story you were hoping for when you contacted Maria Guadalupe Menendez and journeyed out to this hellhole to find a vigilante warrior to fight your battle. We all want the sun to shine in a cloudless sky.

Well, here's a little unit of sunshine for you: I didn't shoot Mr. Maambong in the chest. As the shotgun wavered back and forth over his torso, I pulled the trigger only when the barrel was aimed at the gravel. Sparks flew amidst the gunpowder cloud, but Maambong's raven heart remained unspoiled. You'll want to believe there was something in those beady eyes that stilled my hand, some glimmer of emotion that wended its way into my core, but we've been down that disappointing road before. He simply wasn't worth becoming a killer for. And he still had uses, one of which was as protector of my stake in the coming kidney lawsuit.

"This is the way it's going to be," I said to him. "Once you recover, you and the Principal will come after me again. Do your worst. If I ever let down my guard enough for the likes of you to find me, then I deserve what I get. But you should also know that as long as I'm alive, if anything happens to Cindy Lieu, if she dies through any act of violence, even something as seemingly innocent as a traffic accident, then I will come after both of you and slice you to bits and feed your flesh to the fish in Biscayne Bay. You two need to make it your business to be her guardian angels from here on in." I walked over to where his glasses were lying on the lot, bent over painfully to grab hold, and carried them back before dropping them by his head. "I expect you see things clearly. Now cover your little warty pig eyes, they give me the creeps."

And then we got the hell out of there, all of us, Riley included, who wasn't dead, just blissfully unconscious. The attackers had come in three vehicles, still parked at the mouth of the drive. With Bert's help we found the keys and took the cars out to the open road and scattered. I didn't know where the others were headed; I simply wished them well and sent them packing. All I knew was that I was leaving with Cindy in a pickup with an extended cab. But before we raced away, I stopped in the office and made a call.

"There's been a massacre at a tourist camp outside Morgantown, West Virginia."

"Who is this? Phil?"

"It's called the Maple Mountain Cabins. It's a desultory little spot, but Fallingwater is only an hour away, so there's that."

"Phil? What's going on, Phil? What kind of massacre?"

"The kind where only the henchmen end up dead."

"Where are you now?"

"Leaving. It was all in self-defense, just so you know. Trace the call to get the exact location. I wanted you to have the chance to be the first to get word to your FBI pals. It might give you a leg up on getting a piece of the investigation."

"Why are you telling me this?"

"Because there is one man still alive for now. His name is Maambong, and he's the man who killed Scarlett Gould."

"You're talking crazy now."

"He played the part of a Filipino conservationist at Scarlett Gould's nonprofit to get close to her. He sold her on saving the endangered Visayan warty pig. Someone in her office will remember him, and his DNA will match anything you found on the victim."

"Stay on the line while I make the call."

"I have to go. I'll miss you, Linda."

"Stay on the line."

"Just know none of the bad stuff was personal."

"How about the good stuff?"

"Was any of it good?"

"You dragged me behind you when that woman came at us with a gun."

"And now she's dead with the rest of them."

"My God, Phil."

"Yeah."

"But why did you do that? Why did you put yourself between me and her gun?"

"The good stuff was good," I said. "It would have been interesting to have been able to play it out to the end. The end would have been bad, it always is, but still."

Cindy drove the truck while I lay in the backseat, gnashing my teeth and bleeding into a shirt tied tight around my leg. We were above Morgantown, driving north out of the state, by the time the first responders arrived at the tourist camp. In Pennsylvania, Cindy found me an urgent care center right off the highway, where I paid the moonlighting doctor hard cash to pull the splinter of glass from my deflating eye, to fix my leg on the fly, and to prescribe a mess of opiates, all without calling in the police. My wounds properly bandaged, I fell asleep on a pillow of drugs as Cindy barreled us west.

I check in with her now and then, Cindy Lieu. I call at odd moments from odd locations with burner phones. She's happy, she's healthy, she's in love, the fool. And of course she was made rich by the lawsuit against old Mrs. Wister filed by Maria Guadalupe. Both Maria Guadalupe and I made bundles, too, so all ended well. It would warm the cockles of my heart if my heart had any cockles.

I also keep in touch with Linda Pickering. She's with the FBI now, assigned to the very task force that's hunting me. They've gotten close, but I somehow manage to stay one step ahead of them, and also one step ahead of the henchmen still being sent after me. The price on my head is steep enough to retire on, but apparently the Principal will accept only my head as proof of death. Sometimes I'm tempted to lop it off myself and mail it to her COD.

So what was the answer to Mr. Maambong's question? Or to Linda Pickering's, for that matter. Why did I pull Linda behind me instead of in front of me when I believed Cassandra was out to shoot me dead? Why did I make that spectacularly foolish stand to save Cindy Lieu? What the hell had gotten into me?

There has always been something in my gut shoving me toward failure, even shoving me, I suppose, toward the death foretold by Jesse Duchamp, and that could explain my actions; maybe they were merely errors born of my innate flaw. But I believe there was something else going on.

Words contain and words define and when, for Linda Pickering, I used the word "justice" to contain and define the amorphous cloud of resolve that newly burned in my breast, I somehow set the course of what was left of this rotten life. Mark Twain said the difference between the almost right word and the right word is the difference between the lightning bug and the lightning, and I saw the lightning in Linda Pickering's eyes when they fired with respect, and with admiration, and even with fear, all from one bullshit word. And yes, it is bullshit, rich and resonant, maybe, but manure all the same. For what is justice other than a false construct that billows this way and that in the winds of time? Killing runaway slaves used to be considered the moral thing to do. But the vagaries of the term matter not; it is your reaction to it that matters most.

For this is a truth universally acknowledged: of all the things the world wants, what it wants most is a fighter to stand for justice no matter how shriveled be his heart. Put a cape around your shoulders and a *J* for *justice* on your chest, stand tall with your legs spread and your fists balled at your hips, and suddenly the world will kneel before you.

What more could someone like me ever hope for?

Which brings us back to this moment at this bar. And back to you. The time has come for you to decide on the rest of your life.

The outlaw stared at the magazine writer for a moment, raising the eyebrow over his uncovered eye.

The discouragement she had been feeling had only grown stronger during the telling of the outlaw's brutal stand at the tourist camp. It wasn't just the horror that reached deep inside her, it was the hopelessness. Did she have it within her to risk everything to avenge her brother's death? Could she disregard her own safety and make her stand against the oil-soaked barbarians? Could she ever match even a sliver of the psychopath's resolve?

The answers could only be no and no and no.

The fear in her whispered another plan, a safer, wiser plan. Take the digital recorder with the outlaw's flashy story on its flash memory, ride it all the way to whatever fame and fortune she could garner, and then with the money and the fame go about avenging her brother's death in a way more suitable to the life she wanted to lead. That seemed more than the smart way to play it, even if the result was less certain; that seemed the only way she had it in her to play it.

"Before we get to the nit and the grit," said the outlaw, "what do you say to one more round? Sadly we killed the Samurai, but I wouldn't want you to give up your decision without a final toast." He turned to the barkeep and called out, "Ginsberg, you cur, let's have two more beers."

The barkeep pursed his chapped lips at the insult, before stirring off his stool and beginning to draw two steins of beer from the tap.

"I expect when push comes to shove, you're going to commit an intentional act of journalism," said the outlaw. "And so I'm curious as to the headline you'll draft for me. 'Perk Up Your Love Life with a Bloodbath'? 'Spattered Brain: The Skin Care Secret of the Psychopath'? Do you think I'll get the cover? If you promise me the cover, I'll let you take a photograph. You guys have Photoshop, right? Wipe out the scars, give my jaw a nice unshaven appearance, make me what I once was as you tell my awful story. Everything you need is on the recorder that's been winking at me this entire time. So bring out the camera and let's get to it."

The magazine writer worried for a moment at his reaction when she announced her decision. Though it had almost seemed like he was pushing her to give up the path of vengeance, who knew what was going through a psychopath's brain? Maybe he never had any intention of allowing the interview to be published. Maybe he never had any intention of letting her leave the bar. Maybe all along she had been fated to end up beneath the floorboards. Maybe there were others already buried there; maybe that accounted for the smell. She picked up her bag, opened it, and riffled through.

"Go ahead," he said. "Take it out."

And so she did, she took it out, not the camera he might have been expecting, but the gun, and with her hand on the grip, she placed it on the table among the scattered mugs and glasses, aiming it straight at his malignant heart.

When he saw it, his eye widened nicely before he laughed. "Well played," he said, spreading his arms. "The bounty is as good as in your pocket. Think of all the misfortunate souls you can help with the money. Go ahead, think of them, because I sure as hell won't."

She was ready to stand, using the gun only to protect her exit. But there was something in the way he looked at her, in the cast of his scarred and one-eyed face, that gave her pause.

"Ah, Ginsberg, you grizzled old dog," said the outlaw after the bartender had silently walked two steins of beer from the bar to the table. "Nothing goes better with a gun pointed at your heart than a gulp of your god-awful skunk brew."

The barkeep stopped and stared for a moment at the gun, and then at the magazine writer, before allowing a smile finally to crack his cracked lips as he dropped the mugs onto the tabletop.

The outlaw hoisted his mug high. "To truth," he said. "To justice. To the goddamned American way." He took a long, sloppy series of swallows, slammed down his mug, wiped his mouth with the back of his hand. And then he noticed that the magazine writer hadn't joined him in the drink. "Is something wrong?"

Yes, something was wrong. To her it seemed just then as if the scene in this shack, the byplay with Ginsberg and the other patrons, the whole wild story, had been a test far bigger than her ability to scarf down a pickled egg. It was as if everything had been an act to discourage her, to steer her away from a difficult path. And why would he do that unless she was more than just a knob of wood to him? Maybe despite all that he had done, there was a true nobility in him. Maybe he hadn't just found his purpose, he had also found his soul.

"You're not drinking to our toast?" said the outlaw. "Instead you're staring at me like I'm hanging in a museum."

Could she see the truth in his face? She looked closely, gazed straight into his eye as if the proof of what he was lay somewhere in there, somewhere so deep it couldn't be faked. And then she saw it, yes, as clear as the desert sky.

"What do you see?" he said, his eye widening.

She didn't answer; instead, with the gun still aimed, she picked up the digital recorder and, without switching it off, dropped it plop into her beer. The foam rose up and around it, spilling over the rim and down the sides before spreading across the table. Inside the agitated mug, the digital recorder's screen died.

"I would tell you that was a waste of a perfectly good beer," said the outlaw, "except, well . . . yeah. But I must tell you I am disappointed in your decision. I trusted all the deceit and violence, all the dark and bloody truths would have dissuaded you from your mission. I had been playing to gain your trust all day just so you would walk away. And I did so want the cover of one of your magazines. Don't doubt that you will come to regret this choice in time. But here we are. So what was it that sealed your sad fate, what did you see in my face?"

What had she seen? Nothing. An absence so raw and true it couldn't be faked. An inhuman deadness in the eye that constituted the perfect flower of his condition. And as she admired its utter monstrousness, she remembered what he had told her right at the start, that whatever she saw in his eye would be only a reflection of what was inside of her. Maybe there was more to her than she'd ever imagined, or, even truer, less. It is strange the things in this world that can inspire hope.

"No matter," said the outlaw. "Whatever you think you saw, the die now is cast. So it becomes my turn to listen to you tell the whole sad tale of your brother's death. Together we'll see if there's anything I can do about it. Remember the rules, from here on in absolute secrecy.

"Before we go on, it might be time to more formally introduce these three losers drowning their sorrows at the bar. I figure you might have guessed their identities already, the subterfuge was as subtle as this fake pirate patch on my face, but your mind was undoubtedly on other things. Hey, my fine feathered freaks," he called out, his voice suddenly strong and full of vim, "come and join the party."

As the outlaw pulled off his eye patch and rubbed at the healthy eye beneath, the three patrons at the bar climbed off their stools and made their way to the table, standing in a row.

"As you probably guessed by now, the crab-handed mutant is Kief, missing a few fingers from the accident with his jerry-rigged flame-thrower, true, but still just as deadly with the women. In his time since our own little Agincourt, Kief has proven that when it comes to building complex machinery or rolling joints, five fingers to a palm is probably two too many."

Kief waved one of his grotesque hands as if he were a contestant in a beauty pageant for the damned.

"And yes, the bald motorcycle monster is none other than Gordon, who walked over to our table without a limp, you might notice. The things they do with artificial knees these days, though, as a fugitive, he had to outsource his surgery to Mexico. He used the same doctor, actually, who replaced my own knee. Yes, my limp was as much an act as the eye patch. The embarrassing things we do to remain anonymous."

"Nice to meet you, ma'am," said Gordon in a booming baritone.

"And finally, of course, the cowboy-hatted spark plug known as Cactus Annie is really dear Riley. Still not on Kuta Beach. And I can tell you, this blasted wasteland is not an adequate substitute despite all the sand."

"Howdy," said Riley. "Sorry about all this, but Phil does like his playacting."

"Now, if you don't mind," said the outlaw, "they'll join us at the table and listen in to your tale of woe. They're my crew, loyal to a fault—which is the truth of it, since I have no loyalty to them whatsoever—and they'll be deciding along with me whether to proceed. We're a democracy, a democracy of hyenas."

As the three grabbed chairs and took their places around the table, Riley sitting with the chair spun around so her arms rested on the top rail, the outlaw called out, "Ginsberg, you muck, build a mojito for our guest, pronto, tonto. She's weak with thirst. And a round of lamb eyes for the rest of us. This might be a long slog and we'll need some sustenance. And if there's enough fresh mint, maybe I'll have a mojito, too."

As Ginsberg went to work behind the bar, the outlaw said, "Believe it or not, against all odds, Ginsberg makes a stellar mojito. He learned from the Cubans in Miami. Yes, that's right, Bert Ginsberg. Once we were away from the tourist camp, I gave him the option of returning to the Hyena house and facing the purge or staying with the rest of us, and he decided to stay. He is quite handy to have around in so many ways. Be warned, we might need to check the truth of your story when you're finished. His lie-detector kit is behind the bar.

"Okay, then. Let's get to it. You have a mission of justice for the new and improved Hyena Squad. Go ahead and tell us your story; all of us, we love a story."

ABOUT THE AUTHOR

Photo © Sigrid Estrada

William Lashner is the *New York Times* bestselling author of *Guaranteed Heroes*, *The Barkeep*, and *The Accounting*, as well as the Victor Carl legal thrillers, which have been translated into more than a dozen languages and sold across the globe. *The Barkeep*, nominated for an Edgar Award, was an Amazon and Digital Book World #1 bestseller. Before retiring from law to write full-time, Lashner was a prosecutor with the Department of Justice in Washington, DC. He is a graduate of the New York University School of Law as well as the Iowa Writers' Workshop. He lives outside Philadelphia with his wife and three children.